THE SAVAGE KIND

THE
SAVAGE
KIND

BOOK ONE OF THE NIGHTINGALE TRILOGY

JOHN COPENHAVER

PEGASUS CRIME

NEW YORK LONDON

THE SAVAGE KIND

Pegasus Crime is an imprint of
Pegasus Books, Ltd.
148 West 37th Street, 13th Floor
New York, NY 10018

First Pegasus Books edition October 2021

Interior design by Maria Fernandez

Library of Congress Cataloging-in-Publication Data is available.

ISBN: 978-1-64313-809-1

10 9 8 7 6 5 4 3 2 1

Printed in the United States of America
Distributed by Simon & Schuster
www.pegasusbooks.com

To Jeff, for his love, patience, and inspiration

Strait at these words, with big resentment fill'd,
Furious her look, she flew, and seiz'd her child;
Like a fell tigress of the savage kind,
That drags the tender suckling of the hind
Thro' India's gloomy groves, where Ganges laves
The shady scene, and rouls his streamy waves.

—Ovid, *Metamorphoses*, Book VI

PROLOGUE

If I tell you the truth about Judy and Philippa, I'm going to lie. Not because I want to, but because to tell the story right, I have to. As girls, they were avid documentarians, each armed with journals and buckets of pens, convinced that future generations would pore over their words. Everything they did was a performance. Everything they wrote assumed an audience. After all, autobiographers are self-serving, aggrandizing. Memoirists embellish. It's unavoidable. To write down your memories is an act of invention, to arrange them in the best, most compelling order, a bold gesture. Some of the diary entries that follow are verbatim, lifted directly from the source, but others are enhanced and reshaped. I reserve my right to shade in the empty spaces, to color between the lines, to lie.

You may balk, dear reader, but I don't care. I need to get this right.

I could take different approaches. I could contrast the teenage girls: the black hat and the white, the harpy and the angel, the *cunning vamp and the doe-eyed boob. Or I could draw them together, a single unit: Lucy and Ethel, Antony and Cleopatra, Gertrude and Alice, Watson and Holmes, or even, I dare say, Leopold and Loeb. But neither of those angles would work. The complicated facts are inescapable. These girls are both separate and together, both unified and distinct. They solved mysteries together and, yes, they killed together, but many times, they followed their own paths and even crossed one another. Things are never that simple, never that black or white, that good or evil, or that true or false. I'm not writing this to assign blame, or to ask forgiveness, or to tie it up in a bow for posterity. It's not that kind of book. After all, an act of violence committed by one may have originated in the heart of the other. That's to say, this is a story about sisters, and like many of those dusty and gruesome stories from ancient literature, here sisterhood is sealed with blood.*

I should know. I was one of them.

It's 1963 now, and I'm thirty-one. A few months ago, Khrushchev, Castro, and Kennedy brought us to the brink of apocalypse. There's nothing like flirting with nuclear war to churn up mortal thoughts, to urge you to comb over the past and reconnect with old friends. With that in mind, I hope these pages reach my partner in crime, my only true friend, and nudge her out of hiding. I hope she reads this and knows that I understand her, that I love her, and that more than anything, I want to see her again. It's time.

By now, I'm sure you're wondering who I am: Which girl? Which woman? I should say. The harpy or the angel? Leopold or Loeb? Whose story is this?

Well, I'm not telling. Not yet. I hear you cry: "Don't be so manipulative!" But this story is all about manipulations, so why, dear reader, should I spare you? Sink into it, and don't worry: You'll know everything before it's over. I promise.

CHAPTER ONE

PHILIPPA, SEPTEMBER 8, 1948

No letter for weeks. Maybe they're distracted by the beginning of the school year, or they've moved on, or they're just lazy. If they bothered to write, what would they have asked? "Hey, chum, how's your new school?" Awful, I'd answer—my pen tightly lodged between my fingers, my tongue cocked between my teeth—the kids at Eastern High are impenetrable. They wear blank frowns or phony smiles and drift by like they're on conveyor belts, their eyes looking past you. "And what about Washington, DC? Is it a total lark?" No, I'd say, it's revolting. From the swampy air to the oily bus exhaust to the meaty stench of Eastern Market, it's like being smothered by a big sweaty palm. "But that must be the worst of it, right?" No, erstwhile friends, the worst is our house: It's a cookie-cutter copy of the other ancient row houses on the block. My window overlooks a clothesline-tangled alley and a couple grimy carriage houses, the habitat of feral cats, their nightmarish caterwauls echoing through the night.

I miss our ramshackle, gingerbread Victorian in Pacific Heights. I loved stretching out in the window seat of my bedroom and writing in this and reading the Brontës, Ann Radcliffe, Mary Shelley, Bram Stoker, or anything that blended the supernatural with distraught young women in peril. "So thrilling!" I'd think to myself. "If only I could stumble into drama like Emily St. Aubert or Jane Eyre do." I would pause occasionally and take in the sweep of the Golden Gate Bridge or watch as the fog swallowed the hills across the Bay.

That's why I waited so long to unpack. I was hoping that we'd have a reversal of fortune, that Dad would say, "Hey Phil, I hope you didn't get too attached to DC. They're assigning me back to the Presidio." But Bonnie, ever the fairy stepmother, made it her project to gently—and persistently—nudge me to unpack. With only a week until the beginning of school, I finally dove in, ripping boxes open and flinging stuff everywhere. When I stopped to catch my breath, the spectacle of it was crushing. I slouched against my bed and bawled.

Weeks later, it's nearly complete. The dusty lilac walls and silky window treatments are beginning to feel familiar. My new cream-colored bedspread looks smart and womanish on my bed. I plan to paint over the fussy primrose stenciling on my vanity and its matching chest of drawers. Maybe I'll choose a serious and sophisticated color, like aubergine.

In another gesture of excruciating thoughtfulness, my stepmother unwrapped and displayed on my dresser the framed eight-by-ten of my mother at her wedding reception. Just when I settle into resenting Bonnie, she does something like that; it's always a perpetual game of chess between us. In the photo, my mother's wearing an unconventional outfit for the time—a tailored suit of creamy linen, a white blouse ruffled to her chin, and a wide-brimmed hat, falling over her right eye at a jaunty angle. Her nose is tilted up, her smile furtive, and her visible eye is amused as if she and the cameraman—Dad perhaps—just shared an inside joke. In her white-gloved hands, she's clutching a spray of white roses and baby's breath. I would give anything to have known her, even for a few years. That emptiness never goes away, that ache. She'll always be a thirty-year-old newlywed, preserved like a prehistoric insect in amber.

I tacked my old life on the corkboard beside my bed: movie stubs, theater playbills, photos of my friends, a tenth-grade class photo (the class of 1949 in stiff blue blazers and dour expressions), a letter from Aunt Sophie in her sprawling script, valentines dashed off by silly boys, a smashed and withered corsage from the spring dance, magazine clippings of my favorite stars—Clark Gable, Joan Crawford, Joseph Cotten, Merle Oberon—a postcard of Coit Tower against a faux blue sky.

There it was, a little girl's life—where I'd been and who I'd been. Nostalgia wanted to well up and burst through, but a bewildering question kept it at bay, a question I continued to repeat:

Who will I be *now*?

Who will I be now?

PHILIPPA, SEPTEMBER 9, 1948

Today I met someone remarkable.

I was staring at my mountain of spaghetti at lunch when an elbow jabbed me. A gossipy girl—Betty, Barb, Bess? Something with a B—pointed across the cafeteria and whispered, "Judy Peabody, the one with the bangs. She drops bricks on cats. Kills them for fun." This girl, Judy, held herself erect and gripped her tray like a battering ram. Her jet-black bob sliced across her forehead and fell in sharp angles over her high cheekbones. Over her long black sweater hung a double loop of faux pearls, like a flapper's from an old silent movie. The other kids scattered as she strode to an empty table and sat. She arranged a napkin in her lap, pulled her sleeves back, and tucked her pearls into her sweater. Her every movement felt choreographed, and I wanted to know more: Who *was* she? And why the dated outfit? And what exactly did she do to cats?

Before she ate, she scanned the room. When she looked in our direction, most of my tablemates, the Metro Baptist Bible School contingent (commonly known as the MBBS girls), burst into an explosion of gasps and side-jabs, as if spotted by a vicious predator in the wild. A few of the older, more skeptical girls huffed, rolled their eyes, and adjusted their Peter Pan collars.

I sat perfectly still.

During the first weeks of school, the MBBS girls threw their arms around me, all good cheer and high-toned cooing, but their embraces felt fake—or unsure, like they were pinching my flesh, seeing if I was one of them, the real thing, whatever that was. But I was testing them too, and they were failing. They gossiped and backstabbed and babbled endlessly about boys. None of them read books or even newspapers, just *Seventeen, Ladies' Home Journal,* and of course, the Bible. Their minds were nets, only catching the fluttery and flimsy bits of life.

On the surface, Judy and I are totally different. I have big, messy strawberry blond hair that I trap in a ponytail. I dress in pastel sweater sets, bobby socks, and own pairs of saddle oxfords in various color combinations: black and cream, cream and taupe, taupe and chocolate. It's all a disguise, of course. I want to blend in, a strategy I've learned from moving around as a Navy brat. The blue-haired crone who taught me history my sophomore year told my father that I was "such a sweet and accommodating young lady." It's true. I always check my first impulse and edit it out. Adults do it, so I do it, too. But it wears on you, the politeness, the pretending.

There was *nothing* sweet and accommodating about Judy. Apparently, she kills cats. I loathe them too. They make my eyes water, and my arms and legs break out in hives. Their back-alley screeching slides under my skin. Of course, I'm not going to kill a cat, but from where I stand, it's justifiable homicide or . . . felicide? Seriously, is it even possible to bomb a cat with a brick?

When Judy's black eyes met mine, I smiled. In return, she scowled, and it stung. I bowed my head and began twisting my congealed spaghetti into a tight ball around my fork. For the rest of lunch, I slurped down my noodles, and as I took my last bite, a shadow passed over me. I looked up, and there she was. "Welcome to paradise," floated from her lips, tinged with scorn. But the heat of her glare had been replaced with something else. Confusion? Curiosity? I wasn't sure. Then suddenly, violently, she smiled. It was a cool, inscrutable smile, but all the same, it gave me a strange shock, like accidentally catching your reflection in a mirror. I felt seen by her—or was it that she'd seen some hidden part of me that the others hadn't? It was horrifying and thrilling, and I was temporarily struck dumb. I wanted to say something like, "Nice to meet you," or "The spaghetti is revolting, isn't it?" but before I could, she was gone.

During afternoon classes, Judy's dark eyes pooled around me and seeped into my pores. Her powdered face, her thin lips, her glossy hair, and her slender, craning neck seemed designed to display them, to announce them as her dominant feature. I couldn't stop thinking about them. Staring at me, judging me, wondering about me. They pushed my attention far from trigonometric functions or the Battle of Waterloo. After school, I spotted her beelining up East Capitol Street. I wanted to introduce myself, but I wasn't sure how to go about it, so I stalled out. For a few seconds, I watched her pass in and out of the shadows of overhanging trees. Then, gathering the nerve, I followed her.

"Um, hi," I said, my books clutched to my chest, breathless. "I'm Philippa." I offered her my hand as I walked beside her.

She glanced at it and quickened her pace.

"I know what you think, but I don't like the MBBS crew," I said, struggling to keep up. "They're such namby-pambies." I was trying too hard.

"Good for you," she said, not even glancing at me, keeping her stride steady. "Why are you telling me?"

"You're not like them either."

"So what?" She shrugged, eyes still aimed forward.

"You don't care what they think."

"Look," she stopped and gazed right at me, her pupils black and unsettling, "you've been arm-in-arm with those preening bitches since you got here. I get it. You're new, you're lonely. It's all just a little too pathetic for me."

My heart sank. "Well, I—"

"Go away." She started walking again, moving faster.

"Wait," I called after her. "My father's a Navy lawyer, and anyway, we were just transferred here, and I left all my friends in San Francisco, and my stepmother is driving me crazy. So yes, I'm a little pathetic right now."

Judy halted and muttered, "Hmm."

Did I say the right thing? It'd rolled out like an overturned basket of fruit. The glitter in her eyes told me that she approved of it—or maybe of my rawness, my honesty. I was feeling puny and desperate, and somehow, she seemed like the solution. Then her expression flickered—amused perhaps?—but she didn't smile. On either side of the street, the brick row houses peered out over wrought-iron fences. Their mum-stuffed gardens stirred in a breeze, and their old, uneven windowpanes reflected patches of irritating bright white light. Aside from a few parked cars with their chrome grills flashing in the sun, East Capitol was oddly deserted for mid-afternoon. We were the only people within blocks.

Judy began walking again, slowly. I kept pace beside her, but I didn't say anything. I hoped she wouldn't speed up again and dash off. One thing was true: her magnetism—if that's the right word for it—was unmistakable. Aunt Sophie told me that some people have stronger auras than others, that if you have "the gift," you can see another person's aura. Judy's aura must be blazingly intense, but I had no idea what color it was. Blue? Purple? *Black?*

East Capitol Street gave way to the wide, tree-lined expanse of Lincoln Park. Silhouetted by the yellows and oranges of the turning trees, the Emancipation Memorial loomed at the far end, depicting an imperious Lincoln waving his hand over a kneeling slave. Behind it, fifteen blocks away, the dome of the Capitol rose to the sky like a giant igloo. Judy nodded toward the memorial's dark bronze figures: "Is he freeing him or making him beg for his freedom?"

I didn't know how to respond, worried that I'd say the wrong thing and scare her off, so I squeaked out, "I don't know."

"No, you wouldn't. Well, I *would* know. I understand what being shackled is all about."

What a thing to say! I smiled, but she didn't, her face as grim as a tragedian's mask. "Do you?" I said quietly.

"I do," she said with a kind of finality, as if stating a fact.

I wanted to respond but held my tongue. I didn't want to blunder. But seriously, what *did* she mean? Why say something like that? The tendrils of her strange energy were curling around my feet and twisting up the backs of my legs. A quotation popped into my head—something we'd studied last year, *Jane Eyre*—and I blurted it: "I'm no bird, and no net ensnares me—"

Judy whipped around, and her eyes flashed. "You're a reader," she said. I couldn't tell if it was a question or a statement, but I detected a glimmer of interest.

"I love Gothic literature," I said. "The moors, the castles, ghosts wailing from the battlements. You know."

"Well," she said, "that's not what I was expecting." Her eyebrows lifted, but she didn't offer anything more.

When we reached the end of the park, I said, "I have to go this way." I stretched out my hand.

She gave me a brief, puzzled rumination and sighed. "You don't want to be friends with me. Trust me." She didn't wait for a response. She just turned on her heels and walked north, leaving my hand extended in the air.

I didn't know what to make of it. Was it a brush off? A challenge?

There's just something about her. She's so confident and singular. She doesn't waffle; she doesn't prevaricate. She floats above life, judging everything and everyone absolutely—and with good reason. The MBBS girls are skin-deep and brainless. Beyond them, the entire concept of high school deserves contempt. It's full of old fools teaching young fools, tedious routines, and absurd rituals, like pep rallies and football games and Sadie Hawkins dances. Like Aunt Sophie says, "The only true faux pas is to be boring." Well, Judy isn't boring. She's no dim housewife-in-training, no serial placater, like the MBBS girls, like Bonnie, like my old friends in San Fran. No, she's not that at all.

JUDY, SEPTEMBER 11, 1948

Miss M is a standout. She's not a crusty schoolmarm wearing stiff wool like an exoskeleton. She doesn't pin a dusty felt hat to her head like a dead butterfly and pine for the war—or worse, the goddamn Depression. She doesn't preach about "moral correctness" and "ladylike aplomb," and being "an obliging conversationalist." None of the bullshit the other teachers spew. She insists that I should be forward-thinking like her and not chained to some boy. She's cultured, wry, and whip smart. She's the future.

She swoons over nineteenth-century French composers, especially Satie, Debussy, and Emmanuel, and when we talk, she goes on about jazz, its layering of rhythms and the "sublimity of improvisation." *Sublimity.* I'm sticking that one in my pocket for later. She usually reaches for Ellington and Fitzgerald, but has been working her way into Parker, Gillespie, and others. When we're together, I don't want it to end.

She's nuts about poetry, particularly Wordsworth, Byron, Shelley, and Rossetti, and recites it for the class, swaying and gesturing, her voice drifting out over us, spellbinding and ethereal. In those moments, she's a dream.

So, is it wrong of me to hate her a little for what she did today?

In class, she laid her book down and said, "Keats accomplished so much in his short time. He died when he was young, only twenty-five. His poetry was very sensual, very passionate, but unappreciated in his life."

"Did he write love poetry?" Ramona Carmichael, the MBBS's catty doyenne, asked, muffling a giggle with her well-moisturized hand. Her nails were blood red like she'd just dipped them in the wound of her last victim.

Wrinkling her forehead, Miss M said, "The love of his life was a woman named Fanny Brawne."

The class clown, Jake Wallace, called out: "Did he do a lot of Fanny kissin'?"

The room burst into laughter, and Miss M shook her head wearily. I folded my arms across my chest and cocked my head: I wanted them to know they were being idiots.

Ramona glared at me.

I glared back and spat, "He wrote death poetry," and immediately felt stupid. Death poetry! Really?

"Okay, Judy Peapod." Ramona smirked and ran her tongue between her lips like a pink snake.

Jake moaned and slumped in his seat.

They're a waste of flesh. If I could, I'd save the world and drop a pound of arsenic in their sloppy joes.

Cleveland Closs—aka Cleve—didn't laugh either. He's a bit of a dim bulb, like he's sleeping with his eyes open. He rarely speaks, and when he does, he stutters. He's handsome, but in a spooky way. With his glacial blue irises and shock of white-blond hair, the Nazis would've adored him, his Aryan shine marred only by the flourish of acne across his cheeks. However, today there was a change: his icy pools were boiling, popping brightly, and focused on the front of the room. Something had his attention. Maybe it was Ramona and her minions. For a moment, I wondered if I had an ally.

"Judy's right," Miss M said. "In a sense, some of his poems are about the tension between mortality and immortality, transience and permanence." She smiled at me, flashing her eyes to let me know she was with me. "He seemed to know he was going to die young. Open up your books to page forty and follow along as I read 'Ode to the Nightingale.' Tell me, class, how would you describe Keats' sentiment here?"

I'd read the poem before. Keats is musing on pleasure and pain, and life and death inspired by, of all things, a bird in a plum tree. When I heard Miss M read it, though, she transformed it, making it soar while simultaneously grounding it in sadness:

> Darkling I listen; and, for many a time
>   I have been half in love with easeful Death,
> Call'd him soft names in many a mused rhyme,
>   To take into the air my quiet breath;
> Now more than ever seems it rich to die,
>   To cease upon the midnight with no pain,
>   While thou art pouring forth thy soul abroad
>   In such an ecstasy!
>   Still wouldst thou sing, and I have ears in vain—
>   To thy high requiem become a sod.

As she read, something cracked open inside me and air rushed in. The dark lava that usually swirls around my heart, all that bubbling murk that constitutes my shitty past, the Peabodys, Crestwood, everything, cooled a little, and a particle of the gloom trapped inside me escaped like a floating bit of ash. Immediately I wanted more.

When she finished, she said, "Now, Jake Wallace, tell me what you see in these lines?" She winked at me conspiratorially.

Jake gaped back at her. I imagined a thick rope of drool slipping from his bottom lip and pooling on his desk.

"No? Nothing?" she asked.

"I—something about a bird . . ." he stammered.

"Thought so," Miss M said, giving him a chilly smile. Her eyes broke away from him and drifted across the room, pausing on Cleve. His face was tight, angled. His nose was tilted down, and his eyes were damp now and boring hotly through her, brimming with hostility. What was eating him? Clearly, she was unsettled by him. A faint furrow between her eyes twitched. "Cleveland," she said, forcing her composure, "what do you think?"

"He's li-listening to Death." His intense emotion, whatever it was, seemed to be melting him from the inside out. Almost comically, he spat, "He's done something ter-terrible and wa-wants to die." Miss M flinched, sucking in her breath. There was a strange electric current sparking between them, but I couldn't tell what it was. He'd thrown her off-balance, something that *never* happens. A defensive impulse surged through me, so I blasted this at him: "What are you talking about? Keats isn't suicidal—or guilty."

He turned his death-ray stare on me, flexing his jaw.

"It's just a poem, friend," I said, shrugging.

"That's right, Judy," Miss M said. Her tone was light, an attempt to disarm the tension, but her voice still trembled. "But it's an understand-able mistake," she added, nodding and smiling in Cleve's direction, but refusing to make eye contact with him.

Out of nowhere, Philippa, the new girl, piped up: "The bird's song is so beautiful that it's almost unbearable." Sitting two desks to my left, she was aggressively poised: her shoulders back, her posture perpendicular to her chair, and her breasts pert. Both Cleve and I looked at her. She smiled at us, but it wasn't the prissy know-it-all smile that I'd anticipated. It was open but bashful. For the life of me, I couldn't get a read on her.

She looks like all the other girls—bobby socks, plaid A-line skirts, sweater sets—but she has a queer way about her. She's pushy, then shy, then bumbling, then sharp. "He wishes he could be like the nightingale or the nightingale's song," she added. "He wants to be transformed, I think. Made immortal, but he knows that's not possible."

Ramona rolled her eyes, and Jake smirked.

I expected Miss M to offer her a gentle correction, but instead, a smile of relief lit up her face. So, that's the answer she was searching for? He wants to be transformed? "Yes, Philippa," she said, her gray eyes beaming. "What an excellent read of those lines!"

Cleve dropped his chin, vanquished by Philippa's strident perkiness, and then, as if his mysterious ire were contagious, I felt a rush of anger at Miss M. Did she have a new favorite student? Was this girl her new protégé? Why did Philippa chase me down East Capitol Street and pester me to be friends? Was it a play at something?

At the end of class, I gathered my books quickly, avoiding Miss M's gaze, hoping she would notice and feel a little wounded. Before I could leave the room, Philippa was right there, blocking the door. Damn. "You're right," she said, blasting me with earnestness. Her face was smooth and dotted with freckles. A tendril of her strawberry hair lay loosely across her forehead. "It *is* death poetry. Death is a kind of transformation, right?"

I grumbled—I might've even growled—and pushed past her.

Now, I wonder: Am I getting this wrong? Maybe I shouldn't be jealous. Perhaps there's something to her, and that's what Miss M sees in her. After all, she wants to be my friend. And she's right. Keats wants to be transformed like a character at the end of a Greek myth. A tree. A bird. Whatever. Death *is* a kind of transformation, I suppose. The ultimate kind. If this Philippa girl were just like any other girl, Miss M's attentions wouldn't have cut deep. But if she's different—even brilliant—Miss M is pointing me in her direction: "This one, Judy. She might be one of us."

PHILIPPA, SEPTEMBER 13, 1948

The MBBS girls are closing in on me, whispering about who's inviting whom to homecoming—"If you don't have someone in mind, Philippa, I can put in a good word."—and I've received three separate appeals to attend the Metro Baptist Bible Study on Wednesday nights—"All denominations are welcome! Do come! We don't bite." I bet!

When I saw Judy in the cafeteria today, I plopped down in front of her, if for no other reason than to ward off the MBBS prowlers. She was resistant to me, wary even, but I'd rather shelter in her chilly sphere than field questions about homecoming. She looked up, and her jaw froze mid-chew. Her silky black bangs were combed with geometric precision, and she was wearing dark eyeliner and smears of moody mascara. Horus's eyes. Egyptian, that's totally her look.

After she finished chewing, she said, "What do you want?" and rested her wrists on the side of the table, fork in one hand, knife in the other.

"I just need a quiet place to eat my lunch," I said, as if the cafeteria fare of creamed potatoes, withered green beans, and meatloaf smeared with ketchup warranted my deep contemplation.

"No," Judy said, "you're here to bug me."

True, but I said, "I won't. I promise."

"You're already bugging me."

"Fine, I'll move." I began to stand up and thought, Well, that was quick.

"Sit down."

Okay? She glared at me, squinting like she couldn't quite make me out. I forced a big bite of meatloaf in my mouth and chewed it slowly, staring across the room out the windows.

"So, you really want to be my friend?" she said.

I nodded vigorously, my mouth still full, and swallowed. I didn't want to miss my moment. The window to make a good impression was brief, I was certain.

"Fine," she said, a shimmer of pleasure passing through her eyes, "you'll have to interview for the position."

I patted my lips with a paper napkin and straightened my back like a plucky secretary poised to take a memo. Here we go. I was ready.

"First question: What's your full name?"

"Philippa Ann Watson."

"Date of birth?"

"July 8, 1931."

"Astrological sign?"

"Cancer. Or . . . ? Yes. Cancer."

"Mine's Virgo, as far as I know."

As far as I know? I wondered. What does *that* mean?

She continued: "Place of birth?"

"Oakland, California. But I've lived all over."

"Where?"

"Mostly on the West Coast, but when I was a girl, I'd spend the summers with my aunt in Harpers Ferry, West Virginia."

She sighed impatiently and said, "Favorite color?"

"Pink."

She wrinkled her nose.

"Purple?"

"Favorite book?"

"*The Boxcar Children.*"

She picked at something on her plate. "I'm bored."

I panicked. "It's fun! *Come on.*"

She rolled her eyes. "Favorite pet?"

"I don't have a pet. Detest cats, though." I knew my audience.

"Really. Hmm . . . Music? What's your favorite song?"

"'Little White Lies.' The Fitzgerald version—not the recent Dick Haymes recording."

"Good answer." Her eyes sparked with interest. "Favorite food?"

"Meatloaf." I waved my hand over my plate as if it were a chocolate soufflé. "Voilà!"

Judy smiled—it was a brief flicker, but a smile nonetheless—and said, "What's the worst thing you've done and never gotten in trouble for?"

"I don't know," I said, overwhelmed, feeling as though I needed just the right story, daring enough to impress but not so bizarre that it would repel her.

"Yes, you do."

"It's just that I—"

"I'm sorry, miss," she said in a matronly voice, "but you don't have the level of experience or other requisite qualifications to accept a position with such a demanding—"

"Okay, okay! My father gave my stepmother a locket. My mother died, and it belonged to her. I stole it and hid it." And there it was, my deepest darkest secret. It's not very impressive as deepest darkest secrets go, but it was the first time that I told anyone about it. It's been a while since I even thought about it.

"Why did he do that?" Judy said, raising an eyebrow.

"I don't know. It's a family heirloom, passed from mother to daughter." Although it would've been mine one day, Dad should've given it to me, not Bonnie. I even asked him to. "It's still hidden," I said, pleased that I'd piqued Judy's interest.

"Where?"

"I sewed it up in Mr. Fred."

"*What* is Mr. Fred?"

"A stuffed bear. Well, I've never been sure what he is. He looks mostly like a bear. But there's some otter in there too. He's scrawny."

"Jesus," Judy said and returned to her food.

I waited for her to say more, to receive her stamp of approval, her blessing, but she just started eating again, chewing her food methodically. I grew impatient and said, "So, what happened to the interview?"

She swallowed, and her dark eyes lingered on me. What was her verdict going to be? Was I in or was I out? Was I doomed to be an MBBS girl?

"Interview's over," she said.

"Well, how did I do?"

She cocked her head. "You *are* relentless, aren't you? Why do you want to know me?"

"Honestly?"

"Yes. *Honestly.*"

"You remind me of a character in a book."

I hadn't thought of her that way until that moment, but she did—perhaps a hellbent flapper at the wheel of a roadster or a fan-toting French mistress from a nineteenth-century romance or one of Shakespeare's heroines, Rosalind or Viola? She's a female protagonist in the driver's seat, a daredevil, an adventuress painting her outline with a thick brush, boldly standing out against the background scenery. I like what she stands for—or I guess, what she stands against: the sad frauds, the smug fakers, the happy fools. She's a pylon in a shifting sea of new faces, a definite locus, a hard truth to hang on to—but she is that, a truth.

"You really are pathetic," she said. "But okay, you're hired."

JUDY, SEPTEMBER 13, 1948

"So, is it true?" Philippa said, leaning against the locker next to me, hovering too close. The hall behind us was swarming with kids on their way to practice or home. For a moment, I regretted taking her on. She's throwing herself into this friendship thing with gusto.

"Is *what* true?" I asked but didn't look at her. I was trying to squeeze my history tome between my biology notebooks and my stack of overdue library books. The lockers are the size of baby coffins.

"That you kill stray cats with bricks," she said, standing back a little, as if to brace for my answer.

I shut the metal door with a bang. "Is that what those bitches say?" I spun the lock.

"It's the first thing I learned about you," she said as if she deserved an explanation.

I held my hands out like "What?"

"The MBBS crew are ridiculous," she said, shaking her frazzled strawberry curls. "You know Ramona Carmichael is the type who recites biblical affirmations in front of her mirror—'I am complete in Christ'—then goes out and kicks a puppy."

"You don't like hypocrites, do you?"

"No, I don't."

Intrigued, I said, "Well, I've never killed a cat with a brick."

Her shoulders drooped in relief. "They're horrible creatures, but—"

"I didn't say I'd never tried."

She laughed, only three-quarters convinced I was kidding. That's when an idea struck me, and I said, "Let's do it. Let's drop a brick on a cat!"

Philippa's face drained of color. I grabbed her hand, not giving her time to make an excuse. Moving deeper into the building, we parted the throng of students flowing out of the front entrance. I knew where we could find a cat—the theater. I hadn't set foot inside it since my performance as Lady Bracknell in *The Importance of Being Earnest* last spring: "A *haaandbag*?" Today, Mrs. Q was auditioning for the fall play, *Cyrano de Bergerac*, and I'd overheard Ramona proclaiming that she was going to audition for—you guessed it—Roxane. After all, it was her queenly duty. She couldn't let her "people" down.

When we arrived, I turned to Philippa, held my finger to my lips, and then led her in through the backstage door. Auditions were underway on stage, muffled by the thick velvet curtain dividing us from the auditorium. We made our way through a clutter of residual set pieces, even some lattice work and faux ivy from the set of *Earnest*, and to the narrow spiral staircase stretching up into the fly space. Philippa slowed as we approached the rickety metal stairs and gave me doubtful eyes. "It's okay," I whispered. "I've done this before." I reached down and hoisted up a twenty-pound burlap sandbag, which lay discarded under the stairs in a mound of counterweights, ropes, and pullies. A severed rope was still attached to it, so I draped it over my shoulder and let the bag dangle down my back, like the carcass of an animal.

"What are you going to do with that?" Philippa asked, her face scrunched and dark.

She had some idea, certainly, but I wasn't going to spell it out for her. If I did, it might spook her. When you say a thing, it's more real. I wanted to see if she believed I was capable of doing something terrible: Would I drop a brick on a cat? Or a sandbag—a saaandbag!—on a simp? And was she okay with it? That's what I *really* wanted to know.

So, I just smiled and started up the stairs, feeling the wobble of thin metal and the groan of the risers. We climbed about forty feet into the tangle of rigging, ironwork, and dusty backdrops. We emerged on the catwalk and crept out over the stage. Below us, Mrs. Q, with her usual officiousness, explained the audition scene. She always drains the life out of a production. Whenever I mention her to Miss M, she smiles knowingly, but says nothing, perhaps out of professional courtesy. "This scene," Mrs. Q bleated, "is rich with dramatic irony. Roxane is complimenting the artistry of a love letter she believes was written by the handsome Baron Christian de Neuvillette to the man who *actually* wrote it, Cyrano. Isn't that *just* marvelous, girls? What a hoot!" Philippa glanced over at me and rolled her eyes. She understood my aversion to Mrs. Q. But my ex-drama instructor wasn't why we were here.

We waited, leaning against the railing and staring at the tops of the heads of the student auditioners, listening to the scene over and over—"To my mind, no finer poets sing those pretty nothings that are everything. . . .

You men are always so cruel: He can't have wit, because he's beautiful."
Ugh, Roxane is such an idiot.

Then Ramona ascended the stage—and when I say ascended, I mean
she floated up there like she was accepting an award for best actress. I
slung the bag over the catwalk railing, holding the rope tethered to it. In
all her preening glory, Miss MBBS was just below us, and I aimed the bag
at her. I could easily release it and smash her skull.

That's the moment I thought that Philippa would flinch, scamper back
down the stairs, and escape into the sunny afternoon—or gasp that I might
kill her "friend" and beg me to stop. But she just stared at me, offering me
a slight "oh well" shrug. Was she going to let me release twenty pounds
of grit on Ramona's well-coifed noggin? For a moment, we locked eyes,
and she said, "Go ahead. Do it." A subtle smirk crept into her lips. She
was calling my bluff. Damn it. The tension in her shoulders released, and
she said, "I get it. You're still testing me."

"If this is a test," I said, "then here." I shoved the rope at her, and she
took it, its weight jerking her upper body forward; the sandbag started
swaying. Below us, Ramona had begun to coo Roxane's lines, destroying
any hope that her Roxane—a role she was sure to land—would be anything
other than a superficial twit. As Philippa listened, an unpleasant grimace
spread across her face, like she'd just smelled shit. It wasn't a pantomime
to ingratiate herself with me. She was *really* disgusted at the spectacle of
Ramona and, I imagined, would feel the same about those other fools. At
that moment, I knew we were going to be friends. Then the rope slipped
through her hands—or she let it go. I couldn't tell which. I lunged for it, grabbing it inches from its frayed end. The bag swung wide, struck the edge of
a piece of scenery or lighting rig, and split open, raining sand down on the
stage. Even the universe was protesting Ramona as a casting choice! I pulled
up the empty bag quickly. Mrs. Q and the others stirred with confusion.
I glanced at Philippa, and she offered me a faux cringe and threw up her
hands. I smiled, shook my head, and said, "We've got to get out of here."

We plummeted down the stairs and slipped out the stage door before Mrs. Q and the presumptive cast members figured out that, perhaps, the sandstorm was a critique, not a random prop malfunction. On our walk home, we replayed the scene, each time reveling more in what we imagined to be the expression on Ramona's face—a red-lipsticked gape of horror—as the stream of sand swept across the stage from the pendulating bag. Fate had intervened, and everything happened exactly as it was supposed to.

When I first saw B and E's stately three-story townhouse, I was eleven. The car door swung open, and there it was, dominating the 100 block of Tennessee Avenue, as unreal as the facade from a Hollywood melodrama: large bay windows, a romantic balcony, a glossy red front door, and smooth walls the color of mouse fur. I gaped. I was suddenly a fairy-tale princess. Dyspeptic and sullen and full of shit, but a princess, nonetheless. Inside, sumptuous dark velvets, shantungs, and taffetas draped every window and covered every sofa, love seat, and armchair. Stuffy oil portraits and dim bucolic landscapes hung in gilt frames. A staircase rose in a dramatic semicircle to the second floor. In the center of the hall, the chandelier dangled from an elaborate plaster rosette, scattering light across the woodwork. Boy, I ate it up: I was saved! All this was mine! I was a fool, too blinded by the polished silver and Austrian crystal to realize that it was a trap.

When Philippa stepped into the front hall after our narrow escape from Mrs. Q, I said, "Welcome to Château de Peabody!" with a sharp punch of sarcasm. I wanted her to know how I felt about all this, about where I stood in relationship to it.

Playing along, she curtsied.

"This way, madam," I said, like a prim lady-in-waiting.

Dropping the act, I said, "Thank God B and E aren't in," as we walked up the staircase. I waited for a question: Who are B and E? Are they your parents? If she asked, I could begin to explain how all this came to be. Not the wealth from the drugstore franchise—that was obvious—but how I ended up here, surrounded by it. But she remained mute, mesmerized by the surroundings, or still reeling from the sandbagging of Miss Carmichael.

"I want to show you something," I said at the top of the stairs. She trailed me into the bathroom at the end of the second-floor hall, and I swept back the shower curtain. She flinched but didn't demand an explanation. As she had in the theater, she followed me, but not as a brainless lemming. She had a flaneur-like curiosity. I sensed that about her, that passive daring. She wasn't going to charge into a risky situation, but she was happy to be led. Deep down, I think, she wanted to feel what it was like to disobey her social mores and break the rules, but she didn't want the responsibility for taking the first step. I hopped into the clawfoot tub and tugged on the sash of the room's only window. A blast of warm air rushed in.

"Watch your step," I said as I heaved myself across the windowsill.

"Where are we going?" she asked.

"It's a secret."

I stepped onto the fire escape and mounted its wobbly, rust-coated iron stairs. Philippa hesitated. Was she reconsidering? I imagined her thinking: "Enough climbing already." But I wasn't about to slow down. Not my style. As I started on the stairs, I heard her clamor over the tub. Curiosity killed the cat. (Better curiosity than a sandbag!)

Once we made it to the top, I headed toward Hill Estates, crossing four townhouses to get there, hopping up eight inches for the Cranes' house and then down again to the Webbers' roof. Philippa trailed me, navigating the chimneys and furnace pipes, huffing and puffing. I called over my shoulder: "If you want, you can use the plank." I nodded toward the wide twelve-foot-long board propped against a large vent. I wanted to see what she'd do. I dashed forward, leaping over the ten-foot gap between the Smiths' townhouse and the apartment building's roof.

She slowly approached the lip of the roof and peered over, rubbing her hands together, wary. After all, it's a four-story plunge into the alley below. I wanted to tell her that she could make it, that I'd done it thousands of times, but I held back. She looked at the board and then the gap again. She backed up several yards, planted her right foot behind her, leaned forward, placed her hands on her thighs, breathed in, and began the dash to the edge. Only a few feet from the alley, she screeched to a halt, spraying bits of the crumbling roof. She shook her head, smiled apologetically, and went to get the board. I was disappointed, but hell, maybe I was expecting too much.

On the other side of the plank, she dropped down to the roof and said, "Where are we?" as she scanned the uneven expanse of tar and gravel dotted with fat pigeons and lined with corroded stovepipes.

"The roof of Hill Estates apartments. I come here to get away from B and E," I said. "Not very romantic, but you know . . . "

"Who are B and E?" she asked, adjusting her blouse. "Your parents?"

"Bart and Edith Peabody. Peabody isn't my real name," I said. "I don't want to have anything to do with the Peabodys and their damn drugstores." That's not entirely true. What I want is to be free of them, but I need them—well, their means.

"Peabody Drug! That's you?"

I frowned. "Cigarette?"

Without waiting for an answer, I crossed the roof to the chimney that was pitched forward like the Tower of Pisa, kneeled, and wiggled a brick loose. I fished out my crumpled pack of Chesterfields and offered one to her. She hesitated, a little afraid of it, and took it. I struck a match on a brick and lit the cigarette for her. We smoked in silence, leaning on the backside of the raised brick cornice and peering out at Capitol Hill. The streets below swirled with noisy traffic. The smell of exhaust and baking bread wafted up. Lincoln's dark head shone through a break in the fiery oak trees lining the park. I glanced over at her. She was attempting to hold her cigarette just so, like she was Lauren Bacall in *The Big Sleep*—head cocked back, an ironic smirk, smoke drifting from the lips. But she wasn't pulling it off. After a minute or two, she gave up on the cigarette-smoking routine and held it off to the side. "So, who are they again? Bart and Edith?" she asked.

"They adopted me when I was eleven," I said. "When I turn eighteen, I'm going to change my last name." The name "Peabody" feels unnatural, like living in someone else's skin. I want to slough it off and start over.

"You don't like them?"

"They're miserable. It's a long, painful story."

Philippa's gaze fell on something in the distance, a bird maybe, and she said, "Do you remember your birth parents?"

"I don't remember a damn thing before I came to live here."

She looked at her with wide eyes. "Nothing?"

"Well, almost nothing. I was just a kid."

"Still, that's strange," she said, lifting an eyebrow.

"Is it? Really?" I frowned at her. "Here, hold my cigarette."

She took it between her fingers, and I pushed my sweater's droopy sleeves past my elbows. There, angled in all directions, were my scars—short pink ridges, a half-of-an-inch to an inch long, etched into my skin like hieroglyphics.

"Ouch," she said, captivated. "It looks like you fell in Br'er Rabbit's briar patch."

I tugged open the collar of my blouse and showed her more scars around my throat. "I've had them since I can remember," I said. "They're all over me. I have no idea how they happened."

She craned in for a closer look. Before she could ask a stupid question or say something tactless, I adjusted my collar and demanded, "Cigarette, please." She returned the Chesterfield to my lips.

I turned away, a little worried that I shouldn't have shone her my graffiti. I'm used to my scars, but they can have a dramatic effect on people. Either they're revolted, smile, and go on their way, or they start digging for an explanation. But there's no explanation—well, at least none that I can recall. Anyway, I decided to point us in a different direction: "So, you must hate your stepmom," I said. "Is she a total monster?"

Philippa seemed baffled. "What? God no! She's okay, but I liked it better when it was just Dad and me. He married her because of the war, I think. He was the captain of a destroyer, and he knew he'd be insanely busy. He needed someone to look after me." She picked at a crumbling brick by her hand. "I would've preferred to live with my aunt, but Dad, he thinks she's off her rocker. I suppose she is, a little."

"What about your mom?" I said and added, "Your birth mom?"

"Never knew her," she said, biting her lower lip. I'd hit on something. Her eyes drifted out over the park, and she took a long, uneven drag from her neglected cigarette. How did her mother die? What happened? Perhaps, like me, she has a dark place in her heart, a little fissure that's never fully healed. God, that would be such a relief. Someone who might understand how it feels.

"Hey," I said, flicking my butt out over the street and watching it disappear. "What do you make of Cleve Closs?"

"The guy who sits at the back of the class like a broken desk?"

"That's the one."

"What's his story?" She pulled her hair back into a ponytail, exposing her pale, freckled neck. Is she freckled all over? I have my scars; she has her freckles. Both branded with the mark of Cain! Not the same thing, but *still*.

"He gives me the creeps," I said.

"Me too. He must hate English." She plucked a pink ribbon out of her dress pocket with her free hand and began winding it around her captured hair.

"It's more than that."

Her expression narrowed. "He doesn't like Miss Martins?"

"Maybe."

"How can anyone not like Miss Martins?" she said, finishing with her hair and swinging her ponytail back and forth, showing it off. "She's so smart and kind and not, not—"

"Crusty."

She smiled. "I love her voice, the way she recites poetry."

"'Darkling I listen; and, for many a time. I have been half in love with easeful Death,'" I said, trying and failing to approximate Miss M's modulating tone.

"Oh, that's good." She gave her nose a coy twitch. "Those lines suit you."

"What do you mean?" I said, a little annoyed.

She crossed her arms and gave me a once over. "Your style. Flapper-vamp, circa 1920. The moody lines fit the moody look."

"Okay?" I said, put off.

"Why do you dress that way?"

"Why do you wear pink bows and saddle oxfords?"

"To blend in."

"Well . . . "—I thought about it—"I like to stand out."

She smiled. "I mean, why a flapper?"

I didn't want to explain my Louise Brooks infatuation. How I'd stumbled on an article about Brooks in a disintegrating edition of *The Red Book* that I'd found in B and E's attic. With her severe black bob, wry smile, and sparkling eyes, she seemed so exotic and direct. She didn't suffer fools. I read about her famous movies, notably *Diary of a Lost Girl*, which had been made and then banned in Germany before the war. There was no way to see it in the US, so I tracked down the book it was based on. It felt like my story: a girl cast out from society, then lured back in, only to be tortured again, broken again . . . and finally triumphant! Two years ago, despite B and E's protests, I chopped my hair off.

Philippa tightened her mouth. "Sorry. I didn't mean to strike a nerve."

"'Half in love with easeful Death.'" I repeated, a little to myself, a little to her. "They *are* moody lines. I think of Cleve when I say them. Why was he staring at Miss M that way? His eyes were so full of . . . What? Something?"

She shook her head and breathed in. "I didn't see them," she said and, humoring me, added, "but I'm sure there's something to it."

"Menace," I said as it popped into my head. "That's it. That's what I saw."

JUDY, SEPTEMBER 15, 1948

This afternoon, as I waited for Philippa on a bench in Lincoln Park, I read another of Keats's odes, "Ode to a Grecian Urn," and scribbled a few thoughts in the margins. Keats's lines are so dreamy and intangible. As soon as you've looked up the words you don't know, picked apart the grammar, and are certain you know what he means, they change, as if the letters are alive like ants and are now marching in a different direction.

A shadow drifted over me, and I glanced up, expecting Philippa. I was surprised to see Miss M. "I was just on my way home," she said. With the sun behind her, her face was shaded. A few hairs from her updo caught the light like a fiery spider's web. She pointed to the open pages on my lap, "But now I'm saving you from too much sweet melancholy. You can overdose on that stuff, you know. It's more addicting than opium."

I wedged a piece of paper into the book and closed it.

She sat beside me, crossing her legs and adjusting her skirt over her knee. A fresh, floral scent wafted from her skin. It reminded me of something, a memory, but I couldn't put my finger on it. She didn't say anything at first. She just breathed in and observed the other park-goers, the cloudless blue sky, and swaying trees. A round art deco pin in the shape of a waxing moon held her scarf around her neck. Dark pearlescent enamel coated the eclipsed portion, and paste diamonds dazzled in the silver crescent. It was a bit glitzy, but it worked for her. She rotated through a colorful array of scarves—raspberry, peacock, lavender, chartreuse, tulip yellow—and she always held them in place with that pin. "So," she said at last, "how are you?"

"Fine."

She turned to me, her eyes alert. "Really?"

"Horrible, then. Is that the right answer?"

She smiled. "No, there's no right answer."

Come on, Judy! She'd just dragged me out of my pensive mood, but I shouldn't have snapped at her. I didn't want her to go. I combed my mind for conversation topics. Perhaps music? Had she gone to the National Symphony lately? Or maybe she'd taken in a show at Club Caverns? Or perhaps something about class? Or Keats? Or . . . ? Ugh, I felt so stupid. Finally, it occurred to me that I should ask about Cleve. She'd been rattled by his bizarre behavior, his eyes like daggers. But before I could ask, she said, "Are you friends with Philippa Watson?"

I blinked and said, "I am now."

"She's a nice girl. Smart, too." Her gaze drifted out over the park. "I like seeing you with a friend. You need a good friend. We all do."

My mind turned to the incident in the theater. I thought of Philippa's expression of horror when she overheard Ramona auditioning for Roxane. Did she let the rope slip intentionally, or was she just startled by Ramona's bad acting? I don't know, but it was a sign: Sure, she wore a kind of camouflage of sweater sets and bobby socks and strawberry blond curls, but underneath lurked something darker, coarser, and more honest. Yes, I *am* happy to have her as a friend.

"I'm glad you gave her a chance," Miss M said, gripping her slim leather purse and turning to me. "You're not the easiest person to know." Her eyes were parsing, edged with something: frustration?

I pulled back, just a millimeter, and she noticed.

"You've studied Greek mythology, right?" she said, her voice bright and teacherly.

"When I was twelve, I was obsessed with mythology," I said. "Norse myth, too. My favorite was Freyja, goddess of love, death, war, and . . . sex."

She laughed warmly. "Well, do you remember the three fates of Greek myth? The Moirai?"

"Vaguely."

"There are three sisters. Clotho, who spins the thread of life, a mother of sorts, Lachesis, who directs it, shapes it, and Atropos, who cuts it." She started moving her right hand in little circles, a tic she has when she lectures. "Gods and men had to submit to them. They were the weavers of history and all-powerful. Lachesis, the drawer of lots, is the most important to understand. She determines what a life is going to be." She leaned toward me, resting her hand on my forearm. Her touch was electric, and her voice pulled me out of myself and drew me in. If I'd still felt any trace of jealousy for Philippa, like I had that day in class, it'd vanished. We're connected by something profound, beyond Philippa's grasp—beyond mine, really.

"Now, I don't believe in Greek gods or inflexible fate," she continued. "And I don't believe we can be in control of how we are born, or for that matter, who we are born, or when or how we'll die. But we have some control over how we live. We can pray to Lachesis and sway her to choose better lots for us."

"What does that mean?"

She squeezed my forearm, and energy from her grip coursed through me. "You can transform yourself, Judy. You can take control. Let your relationship with Philippa guide you. Friendship is like a prayer to the gods."

"Okay?" Her hand was tightening around my arm, and I was beginning to feel overwhelmed.

"But be wary of family. Families are in Clotho's domain—and Atropos." Although her eyes were motionless, I detected a wild feeling stalking behind them, caged in. "They are the beginning and the end, but they don't have to be the in-between. They don't have to determine us." She seemed to be talking about herself, about something painful. She wanted me to respond, perhaps something clever or knowing or just considerate, but I couldn't find the words. Emotion continued to pace behind her gaze. Abruptly, her eyes fell away, and she released me. Jesus. What was all that about? "Philippa's good for you," she added. "That's all I mean."

"Sure," I said, noticing an old Negro woman hobbling toward a bench on the other side, hunched over a cane, her coat bulky and stained, her hair tucked into a dingy purple hat. "What about her?" I said, and Miss M watched her inching forward, her cane tapping the pavers in metronomic rhythm. "Do you think she prayed to Lachesis?"

"Every day of her life," Miss M said, smiling sadly.

Just beyond the woman, as if in counterpoint, Philippa was striding toward us, her ponytail swinging back and forth. She gave us a little wave, and Miss M said, "Ah, her ears must be burning!" Philippa was in a pale blue cotton dress and light cream sweater, and her cheeks were rosy from her hustle across the park. "Miss Martins?" she said, nodding with a touch of deference, "I didn't know you were—"

"I was just passing by and spotted Judy bent over her book. I felt duty bound to save her from sweet melancholy!"

Philippa smiled, perplexed. "Well," she said, "I lost track of time. I was journaling in the library, and suddenly, it was five o'clock!"

"That's wonderful," Miss M said, her eyes lighting up. "It's good to know you keep a journal. All girls should keep journals. I've kept one off and on for years. Dipping in and out as I needed to. It's a great place to get things out of your mind and onto the page."

"I've always kept a diary," Philippa said, adjusting the stack of books clutched to her chest.

Miss M stood, stretched out her arms, and said, "Let me treat you both to a snack. Perhaps a soda or something."

Philippa and I glanced at each other to verify the change of plans. We followed Miss M across the park to a small café that I'd never been to: the Bright Spot. The inside of the café was cramped, but in front of it, spread across the sidewalk, were clusters of small café tables. We ordered sodas, pulled a third chair up to the table, and gathered around it. A breeze glided across the park, and the sun warmed us.

At first, the conversation was halting. Philippa treaded carefully, either wanting to impress Miss M or at least not embarrass herself, which I understood but was irritated by nonetheless. I yearned for the intimacy Miss M and I had when it was just the two of us. Understanding how to drive a conversation, our teacher began asking us questions about ourselves, but not the usual questions. She didn't ask what we were studying in history or what we like to do for fun. She asked us: "Who do you think is the best writer of the twentieth century?" I said D. H. Lawrence, and Philippa said Daphne du Maurier, who was a little too popular to have the proper ring of sophistication, but Miss M thought both of our answers were "splendid." Then, she asked us, "Where would you most like to travel in the future?" We rattled off every exotic location we could think of, but Paris topped my list. Something about its mixture of culture and ruin appealed to me—a phoenix rising from the ashes of war. So romantic! Philippa mentioned Scotland, citing its steely gray skies and rugged highlands, its ghosts and castles, its literary mood, but in the end, she found herself agreeing with me on the City of Light. Miss M told us that she wanted to visit San Francisco, and Philippa lit up and began listing its merits, bursting with enthusiasm. Then, the conversation shifted, deepened. After taking a long swallow of her soda, Miss M said, "What do you two make of the opposite sex?" The question seemed to throw Philippa, but I piped up: "They're more an obstacle than an opportunity."

Miss M laughed and said, "You're not wrong."

Philippa smiled and sipped her drink primly.

"I don't give boys much thought," I said. "I never want to depend on one."

Miss M raised her eyebrows, impressed. "It's not easy, but you can do it. Both of you can."

Philippa absorbed all this but said nothing. For a moment, we were quiet, soaking up the beautiful afternoon, ruminating on the problem of men. Ending the lull, Philippa perked up and asked Miss M: "Where did you go to college?"

"Mary Todd," she said, tilting her chin up. "It's a women's college just outside Richmond, Virginia. Are you serious about college?"

"I'd like to study literature," she said. "My mother was a literature major. I've read quite a bit. Austen. Dickens. The Brontës."

Miss M set her elbows on the rickety table and leaned toward her: "Have you read *Wuthering Heights*? It's our next book. It's delicious."

"It's one of my favorites. It was one of my mother's favorites, too."

I was curious about what had happened to Philippa's mother. She'd clammed up about her before.

Miss M sized her up, eyes sparkling. "You have a passion for literature, don't you? You both do." She glanced at me. "You write wonderfully, Judy—very close to the bone. I appreciate your directness. And Philippa, you have a way of drifting into and out of intriguing ideas without losing your way. You have what I call a strong 'thought compass.' These are gifts. Don't underestimate them." She smiled at each of us, lingering a beat on our faces, as if to make sure her words sank in. "You know what I would love?" Her gray eyes danced, and we were alert with anticipation. "I'd *love* to hear you read from your own writing. A sentence or two."

"I just have a few of my random notes about Keats," I said, feeling a bit thwarted.

"Read one!" she said, as if it was a lark. "Don't worry, I won't judge you."

I flipped open my book, and at the bottom under "Ode to a Grecian Urn," I'd written a few trailing thoughts. I didn't want to read them. If I came across as stupid or, worse, naive, I'd be embarrassed. But her gleeful eyes wouldn't let me off the hook, so I read this: "Keats is addressing the images on the side of an urn. He pelts questions at it, even though, of course, it can't respond. He likes its contradictions: the scenes it depicts are full of action, but none of those actions are completed. The urn itself is ancient, timeless, but his interaction with it is fleeting, diverting. The urn is both satisfying and unsatisfying. All art is that way, I think, both resolved and unresolved."

"Brilliant!" Miss M put her hands together, her manicured nails glossy, impeccable. She looked at Philippa: "See, she gets right to it. The kernel!" I sat up straight, proud, beaming—and then a little embarrassed that I'd allowed her approval to affect me so much. "And now, Philippa. What are you going to share? Perhaps something from your journal you've been furiously writing in?"

Philippa glanced down at the stack of books that she'd placed beside her chair. I could tell she was uneasy about reading, for the same reason I was, I imagine. She smiled meekly and fished out her diary. It had a delicate cherry blossom design on it—very pretty, very *her*. She opened it up and began flipping through the pages, her eyes scanning and skipping, making a restless search for something suitable for our teacher's ears. "Philippa," Miss M said, lightly chiding. "Close your journal and open it to a random page and read it. If it's too private, just do the same thing again. I want to hear your voice unfettered. *You*, on the page." Philippa turned white, forced a smile, and then did as she was instructed. The pages fluttered through her fingers. "Stop. Just there," Miss M said. Philippa craned over the milky paper, covered with her loopy script. She blinked, swallowed, and shook her head no. She repeated the gesture, stopping again at Miss M's command. She took a breath, and said, "This is from the end of the summer, just after we arrived in DC." She flicked her eyes at me, then read, "Today, I started unpacking my things. It's a miserable task. I found some of my mother's keepsakes." She paused, worrying the edge of the page.

"It's okay, dear," Miss M said, her voice at once soothing and tinged with anticipation.

Philippa went on: "It'd been a long time since I leafed through the yellowing and brittle human-interest articles she wrote for local newspapers—pieces about piano protégés, spelling bee winners, struggling single mothers, down-and-out Dust Bowl farmers, women scientists, and dock workers. When I read through them, I imagined, not just who she was, but who she might've been." Her cheeks flushed, but she continued. "According to Dad, she wanted to be a novelist and tell stories about the lives of everyday women doing extraordinary things. Because of me, she never wrote a novel. That is, because she *had* me, because I killed her, because having me killed her." She halted, closed her diary, and looked away from us and out at the street. So, that was it: her mother died in childbirth. Her eyes were dry, but I understood she'd just offered us a secret part of herself, something she didn't tell just anyone.

Miss M leaned toward her and took her hand. "You are so courageous to share that with us! It was beautiful."

Philippa smiled at her, her eyes expressing a mixture of gratitude and relief. For a moment, I shared that gratitude. For Miss M *and* for Philippa. We formed a circle, a version of the three fates, and the thread connecting us was our writing, our private thoughts, like an unbroken line of cursive.

PHILIPPA, OCTOBER 9, 1948

We've been bonding over the Romantics. We smoke, sip whiskey that Judy pinched from Mr. Peabody's decanter (I do a terrible job pretending to like it), and we revel in the flamboyant lives of these poets—their drug addictions, sexual exploits, and socially radical ideas. We swoon over their indulgent language and weigh the pros and cons of an opium addiction:

inspired lyricism versus early death? Half of the time we're making fun of them, the other half we're taken with them.

Occasionally, we vent about school or parents or *The State of Things*. We chat about the fallout of the war, about the upcoming presidential election, and about what we want to do with ourselves. I told Judy I wanted to write like my mother. She told me she'd thought about writing or maybe music but said what she really wanted to be was a flaneur and "cast about Paris, drinking absinthe, skipping stones across the Seine, and studying human nature."

Most days, literature demands our attention. Language of any sort—poetry, novels, essays, songs. Even single words stir us. For instance, Judy came up to me today, leered at me, took a dramatic inhale, and said: "unravish'd," and then, "refulgent," and, in a deep throaty tone, "disquietude." I laughed and began improvising: "The unravish'd bride's restless and . . . refulgent eyes exposed her . . . deep disquietude." Judy added, "In other words, when the groom dropped his pants, his prick was too small!"

Miss Martins senses us growing close. When she glances our way, I catch warmth in her eyes. Although she doesn't fawn over us—it's not her style—she makes subtle gestures, gentle nods and half-smiles, that tell us that she's with us, that she remembers that day a few weeks ago when I read from my diary about my mother at the Bright Spot, that doing so fused us together. It's like we belong to a secret society, just us three, and Miss Martins is our guide, our inspiration.

Judy nabbed a book of Keats's letters from the school library today. We read them to each other and debated their meanings, attempting our best approximation of a British accent—very Ronald Colman, I think.

With a cigarette between her lips, Judy read one from December 1817. When she finished, I said, "What *is* Negative Capability?," a concept he'd mentioned but not clearly defined.

"Opposites attract," she said, taking a drag.

I must've seemed baffled because she shook her head and added: "Why two things that shouldn't fit together somehow do—like us."

"Genius," I said.

PHILIPPA, OCTOBER 13, 1948

Because of a stupid filling, I had to make up my test after school, but it was difficult to concentrate. Perched behind her desk, lit by a beam of the afternoon sun, Miss Martins looked impossibly fresh in her trim dove-gray suit, mauve scarf, and yellow wedges. She must shop at Woody's or Garfinckel's. She's no penny-pincher, that's for sure. Where Judy wants to create mystery with her formless sheaths and bulky sweaters—like she wants to keep the exact dimensions of her body a secret—Miss Martins aims to be seen. When I have my own money, I want to shop for darted blouses, form-fitting pencil skirts, and tailored slacks like hers. A real woman's wardrobe. Judy would say that I'm unforgivably materialistic. But being surrounded by the bourgeois opulence of Château de Peabody, she can't talk.

I should've studied harder. I only took a brief glance at my notes during lunch. For the life of me, I couldn't remember if Wordsworth or Coleridge wrote "The World Is Too Much with Us." I could quote Keats—"Nothing ever becomes real till it is experienced. Even a proverb is no proverb to you till your Life has illustrated it"—but I couldn't recall who wrote that poem. So, when I turned in the test, I asked Miss Martins.

She closed her grade book, set aside her pen, removed her delicate wire-rimmed reading glasses, and said, "What did you write on your test?"

"Wordsworth," I said. "That must be it, right?"

She beamed.

"Sordid boon!" I blurted.

"Yes, that's from the poem. It's funny you latched on to that phrase."

"Sordid means 'morally questionable,'" I said. It was all rushing back. Memory works in strange ways. You pull back the curtain on a memory, and then an entire mob comes crashing through.

"It does. And 'boon'?"

"Hmm . . . A gift."

"An immoral gift." She offered a sly smile.

I shrugged and returned the smile, a little embarrassed.

"Well, I hope you answered all the questions about Keats correctly. At this point, you and Judy are devotees."

"The question about 'Ode to the Nightingale' was a gimme."

"For *you* it was," she cooed proudly. "Speaking of 'Nightingale' . . ." Her voice softened, her head and shoulders dropping into a conspiratorial posture. "Did you know that Judy wants to change her name?" Everything about her gesture felt intimate and secretive.

"She's adopted," I said, wondering if I should've offered that information. As far as I could tell, it wasn't a secret, but she might not know that about Judy.

She sensed my concern and said, "She mentioned it in one of her compositions. She wants to be called Judy Nightingale."

I considered it. "Gee, now I need a literary name."

She clapped her hands together, thrilled. "You have one! Sherlock Holmes and Dr. *Watson*."

"Not the same thing." I waved a hand at it.

"Why not?" She smacked her desk in teasing reproach.

"Watson's such a common name, and detective fiction isn't serious literature."

"What?" she protested, wrinkling her forehead. "I love a good detective story." She beamed at me.

"You do?" I'll admit, I was a little shocked. Miss Martins deigned to read popular fiction? Unbelievable, especially considering her swooning poetry recitations. I hadn't taken her for a lover of the lowbrow. She floated above such things. Her lilac perfume swam around in the air, as if little by little, her beautiful skin was dissolving, becoming ether.

"Nothing gives me greater pleasure," she said. "I'll stay up late if it's good enough. I just finished Ray Kane's latest, *Love's Last Move*."

She opened up her desk drawer and extracted the novel. "Would you like to borrow it?" she said, handing it to me. "It has a wonderful surprise ending," she added, her smile becoming furtive, as if recalling the delicious pleasure of the plot twist.

I didn't know what to do, so I took it, holding it out at arms-length. On the cover, a stream of smoke drifted from the barrel of a polished black revolver artfully positioned on a scattering of blood-red rose petals.

"Take care of it," she said, winking at me. "I want it back."

I said thank you and goodbye, and, still astonished, tucked the "sordid boon" under my arm.

As I walked out the south doors, Cleveland Closs was sitting on the wall's edge under the portico, reading a textbook, which was strange. It was unseasonably warm and perfect for the park. Everyone else had fled. I caught a glimpse of a lobster diagram. Biology. I tucked *Love's Last Move* out of sight, and said, "Hello," a bit formally, then added, "Why are *you* still here?"

He didn't say anything. His thick blond hair was disheveled, and his iceberg blue eyes were unfocused but somehow intense. I startled him, I think. Over the past few weeks, I've watched him from a distance as he sulked with determination in the back of English class.

He's striking, milky skin and a prominent jawline, very Nordic, but he's always hiding out, a lobster under a rock. He's out of place amid the MBBS girls and football jocks at Eastern. He reminds me of Blake Le Beux. I never knew Blake properly, just by reputation. He looked different than Cleve—dark hair, slight features—but his demeanor, particularly his aggressive moodiness, was similar. You always sensed that just beneath the surface anger shifted like black ooze, building up pressure. I steered clear of him. He frightened me, but at the same time, I felt sorry for him. Two weeks into my sophomore year, he committed suicide. We were all shocked, but I wasn't surprised. That same intensity—that promise of violence—looms over Cleve.

Eventually, he answered me: "I'm just doing homework."

"I see that. I meant, why are you still at school?"

"Not interested in going home." He sniffed, plucked a tissue from his coat pocket, and wiped his nose.

"Why?"

"I-I—" He faltered. "It's . . ." He stuffed his tissue back in his pocket. A brief tremor of frustration flashed across his eyes.

I didn't realize he had such difficulty forming words. On the rare occasion he answered a question in class, he'd blast it out—for instance, what he said about Keats: "He's done something terrible and wants to die."

"None of my business," I said, trying for cheerfulness.

He deflated a little.

His clothes were neat—his white shirt tucked in, his dark wool pants hemmed and pressed with care, his thin red plaid mackinaw loose, but not too big. There was something boyish about him, and it made me feel sad for him. "Do you want to walk with me?" I said. "I'm heading up East Capitol."

"No," he said sharply.

"Okay, I didn't mean to—"

"You hang out with Judy P-Peabody, right?"

"Uh-huh," I said, not understanding why he was asking.

He scowled and looked away. "She's rotten."

"What do you mean?"

He glared at me, clamping his mouth shut, driving his blue-eyed boy-ishness away. What I'd read as loneliness or unhappiness was turning hot, morphing into anger. I stepped back from him. "Stay away from her!" he fumed. "She's a damned b-bitch. And so is, so is . . . "

"I'll decide who my friends are, thank you," I said, crossing my arms.

His eyes glazed over, his acne-covered cheeks blazed, and his jawline began rippling. Whatever rumbled under the surface was lava-hot and about to gush through. I thought about what Judy said about him, about his spite for Miss Martins, about the Keats lines somehow suiting him: "Half in love with easeful Death." My heart began racing, and I wanted to get out of there, but I didn't quite know how without triggering him. I had to defuse him. A one-person emotional bomb squad. "What are you studying?" I said, shooting for upbeat but achieving something drier.

He was mystified, and for a moment, he opened his mouth and closed it, as if he was stretching the muscles in his twitchy jaw. Eventually, he mumbled, "Uh, lobsters. Crustaceans."

"What are you learning about?" I said, harnessing the last of my depleting resource of goodwill. "Which lobsters are the best to eat, and which should be tossed back? Or something like that?"

"I'm memorizing their insides," he said, suddenly engaged, buoyant. "Cardiac stomach. Pyloric stomach. Dor-dorsal abdominal artery. Ventral abdominal artery."

"And you don't want to do that at home?"

"Too quiet," he said, blackening again. His shoulders dropped, but it wasn't anger. Very Blake Le Beux. For the life of me, I couldn't figure him out. Moods flashed through him like a spinning kaleidoscope. One minute, he's a bland wallflower. The next, a furious glowerer. And the next, a lost little boy.

"Your parents work late?"

"No—well, Pops does. But Mom, she's just . . . you know." His chin wobbled as he struggled to find the words.

"Don't mind me. I'm nosy. I've had to be. It's the only way you make friends when you move around as much as I have."

"I've never moved, but I'd like to." His voice brightened.

"Do you want to go to college?"

"I want to study marine biology." His eyes lit up, and his forehead released. I saw how handsome he could be. "There's nothing like being out on the Potomac in the boat."

"I'd like to be a writer," I said, remembering *Love's Last Move* wedged into my coat pocket. It felt odd for it to be there, even uncouth.

"If you say so," he said, clearly unimpressed.

"I want to write something dramatic and romantic, but with substance. Something timeless."

He just blinked at me.

"You don't like English, do you?" I said.

"No," he growled and looked away.

"It's a good class, though. Miss Martins is—"

His entire face narrowed, his acne purpling like a bruise. "She is . . . She's . . ." he said trembling. "You have no idea," and he looked away, wiping his sleeve across his mouth. Something was eating at him: Miss Martins? English? Judy? Home? Something else? *Someone* else? I wanted to reach out to him, but then he glanced at me. The muscles along his jaw were undulating, and he was taking in sharp breaths through his nose. His mouth fell open, but no words rolled out, or perhaps they had just bottle-necked in his throat. If I pushed harder, the anger I'd sparked minutes ago might bubble up again—or even explode. I smiled and told him I had to get going. He just sat there, puffing and quaking. As I walked away, I could feel his eyes on me. I sped up.

PHILIPPA, OCTOBER 14, 1948

On my thirteenth birthday, Dad gave me a collection of leather-bound nineteenth-century novels that had been a treasured possession of my mother's. He told me that, when she was younger, she had hoped to write a novel. Other than *Wuthering Heights*, her favorites were *Jane Eyre*, *Great Expectations*, and *Northanger Abbey*. During the summer before high school, I gobbled them up, turning the dusty, dog-eared, and heavily annotated pages at a steady rate. Dad was impressed that the Victorian sentence structure didn't slow me down. I pushed through it, steered by my mother's scribblings until the prose began gliding by. It was as if she were reading beside me, her finger gently dragging across the page, directing my attention to a brilliant line or plot point. Her marginalia were cheerful and frank: "Are we supposed to like Heathcliff?" "You tell him, Jane!" "Is it wrong of me to love Havisham?" "I was so much like CM as a child. Full of horrible fantasies."

I often cast my mother as Catherine Earnshaw, beautiful and remote, wandering the moors, adrift in the night, searching for Heathcliff. Or smart, passionate Jane, able to speak her mind, love boldly, and know herself. Or as a girl, Catherine Morland, foolish in dreaming up dark intrigue where there was none, but full of life and adventure all the same. Even Miss Havisham, full of decay and longing, somehow fit in with the rest. I wondered if she was sprinkling little pieces of herself for me to find. I shivered: Did she know she was going to die?

I remembered those books—and the summer I read them—as I considered how to approach *Love's Last Move*. Yesterday, I held it away from me like an untamed animal that might lash out. It isn't refined, I thought. Or cultured. It didn't match Miss Martins. But after taking a deep breath, I dove in. At first, Ray Kane's writing struck me as blunt, even crude. But there was something to it—an energy or maybe an attitude that wasn't so different from the Romantics. As the clues to a grisly murder fell into place, I found myself sucked into PI Calvin McKey's dangerous world of goons, dames, and private dicks. After the first fifty pages, a spell was cast, and time vanished. McKey was about to enter a house where the suspected murderer lurked in the darkness when I heard a knock on my bedroom door.

I shoved the book under my pillow and responded, "Yes?"

"Phil," Dad said, pushing the door open. "What are you up to?"

Based on his photos, you'd think he was as stern and monolithic as an old battleship, but in life, that's far from true. His dark eyes are wide-set and roam ceaselessly, like he's always picking up sounds at frequencies out of range for mere mortal hearing. His hair is a neat silver bristle, and of course, he carries himself like a military man, shoulders back and chin up. It suits him.

"Just homework," I said.

"Aunt Sophie rang. She wants us to drive up to Harpers Ferry in a few weeks."

"Really!" I said. "Can we?"

"If Sophie calls, we must come," he said, stepping forward. "She has 'important news' to tell us. Whatever that means." His eyes warmed, and he added, "Oh, and Quincy. He officially joined the metro police. I wrote a recommendation for him months ago."

Can you imagine, our own Calvin McKey in the flesh? My first cousin brandishing his weapon in the moonlight to hunt murderers. I hope this means he'll be close by, and we can have adventures like we did when I was younger. I could tell Dad was pleased. "We'll have a detective in the family," I said and suddenly felt self-conscious about *Love's Last Move* under my pillow.

"He hopes to be, eventually." He exhaled. "Well, I should say good night."

That's when I said, "I'm beginning to like it here." It's true, I am.

"Well, good."

"I want you to meet Judy."

"This new friend of yours?" I'd mentioned her in passing.

"She's the one."

"Well, I look forward to it."

"And I want to study literature in college," I blurted. "My English teacher thinks I would make a good writer like Mother."

"She does, does she?" He smiled, but I didn't know what he really thought of my idea. Most likely, he'll proclaim it "impractical." I love him, but he can be frustrating. His emotions tumble and clank behind his iron plate face. I'm often left in the dark about what he feels.

"Maybe I'll write a book one day," I said, nudging him further.

"That's an idea," he said, turning away, his face in shadow. "Now, go to sleep."

JUDY, OCTOBER 15, 1948

So much to report. Damn. It began when I slipped out of lunch, doing my best to dodge the runny Chicken à la King. I wanted to find Miss M and ask her about a poem I'd read last night called "My Last Duchess" by Robert Browning. It's about this duke who shows a representative of his fiancée's family a portrait of his late wife. He tells him that he executed her for being a flirt. At least that's what I think is going on.

As I turned the corner to the southwest hall, I stopped in my tracks. It was empty and dim. The polished linoleum reflected light from the frosted glass window at the end of the corridor. Outside the entrance to her classroom, Miss M stood with her back to the wall, trapped by Cleve. He was leaning toward her, his shoulders hunched and his stance wide. The muscles in his sinewy corpse-gray arms twitched. He was speaking to her in a biting whisper, but I couldn't make it out. Miss M stood tall, but her arms were crossed over her chest and her face was averted, as if she'd just been slapped or was bracing for it. Chills cascaded through me, and a line from the Browning poem came to mind: "I gave commands; Then all smiles stopped together." For the first time, I could imagine Cleve, mute and dull-as-hell *Cleve*, attacking Miss M and driving his balled fists into her stomach, into her face, as if she were some sort of blasphemous idol he was bent on destroying. My heart clanged like an alarm bell. To diffuse the situation, I dropped one of my books, alerting them to my presence. Cleve jumped and looked around; Miss M caught my eye. Her face was bloodless, her eyes dark with fear. He took a step back and, like a rubber band being pulled taut, snapped, spun around, and blew past me, his eyes unblinking and hot with anger.

For a beat, I stared at Miss M, breathless. I started to say something.

"Not now," she stammered, holding her hand out. "I'm sorry, just not now."

I wanted to press her, but the words wouldn't form. I didn't know what to say or how to say it. I was too stunned, too shaken.

I lingered a moment, then left.

I found Philippa in the cafeteria, reading a book and eating, no longer swarmed by MBBS queen bees. "What class does Cleve have next?" I said.

She frowned. "How would I know?"

"I need to find him. Now."

She dropped the biscuit she was about to eat. "He doesn't like you very much, you know," she said, brushing crumbs from her palms.

"I had that feeling."

She closed her book, something trashy called Love's Last Move. "I bumped into him yesterday, and he growled at me for hanging out with you. I told him to mind his business."

"I don't even know him," I said with a twinge of anxiety. "We've never had classes together. Not that I care, but it's just weird." His ire toward me bugged me and still bugs me. I don't care about being disliked, but I want to know why.

"He seems off," she said.

"He's something all right, and I want to know what." My stomach gurgled, so I reached down and snatched up Philippa's neglected biscuit. "Finders keepers!"

After classes, we waited thirty minutes at the south entrance for Cleve, but he didn't show. On our way home on East Capitol, he crossed in front of us on his bike, heading north to south. He was hunched over his handlebars, his red backpack's straps pulling at his shoulders, focused on the road. I called out to him. He slid to a gravel-crunching halt and whipped around. He squinted at us. When he realized who it was, his eyes glittered with rage, and the acne across his cheeks blazed like slashes of war paint. I shivered, but being frightened of him pissed me off, so I stood a little taller and said, "Don't fuck with Miss M! You hear!"

Two nearby girls gaped at me as if I'd just made their ears bleed.

Cleve circled his bike around, slipped out of one of his backpack straps and slung its bulk over on his right shoulder. He stood on his pedals and started pumping his legs, driving the bike forward, toward us. At first, neither of us moved. Perhaps we were frozen in disbelief or maybe just slow to realize that he wanted to hurt us. We were caught in that strange limbo for a moment, but as he gained speed, I murmured, "Run," to Philippa. She didn't move, so I shouted it: "Run!"

It was too late. Cleve dropped his shoulder, slid the straps of his backpack down his arm and clutched them. As he advanced, he swung his book-ladened bag at us like a medieval flail. Apparently, we were jousting. Quicker on my feet than Philippa, I shoved her out of the way. In doing so, I twisted awkwardly, taking the full weight of the bag in the small of my back. I flew forward and hit the ground hard, my breath flying from me. I saw stars and my back cried out, but I raised myself to my elbows. A warm trickle of blood ran down my cheek where I'd scraped it on the pavement.

Cleve slowed his bike, spun around, and adjusted his grip on the straps. More humiliated than afraid, I wanted to scream, "What do you want?!" But I still couldn't catch my breath, so I just glared at him, trying to steady my vision. His feet were spinning, his blond hair was flapping, and his blue eyes were little sparks of hellfire. He was coming—and fast! He wanted to run me over or beat me to death with his stupid bag. With all my strength, I gave a heave-ho and groaned. I pulled my knees under me, so I could stand, but there wasn't time. He was closing in. I swiped my hands across the ground, searching for a rock or a piece of concrete or anything I could arm myself with. If I couldn't dodge him, at least I could be armed.

As we were about to collide, Philippa rushed at him. From over her shoulder, drawn back like a baseball bat, she swung at him with something long and dark. It made an audible, satisfying thwack when it connected with his upper arm. My heart lurched in my chest. He yelled, wobbled, and tumbled over, a tangle of bike chain and book bag innards.

I got to my feet, taking a moment to steady my spinning head. Philippa was breathless, limp. She clutched a wrought iron post in her right hand, an arrow-like rod from a nearby crumbling city-issued fence. I swelled with gratitude. "It was loose," she muttered and looked at it, seeming astonished that she'd just whipped a boy with it. Suddenly horrified, she dropped it. As it clattered over the pavement, I snatched it up. My relief had reshaped itself into something sharper. I strode over to Cleve, who was beginning to stir, and lifted it up. I won't lie. I wanted to brain him with it. He deserved it—and I didn't want him to think that he could come at us again. But passersby were starting to gather. "Leave him!" Philippa cried. "Let's go!"

"Why are you doing this?" I hissed at him.

He stared at me, wide-eyed and scared. His cheeks were tear-smeared, and his complexion blotchy. It was a little boy's face, huffy and tender and distraught. I suppose I should've felt something, some twinge of sympathy—or at least restraint, but I was bleeding, I was trembling. He didn't get to ask for mercy.

"Leave us alone. Leave Miss M alone." I lowered the post, pointing its arrow-shaped tip at his chest. "Or I'll shove this through your goddamn heart."

CHAPTER TWO

I must interject. Philippa and Judy didn't react to Cleve's aggressions in a particularly ladylike manner. I know. Consider your concerns noted. Yes, they should've dodged him and ran, although he was moving quickly. Or, no, you're right: Judy should've kept her mouth shut and never drawn his attention. And what was Philippa thinking vandalizing city property and using the fruits of her savagery to strike a young man? Oh, the horror! Had one of the schoolmarms in their sad hats or bunched stockings witnessed that exchange, they would've swiftly concluded that Cleveland was provoked, that these girls were serious troublemakers, a touch wicked really. Miss Martins wouldn't have thought that, of course. She would've seen it for what it was. She'd already had a taste of Cleve's dark side. But in 1948, that sort of behavior from young ladies wasn't tolerated. At all. Can you imagine threatening to drive a stake through a boy's heart? Horrible.

Not much has changed since then, but Betty Friedan has her finger on the problem—"the problem with no name." I tore through her book and left it dog-eared. I've followed her from the early fifties when she wrote for UE News and reported on HUAC and jackasses like Nixon. Her subject is "the American Housewife" and how she's been molded into a commodity. She's a cash cow, apparently. She's a mechanism of consumption and economic growth—a queen and a prisoner of her domain: suburbia. I wonder what Friedan would think of Philippa and Judy, of everything we did over the past fifteen years. Not very housewifey, were we? We'd murder before shoving ourselves into girdles and crinolines, before making hubby a "Welcome Home" martini ("Extra dry, darling!"), before whipping up grandma's soggy meatloaf recipe, and before squeezing out two-point-five children. We'd murder before we'd do any of it.

Cleve was just the beginning. The tip of the iceberg, so to speak. Inadvertently, he was signaling to us that destructive forces were closing in, about to envelop us. Would we have become what we did without him? Who knows? Could we have saved him had we known the truth? Would we have even wanted to?

PHILIPPA, OCTOBER 15, 1948

So, there I was in Judy's foyer, my entire body buzzing, the adrenaline still surging. Minutes ago, I'd struck—no, *slugged*—Cleve with a piece of metal. I didn't know I could do something like that. I was astonished at myself. I'd been operating on pure instinct. Cleve would've plowed into her; he could've seriously hurt her. My arm ached from the impact, but it felt like an old war wound, a badge of sisterhood.

Instead of whisking me upstairs and out the window to the roof, Judy said, "Wait here. I'll be right back," and disappeared through a small door under the stairs.

I took a deep breath and stepped from the foyer into the front hall. On a table set in front of a sizable gilt-framed mirror, I spotted a spray of lilies. Their spicy-sweet odor was bright and nauseating. Under the bouquet, framed in fine white gold filigree, a young girl of six or seven peered out from a black-and-white photo. Her gray felt tam complemented her houndstooth coat, and a flip of straight dark hair fell across her forehead. She seemed smudged at the edges, a touch out of focus. Since Judy had always rushed me through the hall, I hadn't noticed the photo before. I thought it was a younger version of Judy at first—more subdued, more girlish—but as I leaned closer, I realized it couldn't be. Their eyes were different. This girl's pupils were dim flecks, cooled ashes. They lacked Judy's intensity.

"Hello," a stern but not unkind voice said behind me. "And who are you?"

A man of fifty or sixty—age in older men is always difficult for me to determine—emerged from the hall beside the staircase. He had a bushy mustache, well-oiled hair, and watery eyes. He wore an expensive wine-colored tie with gold geometric shapes, and his tailored three-piece suit held him in like a balloon does air.

"I'm Philippa, a friend of Judy's," I said and shook his damp palm.

"I'm Mr. Peabody," he said, leaning forward.

I caught a whiff of his sour breath. Alcohol? "We met at school. We're in English together."

From the other room, a woman's voice rang out—"Bart, who are you talking to?"—followed by footfalls. Around the corner strode a wide-hipped and big-breasted woman roughly Mr. Peabody's age. Her thick-heeled shoes whacked the floorboards. She was frowning.

"Edie," Mr. Peabody said, "it's a friend of Judy's."

Edith wasn't so much attractive as she was, like Mr. Peabody, fashionable. She wore a navy-blue pleated silk blouse and elegant wool skirt. Her face was smooth and gray and proud like the marble bust of a Roman emperor, and her wavy auburn hair was cropped tightly to her head, showing off a pair of diamond-encrusted opaline earrings the size of half-dollars.

She gave me a nod and said, "I didn't know Jackie had a new friend."

I stared at her—*Jackie?*—then, catching myself, I remembered to smile.

Correcting her, Mr. Peabody said, "*Judy* made friends with Philippa in English."

"Yes, well, she's never spoken of you before," she said, the charm bracelet on her wrist clattering.

"I just moved here. My father's in the Navy."

"I see."

"A lawyer. JAG Corp."

"Impressive." A smile fluttered to her lips and died away. "My uncle Andrew was a JAG. The courts-martial is a more effective judicial system than our civilian one, wouldn't you agree?"

"I'm not sure I could say."

"Our civilian courts are absolutely broken. Damaged. *Damaging.*"

Mr. Peabody sniffed at this, which annoyed the Mrs., but before she could respond, a little black dog with twitchy bat ears scampered through the door under the stairs. Mrs. Peabody groaned, and Mr. Peabody smiled, his grooved and pockmarked face lighting up. The dog darted around his legs, gave a couple sharp barks, and came to me, ignoring Mrs. Peabody.

"Philippa, meet Roosevelt. Rosie, Philippa," Judy said, following close behind.

I kneeled and held out my hand. Rosie had a stripe of white fur that ran from his forehead over his crushed nose and disappeared into his tight cord sweater. He licked my palm, rubbed his back against my thigh, and dashed back to Judy. "He's so cute!" I said, standing again. "Is he a Frenchie?"

"Cute he may be, but intolerable," Mrs. Peabody said. "Judy, I told you not to let him into the front rooms. He'll chew my cushions."

"He's never chewed a cushion," she said, glaring.

"It's in their nature," Mrs. Peabody said. "Dogs are destructive."

"Rosie's a good dog," Mr. Peabody said, adding to Roosevelt, "Aren't you, you rascal?" The dog began pawing at his knee, and he patted his head. Something about the gesture made me feel sorry for Mr. Peabody. He seemed tender, not the nightmare Judy seemed to think he was. Edith must be the primary source of her ire.

"Come on, Philippa," Judy said and scooped up Rosie, who licked her neck and her chin and the side of her face, cleaning away the thin smear of blood on her cheek from Cleve's attack. She laughed openly, something I hadn't witnessed before.

We played with Rosie in the upstairs den for a quarter of an hour. Judy had found him nosing around the trash behind Hill Estates that summer. He'd been starving, encrusted with infected sores, and swarming with fleas. Despite Edith's protests, she nurtured him back to health. He was named Roosevelt because, while the family was listening to a retrospective about FDR on the radio, he stretched out his stumpy neck, threw back his ears, and cooed every time the president spoke.

Growing tired of his friskiness, Judy shooed him away and said, "Let's go to the roof." She fished out a portable record player in a cracked leather case, a stack of records, and said, "Come on."

After a tricky balancing act crossing the board over the alley, Judy popped open the player, dropped a record on, and cranked it. I leaned against the sun-warmed bricks at the roof's raised edge, watched some stray clouds straggle across the sky, and listened to Edith Piaf's dreamy warble over the murmur of traffic and pedestrians. Passersby below drifted back and forth on the sidewalk, vanishing into and materializing out of the canopy of turning leaves. Based on their hairdos and hats, I imagined their life stories. There goes a victory roll (she lost her husband at Midway, poor thing); there goes a queue curl (she's pregnant out of wedlock and hasn't told her family); there goes a brown fedora with a navy-blue ribbon (he's a spy who fell in love with a German woman); there goes a dramatic purple cartwheel (she's the wife of a disgraced senator); there goes a beret and there a crochet snood and there a redhead in a scarf—

"You really let Cleve have it," Judy said, bumping me with her elbow.

"He was going to run you over."

She smirked. "I could've moved out of the way."

"It didn't look like it," I said, a little miffed. She should've been thanking me.

"He deserved it." She shook her head. "God, what a jerk."

"Something's wrong with him."

"Miss M knows why."

I took a deep breath. "So, what do we do?"

She looked at me but didn't respond. She just picked a hair off my sweater, held it into the breeze, and let it float away. Piaf's voice swirled in little eddies around us. I caught a lyric or two, the French that I took before switching to Latin came back a little. Piaf was singing about a girl who'd killed herself. Something about her dreams being full of madness. I glanced over at Judy, who'd propped her elbows on the cornice, still deep in reverie. The sleeve of her shirt was dirty from the attack and ripped to the elbow, but her slender arm underneath was clean, olive-toned, her little scars faint. Still high on the exhilaration of striking Cleve, I had the urge to slide a finger through the tear in her blouse and run it over the delicate ridges of her scar tissue. As soon as the thought entered me, I felt woozy, embarrassed. I shook it off, and I said, "I have a confession to make."

Snapping to, Judy said, "Okay, spill it."

"I've been reading a detective novel Miss Martins gave me, and I can't put it down."

"Detective novels are so boring. I'm always a step—no *five* steps ahead of them. I like the racy hardboiled books best. Chandler. Cain." Her arms were crossed, and she was now regarding me.

"Why do you think Miss Martins would read mystery novels? It's so—I don't know—*beneath* her."

Judy rolled her eyes. "Oh, don't be a snob."

"Dad wants me to read only the classics. Shakespeare. Homer."

"Does he lock you in the closet and make you read the Bible, too?"

"I think he'd rather I read something practical, like a chemistry textbook."

She turned away again, letting the low evening sun warm her features. "At least you're not scolded by Edith every time you break one of her stupid rules. She's a total fascist."

I tilted far over the edge of the building, letting my heels lift off the roof. Piaf was still singing. *Dreams full of madness.* The strange urge to jump tugged on me. I'd had a similar feeling when Dad held me by the waist as I peered over the edge of the Golden Gate Bridge. The frothy chop below had looked like rows of jagged teeth, gnashing, hungry. I rocked back on my heels and said, "I have a question."

"Okay . . ."

"Edith called you Jackie instead of Judy, and Bart corrected her. Is Jackie a nickname?"

Judy sighed. "I need a cigarette," she said, pushing herself away from the wall. "Change the record, would you?"

"Okay, sure." I put on Nat King Cole. "Nature Boy." Soft strings and fluttery flute.

Once we had our cigarettes—I held mine out, smoking as little of it as possible—Judy said, "Do you really want to know why I can't stand B and E? Why I can't wait to leave this place?" Her eyes were level, serious.

I nodded. Of course I did.

"It's because of *her.* Jackie." She took a long drag and blew a thin cone of smoke to the sky.

A sooty smudge ran along her cheek. I suddenly wanted to wipe it away. "Is that why you want to change your name to Nightingale?"

"Who told you that?"

"You did."

She squinted at me. "No, I didn't. Whatever. It doesn't matter." She took another puff. "Anyway, they adopted me because of Jackie."

"Why?"

"Because she was murdered."

It was staggering news. A murder? I didn't know what to say. I just listened to the mournful and sweet piano interlude of Cole's song. "The photo on the table with the lilies," I said. "That's her."

She blinked. "She was strangled by a boogieman when she was nine and dumped in the Anacostia River."

"That's horrible. Did they catch him?"

"No, but B and E are sure it was this man, Bogdan, a mechanic who worked at the Navy Yard. He'd sit outside St. Timothy's and watch the girls come and go. He had a Shirley Temple thing."

A Shirley Temple thing? A ripple of nausea passed through me.

"The police didn't have enough evidence to lock him up, so out he went, back into the world. Caught and released. Who knows where he is now? It's been eight years."

"That's why she was angry about the court system."

"Sounds like her."

"But what does that have to do with you?"

"I'm her replacement. Edith was too old to have more children, so they adopted me. *Presto.* Instant daughter. Back then, I even looked a bit like Jackie. Mediterranean, that is. Dark hair, golden skin. Edith comes from a wealthy Greek family. Georgiou."

As she was speaking, I thought of Jackie's photo. In my mind, it wasn't the blurry image that I'd studied in the hall. No, it was as if she'd been posed like in a Victorian postmortem portrait. I imagined the Peabodys propping her up, sliding a rod under her coat to hold her shoulders in place and strapping her wobbly head to the curtained backdrop. Once her body was secure, they smoothed her hair; adjusted her tam, blouse, and coat; positioned her hands in a deferential pose (always their little angel); and dusted her gray skin with phosphorus to give her a "life-like" glow. But the eyes . . . Well, there was nothing you could do about the eyes. They were stubbornly vacant, beckoning you in as if she were a room for rent.

I expected Judy to say more, but she didn't. She just stood there, smoking. Even after the song ended and the record hissed and crackled, she didn't move to change it.

And it occurred to me: She didn't want to resemble Jackie at all. Her black bob, her pale face, her double strand of pearls, her forced gloom, her choice of music, even Roosevelt, all added up to something—a line in the sand? What was it she said to me? "I understand what being shackled is all about." Perhaps she does.

PHILIPPA, OCTOBER 20, 1948

This morning I woke up late and, in a dash to get ready, left *Love's Last Move* by my bed. After having it for a week, Miss Martins asked me to return it. So last night, I rushed to finish it, which wasn't difficult. I couldn't put it down, and she was right, it had a good twist. The murderer was devious. Can someone conceal their true nature that well?

I arrived early to class and confessed that I'd forgotten it.

"It's all right," she said, shaking her head. Her cheeks were flushed, or perhaps just overly rouged, and her eyes were red-rimmed. "You need to keep your promises," she added, her affect flat. The light she usually shined on me was out, extinguished by her bad mood. At first, I felt angry: How could our guide, our muse, our Miss Martins be so cold to me? But then, I wondered if everything going on between her and Cleve was taking its toll. She seemed to notice my sinking emotion and softened, dusting her voice with levity. "So, what did you think of the ending?"

"I suspected Clarence until the last few pages. I didn't think he was going to be the final victim. And Mabel—she was shockingly vicious."

"Kane based her on Lady Macbeth."

"Oh." I'd read *Macbeth* last year in English, but I hadn't made the connection. "I didn't suspect her. She was so . . . something."

"Appealing?" Miss Martins said. "Kane knows how to manipulate a reader's sympathies. That's the fun of it."

That was true. Kane made you fall in love with Mabel, her brashness, her excellent sense of humor, and then pulled it all out from underneath you. It was cruel but delicious. I wasn't sure I'd agree that it was *fun*, not exactly. More like, *gripping*.

Miss Martins smiled, seeming to sense my ambivalence. "Kane's second book was also very good. It's about twin brothers who are accused of murdering their father," she said, "but I'm not going to loan it to you until you return the one you have."

"Alright," I said, wanting to read it, craving the dark spell of the first book. "I could go home during lunch and grab it."

"You shouldn't skip lunch." She thought about it. "Why don't you drop it by my apartment at Ninth and East Capitol after school? That's near where you live, right? I'll be there after five."

"Well . . ." It did make my life easier, and I could start reading it tonight. "Are you sure?"

"Of course," she said, and her mood shifted, darkening, but instead of shutting me out, she leaned in. "Philippa," she said and took a breath. "You and Judy are tight-knit now, aren't you?"

"I suppose," I said, uncertain where this was headed.

Her eyes were silvery with moisture, and suddenly her makeup seemed as fragile as eggshell. "Lovely. That's what I was hoping for," she said, but there was no brightness in her voice. Whatever was eating at her was disturbing to watch. I wanted to say something, but who was I to comfort her? That's not the usual dynamic between student and teacher, and I didn't want to risk embarrassing her. "And is DC beginning to feel like home?" she added, another smile flickering and fading.

"It's okay," I said. "My mother grew up here. So, I guess Washington is in my blood."

"She did?" Her eyes lit up.

"She and my father met here. My real mother, that is."

"*Real* mother?" She smiled. "You mean your birth mother?"

"Yes," I said. "Dad has a funny story about how they were paired up through a blind date, the matchmaker, some busybody friend of my mother's, was matching up another couple at the same time and crossed her wires. She accidentally paired up Dad and Mom; they were supposed to go on dates with other people. Dad thought her name was Betty most of the evening. They didn't even like each other at first, but it all worked out in the end." Realizing, of course, that it hadn't worked out in the end, I added, "Well, not the *very* end."

"Oh," she said absently, "that's a great story." As I'd rattled on, she'd receded again, like a ghost in a dark passage. She wanted to be present, to be herself, I think, but she seemed to find it impossible. I felt drawn in and then thrust away—first the beckoning finger and then the sudden flat palm. An emotional yo-yo. It's how I feel when I stare at the photo of my mother in her wedding dress: embraced by her smile but rejected by her two dimensions. I sense that her loving expression is for me, but then realize—my heart sinking every time—that that couldn't be the case. I didn't exist to her then.

Something shifted in Miss Martins again and warmth spread across her face. "Thank you for telling Judy and me about your mother," she said, tilting toward me. "I'm sure it's been difficult growing up without her." Then dreamily, as if she were reciting poetry, she added, "The hardest thing in the world, I imagine." I didn't know how to respond. I should've said something like, "Thank you for saying that, and I don't know what's going on between you and Cleve, but I hope you're okay." Instead, flustered by all the emotional push and pull, I told her that I'd see her later with *Love's Last Move* in hand.

JUDY, OCTOBER 20, 1948

I watched from the door as Philippa and Miss M spoke. They seemed surrounded by a golden bubble. It was like seeing myself a year ago in junior English at the moment I knew Miss M and I had a special connection. I'd written a composition in defense of Circe from the *Odyssey*. It was a sympathetic portrait—after all, she was just protecting what was hers. Miss M ripped through it with a red pen and wrote, "See me immediately!" When I approached her desk, she told me that my essay was extraordinary, that sure, my writing was a little rough here and there, but that I had "a remarkable aptitude for reading literature from a fresh point of view." She insisted that I cultivate it and gave me a reading list, everything from Dickens to Fitzgerald to Dorothy Parker and Elizabeth Bowen. We began to meet after school to discuss my extracurricular reading. Although she never confirmed it, I was sure that she pulled strings to have me placed in her class this year. But today Philippa was in my place, and Miss M was beaming at her. I felt cut off, divided from Miss M *and* Philippa. Together, Philippa and I needed to confront her about why Cleve was threatening her. She wasn't talking to us, and it was getting under my skin. As I stepped forward to burst their bubble, Jake Wallace rammed into my side. "Move it," he said.

Having lost my momentum, I walked to my seat and slung my bag on the floor, not making eye contact with Philippa. Miss M stood to greet students as they flowed in. Once we were settled, she instructed us to open *Wuthering Heights* and locate the passage where Catherine's ghost confronts Lockwood. I knew the passage. Philippa and I reread the book a week ago.

Miss M was about to elaborate on her instructions when Cleve entered the room. There was an uncomfortable hush. His head was down, hair flopped forward. He crossed in front of Miss M. Usually, she would've called him on his tardiness—or any student, for that matter—but she let him stalk to his desk with no reprimand, her troubled eyes lingering on his back.

She continued her instructions: She wanted us to write an impromptu essay arguing whether Catherine's ghost is real or a dream. Was she a figment of Lockwood's imagination or an actual ghost? As she spoke, her voice seemed dislodged from her—a ventriloquist act—and she kept nervously eyeing Cleve, who was slumped in his desk.

I set to work, paging through the novel. I ran a finger across Catherine's wail, "Let me in—let me in!" And Lockwood's response: "Who are you?" And her answer, "Catherine Linton," not Catherine Earnshaw, a name far more familiar to him. It was proof the ghost is real, or at least that's what I'd argue.

I marked the line and glanced up. Cleve wasn't working. He was flipping through a red-brown leather-bound book of some sort, pausing occasionally to let his eyes drift up to Miss M, who was grading at her desk.

After removing a clumsy paragraph with my eraser, debris strewn across my desk, I looked at him again. He was glaring at her. His blue eyes, now glittering in the afternoon sun, broadcast pure disdain. Anger churned in me. I wanted to launch out of my chair and shove him against a wall and demand an explanation for this bizarre behavior—but I was also awed by his insolence, even frightened by it. Where was all this headed? I blew the eraser bits off my desk.

Miss M called time, and we laid down our pencils. She stood, walked in front of her desk, smiled uncertainly, and clasped her hands together. "Okay," she said. "Do I have any volunteers to read the first paragraph of their compositions?" She scanned the room, but no one volunteered, as usual. I thought Philippa would, but perhaps the exercise hadn't gone well for her. "Be brave, now," she said. "I'm not going to grade these harshly.

We just need to hear a few examples to spark discussion." She scanned the room again, the corners of her mouth turning up and her eyebrows twitching encouragingly. I was about to volunteer when Cleve's hand shot up. His arm stretched high, fingers wiggling. "Yes, Cleveland," she said, her cheerfulness seeping from her.

"I'll read," he said.

"Read *what*?" I thought.

"Very well," Miss M said. She took a step toward him, then stopped short. From amid the mess of loose notebook paper on his desk, he raised up the reddish leather book. His jaw was set, and his eyes were slits like he was taking aim. He began: "'Today was just extraordinary. The past is indeed not the past at all—'"

"Stop!" Miss M said. Her entire body buckled slightly, as if some invisible force had socked her in the stomach. "Get out," she added. Her face had flushed bright red.

He didn't move or react. Hatred was radiating from him. Both Philippa and I knew what he was capable of. I wondered when he might swing around and try to melt us with his gaze. Or worse, reach into his knapsack, grab something sharp—a pencil, a drawing compass—and fly at us or Miss M. I flicked my eyes at Philippa, who squinted back but offered me nothing. Wasn't she worried?

"Leave your things and—and get out," Miss M said and, in a lower tone, added, "It's for your own good."

"'You never know what a day has in store for you,'" he continued to read, his voice grinding through the words. "'How everything can change in a moment. You're poor one minute, then rich the next. You're alone, then suddenly you're in love—'"

"Go!" she shouted. "I don't want to look at you!" Her eyes were leaking tears.

He shifted in his seat but didn't leave. I wanted him to go, to relieve the room of the weight of his presence. But he seemed determined to have a standoff, as if this was his way of forcing whatever it was to the surface, even if it meant pushing us all over the edge. Miss M dropped her shoulders, her resolve wilting. The rest of us remained on tenterhooks, sensing that we were witnessing something profound or just deeply strange. I wanted to jump up and shake him by the shoulders: "Spill it, damnit! Get it over with!"

Finally, Miss M said, "If you don't go, I'll get Principal Green."

He didn't leave. He just turned the page of the reddish book and glared at her.

The room was the deck of the *Titanic* tilting toward the ocean, and everyone was paralyzed, waiting for the inevitable cold slap of water. I had to do something, so I plucked a pencil from my desk and flung it at him. It struck him in the chest eraser first. It was a childish move, but it worked. It punctured the tension. He leaped up, shooting me his death-ray stare, and spat out, "You're next!" Whatever *that* meant. He shoved his papers, the leather-bound book, and *Wuthering Heights* into his beat-up red backpack in one crumpled wad. He dashed down the aisle and out of the room. In the commotion, my pencil fell to the floor and rolled toward me. A boomerang!

Miss M looked at me, sad and exasperated, and shook her head, as if I'd done something wrong. The gesture stung. I wanted to step forward and be permitted inside the golden bubble that I'd seen Philippa in earlier, that many times before she'd dropped over me like a bell jar. But right then, like some ghoulish harbinger of doom, she was issuing a warning: "Turn back! Cleve is off bounds." An impetuous part of me, deep inside, wanted to scream, to stand up and demand an explanation, but as soon as that emotion welled up, Miss M dabbed her eyes with a handkerchief, threw back her shoulders, and with forced levity, said, "Enough of all that. Let's turn our attention to the melodrama on the page?"

I clamped my mouth shut and squeezed the sides of my desk.

PHILIPPA, OCTOBER 20, 1948

Once home, I flew up the stairs, grabbed *Love's Last Move*, and flew down again, promising Bonnie I'd be back before six. Out on the street, a breeze tossed a few dead leaves into the air, and I slowed my pace. The windows of the townhouses I passed were life-sized puppet shows. In one, an old man in red suspenders was watering his plants. In another, a fresh-faced wife was helping her husband off with his coat. In yet another, a bedraggled maid was cleaning a chandelier from the top of a ladder. In others, shadows shifted across molded plaster ceilings, and cats waited for their owners, tails twitching, and as twilight descended, lights clicked on. The tinny voices of afternoon radio show hosts and even the tinkling of a piano lesson curled through open windows. Warm smells of baking bread, fried chicken, and bacon grease hit my nose and made my stomach growl. I wondered if Cleve lived in one of the houses, and if perhaps it held the key to his odd behavior.

Miss Martins lived in the English basement of a large townhouse with stone siding and a weather-vaned turret, like something out of an *Inner Sanctum Mystery* broadcast. The entrance to her apartment was on the outside of the building, five feet below street level. In the growing dark, it took me a minute to locate the steps. Beside her door was a small metal mailbox: "900 A: Christine Martins." The door was ajar, which was odd. People in the city didn't leave their doors unlocked, much less open. I rapped on it, and loose in its hinges, it swung wide.

Inside, the dimly lit room was modest and neat, everything arranged at right angles. In one corner sat a writing desk covered with stacks of papers, most likely overdue grading. The only light in the room came from a banker's lamp on the desk. Its green glass shade emitted a sickly, underwater glow. A spicy metallic odor hung in the air like a heavy perfume or cologne, stinging my nostrils and rushing to my head. A scratchy and muffled melody—something from a radio or record player—drifted out from beyond an arched doorway.

"Miss Martins?" I said and waited for a response.

Nothing. Just the music, the perfume.

Certainly, she was here. She told me to come. I was on time. Perhaps she was just out of earshot. "Hello?" I said and continued on.

Beyond the archway, streetlights shone through the ground-level windows, revealing the shadowy outlines of a kitchenette with a cramped breakfast nook and thin strip of Formica countertop. Here, the radio was louder, the tune more discernible, some old crooner going on about being a prisoner of love. I told myself that I shouldn't go any farther, that it was invasive, that Miss Martins would be angry with me, but my body was drawn to the cool, lazy notes, so I crept on. Besides, she'd invited me here, she knew I was coming, right? Perhaps after the disturbing standoff during class, she'd forgotten?

The odor—it was definitely a man's cologne—was even more oppressive. My head throbbed; a headache was gathering steam. I took another step, and something crunched under the sole of my shoe. The noise seemed terrifyingly loud, like I'd overturned a tray of glassware, but it was just a small piece of glass. In a puddle beside it were white chrysanthemums, baby's breath, and shards of a milk-glass vase. Something rustled deeper in the apartment; someone *was* there. "Hello? Miss Martins?" I said in a squeaky whisper, unsure I wanted her to know I was there. I'd gone too far. The music and the cologne swirled around me, disorienting me, making it hard to pin down a directive: Flee or plunge ahead? But something was off, something was wrong. If Judy were there, she'd grab my hand in hers and drag me forward.

Before me was another archway, veiled with a sheer curtain. The music, now on to another song, something about madness and love, was coming from behind it. (Seriously, why are so many songs about love and insanity?) Anyway, I stepped forward, over the puddle, clutching *Love's Last Move*, as if ready to hold it up in my defense. I almost said, "But you told me to come! Here's the book!" I heard mumbling, nothing intelligible, then the soft cry of a woman's voice. Shapes were shifting behind the translucent fabric. Imagining Judy's hand in mine, tugging on me, urging me, I drew back the curtain.

Other than a bedside lamp draped with a pink scarf, the room was unlit. Ten or so feet from me, across a floor strewn with women's clothes—dresses in various patterns, vibrant scarves, several pairs of pumps—a man's bare buttocks undulated, thrusting savagely at a dark form under him. His pants were down mid-thigh, and his leather belt drooped from his belt loops, snaking around his left leg. His rumpled white dress shirt hung loosely from his shoulders; its collar twisted away from his neck. His dark-toned fedora was cocked back, obscuring the shape of his head and hair. His arms, thrown forward, vanished into a shadow. To either side of him, a woman's legs were spread, gray and contorted, one of her black suede pumps dangling from a toe. He grunted, and the woman stirred—a slender arm fell into view. Her open palm was a bright cup of light.

I felt like I'd been swallowed whole. The air was humid, and under the cologne, which was so strong it singed my eyes, creeped the funk of body odor. My headache ballooned, making the veins on the sides of my head pulse. The cover of *Love's Last Move* grew damp from my sweaty palm. I almost cried out "Stop!" or "Don't do that!"—something deep within me wanted to protest, to scream, to rage—but instead, feeling Judy's phantom hand detach from mine, I weakened, and the courage drained out of me. I backed away, trembling. I turned and began to run. But as I did, I stepped in the water on the floor and slipped. I fell hard against the counter, dropping the book. It tumbled under the table in the breakfast nook.

My side throbbed and my vision blurred as I began to recover. I gripped the brittle Formica and hoisted myself up. I had to get out of there—and right away! I couldn't let Miss Martins know I'd seen her like that, with him. The thought was just too horrifying. My chest was heaving. A harsh whisper—it was *his* voice—slid out. "Someone's here. Jesus Christ!" The shadow behind the curtain grew larger, man-shaped. He yanked up his pants and turned, his fedora still crooked. He stepped forward, his silhouette blotting out the rosy light from the lamp. I drew in a deep breath and bounded over the remains of the smashed chrysanthemums, throwing myself through the living room and out into the street.

JUDY, OCTOBER 21, 1948

So, here's some news: Philippa walked in on Miss M with a man, not just with a man, not just sex, but . . . what? Something worse? Rape? Of course, she could be exaggerating. She could be that naive, that inexperienced. She *could* be. She seems that way at times, especially the silly way she smokes her cigarettes like she's channeling Rita Hayworth in *Gilda*.

Not that I'm an expert, but my experience with Roy goddamn Barnes taught me a few things, a few lessons. First of all, fucking is painful and weird, not the romanticized nonsense that movies or magazines make it out to be—or literature, for that matter. It's messier too, and not aesthetically pleasing. Midway through my ordeal with Roy, I opened my eyes, saw his doughy face, his features balled up like a baby's fist, and laughed out loud. It was easier than crying. He gave me a confused, desperate look as if to say, "Huh? What did I do wrong?" But he didn't wait for an answer. He just moaned, pulled out, and left his goo on my skirt. That was it. Can you believe it? Since I was his first—or so he said—does he expect girls to laugh at him during sex now? Is he baffled when they don't? Does he think that's normal? Does he care?

Surely Philippa has had some experiences, some idea of what goes on between men and women. Perhaps I should give her more credit. I don't know. She was really frightened for Miss M. That was clear. After all, she wouldn't have pulled me into Eastern High's grimy service stairwell to tell me the news if it was nothing, right?

After she rushed through the story—she was all fluttery hand motions and run-on sentences—I searched her face and said, "Did Miss M see you leaving?"

Humiliation bled through her cheeks, not the brief flash of embarrassment you feel when tripping going up the stairs or giving the wrong answer to simple arithmetic. She was mortified, almost in tears. Then I understood: she'd dropped *Love's Last Move*. Miss M knew who had walked in on her and her paramour? Her attacker?

Recovering, she said, "I think something is wrong. She wouldn't have asked me to drop off the book when she was . . . entertaining someone. She knew I was coming."

"Maybe she forgot," I said, "or maybe he wasn't invited."

"It doesn't seem like her to be with a man that way. To be . . . loose."

When she said that, I thought, "Jesus, she is a virgin!" Only a virgin would say "loose"—only a virgin from a nineteenth-century novel, that is. I stymied a smile.

"What if she was in danger?" she continued, her face growing pale. "What if he was hurting her, and I did nothing?" She looked at me, her pewter-gray eyes brimming. "Jesus, I just ran."

"You don't know what you saw," I said, touching the side of her arm. "It was probably just a passionate sexual rollick."

"A rollick?" she said, a little irritated. "It was rough. Not a rollick."

"Have you ever seen a man and woman doing it?"

She squirmed a little, exposing her inexperience. Trying not to be a jerk—not always easy for me!—I didn't want to make her feel even more self-conscious. Besides, I was charmed by the paradox of her high-minded moral position on Miss M's romantic life coupled with her fear of admitting to being a sexual neophyte. How she holds her cigarette . . . Clearly, it's all for my benefit.

"So," I said, "you don't really know what sex is supposed to look like . . . in action."

"Something wasn't right about it." She scrunched her face at me. "I'm not an idiot."

"If you say so." I shrugged.

She wrapped her arms around herself as if fending off a chill. "I'm horrified."

"Well, let's see how she reacts to you. Class is next period."

She stared at me and said, "Oh boy, I can't wait."

But Miss M wasn't in class. According to our ancient substitute, Mrs. Blandish, she was "a little under the weather."

PHILIPPA, OCTOBER 21, 1948

Judy and I agreed to meet up after school. We needed to make a plan to investigate what happened to Miss Martins. So, there I was, scanning Horsfield's malt shop for her, peering in through the O in the red-enameled script that swept across its wide plate glass window. I felt jittery, nervous that I'd witnessed too much at Miss Martins's apartment and said too much to Judy about it. This afternoon—and still now—my loyalties are strained, even divided, not that I'm somehow beholden to Miss Martins and not that Judy doesn't deserve to know. In truth, I'm not sure what I *actually* saw, but it felt intimate, and I can't shake the feeling that I've done something to add to Miss Martins's pain.

Inside Horsfield's, kids from school were clustered around cafe tables. In their crisp navy-blue letter jackets, Jake Wallace and his buddies were peacocking for a group of adoring MBBS girls, including Her Holiness Ramona Carmichael. The last thing I wanted to do was bump into them, but I wasn't going to be intimidated by Ramona and her entourage. So, I went in, chin-up, shoulders back, blinders on.

The warm, buttery smell of grilled cheese and the sugary odor of malt mingled in my nostrils and roused my stomach. I weaved between the tables, avoiding Ramona and the others, located two empty barstools, sat on one, and dropped my book bag on the other. I caught my reflection in the chrome service station behind the counter—a blurry twist of pink and blond. "My God, who am I?" I thought. "Just a smudge of flesh and freckles?" I wondered what I'd look like if I chucked my pastel palate and started wearing earth tones or even black, like Judy. Somehow that seemed wrong, too. Waking me from my self-loathing reverie, the waitress, Iris Baker, greeted me. She took my order—a vanilla malt and a piece of pumpkin pie with lots of whipped cream—and gave me a wink.

Judy is a regular at Horsfield's, and she and Iris bonded over their mutual hatred of the MBBS crew. Ramona and the MBBS-ers make a point of reminding Iris how "blessed" she is, as a Negro woman, to have the honor of serving such lovely Christian girls as themselves. I can hear them now, congratulating each other on being such generous tippers: "I gave the poor thing a whole extra nickel!" Ramona and her lemmings are fools. The job at Horsfield's helps Iris pay her living expenses while she studies medicine at Howard University. Luckily, Mr. Horsfield isn't a stupid segregationist. As an undergraduate, Iris participated in sit-ins at cigar stores and diners that refused service to Negros. "She knows what she's about," Judy told me. "She's not putting up with bigots. I want to be like that." As far as I can tell, Iris is Judy's only other friend.

I felt someone poking me in the shoulder and spun around. "Hi, Philippa," Ramona said, smiling, her lips freshly lipsticked. Was she on her way back from the bathroom?

I wasn't going to let her cooing fool me: "What do you want?"

"We need to talk," she said, dousing her saccharine voice with a squirt of lemon.

"About what?"

"Your new best friend."

"Don't think so."

She squinted at me, sizing me up. For a moment, I thought she was going to walk away, but instead, she grabbed my book bag and moved it to the floor. My first impulse was to tell her to scram, but I wanted to hear what she had to say.

"What are you doing?" I said.

She tucked her salmon-colored dress under her and slid onto the stool. "I want to be your friend. I really do. I wanted to when I first met you, but you developed such an *attitude*. It's like you're becoming *her*."

"I never asked you to be my friend."

"I have to warn you about her." She touched her cross like she was making a solemn pledge to her Lord and Savior. "It's my duty."

"Go away," I said, sitting up and turning away.

"Judy isn't a good person."

"Thank God!" I glared at her. "Good people are dull."

"She's done horrible things."

"What? Like bombing cats with bricks?"

She seemed genuinely puzzled.

Iris whirled around, unveiling a creamy, frothy malt, and placed it in front of me.

"That looks decadent," Ramona said. "But it would simply ruin my figure."

"I thought you were impervious to sweets," Iris responded. "The Lord willing."

Ramona gave her a dyspeptic smirk.

"Say what you have to say," I demanded. Beads of condensation were forming on the soda fountain glass, and the whipped cream was melting, losing its curled ribbon shape.

"Last year, Judy did something cruel to a boy . . ." Ramona glanced down and smoothed a wrinkle on her dress.

"Okay?"

"His name was Roy Barnes," she said, lowering her voice. "He was a junior, a wonderful wide receiver, and an all-around nice fellow. Good looking, too. Anyway, Judy took a disliking to him. He wasn't the brightest bulb, so that offended her. She enjoys taking offense but never considers how she offends."

"*Ramona.*"

"Okay, so forgive me, this is inappropriate, but Roy got a reputation for going to the boys' room during lunch and well . . ." Her voice dropped to a whisper. ". . . abusing himself."

Abusing himself! I couldn't believe that's where this was headed.

"It's a sin and something us girls shouldn't be concerned with," she continued. "Anyway, Judy was working on the newspaper at that time. She caught wind of his distasteful habit and, one day, decided to prowl the boys' bathroom, looking for headline material. She wore baggy slacks, tucked her hair into a golf cap, snuck past the hall monitor—that old blind goat Mr. Ives—and went into the boys' bathroom, just outside the auditorium, which no one goes in. Apparently, she hid in an empty stall and waited for Roy. When he entered the boys' room, she crept out and into the stall beside him. She'd hidden a camera under her baggy shirt. She climbed on top of the toilet seat, held the camera over Roy, and snapped a photo. The flash scared him so bad he slid off the toilet and banged his head on the partition."

"He sounds like a real catch," I said, growing tired of her gossip.

"He didn't deserve what she did to him next." She let it hang in the air for dramatic effect.

"Jesus, Ramona—what?"

"She sent the photo she took to his mother."

I winced. Embarrassing him at school was one thing, but sending a photo home—well, Ramona had a point, that *was* cruel. It crossed a line. Walking in on Miss Martins was also like stepping over a forbidden border. It was so out of place with what I knew of her, but it wasn't deliberate. I hadn't meant to. I had trouble imagining why Judy would do such a thing on purpose unless there was more to it.

"He was so ashamed that he went to a private school across the city," she added.

Iris set a thick slice of pumpkin pie in front of me. "Hello, honey," she said, making eye contact with someone behind us.

We spun around. It was Judy.

"I was saving you a seat," I said. "Ramona swiped it."

"I was just leaving," Ramona said in a squeaky voice. "Enjoy your food, Philippa."

"Have a God-blessed day," Judy said and gave her a benediction.

Ramona returned to her hive of MBBS girls.

Judy cast her black eyes on me, and I smiled. "I ordered for us." I selected two straws from a chrome-lidded dispenser and planted them in the soupy malt. Neither it nor the pie were now particularly appetizing. Judy bent to her straw and inhaled the liquid. After drinking her fill, she said, "What did Miss Jesucristo want?"

"A question about homework."

"I didn't know she cared."

I shrugged. The story about Roy Barnes was rattling around in my head. Ramona wasn't warning me out of Christian charity. Still, I wanted to understand it—or at least find out if it was true.

After slicing off a piece of pie with the side of her fork, Judy said, "So, where do you think Miss M is?"

"I really don't know," I said, picking up my fork and jabbing it at the orangish-brown filling.

"Who do you think her lover is, if he *is* her lover? Another teacher? Or someone else at school?" Judy raised her eyebrows. "Could it be Cleve?"

"What?! No, he was an adult, much bigger than Cleve."

"Hmm," Judy said, holding her fork up, making little circles in the air. "Why was his shirt on? And his hat? If they were screwing, why was he wearing most of his clothes?"

"I don't know," I said, exasperated. I couldn't summon any theories. The story about Roy was nagging me, taking up all my mental space. Sure, I believed that she could've done that to a boy, but not unprovoked.

"Well, you witnessed *something*," Judy said, plunging her fork into the whipped cream. "But what?"

"He could be a maniac, a pervert, like the man who strangled Jackie—or Jack the Ripper." A few years ago, I'd flipped through a book about the famous killer. I'd opened it to a photo of Mary Jane Kelly's mutilated corpse. It was a horrible abstraction of blood, bedsheets, and limbs, a scorch mark on my brain.

"Can you remember anything else about him?" Judy said.

"His cologne. It was strong. Top-shelf."

"Anything else?"

"I'm not sure . . ." I closed my eyes and tried to blot out the restaurant noises. "He was tall, wide-shouldered." A kaleidoscope spun in my mind: the man's thrusting rear end, Roy in the stall assailed by a camera flash, the black-and-white of Mary Jane Kelly's body. I didn't know what else to say.

"What about *her*?" Judy said.

"I couldn't see her. Just legs." I also remembered her arm, stretching out, her palm catching the light from the lamp. On the one hand, the gesture seemed pathetic, like she was giving up. On the other, it appeared persistent, like she was reaching out *for* something. Help maybe? I was about to mention it, a detail Judy would've sunk her teeth into, but I held back. Somehow, even as I think about it now, it feels too private to share.

Judy's face darkened; she was indexing the information. "She's never missed a day of school, has she?"

"Never."

"We should check on the scene of 'the crime,'" she said, sounding a bit like Calvin McKey.

I pushed the partially eaten pie away from me.

Judy has an I've-seen-it-all air to her that, for some reason, I assumed meant she'd lost her virginity or, at least, had messed around. But I wonder if I have it wrong. After all, she's never mentioned having a beau or even pointed out a cute boy. When she brings up sex, she talks about it with an edge of disdain, as if it was all beneath her. Other than her scrutiny of Cleve or the occasional eye-roll in the direction of the football team—"Dunderheads! Simps!"—she hasn't mentioned a single boy, especially not Roy Barnes.

I've considered telling her about my episode with Danny Barber back in San Fran. Perhaps it would get her to open up. I think about it all the time. He drove me home from the Midwinter Dance and, before dropping me off, turned his father's Buick into a shady alley. He slid over, wrapped his arm around my shoulders, and without warning, smashed his face against mine, forcing my mouth open with his tongue, which began flopping around like a dying fish. "Throw it back!" I wanted to scream, but of course I couldn't, because of his tongue. His left hand crawled up my satin dress and squeezed my breast, which he began kneading like a ball of dough. "Jesus," I thought, "you're not making biscuits!" While it was happening, I ordered myself to enjoy it, that it was something that *should* be enjoyed, but of course, you can't will yourself to enjoy anything; that's not the point.

Yes, he was handsome, even striking. I've checked out other boys, too. I could point to this or that about them—nice straight teeth, beautiful brown eyes, thick dark hair, full shoulders, muscular arms—but I always feel bored by them. The pretty ones seem more like pieces of art in a museum, staged and cordoned off. Perhaps that's why I'm still such a novice. I don't want to touch them or be touched by them. I'm not a prude. I've just never been properly inspired.

When we arrived at Miss Martins's apartment, we knocked, but there was no response. I peered in the small window at the top of her door. The living room was shot through with angles of late afternoon light from the window wells. Its walls were bare, except the dusty outlines of picture frames. Cardboard boxes were stacked in clusters on the floor and on top of the furniture, most of which were everyday, inexpensive pieces. Only a cushioned stool, a ruffled loveseat, a frilly floor lamp stood out as more exceptional, more personal. A metal trashcan over-stuffed with garbage sat by the front door. No lights were on.

"She's moving?" Judy said, cocking an eyebrow.

"But why?" Clearly, something was very wrong. I wondered if what I'd witnessed had brought all this about—or whether my witnessing of it set things in motion. Perhaps both.

We listened for movement from inside but heard nothing. No one was at home. Judy tried the door; it was locked. "Follow me," she said, leading us to the sunken windows on the East Capitol Street side of the house.

"What are you doing?" I said with a huff.

Judy hopped down in a well and began tugging at the frame, testing it to see if it was bolted. "What does it look like?" she said.

"We could get caught!" I said. Even though we were below street level, we were still visible. My heart was in my throat. I'd never done anything like that before.

"We'd still have less to explain than Miss M."

"She's not going to see it that way," I said, crossing my arms. "Neither are the police."

We hopped out of the window well and dropped into the next one. This time we were obscured by a large boxwood. The pungent stench of the bush—like a thousand dogs had urinated on it (or one cat!)—flooded my nostrils. The smell didn't faze Judy, though. She yanked on the window sash, and the grimy frame banged open, a crack splitting the glass. "Great," I said. "Now we've damaged property. What next? Theft?"

"Do you think I like squeezing through a window into someone's basement? A few days ago, you were a Valkyrie wielding an iron spear, and now you're worried about a little snooping. Come on."

Judy wriggled her thin body through the small window and landed lightly on a toilet lid. I stalled, giving the wisdom of breaking and entering serious thought, such as how getting caught might affect my future. But, as she always does, Judy demanded I take action, so I buttoned up my cardigan and, bracing against the frame, lowered my body through feet first. Judy steadied me until I was balanced on the lid.

The bathroom was lined with black and white tiles and outfitted with dull chrome fixtures. A claw-footed bathtub dominated the far corner; its faucet dripped steadily and a rusty streak stained its enameled surface. The odor of ammonia cleaner was intense. There were no personal effects. She'd already begun to move. Clearly, she'd been in a hurry.

The bedroom was also void of personal items, save a bare mattress, a box spring, and a simple oak headboard. Its soft rose-colored walls and the faint fragrance of lilacs were the only signs this had been Miss Martins's bedroom. I shivered. I remembered the man, whoever he was, attacking her on the mattress, crushing her against the springs. I could still see his angry, jagged movements and his shadow over the bed. I could hear him say, "Someone's here. Jesus Christ!" The panic I'd experienced that night surged through me again, that impulse to flee, matched only by my strange tractor beam–like fixation on the scene. Why had I walked deeper into the apartment? Why I had I lingered even a second? My stomach felt hollow, caving in on itself.

Judy paused at the door to the kitchen and looked back at the bed. "Is this where you stood when you saw it—*them*?"

"Yes." My head began to ache.

"And he was covering her?"

"Yes." My pulse thrummed in my temples.

I'd seen her legs akimbo, her outstretched arm, and her hand—I knew its long graceful fingers. I'd watched them hold a piece of chalk and write,

"Was it a vision, or a waking dream?" on the board in a script that was both exact and fluid, an extension of her.

Judy drew back the curtain. Its scraping sound yanked me out of my memory.

The kitchen's celadon walls and white cabinets were warmer in the daylight, but other than the small table and chairs, it was empty too. The spot where I'd slipped on the puddle from the broken vase was clean. I stooped and looked under the table, hoping by some miracle that *Love's Last Move* would still be there. Of course, it wasn't. Judy ran her hand down the Formica countertop, inspected her fingers, and went into the living room.

I looked back into the bedroom, and something beside the bed glinted in a strip of sunshine from the kitchen. I went to investigate it. For a moment, I stood over it, a little astonished. It was Miss Martins's beloved art deco moon pin. It seemed to be flattened, as if someone had crushed it underfoot. It was missing several faux diamonds, but the crescent was still in place. When I picked it up, I noticed that the fastener on the back was bent out of shape. "Look at this?" I said to Judy, who'd come to find me.

She examined it. "It would take some force to do that much damage, like someone meant to destroy it. Strange." She slipped it into her pocket.

"I guess we're stealing something after all," I said.

Judy wiggled her eyebrows at me. "We need to look one other place."

JUDY, OCTOBER 21, 1948

We snuck into Eastern High a little before 5:00 P.M. Facilities hadn't locked the doors yet. After discovering that Miss M had packed up her apartment, we couldn't waste time. Her classroom was the next logical stop. We made our way through the labyrinth of dark and empty halls, peeking around corners to avoid teachers or administrators who were lingering late. Philippa's saddle oxfords squeaked unbearably on the freshly waxed linoleum. I demanded that she take them off. She gave me a look like I was asking her to donate an organ, but she obeyed. As we rounded the corner to Miss M's room, I held out my hand, and we stopped.

Light was spilling out from the door, and we could hear two voices. They were shrill and uneven, warped by the echoing hall. We crossed the corridor, pressed our backs against the wall, and crept closer to eavesdrop. The transom above the door was tilted, and in its reflection, I could see Miss M and Cleve. She was alright; she hadn't vanished. But something was up. She was in her chair with her hands in front of her, gesturing back and forth, fluttering like a bird. Cleve stood above her, his backpack slung over a shoulder. He's never apart from that damn bag. "Just try to understand," she pleaded, her voice breaking in fear. "I know you're a young man, and it's difficult for you to—"

Cleve said something sharp and unintelligible.

Philippa tugged on my sleeve, but I ignored her. I was running scenarios in my head. My first impulse was to barge in and whack Cleve over the head. As before, everything about his body language—his looming, his glowering, his twitchy energy—foreshadowed violence. Eventually he was going to snap and let loose on Miss M like he had us. But I was also frustrated that Miss M hadn't been more forthcoming; after all, we wanted to help her, so I decided that we needed to linger a beat or two and listen.

"Please, return it to me," she said.

What did she want returned?

"No! Why should I?" he barked.

"It's not yours. You stole it from me."

"Go to hell," he said, spitting it at her. "You're a horrible person. A-a whore!"

Her shoulders drooped. "That's unfair."

"You've ruined my life."

Miss M looked up at him, her eyes softening. What was going on between them? She reached out for his arm as if she was trying to console him and started to rise from her chair. He lurched forward and shoved her back into it. She cried out—and that's when I cracked. I couldn't take it any longer. He wasn't going to do that to her! I lunged into the room, screaming, "Leave her alone!" and grabbed him by his backpack, yanking him away from her. He flailed, spinning his arms in helpless semicircles. His left forearm shot out and clocked me in the ear. I let him go and stumbled back against Miss M's desk. Cleve tripped over his feet and collided with several student desks in the front row, tipping them over in a clamor of metal and wood. Philippa stepped forward, and in a burst of authority, shouted, "Stop it! Now! Just stop!" as if she were everyone's bossy older sister. Dazed by the ringing in my ears and the flood of pain in my head, I braced myself against Miss M's desk and slouched to the floor. As I was sinking, Cleve, driven by fury, hoisted himself up. He clumsily slipped on the waxed floor but caught himself before falling down again. He glared at Miss M and then at me. His face was flushed bright red, and his eyes were twin hot pokers, but some detail—a wrinkle along his forehead, a slight tremor at the corner of his mouth—made him seem wounded, like at any minute he might crumple into a ball and blow away. "You, you, both of you . . ." His words faltered, adding to his rage, short-circuiting him. He shook his head and bolted out of the room.

It took me a minute to recover. My vision was blurry, and my voice felt far-flung like it was coming from some dark corner of the school. I tried to say something comforting to Miss M, but it must've come out oddly. In response, she just stared at me, empty-eyed. She was slumped in her chair, and her eyeliner ran down her face, ruining her meticulously blended makeup. In one nasty gesture, Cleve had diminished her poise, the smart figure she cut in a room, and most of all, her Romantic optimism. The sparkling cloud of beauty that surrounded her had dispersed, blown away with a single puff. I remember her calling me to her desk and telling me that I was a good writer for the first time. It wasn't just the compliment that mattered but how she said it. It was as if, from some heightened place, she was anointing me: "If you can find sympathy for Circe, you can take over the world! Go forth!" Now, Cleve had reduced her, embarrassed her, and I hated him for it. I wanted to hunt him down and choke him with his backpack straps. How could he treat her that way? What's wrong with him?

Philippa took a step toward Miss M.

With almost a flinch, she rose from her chair, fidgeted with her handker-chief, and began dabbing her eyes, smoothing away the tears and cleaning up her streaks of mascara. "Please, girls," she said. "I need to be alone."

"Cleve tried to run us down the other day," Philippa said with surprising calm. "He was very angry."

"He's not a bad boy. He's just . . . upset," she said. "Give him a wide berth."

"Wide berth?" I said. "He's out of control."

She approached us, taking a moment to look at each of us in the eye. "Leave him alone. Promise me." Her gray irises silvered over again with tears, and she gave us her back. "You need to stay away from me, too," she said over her shoulder as she wiped her cheeks with her makeup-stained cloth. She turned to us again and attempted a smile that died before it began. "I've given my notice." Her tone was flat, drained of its art. "I'm no longer your teacher."

"Where are you going?" Philippa said, her voice trembling.

"I'm sorry, Philippa, but I can't . . . I can't say, okay?"

"What?!" I said bitterly. "You have to tell us *something*." After how she drew us in, told us we were brilliant, and gave our friendship her blessing, she couldn't just walk away, especially with no explanation. We deserved that much.

"I'm sorry. I can't."

I squinted at her. "What's going on between you and Cleve?"

She crossed her arms and iced over, her soft lips a hard line.

"He's dangerous," I added.

"I appreciate your concern, Judy, but I can take care of myself. Thank you."

Concern? I remembered the pin in my pocket—a favorite object of hers smashed and discarded. Right then, I nearly pulled it out and confronted her with it, but my wooziness made me cautious, hesitant. I wasn't ready to explain where we'd found it.

"Will you let us know you're safe?" Philippa said, still shaken. "In some way?"

Miss M offered her a faint, resolute smile. "I will, but for now, I must say goodbye, and you . . . you two need to go home. It's dinner time." She was shooting for cheerfulness, but it came across as playacted, a thin veneer. Why was she trying to shut us out? Fear or frustration or some combination of both rattled through me. I wanted the truth; I *deserved* the truth. "Why does Cleve hate you?" I wanted to demand. "Who was the man Philippa saw you with? Why are you really leaving?" I took a step forward, my fists balled, nails biting my palms, hoping the pain would hone my purpose. But before I could speak, Philippa touched my arm, and just like that, I felt incredibly weak, like I might pass out. I whispered, "Jesus," and uncurled my hands and let the anger and questions go, for now. I turned away, leaving Miss M standing in that empty classroom, a pale shadow of herself.

CHAPTER THREE

We were infatuated with Christine Martins. I see that now.

There, in her smart suits and fashionable scarves, her tailored glamour, she was a model for us, a Roman standard held high, a bas-relief carved out of the dull material of our teenage lives. She shines out from my memory like something we invented, indelible like a storybook heroine whom young girls dream up and spin fantasies about on long summer days. We were girls looking for a mother figure—or maybe just an older sister—someone, anyone, to tell us about the world, to hint at its beauty, what pleasures and excitements it had in store for us, from hedonistic pursuits, like designer outfits to new shades of lipstick to the mysteries of sex, to an appreciation for ourselves as creative, passionate, and, most of all, worldly. Like Miss Jean Brodie does her set of devoted pupils in Spark's novel, she was the would-be vanguard, leading us out of ignorance, shaping us into modern women.

But like Brodie, her insecurities were all too real, her facade cracked and chipping. We were so intent on interpreting what we saw—the drama, her tears, Cleve's anger—that we forgot that she was looking back at us, predicting our next move, using us. We didn't understand she was full of grave secrets, that she sensed the horrors just ahead, that on some level she knew what we were capable of—that our loyalty to her was ferocious, even murderous. But that's how teenagers think. They can only envision the world in terms of themselves. We were no different. Like the Brodie set, those spellbound girls in Spark's novel, we could only understand our teacher as far as our imagination allowed, and she fiercely guarded her version of the truth.

JUDY, OCTOBER 23, 1948

Cleve was absent from school Friday. Another vanishing act. Something's in the air. No chatter about where he was. I assumed it had to do with his argument with Miss M. What he said to her continues to echo through my mind: "You're a horrible person. A whore! You've ruined my life." He was so upset, violent. Then, from his fire to Miss M's ice: "I'm no longer your teacher." The news landed with a dull thud, and her tone gnawed at me. It revealed something about her, a hard edge under all that dreamy idealism. Maybe that's okay—I have a similar edge—but why didn't she show us this part of herself sooner? Why not invite us in?

I was still spinning myself up when Philippa rang and invited me to go with her to Harpers Ferry. "Come on!" she said, perky as ever. Jesus. "It's my aunt Sophie's place. She'll love you—and she's an amateur medium. She says things like, 'Philippa, there's a blue cloud nestled on your shoulders like a cat in a tall tree. You must be melancholy today,' and she gives the best tarot readings. She's a lark." Without thinking it through, I said yes, anything to avoid brooding. I didn't know the Watsons or what they'd make of me, but what the hell, it's better than a weekend locked in my room, fending off B and E as they nagged me through the door.

As we drove up to Harpers Ferry in Mr. Watson's cranberry red Chrysler Town and Country this morning, I rose to the occasion, made like a social butterfly, and chatted up the Watsons. God, I'm becoming Philippa! I steered the conversation away from school-related topics and babbled about everything from the best restaurants in town ("The Oysters Rockefeller at Naylor's are shockingly good!") to movies ("Are you a blond or brunette fan? Declare yourself: Veronica or Rita?") to the election ("Truman is a feisty candidate. He's got Dewey by the ankle like a terrier."). I thought Mr. W might be a Dewey man.

"Give 'em hell, Harry," Mr. W said and shook his head. "He's not likely to win. But I agree with you."

I was surprised.

"Neither candidate is moving fast enough on civil rights issues if you ask me," I said, wondering if I was making Philippa nervous. Was I poking and prodding her father too much?

Mr. W smiled condescendingly and said, "What do you know about civil rights?"

Which made me think of Alice, the principal housekeeper at that hellhole of an orphanage, Crestwood, and one of the few people I remember. Alice chatted with me, asked me about myself and about what was troubling me—a rare occurrence in its hallowed halls. She even brought me snacks when the other girls were napping. Slices of brown-sugary pound cake, snickerdoodles, and homemade peanut brittle. Each bite, a brief escape.

Crestwood's little daily traumas have blotted out most of my memory of the place. I can only recall images and sensations, like the dreary green paint in the halls, the musty boarding chambers, and the lye-based soap that burned my eyes. But Alice cuts through the mental static. I became aware of racial discrimination—or at least I began to understand that Alice's being Negro made her vulnerable—when she was accused of stealing a broom (or was it a mop?). She was tossed out like garbage and not allowed to say goodbye to us. She wouldn't have stolen a dime. Iris told me: "If you're a Negro in this country, you're presumed guilty until proven innocent." She was right.

Part of me wanted to tell Mr. W all that, to challenge his tone, but I didn't for Philippa's sake. Instead, I lobbed opinions at him: "The Soviet Union's blockade of Berlin is a complete disaster. Communism is a ruse for power-hungry bureaucrats to hide behind. HUAC better ferret out all the spies in Hollywood."

Philippa gave me a look that said, "Shut it, now."

But I went on: "I mean, *why* would anyone want to make a commie movie anyway? Can you imagine? All the actresses would be wearing sackcloth dresses and headscarves. Who'd want to see that?"

Mr. W didn't think fashion was the point. *Of course*, fashion was the point! It's Hollywood!

When we arrived, Philippa was partway to the house before I'd even flung open the Chrysler's door. A complicated tangle of towers and steep-angled roofs, the old sprawling house clung loosely to the side of the hill, as if at any minute it might let go and slide into the gorge. Behind it, the changing leaves flared in bright bursts across the mountain. The sky was fading to a pale periwinkle. I followed Philippa to the edge of the porch, where she was leaning against the balustrade. Fall decay and chimney smoke stirred in the air. The Potomac River shimmered like a black snake below us. The evening landscape was beautiful but sad. Miss M's words crept into my mind again: "I'm no longer your teacher . . . I must say goodbye."

Philippa smiled at me, her eyes brimming with enthusiasm, and gave me a hug. I froze. I had no idea what to do with my arms pinned to my sides.

"Isn't it just wonderful?" she said and released me. I shivered, glad to be free of her.

"It's fantastic," I said, mocking her lightly, but happy I was no longer thinking about Miss M.

PHILIPPA, OCTOBER 23, 1948

Before I could knock on the front door, Sophie opened it. I rushed to her and gave her a big, long hug, my eyes watering from her intense gardenia perfume. She stood back from me, touching me gently on the elbows. "My oh my," she said, "you've grown a foot since I last set eyes on you."

Usually, she wore loose, colorful clothes, like lace shawls, wool wraps, billowy blouses, and dresses in busy flower patterns. She was never chic, but always put-together. But this time, she'd wrapped herself in a bulky wool duffle coat and a thick purple scarf, like she was on her way to make snow angels. Her round face had thinned, and her translucent skin stretched across her cheeks, exposing a delicate web of veins underneath. She seemed more seventy-seven than fifty-seven. Golly, how had she grown so old so fast? How had I missed that? Still, behind her horn-rimmed glasses, her light brown eyes sparkled, unflinching in their sockets.

"Now," Sophie said, releasing me and directing her attention toward Judy, "who are you?" She held out a hand, which trembled as if from a palsy. My heart swelled with sadness. You expect parents and proxy-parents, like Sophie, to stay fixed in time, like only you, not they, are allowed to age. It's stupid of me, really.

"I'm Judy, a friend of Philippa's."

When Judy took her hand, an odd look passed through Sophie's face, like a sharp pain had seized her briefly.

After we retrieved our luggage, we filed into the house. I grabbed Judy's hand and led her to the room we'd be sharing. After we freshened up, I took her on a tour. "Over there, in that window seat, is where I read hundreds of books," I told her, "and over there, that's where Sophie taught me piano. There's Quincy's bedroom. It's out of bounds. At the end of the hall, that's Sophie's library, where she does tarot readings." I twirled around too much and talked too fast, as if the girl who I'd been over the many summers I spent there had emerged and possessed me. A place can do that, I guess. I'm sure that I annoyed Judy, but I wanted her to love it as much as I did. It's magical. I explained to her that the central eight rooms of the house were constructed before the Civil War by a semifamous railroad architect, Thaddeus Bartlett, who, according to Sophie, haunts the premises. I told her that whenever floorboards creak, Sophie says, "Quiet down, Mr. Bartlett!"

"Terrifying," she said drolly.

"Over the years," I went on, leaning into my role as tour guide, "the house's rooms grew like limbs, stretching across the hillside. Each addition was at odds with the previous building, giving the floor plan a strange flow. It's easy to lose your direction."

In the dining room, I gave a panel in the wainscoting a firm shove. It popped loose, and with a touch of wonder, Judy said, "Where does it go?" *Finally*, I thought, I'd captured her interest.

"A secret cellar," I said, as a rush of musty air wafted up the cobweb-laced, spiral staircase. When I was young, I loved the passage and its Gothic intrigue. It was straight out of Nancy Drew. "They added it before the Civil War," I said and launched into the complete history: "The Bartletts were white abolitionists and used it to hide slaves escaping to the North. During the 1930s, Bartlett's son stashed spirits in it, particularly local wine. According to Sophie, it tasted like moldy vinegar. After Prohibition, they knocked down the wall between the two cellars to make a single room. Now it's full of dust and Christmas decorations."

I waited for a response, but Judy's eyes glazed over. She had something on her mind. Miss Martins, perhaps.

"Want to go exploring?" I said, trying to nudge her out of her plummeting mood. "Down the stairs?" I thought she'd jump at the chance for an adventure.

"No," she said sharply and took a step back.

Why was she resisting me so much? I couldn't figure it out. There I was, trying to reveal something about myself and share it with her. I am Bartlett House, Judy. Don't you see! At very least, she could pretend to be interested.

"Oh, come on," I said cheerfully. "It would be a lark. Who knows what we'd find down there? Maybe even moldy wine."

She crossed her arms and shivered. "It's like being buried alive." Her face was sickly pale. Something was wrong. I'd struck a nerve—but what?

"You really don't want—" I stopped myself.

Her expression had hardened into a mask. She wasn't having it, so I let the door close.

At dinner, Judy and I sat side by side, Sophie at one end and Dad at the other, with Bonnie to my father's right. One chair with a place setting remained empty. "Who's that for?" I said. "Mr. Bartlett?"

"Quincy," Sophie said. "He's running late."

I was thrilled—and surprised. Quincy was at the top of the list of things I missed about my summers in Harpers Ferry. Six years older than I am, he taught me how to play gin rummy, build a campfire, catch a frog, and hold a tennis racket, although I never could manage to hit the ball—or catch a frog, for that matter. He loved war stories and spy novels, like *The Red Badge of Courage* and *The Thirty-Nine Steps*, and he read them to me with gusto. I remember when he told me about the secret passage and led me down the stairs to the cellar. "The catacombs," he called it. We spent hours speculating about whether or not there were other secret passages. We invented melodramatic stories about the Bartlett family: We mused

about Old Thaddeus's missing rare coin collection, which we were sure
was hidden somewhere in the house. We hunted for Miss Nancy Bartlett's
woeful spirit, who still roamed the halls searching for her dead baby.
When Quincy turned eighteen, he joined the Coast Guard but never
saw any action in the war, which, according to Dad, is why he joined the
police academy. I was dying to see him. I wondered if he'd have changed
as much as Sophie.

"We've wanted to have him over for dinner," Dad said. "Isn't that right,
Bonnie? But he never dropped us a line."

"He's not watching his manners," Sophie said with a little tut.

"Young men get caught up in their own lives," Bonnie said. "It's only
natural."

"His new job—it must be difficult," I said, feeling loyal to Quincy,
especially since he wasn't there to defend himself.

"Yes," Sophie said, laying her shaky hand on mine. "From what I can
tell, he's been quite busy. He's had to cover shifts and work long hours."

Sarah Yolland, Sophie's help from town, bustled into the dining room
with a tray of soup bowls. She placed the creamy, onion-scented broth
in front of each of us and garnished it with parsley. The formality of it
struck me as funny. Sophie was so old-fashioned—not narrow-minded,
just nostalgic—and somehow, she'd roped Sarah into playing the role of
the dutiful servant in their little period piece. In truth, Sarah and Sophie
spent most mornings drinking coffee and gossiping and laughing, more
peers than employee and employer.

While we slurped soup, we chatted about current news. Judy asked
everyone if they thought Alger Hiss was a spy. Most of us agreed that he
is; Judy believes he's only the tip of the iceberg. Dad mentioned Babe Ruth's
death, shook his head, and said, "End of an era." Sophie asked us if we'd
seen Olivier's *Hamlet*. She just adores Lawrence Olivier. None of us had.
Aiming to be the most outspoken person at the table, Judy asked us what
we thought about California ending the ban against interracial marriage.

No one responded. Bonnie just smiled politely and glanced at Dad. Terrified that Judy would think me backward, too, I said, "Well, I guess it's overdue." Sophie winked at me. Dad frowned and, clearly sarcastic, said, "Truman desegregated the military, so why not continue to shake things up? It's sure to go smoothly." Then Judy said, "Has anyone heard about the Jackie Peabody murder case?" Suddenly, we'd leaped into ancient history—and personal territory. What was she up to? "She was my adoptive parents' only offspring. She was violated and murdered and dumped in the Anacostia." Sophie was taken aback; the wrinkle on her forehead gave her away. She was well acquainted with death. She'd lost her husband to the bottle and my mother to childbirth. She didn't approve of talking about dead family members so casually. I was embarrassed for Judy.

"Well—" Sophie said.

"My parents, Bart and Edith . . ." Judy interrupted. "They were so knocked out by Jackie's death that they needed a replacement quick." I detected a shift in her voice, a crack. "Ta-da! I was the new, replacement Jackie. Everyone wins." The bile was seeping through. "All's better, everything's dandy."

I didn't know what to do or say, but I was sure this was connected to her sudden shift in mood earlier. She wiped her lips with her starched napkin. Sophie broke the silence, once again regaining command: "I'm sorry for you, honey. It must be so awful for you."

Judy smiled at Sophie, but it was a false, vampish smile.

We were about to dig into apple pie à la mode when Quincy strolled through the dining room door, out of breath. "Apologies!" he said. "I ran from the station. Did I miss dinner?" He had a duffel bag slung over his shoulder, he was still wearing his patrolman's blues, and his thick black hair was mussed and cowlicked from his patrolman's hat. He dropped his bag and kissed Sophie on the cheek. In turn, she gave him a gentle hug, her hands hovering before touching his back. She was clearly in pain. Something *was* wrong. Dad rose to shake his hand, and Bonnie pushed back her chair and greeted him. When I stood, he turned to me: "Wow, it's hard to believe! You're all grown up. I haven't seen you in . . . how long?"

Feeling strangely shy, I muttered, "Four years." Quincy looked taller and thicker through the neck and shoulders. Perhaps it was his uniform.

He smiled and opened his arms, and the tension broke. I hugged him, feeling his solid body under his uniform. "How are you?" he said in my ear. I didn't answer; I just clung to him as if I held on tight enough, he and everyone around us would stop changing. "You look great," he said, releasing me. "I can't believe it's been so long."

"Who is this?" he said, looking at Judy, who was standing behind me.

"My friend, Judy Peabody."

Judy held her hand out, palm down, which briefly confused Quincy. As he took it, he bowed his head as if he thought he should kiss it but caught himself. It was her sly criticism of Sophie's formality and his earnestness. She was testing him, and he'd almost failed. I wondered if I'd made a mistake in inviting her. Nothing about Harpers Ferry or my family seemed to suit her. Quincy, despite his initial awkwardness, didn't seem fazed by her now. He took her as a matter of course. I wondered if he knows girls like her.

"I made it in time for dessert," he said, scanning the table.

We sat again, and Sarah brought out a foil-covered plate of the baked chicken, potatoes au gratin, and string beans saved from dinner for Quincy. The rest of us devoured the mushy, creamy, brown-sugary apple pie.

"We'd love to have you over for dinner in the city," Dad said, wiping crumbs from his mouth. "If you can spare the time, that is." Dad has genuine affection for Quincy; he's the son he never had, I guess.

"I should've reached out sooner," Quincy said, glancing at Sophie. "I've been busy. Today has been no different. I almost didn't come. A prominent Washington family has reported their child missing. He's been gone for twenty-four hours. There's serious concern, of course, but we're not all-hands-on-deck yet. But, you understand, we have to be accommodating to the prominent locals."

"Of course," Bonnie said dimly.

Dad nodded.

Judy perked up: "So, who's missing?"

"Hmm," Quincy said, squinting at Judy. "I'm not sure I should say."

"Come on," I said, smiling. "We're not the press."

"Philippa," Dad said sternly.

"He may not even be missing," Quincy said. "You know how these things go."

"Then it won't hurt you to tell us," Judy said, her manner direct, even pushy. I glanced over at her, and her dark eyes caught mine. I knew what she was thinking: She wanted to know if the missing person was Cleve. He hadn't been in school on Friday, which given his confrontation with Miss Martins wasn't surprising, but recently, he'd been so reckless and distraught. Maybe he'd run away from home—or done something even more rash.

"Don't let the girls pressure you," Dad said, scowling at me. "We don't want you to get into trouble."

"It's none of our business," Bonnie said.

"Was the missing boy Cleveland Closs?" I blurted out impatiently.

Quincy's eyes grew wide, and he blinked. "How do you know that?" he said. So, it *was* Cleve.

"We're schoolmates," Judy said, saving me. "He's been a mess lately."

"And he wasn't in school yesterday. He never misses school," I said, further justifying our lucky guess.

"Howard and Elaine Closs—well, just Mr. Closs—called in, worried that he hadn't come home Thursday night."

Dad, Bonnie, and Sophie wore expressions of concern.

Quincy set down his fork and asked, "How well do you know him?"

Judy knocked her knee against mine. "Not well, but he stands out. He has white-blond hair," she said, as if that explained everything.

Adjusting her napkin in her lap, Sophie said, "Terrible news."

Was it terrible news? Strange news, for sure. The skirmish between Cleve and Miss Martins was still fresh in my mind. He'd called her a whore and a horrible person. He'd attacked her—and Judy. But maybe there was more to him. Did I actually believe that? Did I care? What if something *had* happened to him? Gee, what if he'd done something to himself? And we might've been the last ones to see him before he vanished. Chills crept up my spine.

"Are you girls alright?" Bonnie said in a maudlin warble.

"We're fine," Judy said, looking at me. "Like I said, we don't really know him."

Sophie's eyes narrowed, and she clamped her lips. She didn't like Judy; I could tell. Perhaps it was Judy's gaffe of talking too bluntly about Jackie or all this about Cleve. I didn't want her to sum Judy up like that, and I didn't want Judy to judge her either. My aunt stood from her chair and gave us a flickering smile. Dinner was over.

JUDY, OCTOBER 24, 1948

The second that I stepped inside Philippa's aunt's house I knew I shouldn't have come. It was full of Philippa's history; it was all about *her*. I have no home to speak of, no place stocked with good memories—or memories at all. Crestwood is my only constant, but its shabby halls hardly count. As for Château de Peabody—well, it's a little like sleeping in a mausoleum.

Then Philippa thought it would be a lark to go spelunking in the cellar. Staring down those stairs was like staring at the pit of hell. The thought of going underground gives me the shivers. I've always been that way. Needless to say, a mood grabbed ahold of me. At dinner, I lobbed opinions out over polished silver and the severely starched white tablecloth, hoping something exciting would happen—and finally, something did. Quincy, Philippa's first cousin, arrived and brought news: Cleve is missing!

Once we were back in our room, Philippa flopped on her bed and said, "I think we may have been the last people to see him before he disappeared."

"Hmm."

"We could help," she said, grabbing her pillow and hugging it in her lap.

"If we're going to help anyone, it'd be Miss M," I said, sitting on the twin bed across from her. "Let's lay it all out." I took a moment to collect my thoughts. "First, we noticed that tension was running high between Cleve and Miss M. He was threatening her. Then he attacked us on his bike."

"Soon after that, she kicks him out of class."

"And you walk in on her and a man—not Cleve—fucking."

"Jesus." Philippa pursed her lips.

"You're such a prude." She glared at me. "Okay, 'making love.'" I threw my hands together in prayer, doing my best impression of an ironic angel.

Philippa rolled her eyes and said, "The next day, she isn't at school."

"And her apartment is empty."

"And now we're up to the night in question." Philippa released her pillow, stood, and began to pace. "It gets physical between Cleve and Miss M. We witness the tussle. He wants something from her, or he knows something about her." She looked at me, her eyes unseeing and whirling with thought. "There's definitely something wrong." Then her face crumpled a little. "Poor Miss Martins."

"And . . ." I said, waving my hand like a magician. "Poof! He is vanished."

Her face snapped back, smooth and white. "So, do you think she did something to him?" She blinked nervously.

Annoyed that she'd jumped to that conclusion, I said, "No, never." This was about Cleve's erratic behavior, not Miss M's.

"What happened then?"

"I don't know. Cleve will turn up."

"I hope so."

"Do you?"

Philippa flopped on her bed and said, "He's a jerk, but—"

"But what? He ran us down. Jesus, Philippa. Who cares what happened to him?"

"Okay, but there's more to him. He struggles with that stutter. It can't be easy." I couldn't believe she had even an ounce of sympathy for him. I wondered if I'd misjudged her character. Cleve wasn't someone we should waste time trying to empathize with. Then she added, "And he reminds me of someone I once knew."

My curiosity was piqued. "Who?"

"This boy—Blake Le Beux."

"Oooh, do tell!"

Philippa's face darkened; something was bothering her. Despite her pink sweater sets, saddle oxfords, ankle socks, and irritating bows—God, the fucking bows!—this ripple in her smooth waters suggested something—gravity or sincerity or both. It was strangely reassuring.

She approached the window and looked out at the night. "He committed suicide," she said. "I didn't really know him, but I noticed him in the hall, in some classes we had together. He never seemed like someone who would do a thing like that, whatever that might look like, but he did seem . . . burdened by something, like it physically weighed on him."

The wind stirred the trees just beyond the panes of glass.

She turned abruptly and said, "Tell me about Roy Barnes."

My stomach lurched. How the hell did she know about him? Then I got it: "Did that bitch Ramona tell you?"

"She said you took a photo of him . . . "

She was judging me, deciding I was some sort of bully. I had no doubt that Ramona had told her about the photos, so I said, "Did she tell you why?"

"She said you didn't like him."

"Didn't *like* him?"

"That's what she said."

I gazed up into her blue-gray eyes, measuring their receptiveness, searching for a way to explain myself. The silence between us grew thick. Eventually, she let out an impatient gasp, which I responded to by blurting: "He forced himself on me! Are you happy?" Her freckled forehead wrinkled, and her bottom lip dropped open. "Last year, when I played Lady Bracknell in *The Importance of Being Earnest*, Roy was on the carpentry crew. He'd been flirting with me for weeks. One afternoon we were working after school, and he found me backstage, cornered me, and he . . . that's when . . ." I left the rest for her to imagine.

He hadn't forced himself on me, not exactly. He had propositioned me, and I'd agreed to it. I wanted to know what it felt like. He seemed like a nice fellow, like he'd guide me through it. But he just shoved down his pants, flopped on me, and entered me like I was beside the point, an excuse to validate his manhood, a trophy. I was furious—and full of regret. I told him to stop, but it was too late. I was trapped. I had to watch his face twist upward as he came, his eyes lost in the fly rigging overhead. So yes, I embarrassed him. I ran him out of school. Let that be a lesson!

"I'm so sorry," Philippa said, sitting next to me and sliding her arm around me.

"It's okay," I said, hanging my head. I didn't want to lie to her but didn't know how else to explain it. I pulled away: "So, tell me more about this Blake fellow."

She smiled and said, "There's nothing more to tell."

PHILIPPA, OCTOBER 24, 1948

This morning, Quincy and I took Judy on a tour of Harpers Ferry. The sky
was high and blue, and the air chilly. We wandered down the steep streets
to Arsenal Square and over to the site of the old armory where, during
the Civil War, Union soldiers, outnumbered and without reinforcements,
had set fire to their own stash of supplies and weapons. As we climbed
the steep hill and wandered through Harper Cemetery with its ancient
tombstones sprouting up at angles, Judy took my hand and, in her best
brooding Heathcliff, whispered, "You lie to say I have killed you. Catherine, you know I could as soon forget you as my existence! While you are
at peace I shall writhe in the torments of hell?" It was Cathy's deathbed
scene. I paused a moment, noting our Gothic setting, the hillside strewed
with weather-beaten graves, and then clutched my chest and wailed, "I
shall not be at peace! I'm not wishing you greater torment than I have,
Heathcliff. I only wish us never to be parted!" Quincy lagged behind us,
baffled by our behavior, I'm sure. Holding each other's hands, we flung
ourselves through the cemetery, weaving through the graves as if they
were an obstacle course and laughing. God, how we laughed! When we
reached the top, palms still sealed and breathless, I didn't want to let go.
The gap that had grown between us over the past day had closed, and I
didn't want to risk opening it again.

After lunch, Judy and Quincy paired up for a game of checkers, and
Sophie asked me if I wanted a reading. She led me into the library, a book-
lined parlor, once Mr. Bartlett's study. The room smelled of moldy books
and sun-warmed leather. It soothed me and made me drowsy. Sophie gestured toward a small oval table in the corner. "Sit," she said. "Clear your
head." I sat, but my mind drifted to a reading that she'd given me when
I was ten or eleven. I couldn't remember all of the cards she drew, but I
recall the Empress, pregnant on her throne, and Aunt Sophie reaching
over and laying her hand on mine. I realized then that, to her, I was that

hope that had been plucked from a pyre of tragedy. I felt special and loved and burdened with an immense weight. Like Judy, I guess, I'd inherited something I neither understood nor asked for. Was it a blessing or a curse?

Sophie positioned herself opposite me and shuffled her beloved tarot deck, the worn cards falling smoothly through her fingers. "Have you cleared your mind, dear?" she asked. I nodded but hadn't—and couldn't. Thoughts of Cleve rose up. Where was he? And how was Miss Martins involved? Then Judy. What an awful thing Roy Barnes had done to her! And even Sophie. Her makeup so thick, so much more than she typically wore. Why?

Sophie asked me if I had a specific question for the cards or whether I wanted a general reading. I requested the overview. I had too many questions to decide on one.

She asked me to hold the deck and shuffle it. I did, and she took the cards from me, held them to her forehead with a touch of melodrama, and began laying out a Celtic cross formation on the table. She spaced two cards in the center, one over the other, then one card for each end of a crossbar, starting at the bottom and moving clockwise, ending with four cards, bottom to top, running up the right side of the cross.

I don't usually take her readings seriously, but I love how she interprets the cards—like the mysterious blind swordswoman in Two of Swords or the surrealistic collection of gold goblets in Seven of Cups—and threads together the present, past, and future. They don't provide a map of my fate (if you believe in that sort of thing), but an arabesque of possibilities. Each reading soothes me like my mother's handwritten marginalia. Each card or each note, a gentle nudge or hint, never a command or an absolute.

The first card she laid down was the Chariot, which seemed positive or, at very least, neutral. On it, a warrior in full armor faces forward with a canopy of stars behind him. Two Egyptian sphinxes, one black and one white, tow his chariot. Horizontal over the first, the second card was the Devil—a cat-faced monster with swirling horns, bat wings, hairy legs, and taloned feet, squatting on a pedestal. He grips a torch in his left hand and points it down toward—what? Hell? He holds his right hand high, his middle finger and ring finger split in a perverse blessing. A white pentagram hovers over his head, and a naked horned man and woman pose at his feet, a chain looped around their necks. It was horrifying—and had never surfaced for me before.

"Now," Sophie said, detecting my concern, "remember, there are no good cards or bad cards." Yeah, right.

"What does it mean?" I said, my distress spilling over.

"The first card is your present," Sophie said, smiling kindly. "The Chariot is about articulating a wish—or to be more specific, it's about how articulating your wish will give you direction, even momentum. The sphinxes represent mysteries, riddles. You must find your way through the labyrinth in your heart by saying what you want—it's the cord that runs through your life and guides you. Perhaps this is about school? Or even your missing classmate?"

"And the Devil?"

"Well . . ." Sophie took a deep breath. "The Devil is a heavier card." Heavier!

"But *what* does it mean?"

"It's both 'the vampire' and 'deprived child.'"

"Wonderful." She was failing to reassure me. Of course, arguably that was not her job.

"It suggests something is burdening you, something is weighing on you. Like a vampire, it's draining positive energy from you."

"And what does the depraved child mean?" I stuck out my bottom lip like an ugly baby, trying to make a joke, trying to remember I didn't take this stuff seriously. "Is that supposed to be me?"

Sophie laughed. "*Deprived*, not *depraved*."

Queen of Wands surfaced next. On the card, the queen sits on her throne, grasping a long wooden staff and sunflower. At her feet, a black cat stares out with sinister yellow eyes. Sophie had drawn Queen of Wands for me many times. In this position, it suggests a warm memory. I thought about my recollection of Sophie doing a reading for me years ago. Her kind eyes came to me, not as they are, but as they were.

Then came the Moon, a bright gold disk in a blue sky between two stark towers. Its crescent face is downcast, somber. A wolf and dog look up at it longingly, and at its center, a lobster or crayfish crawls out of a stream. Sophie had never drawn the Moon for me. It was a reading of firsts.

The study door swung open with a bang, and Judy plunged in. "Checkers was a bust," she said, bearing down on us. "We couldn't find the board."

"We're in the middle of a reading," Sophie said, straightening her back. Judy loomed over the table. I wanted to tell Judy to knock it out, that she was being rude.

"So sorry," she said with a false ring. "Wow," she added, snatching the Devil from the center of the spread and holding it at arm's length. "Phew. You're in trouble!"

"Judy," my aunt snapped, "put it back. Readings are personal."

"Oops," she said with an exaggerated shrug. She replaced it gingerly.

"The checkerboard is stored on the bottom shelf of the cabinet in the hall," Sophie said. "Now, please . . . "

"Sorry for the intrusion." As she turned to go, she winked at me.

After the door clicked in place, Sophie looked at me; her kind, expansive eyes were now drawn together, incisive. "Philippa," she said, glancing down at the spread as if it were a broken piece of china. "She's bad news. All around her, there's a backdrop of shadows."

"You're kidding, right?" I asked. Judy had been rude, but she shouldn't be dismissed so sharply.

She frowned. "Do you really like her?"

"Yes, I do."

"Trust me," she said, shaking her head. "She's dangerous."

"So, what are you saying? *She's* the Devil?" I gave a little forced laugh.

"No—but she carries him with her."

I started to get up. I'd had enough. Sophie picked up a card that she'd laid to the side, seized my wrist, and shoved it into my hand. It was Justice, cloaked in red, crowned in gold, holding a sword upright and, of course, her balancing scales.

"You should make your wish, articulate your intention," she said, still gripping me, her skin clammy. "This is your personality card, remember. The sum of the digits of your birthday."

"Dad doesn't approve of this," I said, shaken. "He says it's all nonsense."

She released me. "He's never believed in my gifts."

I remembered her hand on mine all those years ago, reminding me I was special—and burdened. "Did my mother believe in them?"

"I wasn't paying attention to that part of myself back then," she said, her face draining of color. "It was only after her death that I—" She suddenly gritted her teeth; her chin began wobbling and a tremor shook her body.

"What's wrong?" I said, panicking. "Are you okay?"

Her eyes were damp, but her cheeks began to regain their color. "I'm in a bit of a predicament, Philippa—a physical predicament." She smiled wearily.

"I don't understand."

"I have cancer."

"Oh, god." I steadied myself against the table and willed myself not to cry; I wasn't going to do that to her; she's been strong for me over the years, hiding the depth of her loss.

"I was going to tell you last night, but the time just wasn't right. I told your father and Bonnie today, and of course, Quincy knows." Her eyelids fluttered, and she raised her hand to her mouth. I squeezed the edge of the table harder. "It's bone cancer. I've found a wonderful doctor in Frederick, and I've started Koch's antitoxin therapy. I'm hoping for the best, but it's . . ." She glanced down at the unfinished tarot reading. "Oh, who am I fooling?"

I went to her and wrapped my arms around her. I breathed in her gardenia scent. Under it, I smelled the ripe odor of sickness, a faint whiff of mothballs and urine. I couldn't hold it in; I burst into tears.

"Now, honey, don't cry," Sophie said. "I'm not gone yet."

I wanted to fall to the floor and roll around and pound it with my fists! So much had been taken from me: my mother, my home in San Francisco, Miss Martins, and now Sophie.

"Now, niece," she said, pulling away. "We should finish this reading. What's your intention, your wish?"

I wiped my eyes with my sleeve. "Please don't die, Sophie. Promise me."

She hung her head and said, "I can't promise that. No one can promise that."

A sob ballooned in my chest, but before it burst, Judy's flushed face as we plunged through the cemetery flashed through my mind, and I thought, "Whatever happens, don't take her from me? Not her, not ever."

I should've wished for Sophie to live or Cleve to turn up or Miss Martins to return to school. I should've prayed, not flung a wish out into the cosmos. A wave of guilt crested in me, but then, like that, it dissolved. What I'd thought felt right and good—and now it feels more like a fact than a wish, like it's already happened, that it just *is*.

PHILIPPA, OCTOBER 25, 1948

As I walked into the kitchen this morning, Bonnie said, "My goodness, Philippa"—she was facing the stove—"you slept nearly eleven hours. The drive home knocked you out." She pivoted and scraped scrambled eggs from the frying pan. She was wearing an ill-fitting floral housedress, her hair was a nest of tight curls, and her face was strained, lacking makeup. I didn't respond. Dad was at the kitchen table. He slowly lowered his *Washington Post*. His mouth opened like he was about to speak. Instead, he squinted, nodded, and took a sip of coffee.

"Would you like some eggs?" she said cheerfully.

"Sure," I said, still watching Dad, intrigued despite my bleariness. He pulled his paper back up, walling himself off.

"How are you feeling?" she said, her voice syrupy. "I know this news about Sophie is—"

I glared at her, wanting her to spit it out and get it over with. "Is what?" I said, and she seemed deflated. "I'm sorry," I said. "I'm fine. Really."

"Well, your father and I, we'd understand if you weren't. We're all struggling with the news, but I'm sure it's particularly difficult for you."

Bonnie's over-solicitous treatment of me must be motivated by her endless desire to please Dad. She adores him, and I suspect she fears he might throw her over one day and move on to someone prettier and more sophisticated. I never want to be trapped like she is, afraid of being cast away. I pity her, but this dynamic gives me leverage.

She handed me a plate of fluffy eggs and buttered toast. "Well, if there's anything I can do. Maybe your favorite meal tonight? Rarebit on toast?" she said, her lips quivering. "We love you, dear."

"That'd be nice," I said and took the plate.

"Carl, do you want some eggs?"

"No, no, thank you," he muttered.

She turned to do the dishes.

He fidgeted with the paper and folded it closed. His gaze lingered on a landscape of the San Francisco Bay on the wall across from us; the bright blue of the water was intense in the morning sun. He was probably processing the news about Sophie. He finds her flighty and impractical, but he loves her—and I know he feels indebted to her for her support during the early days after my mother died. He took a measured sip of coffee and cleared his throat. He always struggles to say what he feels. When he told me about his engagement to Bonnie, he couldn't glue two words together—a seasoned JAG!

"Philippa," he said grimly.

"Yes?"

He studied me. Something was bothering him.

"What is it?" I said, nudging him along.

"The young man has been found. Your classmate."

"Cleve?" I said. "What happened? Is he okay?"

His posture stiffened. "No, Philippa," he said, shaking his head. "He's dead."

Before I said, "What?" I felt a catch in my throat—a glob of messy emotion. I remembered Cleve sitting on the school steps rattling off the scientific names for lobster parts. I remembered his momentary exuberance and the tenderness that I'd felt toward him when he stuttered. But later, practically frothing at the mouth, he'd attacked us. I'd wanted to hurt him—and I'd struck him, which felt good. The reverberation still echoed in my arm bones. How should I feel now? Sad? Horrified? Even guilty? No, not guilty.

"It's in the *Post*," Dad said softly. "I'm sorry."

His grip tightened on the folded paper, crinkling it. I reached across the table and held out my hand for it, but he didn't move.

"*Dad*," I said in almost a whine. "Please."

He relinquished it. "I suppose you should read about it now rather than hear about it at school."

The paper had printed Cleve's school portrait. He had carefully oiled and combed blond hair, distant eyes, and a fixed smile. Beside the photo, it read: "WASHINGTON, DC—Boy found dead on Sunday has been identified as seventeen-year-old Cleveland Closs of Capitol Hill. He was reported missing by his parents, Mr. Howard and Elaine Closs, on Friday morning. Lunchtime picnickers Rody James and Linda Wells discovered the body on the bank of the Anacostia River, just below the Sousa Bridge on the District side. Foul play suspected."

I scanned the article.

The Wells woman said, "When I first saw him, I thought he must be sunning after a swim. For heaven's sake, I thought, it's October, and he's shirtless!"

An armchair detective, Rody James said, "He must've washed up from the river. He had something on his arm, writing, but I couldn't make it out."

E. G. Thomas of the *Washington Post* described him as a senior at Eastern High School, who "planned on attending college and studying to be a doctor." *A doctor?* That sounded wrong—a wish his parents had, perhaps, but not him. The article also mentioned his grandmother, local socialite Mrs. Moira Closs of Chevy Chase, the wife of the late Mr. Cleveland Closs, owner of Capitol City Hardware, a regional chain. Cleve was the grandson of an important person.

"Phil," Dad said, touching my arm, "are you okay?"

I recoiled from him, my head spinning. "Excuse me," I said, pushing away from the table, "I need to . . ." and then I stood and left the room.

As I'm writing this, I'm trying to imagine Cleve lying there in the grass and mud. Not to be morbid, but just to find a way to believe it. I close my eyes, and I can hear the lapping of the river, the traffic behind me, and the gulls swooping by. I can smell the earthy, squishy shoreline sod. I look out, then down, and his pale body shimmers past me like a few frames of a filmstrip, like something I once saw in a tabloid rag and quickly turned the page. The colorless sunlight briefly shines on his damp skin before a cloud passes overhead—or is it before the police cast their long shadows over him? He's there, then not there. But I can't imagine his lifeless face. It's beyond me. I just see him after I struck him with the iron slat or after his tussle with Miss Martins. His face was hectic and perplexed and furious, but very alive, its heavy-lidded gaze challenging me, taunting me.

JUDY, OCTOBER 25, 1948

Eavesdropping is a bad habit, or so I've been told. I can't help it. It's how I turn enmity into entertainment. As I spy through cracked doors and around corners, B and E transform from my bitter stewards into dreary characters from a Eugene O'Neill tragedy, "Long Day's Journey into Cocktail Hour" or "The Iceman Stumbleth." They seem to drift around freezing intermittently, each tableaux depicting a big emotion: "Rage" (gritted teeth, balled fists, sweaty forehead) or "Melancholy" (drooped shoulders, empty tumbler in hand, lips moving soundlessly) or "Pity" (one parent staring queerly at the other who is staring at nothing). This morning, I leaned on the frame of the kitchen door and witnessed Bart read to Edith the *Post* article about Cleve.

"Dear God," she said after he finished. "Where he was found, down by the river . . . Could it be another victim?" With the newspaper spread out in front of him, Bart sat there, petrified and mute. Hovering over his shoulder, her fussy Limoges coffee pot still in hand, Edith scanned the article again, as if she was unable to digest its contents the first go-around. "The Closs boy," she said, setting the pot down with a clunk, forgetting to finish filling Bart's cup. "Not only a child but a grandchild of a prominent citizen. You must reach out to Moira. This is terrible."

"It brings it all back," Bart said. "Oh, Christ."

"Yes," Edith said, placing her hand on his shoulder. "But it's an opportunity. Perhaps we can prove it this time."

"That bit about the writing on the body," Bart said. "It sounds like Bogdan. God help the Closses if he defiled their boy the way he . . ." He bowed his head, unable to go on.

"We should go to the police," Edith said. "Today."

Right then, the doorbell rang. They looked up and caught me observing them, a little unnerved I'd been snooping on their private moment. I wanted to say something encouraging; then I wanted to say something biting. I did neither. I just went to the door.

To be honest, I don't know what to make of B and E. When I was younger, they inflicted Jackie on me day-in and day-out. Edith forced me into the mold of a dead girl, a prissy princess in velvet hair bows, white stockings, and patent leather Mary Janes. It was a nightmare trying to live up to her, but far worse was trying to be her in the conditional tense: Who might've she been? A flute player? A calligraphist? A Francophile? A flirt? A showboat? A pleaser? Always a pleaser. Still, during all of it, even when it was utterly humiliating, even when I imagined shoving B and E down the staircase or setting the house on fire, I couldn't bring myself to hate them outright. At times, I wanted to—and perhaps I even did—but it would pass into something stranger: revulsion. Now, I just want to get the hell out of this house, escape this suffocating cocoon, and become someone else, no longer a Peabody.

I swung the door open, and there was Philippa. She'd heard the news, too. I grabbed my bag and coat, but instead of heading to school, we circled back and, using the fire escape stairs, climbed to the top of Hill Estates. The wind was up, and it whipped hard at our skirts and hair. I lit a cigarette and gave up on it, tossing it over the side. The butt almost hit an old woman walking a toy poodle. The dome of the Capitol played peekaboo through the shifting tree limbs.

"What do you think?" she said, full of wonder.

"B and E are ready to storm the police station," I said.

"What? Why?"

"Jackie died under similar circumstances."

A few strands of strawberry blond hair flapped across her face. "Okay?"

"Remember, Bogdan strangled her and dumped her in the river. She washed up not far from Sousa Bridge, naked. He'd done the worst to her."

"The worst to her?"

"He assaulted her," I said, irritated by her naivete.

It didn't seem to be sinking in.

"Sexually," I said, but she still looked confused. "Jesus, Philippa. He raped her."

"I'm sorry. I didn't—" She bit her lip. "Oh, my God. She was only nine."

"Like I said, Bogdan had a Shirley Temple thing."

"What does that even mean?"

"B and E see similarities between Cleve's and Jackie's deaths and are jumping to conclusions. They've always been convinced Bogdan is still out there, hunting children. The boogeyman."

Philippa rested against the crumbling chimney and sheltered herself from the wind. The sky was beginning to darken. Rain was coming. She crossed her arms and gazed at me, her slate-colored eyes grave and earnest. "But Cleve's seventeen, not nine," she said.

"That's right."

"And he wasn't completely naked like Jackie."

"That too."

"And somehow, all this might be connected to Miss Martins."

"Maybe."

Sure, Cleve and Miss M were at odds. I still see them in the classroom: Miss M's defeated slump, her tear-stained face, and her hollowed-out expression, and then Cleve's flailing arms, his irate stutter, and his stupid wounded eyes. If I'd had that iron stake, I would've driven it through him, then and there. But that wasn't Miss M's style. No, she didn't do it; she couldn't have done it. I'd suspect myself before I'd suspect her. As for Cleve's death being linked to Jackie: B and E are desperate to find a connection, to grasp at some hope. But who knows? Maybe they're right.

"Shouldn't we do something?" Philippa said, leaning in and blocking the breeze. "We need to do something."

"I know where to start," I said.

Her eyes urged me on. "Well?"

"Cleve's family. The Closses."

PHILIPPA, OCTOBER 26, 1948

I was on the edge of the river, the brackish water slurring and shifting against the tree-lined horizon. Behind the trees, the sky deepened from pale purple to indigo to bruise gray. A storm was about to break. My feet were sinking into the muck—twin white slivers with toes wiggling, then just ankles, then knees—I was being swallowed up and couldn't move. Twenty feet in front of me, I spotted debris of some sort, moving in and out of the choppy waves. I strained to make it out. A fish? A part of a boat? Garbage? Suddenly, I was near it, above it, floating, magically freed from the mud. Under the surface, a human form darted away like a skate or a ray. Was it Cleve? I followed him, worried I was getting too far out; the river was vast, oceanic. I caught another glimpse of it, *him*. It wasn't Cleve, it was Jackie Peabody. As soon as I was close enough to glimpse it, it glided away again, a limp hand casting a spray as it sliced the water. I zipped after it, flying like a character from a comic book—or maybe I was on the bow of a boat? When I saw her, it was my mother—pale and lovely and smiling. I was close to her, leaning toward her, a glass-thin layer of water between us. I reached out for her. But the boat rocked (it was a boat!), and I lost my grip and tumbled in, headfirst.

I've never had a dream like that before. I was terrified when I woke up. Every time I closed my eyes, I saw Jackie's small, bare body, a pale fish slipping away under the surface of the Anacostia River. Like Cleve, she was unfathomable. For a long time, I just lay there, listening to the trees sway outside my window and the patter of rain against the glass. Then I got up to use the bathroom.

Dreams are like scattered jigsaw puzzles, pieces flung under tables, between cushions, and behind radiators. Maybe my mind was picking up pieces as I slept, trying to complete the picture. As I scribble this down, I no longer see Cleve or Jackie or even my mother submerged in the river, but instead, Miss Martins. The water is rushing over her, becoming foamy and opaque. Her face is slack, and her eyes mascara-streaked. She's sinking away from me. I see the back of a man, her attacker, his naked rear end thrusting, his cologne singeing the air like mustard gas. Her hand is stretching out to me. Does she need my help? No, that's not it, is it? She's reaching out to me, her palm cupping the light. "Take my hand," she seems to be saying, "and I'll show you everything."

CHAPTER FOUR

Philippa relished recording her dreams, as did Judy. In college, both of them—us, both of us—thumbed through Freud's writings, but long before then, our gut told us that dreams were "the Royal Road to the unconscious." Our own minds, especially the secret impulses we harbored there, were fascinating to us. Like the Romantics and teenagers everywhere, we were self-absorbed, endlessly entertained by our own enigmatic natures. Perhaps that's why we tore through journal after journal, trying to get down every detail, impression, and opinion. We knew we could pick through them in retrospect. Unlike adult diarists who claim to be writing for themselves but in truth are writing for posterity, we were writing for our future selves, as if we knew this moment, the occasion (and necessity) of this book, would come.

We each had our own style: Philippa favored little hardbound books, with dainty string ties and floral print covers. She always wrote with smooth, thick black ink, her script tight and orderly, almost as if it were typeset, with the occasional smudge. On the other hand, Judy was drawn to large-format journals, like artist portfolios or sketchbooks, where she could scrawl her thoughts with whatever writing implement was within reach and paste in memorabilia, part record keeper and part art project.

Both of us saved and protected our journals compulsively: Philippa in a large tapestry suitcase under her bed. It's now frayed and worn at the corners, the handle is broken, the locks rusted and warped. And Judy in a secondhand steamer trunk until a mouse clawed through the laminated paperboard exterior and ransacked it, making a cozy nest out of 1951–52. Now what's left of both collections is organized and cataloged on a bookshelf in my office.

I've read them many times, even my own. I've taken reams of notes about 1948 and the years before and after. It was tedious reading. You have to slog through weeks and weeks of "Bonnie baked me a pineapple upside-down cake. I just HATE pineapples. She knows that!" Or "I wonder if B&E actually love each other—Oh God, imagine them having sex!" Or "Can't sleep. The news about that woman cut in two by a psychotic killer in Los Angeles has me all nerves." Or Mother Wore Tights is all technicolor fluff and . . . I really can't tolerate musicals. The Lady from Shanghai is killer-diller, though."

The daily record-keeping has its use: every flourish of the pen, every smear of ink, and every pencil scribble brings me closer to the past. After all, didn't honest Abe say, "No man has a good enough memory to be a successful liar." These pages are our memories, shuffled together to make a whole—one story. Sure, I've excised the redundancies and dull bits. I've filled in the gaps here and there. But I'm aiming for the truth.

JUDY, OCTOBER 27, 1948

Mrs. Whitlow didn't notice me as I peered in. The old snoot was typing at her big wooden desk, her fingers striking the keys furiously, and her eyeglasses perched on her nose. It was lunchtime, so no one was around. I signaled to Philippa. She hesitated, a worry line creasing her forehead. "Don't chicken out," I thought. "Come on, damn it!" Then she leapt into action, dashing into the room, clutching her chest, and gasping, "Mrs. Whitlow!" Pure melodrama.

"Yes, Philippa?" Her voice sugary, full of thinly veiled contempt.

"This girl, Ramona, tripped and hurt herself on the steps out front! She's bleeding from the mouth and the ears!"

"Oh, dear!" Whitlow said, popping up from her desk, her chained reading glasses dropping from her nose.

Philippa was getting the job done, even if she was laying it on a bit thick. Whitlow careened across the room, half-drunk with panic. To me, she said, "Go find the nurse!" To Philippa: "Show me where Ramona is."

As Philippa passed by me, I mouthed "ears?" to her.

She shrugged and followed Whitlow out, calling to her, "The *front* steps, Mrs. Whitlow! The front!"

To my right stood a large, three-tier file cabinet that must weigh as much as an army tank. With no time to waste, I slid Whitlow's chair over to the cabinet and climbed on its seat, wobbling, tightening my abdomen to steady myself. I needed to see into the A–G drawer at the top. Using the excuse that we wanted to send condolence letters, we'd asked for the Closses' home address. Principal Green told us that he wasn't sharing it out of respect for their privacy, but he'd be happy to convey any notes to the family. Well, that wouldn't work. We needed to know where the Closses lived. So, we concocted a plan. This "brilliant" plan.

I yanked on the drawer, and it slid out with a bang. I lost my balance, stabilizing myself by grabbing the top corner of the file cabinet, the sharp metal biting into my palm. I peered in and began searching the files: Cline, Cooper, Crane, Cromfield, Cross, but no Closs. I heard footfalls and voices in the hall and jumped down, forgetting to close the drawer. I fell to my knees behind Whitlow's desk. My heart thumped against my rib cage. Someone was in the room: students murmuring something about whether or not the football players would get their uniforms in time for the game. I thought, "Go the hell away! *Now!*"

Luckily, they left as quickly as they had arrived. Making sure the coast was clear, I rose up. I stood on the chair and flipped through the files again. No Closs. Had the police already claimed it? Or maybe Principal Green had it in his office? I shut the drawer and dragged the chair back to Whitlow's desk. I noticed a piece of paper scrolled in the typewriter, a condolence letter from Green to Mr. and Mrs. Howard Closs. She'd typed the address: 610 A Street SE! Not far from Philippa's house.

Footfalls again.

I was on the other side of the room sitting calmly in the waiting area when Principal Green, who hadn't heard about the mortally wounded, brain-bashed, blood-gushing Ramona Carmichael, appeared and said, "Hello, Miss Peabody. What can I do for you?"

PHILIPPA, OCTOBER 27, 1948

We'd been spotted.

Beyond the bright scarlet-leaved maple in the front garden, I detected a flash of white in the large bay window of the Closses' three-story Victorian townhouse. I scanned the scraggly bushes clustered around the iron stairs leading up to the front door. To the right of the steps, jammed crookedly into the ground, was a grimy birdless birdbath. Nearby, a moss-eaten marble figurine of Pan as a boy puffed on his pipes, his horns snapped off, perhaps by a young Cleve.

I remember thinking: How are the grief-stricken Closses going to respond to a knock on their door from two "friends" of Cleve's? I mean, who are we to them? And what are we *really* attempting to do here? Are we investigating Cleve's murder? Or who attacked Miss Martins? Or both? Isn't that pretty pushy of us? Or just foolish?

I paused on the sidewalk, registering my quickened breath and the thrum of my nerves. Judy seemed so cool, so confident. Her impatient glance was enough to unglue me. We trudged through a sea of red leaves and up the steps, the soles of our shoes clattering across the filigreed metal. Judy's finger shot out, stopping just short of the doorbell. "Here we go," she said. "Remember what we talked about. Keep to the plan."

I nodded, and she pressed the doorbell. Behind the doors, from a far corner of the house, it chimed a hollow, mournful sound. I waited, still breathless and tense. Nothing. Judy glanced at me, scowled, and pressed it again. Again, *that* noise—like a gong at the bottom of a well. We could retreat to the street, to safety, I thought. It wasn't too late. Then the bolt on the other side of the door slid back, and the thick door opened, scuffing against its frame.

Smiling grimly before us was a woman in her mid-sixties or so. She had a large, elegant bouffant that flared out from the sides of her head like a silvery crown. She wore a navy-blue cape trimmed with lustrous chinchilla fur. Costly, no doubt. She tilted toward us, insisting that we speak first.

"Are Mr. and Mrs. Closs in? We're friends of Cleve's," I said, all jitters.

"And I thought the reporters had finally found us." Her remark fell like a dead weight between us. "Your names?" she said with an impatient sigh. "Let's begin there." Her makeup was thick and expertly applied to smooth out any wrinkles. Her sculpted eyebrows arched over her moist protuberant eyes, giving her a look of constant surprise—or was it perpetual shock?

"Philippa Watson, and this is my friend—"

"Judy," she said, thrusting her hand out like a dagger.

The woman winced. "I'm Moira, Cleveland's grandmother."

The article in the *Post* mentioned that she was rich and that her husband had built Capitol City Hardware from the ground up. It was the largest chain in the city, with a store in every major neighborhood. Cleve's parents must have money too, although the size of the townhouse didn't suggest significant wealth, not like Judy's.

Moira held out her well-manicured hand to Judy. It bobbed between them like the head of a snake, her huge pear-cut diamond glittering like a spectral eye.

"We'd like to pay our respects," Judy said in a muted tone, constructed, it seemed, to suggest deference, even pliability. She shook Moira's hand. I did too, cautiously. My nerves were subsiding.

"That's thoughtful, but it's not a good time. His mother is—we all are—terribly upset," she said, not seeming remotely upset.

"We're torn up, too," Judy said, using that voice again.

"Perhaps another time." Moira began to close the door.

"Please," Judy said, stepping forward. "We may know something about what happened to your grandson." We didn't know anything, or if we did, we didn't know what we knew, but it was clear Judy was determined to get inside and meet Cleve's parents. Moira squinted at us as if she couldn't quite make us out, but her curiosity seemed piqued. "Very well," she said. "Come in. But you'll need to be brief. Elaine isn't well, and my son isn't here."

Moira led us into the front parlor. The scarlet maple radiated through the bay windows, but the drab emerald-green wallpaper and the heavy velvet upholstery on the sofa and wingback chairs swallowed its brilliance, leaving the room filled with a dull pink haze. A vase of dingy silk flowers—red and white roses, and thin plumes of baby's breath—like a remnant from a decades-old Valentine's Day bouquet, moldered in the fireplace, a sad substitute for a fire. No light, not even the ornate Victorian chandelier, was on. The low murmur of classical music hissed from an art deco radio console in the corner. The unease that had lifted briefly wormed its way back into me.

"Have a seat," Moira said, gesturing toward the sofa, over which hung a landscape of a vast plain with a dark river running through it. In the background, a wall of rain was consuming the low rolling hills. It looked like the moor in *Wuthering Heights*. I thought of Catherine's ghost scraping at the window, and I shivered. We sat down, and Moira marched out of the room, her cape rippling.

Opposite us, a large oak grandfather clock with a tarnished moon dial and elaborate finials glowered. Its pendulum swung, glinting in the gloom of its casing. "Go away," it seemed to whisper. "The Closses have suffered enough." Its gears rotated, a creaky mechanical noise, and it chimed—a quarter till four.

I was aware of someone staring at us.

The silhouette of a woman lingered in the threshold of a second entrance into the room. Judy shifted beside me, and the sofa's springs squeaked. Moira materialized behind the woman and, with assertive, carpet-ripping energy, swept the shadow toward us. "There, there, Elaine, no need to be skittish," she said, her arm across her back, guiding her. "These children were friends of your son." Moira smiled at us. "As you can imagine, this has been difficult for us, but especially for his mother. Why don't you join her at the window? The light is better over there and, unlike the harsh electric lights, won't agitate her. She gets furious migraines." She released Cleve's mother and waved her hand at the window seat, upholstered in dusty velvet. "I'll gather some cookies and milk," she said, stopping by the radio to switch it off. "Or would you prefer tea?"

"Milk is fine," I said.

We positioned ourselves on the U-shaped window seat. Between Cleve's mother and the two of us was a dainty, thin-legged tea table. In her mid-thirties—I'm guessing—Elaine might've struck me as an attractive woman, but her gaze was averted, focusing on her lap, and her tight, high-collared dress was propping her up like an exoskeleton. "You knew him?" she said, glancing up. Her eyes were damp and startlingly vibrant, the color of green jasper.

"He was in our English class," I said.

She brightened. "Oh, really? Cleve doesn't care for school much. It's difficult for him." Her face fell. "It *was* difficult for him. He was so different from me. I always loved literature, especially classical literature. I studied it in college." She glanced up, her eyes rolling back to access a memory. She puffed up a little and said, "'Res est soliciti plena timoris amor.' Do you know what that means?"

I shook my head.

She frowned. "Why have they stopped teaching Latin in our schools? It means: 'Love is a thing ever filled with anxious fear.'" As she considered it, she began retreating again into a fog. "All lovers understand that," she mumbled. "And mothers, too."

"I'm sorry Cleve didn't like English," I blurted stupidly and then tried to recover: "It's terrible what happened to him. You must be just . . . I can't imagine."

She perked up. "I don't know what to say," she said, smiled meekly, and crumpled again. "Nothing will be the same. There are no words . . . "

Her sorrow—its inexpressibility, really—made me think of my mother. I thought of her in her wedding photo, smiling out at me, at everyone, but somehow, at the same time, she was smiling at a certain someone, maybe Dad. When I look at the photo, I don't know how I feel, and I don't have a pithy quotation to sum it up. It's just a messy mixture of longing and hope, I suppose. One thing I do know: the woman in the photo was the opposite of Elaine, who was swooning before me, as if her sadness were a disease spiraling through her. We were just interlopers, stomping on her grief.

"He'll be missed," I said. It was a lie, but it seemed necessary to say.

"Yes," she said, and her face tightened as if she'd been seized by pain. She raised her hands up as if she were trying to fend off an attack, as if some creature were dragging its claws across her skull.

"Are you okay?" I asked softly.

Then, whatever it was seemed to vanish, and she dropped her fists into her lap. Her clenched eyes relaxed and flicked open. "Cleveland didn't care much for English," she said, her tone disappointed, even critical. "He had trouble with his speech. A stutterer."

"He told me he wanted to study biology," I said. "He liked marine life. Lobsters."

"He loved going out on the boat. He adored the ocean. All Closs men adore the ocean, the water. So sad that . . ." Grief yanked the thought away from her. Her gaze drifted. I wondered if she was staring at the dramatic landscape over my shoulder, finding solace in its brooding clouds.

Judy leaned in and, attempting to draw her focus, said, "We were wondering if you could tell us what happened. No one will tell us. The paper—it didn't go into detail."

"I don't know," Elaine said, withdrawing, her palms out, pushing at an invisible wall between them. "I don't know who would want to hurt him. It all seems pointless—and unnecessary. So unnecessary."

We'd come to retrieve information, to discover a clue, but it felt like we were crossing a sacred boundary—and that it could easily backfire.

"When was the last time you saw him?" Judy said, her eyes locked on her.

"She asked him to pick up dinner," Moira said, entering the room. "It was Thursday, the twenty-first." She was carrying a tray that she positioned on the table in front of us. It held two glasses of milk on doilies and cookie sandwiches oozing strawberry jam, artfully displayed on fine china.

"I asked him to go for me," Elaine said. "I was very ill."

"We saw him that night," Judy said, which surprised me. Was she going to tell them about his row with Miss Martins?

"You did?" Moira asked, her nostrils flexing and eyes narrowing. "Where?" She sat beside her daughter-in-law.

"We bumped into him on East Capitol Street," Judy said, which was a lie, "at the corner of Ninth."

Why bring it up, then lie? What angle was she playing?

"Where were you headed?" Moira said and, with forced levity, added, "Please, have some milk and cookies. They're shortbread, my mother's recipe."

"The grocer's," Judy said, snatching up a cookie. "My mother needed butter."

"And when was that?"

"Five or six. I can't remember," Judy said and bit into the cookie. Jam squished out and dribbled in globs down her white blouse. "Shucks!" she said, after swallowing. "It will stain!" She tossed the cookie back on the plate, spurned for its offense. "I need to clean it right away."

The plan was kicking in: We'd decided that if we were invited in, Judy would make an excuse to use the bathroom. While I kept them distracted with chitchat, she'd snoop. I *really* didn't want her to leave me, though.

"I'll get you a towel," Moira said, beginning to get up.

"It's okay," Judy said firmly. "I'll do it. The bathroom?"

"Down the hall and to the right."

And she was gone.

Both women glowered at me. My throat tightened. Moira was haughty and disbelieving. She seemed on the verge of demanding the *real* reason for our visit. Although still slumped like a collapsed puppet, Elaine seemed more assertive, as if she was trying to communicate with her jasper eyes, blinking out Morse code or something: H-E-L-P!

"So, dear," Moira said. I shifted back in my seat. "You said that you may know something about what happened to my grandson."

She wanted her quid pro quo. She wanted information in exchange for the access she'd granted us—and for the cookies and milk, of course. I took a bite of a cookie, giving myself time to think. "Well," I said, wiping my lips. "We were all in the same class."

"English," Elaine said.

"Our teacher, Miss Martins. She and Cleve had a quarrel of some sort, an ongoing squabble."

Elaine's eye sockets seemed to sink deeper into her face, her damp eyes glittering.

Moira said, "What sort of squabble?"

It was much more than a squabble, but following Judy's example, I wasn't going to offer the Closses everything I knew. I wasn't going to mention the bicycle attack. "Maybe it was about a grade or something."

"Well," Moira said, "Cleve could be volatile, like many young men."

"Capricious," Elaine said with a touch of bitterness, even spitefulness, "like his father." That shocked me a little. I got the sense that under Elaine's grief, there was something else. Resentment, or even anger.

"Where is Mr. Closs?" I asked.

"Nowhere, everywhere," Elaine groaned and let her chin fall forward. The puppet's string was now severed.

"He's making funeral arrangements," Moira said and, shifting her tone, added, "Would you like another cookie before you go?"

"Thank you, but I should check on Judy." We needed to leave.

"We're going to have to end this visit soon," Moira said. "As you can see, Elaine needs her nap."

I stood and, to Elaine, said, "I didn't—*we* didn't mean to tire you out."

To her lap, she said, "Don't worry, dear."

I excused myself to the hall.

The murky corridor was lit with sconces. Judy was at the far end, inspecting something on the wall. I went to her and whispered, "We've overstayed our welcome."

"Look," she said, pointing to a photo among a collage of family photos. It was a black-and-white of Elaine Closs. She was much younger, perhaps in her late teens or early twenties. She was in tennis whites, standing in the middle of a groomed lawn. She held a badminton racket in her right hand—I've played once or twice, but because of my lousy coordination, I couldn't hit the birdie. To Elaine's right were trimmed hedges, a stone bench, and the street curb; in the background, a net on poles and a blurry figure, her opponent, who looked to be another young woman in white. Elaine was fresh-faced and beaming, not a trace of foreboding. However, her green eyes seemed to emerge from the grays of the photo, as if the black-and-white film couldn't resist their color.

"We've got to go," I said. "Come on." I didn't want to run the risk of angering the Closses and unleashing the strange energy they possessed.

"And there," she said, pointing to another photo. "That must be Mr. Closs, Cleve's dad."

This photo was a wedding photo, also a black-and-white. Elaine wore a brimless hat with large silk rosettes (which from the angle of the picture looked like Mickey Mouse ears), a floor-length white gown, and white gloves up to her elbows. Beside her, in a dark, double-breasted suit, was Mr. Closs, a handsome man in his twenties with an angular jaw, a broad smile, and a slick of thick blond hair. Etched at the bottom of the frame was "The Happy Couple, H & E, 1931." They were a striking pair and, from the look of it, in good spirits. My father has a similar photo of my mother and him; they also look so happy, so in love.

"He looks artificial," Judy said.

"They seem good together," I said, glancing over my shoulder. "We need to go."

"I want to meet him," she said.

"Girls?" Moira was at the end of the hall in silhouette, her cape swaying. "Elaine needs a rest," she said, drifting closer. "Thank you for dropping in." Her voice was low. The perfume of sociability had burned off.

"Of course," I said, forcing a smile. I started down the hall, but Judy didn't budge.

"When will Mr. Closs be home?" she said. My heart skipped a beat. Judy clearly didn't like Moira Closs—and she wasn't concealing it.

Moira stepped forward, light falling on her meticulously applied makeup and shapely updo. Her eyes, bright and forceful, scrutinized us. She hadn't been fooled; she knew we had ulterior motives. "Not for a while."

I grabbed Judy's arm and pulled her after me, saying, "Thank you for the cookies," as we blundered out the door.

JUDY, OCTOBER 27, 1948

Philippa is the type of person who thinks the world is basically a good place, who's blind to the danger of someone like Moira Closs. It's not her fault. I've been through hell and back, from Crestwood to the Peabodys to Eastern High's social gauntlet. Philippa grew up without her mother, so that gives her some . . . texture. There's an empty place in her life, but she knows where she came from and who her parents are (or were). My point is: She knows *who* she is. I can't remember entire periods of my childhood; years have been stripped away like a poorly peeled wheat paste poster.

That's why, once we'd left the Closses, I snapped at her: "Don't *ever* do that again!" I was standing in front of her, and the red maple was blazing behind her. "I'll go when I'm ready to go."

"I didn't mean to," she said, meekly. "But Moira—she insisted."

We walked on in silence. I wondered if I'd been too harsh. After all, she'd just learned that her aunt is sick with cancer. "Okay," I said, softening my voice. "But don't be scared of the Closses. Don't be scared of *anything*. If we're going to do this, to find out what happened, we can't be afraid."

"I know," she said, showing a little temper.

"I've seen Moira Closs before," I said. "She's attended several of B and E's parties. She and Bart know each other somehow. They run in the same circles."

"Hmm."

"When I was snooping, I searched the bathroom and found a cabinet full of pills and syrups, most of them for sleeping, and all of them prescribed for Elaine. Some of the bottles were old, caps crusted over. She must've been a nervous Nellie long before Cleve was killed."

We trampled across the fallen leaves, and Philippa stared gloomily at the sidewalk. Without looking up, she said, "Why did you lie about where you saw Cleve on Thursday?"

"I don't trust them, especially Queen Closs. She's a viper."

"In chinchilla's clothing," Philippa said, enjoying her joke a little too much. She glanced up. "Speaking of clothing—your top, it's ruined." She reached out, grazing my breast, and touched the red spot on my blouse.

Flustered, I batted her hand away. "Don't worry about it."

"I hope it's not an omen," she said with a wry twist of her lip.

I inspected the stains. "Bullet holes or stab wounds?" I said. "What do you think?"

Philippa smirked. "Bullet holes. You're a bullet hole kind of girl."

PHILIPPA, OCTOBER 27, 1948

When I returned home this evening, I wasn't greeted with the warm smell of pot roast or fresh-baked bread, or Dad in his chair with a whiskey at his side and the evening newspaper in his hand. Not even the radio was warbling out a tune, some Peggy Lee number. Instead, Dad and Bonnie were seated at the kitchen table, their eyes shaded with anger, silent. After a beat, Dad stood, his chair scuffing against the linoleum. "Where have you been?" he said.

Bonnie smacked her lips in disapproval.

I was baffled. I didn't understand what was the matter. "I've been with Judy," I said. "Am I late for something?"

"Principal Green called us," Dad said. "You and Judy pulled a prank on his secretary, and most likely you'll be suspended."

I'm such an idiot! Of course there were consequences! I don't know why I blotted it out. When I took Mrs. Whitlow to the scene of Ramona's "accident," I feigned confusion: "Where did she go? She was just here, a bloody mess. What happened?" Mrs. Whitlow gave me a peculiar look like I was out of focus, or she hadn't quite caught what I said. I should've understood then that I'd—that *we'd*—be in trouble.

"Tomorrow morning, Bonnie will take you to meet with Principal Green and apologize," Dad said, his mouth creased with disappointment. His eyes lingered on me, and their pained, brow-heavy glare dug into me, churning up shame, even a smidge of remorse. "This isn't the way a young woman behaves, especially not one with as much sense as you," he said. "These are schoolgirl antics."

I was embarrassed, but not for having tricked Mrs. Whitlow (that was necessary) or even for having been caught (that was unavoidable), but for not being prepared for the consequences, for not having a plan.

"It's so unlike you," Bonnie said, shaking her head. "You've never been a prankster. Always a good girl."

Her naivete annoyed me—I'm not a "good girl," whatever that is!—and I almost snapped at her. But I needed to do something to break the tension, not crank it up, so, thinking like Judy, I lied: "Ramona Carmichael put us up to it. She said if we didn't trick Mrs. Whitlow, she'd say we'd cheated on our poetry tests."

Dad's expression remained hard, and it was still wilting me. I didn't want him to think I was a bad girl or whatever Bonnie was implying. What can I say? I'm susceptible to his judgment, even when he doesn't have the full story. I had to appeal to his sympathy, so using what little I know about acting, I tapped into an unrelated event, the news of Sophie's illness, and summoned tears.

"Why would the Carmichael girl want to do that to you?" he said, his tone a shade lighter, although still unconvinced.

"She's a queen bee." Which is essentially true.

His shoulders loosened, and he dropped his chin, but he wasn't entirely thawed. "That's no excuse. Don't give girls like that the satisfaction. Ignore them. Don't let them pull your strings."

This was a lecture for a girl half of my age. "I know," I said, wiping away my crocodile tears.

"She won this round," he said. "Don't let it happen again."

"I was foolish."

"Well," he said. "You've learned something."

During dinner, he told me that, in addition to the school's punishment, I had to be home by nightfall all week. As soon as he excused me, I phoned Judy. We needed to get our story straight before we were questioned by Green.

Fortunately, her parents weren't home, so she hadn't been forced to tell a story that would conflict with mine. "Barty-boy is getting smashed at the club," she said, "and Ol' E is at a Daughters of the American Revolution meeting."

I imagined Edith in a room full of women in long bustled dresses and lace bonnets armed with muskets and frying pans.

"Your lie," she said, "it was smart."

PHILIPPA, OCTOBER 28, 1948

What a relief! Principal Green wasn't the sanctimonious scold I thought he'd be. I'd feared being talked down to more than being punished. He "sentenced" me to two days of suspension and asked me to write an apology to Mrs. Whitlow. He didn't quite believe that Ramona was a queen bee with a barbed stinger, but he didn't challenge me either. He must've sensed an air of truth to it.

Once home again, Bonnie suggested that we fix Dad lunch and deliver it. She hated for us to be at odds as if somehow it meant she was failing at her job of harmony-making homemaker. Anyway, we threw together ham and mustard sandwiches, whipped up potato salad, grabbed a ginger ale from the refrigerator, and stuffed it all in a gingham-lined basket.

It was chilly out, and the sky was bright blue through the tree limbs. To be honest, I felt as if I were playing hooky instead of being punished. Less energized by the cold weather, Bonnie had buttoned her coat up to the collar and scrunched her shoulders up to her ears. Judy was probably wrapped in a big sweater on top of Hill Estates, smoking cigarettes and staring at the same sky.

We crossed Pennsylvania Avenue and made our way down 8th Street, at the end of which stood Latrobe Gate, the dignified entrance to the Navy Yard, shining white in the sun. Although I want to be a writer when I graduate college, sometimes I wonder what it would be like to be a JAG like Dad and prosecute Japanese war criminals for the Navy War Crimes Office. I'd like to be someone who commanded that sort of respect. Of course, he probably wouldn't approve of that either.

After a streetcar rattled by, we approached the gate, checked in at the guard station, and made our way through a courtyard, up a flight of stairs, and down a long squeaky linoleum hall. Dad greeted us and showed us into his office. It was clean and spare, except for a desk, file cabinets, two potted rubber plants, a photo of President Truman, American and US Navy flags on staves, and photos of Bonnie and me on his desk. He took his lunch, and we all sat. He seemed stiff, even a touch nervous.

"How did your meeting with Principal Green go?" he said.

Bonnie recounted it, and Dad took it in.

"That's just a slap on the wrist," he said.

"I'll catch up on all my homework," I said, shooting for a positive spin.

He frowned. "I wonder about Judy."

"What about her?"

"Is she the best influence? Sophie doesn't think so."

"Now Carl," Bonnie said, always the peacemaker. "Philippa behaved well today and accepted responsibility for what she did."

"I don't want you to see or talk to Judy for a week," he said.

"What?" I said, my heart leaping up. I began bargaining: "What about just for the two days of suspension?"

He studied me, an eyebrow raised. "Okay," he said and after a long pause: "You've never done anything like that, so spend time reflecting on it."

"I promise."

He unpacked his lunch, unwrapping the foil around his sandwich. "Do you remember how you'd save your gum wrappers for the metal drives during the war?"

"Yes," I said. "It was ridiculous." I collected wrappers during junior high and pressed them together until they created a four-inch-wide foil ball. It took months, and I was so proud of it. I was sure that I'd singlehandedly win the war by mashing foil together. If we just saved enough aluminum, we'd blow the Axis out of the skies! Sure, Philippa.

He handed me the foil. "Here," he said. "Just because the war is over doesn't mean we should be wasteful."

I took it, slipped it into the pocket on my coat, and smiled, but what I wanted to do was scream: "Are you blind? I'm not your little girl anymore! I don't skip rope or play jacks or collect foil."

He doesn't *really* care about the Whitlow incident. I see that now. He just doesn't like me growing up, thinking for myself, and taking action. Most of all, he doesn't like me wanting things: like college and a career, like my friendship with Judy. I wonder if my mother ever felt hemmed in by him—or did she just accept her fate like Bonnie?

JUDY, OCTOBER 28, 1948

Miss M and I talked about everything: Literature, politics, art, movies, music. Everything. Just a month ago, she was urging me to give Charlie Parker a chance: "Yes, he meanders, but that's the point. He's so restless and alive. Listen and go with it." When I told her that I didn't want to keep the Peabody name when I turned eighteen, she didn't argue with me or attempt to persuade me to reconsider, to give B and E a chance. She just said, "Well, what about a literary name? Something poetic? A flower or an herb? Perhaps Judy Oleander or Judy Rose, or wait, what about Judy Parsley?"

I smirked. Although our conversations often had a heightened feel, as if they were happening in a dream, smudged at the edges and surrounded by a haze of lilac perfume, occasionally, she'd drop below the ether and crack a joke or wiggle her nose. More than all the poetry tutorials and music recommendations, those moments have clung to me; I wonder if we'll ever have them again.

"Okay, okay," she said, "if that doesn't suit you, what about a bird? Cardinal? Robin? Judy Robin."

It was absurd, but I played along: "Judy Pelican or Judy Woodpecker. Mademoiselle Albatross."

She broke into a wild laugh. "Judy Finch?" she said, recovering. "That's better, right?"

I cringed.

"Or wait, I have it!" Her eyes sparkled. "Nightingale, like the poem."

And that was it. The perfect name. Judy Nightingale. I'd even researched the bird and wrote about it in a paper. It was an important poetic symbol from Homer to Keats to T. S. Eliot. Most of all, it suited me. After all, I want to transform—to metamorphose—like the characters do at the end of Greek myths. I want to be a Nightingale and leave my mortal Peabody behind.

Today, after a predictable brawl with Edith about being suspended from school, I stormed out of the house, nearly knocking her down. I went to Miss M's old apartment. Philippa is temporarily off-limits, so I couldn't go to her place. I'm not entirely sure what I was doing. Miss M had moved by now, but maybe she'd be lingering, or there would be traces of her, something that would give me hope of seeing her again.

As I stood in front of it, the city bore down on me. Cars honked, businessmen flagged cabs, and girlfriends squealed into each other's arms. Down the block, little girls were fighting over a game of hopscotch. The thin vertical faces of the row houses loomed, the ripe odor of sewage hung in the air, and roots from the old oaks seemed to shift and break through the sidewalk bricks, gradually unburying themselves under my feet. No sign of Miss M, none of her lightness, her serenity. Just the goddamn pressure: where was she? What had happened between her and Cleve? What had Philippa actually witnessed?

Police cars barreled by, and I glanced across the street. On the other side, a tall man was staring back at me. He was well dressed in a charcoal suit and gray fedora and gave off the impression of being good-looking, although from that distance, I couldn't make out his face. I didn't think anything of it. He was just another businessman or government Joe headed home. But when I started down East Capitol toward Lincoln Park, he was still behind me, thirty yards back. Okay, but that's not unusual. Be calm. We could've been going the same direction, or maybe—although this wasn't particularly reassuring—he was trying to pick me up. When I crossed to the park, he crossed too. Shit. When I walked faster, he walked faster. What does he want? My heart was racing. I cut through the trees for a more direct route to Tennessee Avenue.

Once home, I slammed the door and locked it behind me. I went to the parlor, peered between the window sheers, and scanned the street: evergreen hedge, iron fence, brick sidewalk, blue Buick, black Packard, rusty delivery truck, towering yellow oak, snooty woman walking her schnauzer. My heart was still pounding, but he wasn't there, vanished like a ghost. A gray ghost. Briefly, I wondered if I'd made him up, but as I withdrew, I saw his silhouette through the gauzy fabric, and I jumped like I'd just spotted a spider in the middle of the floor. He stepped out from between the truck and the Packard and glanced around, pausing to take in the house. Then the shadow of a passing car swallowed him, and he was gone.

PHILIPPA, OCTOBER 30, 1948

Today our suspension was over. Thank God. As soon as I stepped through Eastern High's front door, an arm slipped through mine and tugged me forward. "Come on," Judy said. "I have news." Her touch was reassuring. I hadn't realized how much I'd missed her.

We found a table in the library, and in a heated whisper, Judy told me all about the man who followed her home. It was thrilling news, but neither of us knew who he was or what it meant. "He was probably a government spook," she said with a chuckle. "He looked the part—gray suit, gray fedora. A gray ghost. J. Edgar is following everyone else in town, why not me?"

Sure. J. Edgar Hoover. Why not?

"He's everywhere," she added. "The puppet master."

Judy has strong opinions. She reads the newspapers and listens to the radio collecting tidbits of information so she can shape them into grand theories. I'm never quite sure what to make of her ideas—from her conviction that Alger Hiss is a spy ("Whittaker Chambers would know a spy when he saw one, right?") to her certainty that the spread of communism in Europe will end in war ("Trust me, it's not like the Soviets are content with their shitty slice of Europe.") to her casual prophesy about the deadly smog in Donora, Pennsylvania ("It won't be the last time an American company poisons its own. But hey, it's better than communism!"). She knows about these things, and she relishes making up her mind about them. Dad and Bonnie would prefer that I live with my head in the sand, as if glancing at a headline or newsreel would shatter my nerves. Girls with minds of their own don't fall to pieces when faced with ugly truths. Judy's right: we should look at the world squarely, take it all in.

"I'm meeting Quincy at Horsfield's after school," I said. "Wanna come along? He phoned last night trying to reach Dad."

"Are you pumping him for information?"

"For malts—and information."

"I'm in."

Quincy wore pedestrian clothes on his day off—a brown leather jacket, a plaid flannel shirt, and jeans. His cheeks were puffy, his face unshaven, and his hair uncombed like he'd just rolled out of bed. Stress seemed to be percolating behind his cheerfulness. I wanted to ask if he was okay, but I didn't want to embarrass him.

In contrast, Judy had spruced up in the bathroom at school. Her eye makeup was fresh and feline, and her lips were lined, something she rarely did. Despite the brisk weather, she removed her black sweater, which was thrown jauntily over her shoulders, exposing her arms. Grouped in threes and fours, her scars ran from her wrists to her elbows, marring her olive skin at various angles. Some were as long as two inches and others as short as a half inch. Some were pink and bulbous, others only faint red lines. She seemed to be offering up a comparison: the makeup versus the scars. Beauty versus the beast. I wondered if she wasn't doing it to invite mystery, to spark Quincy's curiosity—or at the very least, throw him off balance.

Horsfield's was packed. We found a booth against the back wall which was shielded from the chatter by a partition. Overwhelmed by the after-school rush, Iris briskly took our orders, giving us a distracted smile and Judy a quick wink. Quincy ordered a chocolate malt and a cheeseburger, and we had vanilla malts. Judy requested extra whipped cream.

"How's school?" Quincy said, after Iris had left us.

"We wouldn't know," Judy said.

"Why?" Quincy said.

Judy leaned in, smiling coyly. "We played a practical joke on the school secretary, Mrs. Whitlow, and they suspended us." I didn't understand why she was acting this way. Where was flirting with Quincy going to get us?

He shrugged, baffled.

"We did it for a good reason," I added, not wanting him to think we were crazy—or spiteful.

"Like I said, it was a *practical* joke." Judy smirked. "*Practical* because we needed Whitlow out of the way, so we could find Cleve's address. We wanted to pay our respects to Cleve's parents."

Quincy looked at me. "Why not just ask?"

Judy leaned farther forward, stretching her scar-emblazoned arms across the table. "They wanted us to write condolence letters, not drop by. We wanted to meet his mother and father and see where he lived." I wanted to drape my napkin over her arms, not because they were ugly, but because they were so intimate. It felt like a striptease.

"You shouldn't be doing that." His eyes flicked to her arms.

"Cleve was my friend," I blurted. "I wanted to talk to his parents and tell them I knew him, that I was sorry." It was a lie, but it felt necessary. Something to focus Quincy back on me.

"You could've accomplished that with a letter," he said.

"We want to figure out who killed him," Judy said, sitting back in the booth and retracting her arms. "In child murder cases, you're supposed to start with the parents, right? I read that in *True Crime*."

Quincy glanced around as if he was worried about being overheard. She had touched on something. "Yeah," he said. "That's usually where we begin, but not in this case."

Judy lit up. "So, where then?"

"Well, *I'm* not beginning anywhere. I'm just learning, doing grunt work, paying my dues. The lead detectives call the shots."

Judy sized him up. "But you know the direction of the case." She smiled, her lined lips prominent and sensuous. "They've been relying on you, haven't they?" She smiled, giving her nose a little seductive scrunch. I could only guess that she thought flirting with him would make him more pliable and willing to divulge information. He was just another boy to her, and his red cheeks told me that he wasn't proving her wrong.

"I can't talk about it," he said. "I'd lose my job."

"It's okay," I said. "We don't want to get you in trouble. We want to help."

"Well, can you tell me something?" he asked.

I looked at Judy. "Sure."

"What were his parents like?"

"We only met the mother and the grandmother," I said. "Cleve's mother was devastated, on the verge of crumbling. But his grandmother, she was—"

"A queen bitch," Judy said, her eyes narrowing. "Definitely running the show."

"Did they say anything unusual? Something that surprised you?" Quincy asked.

"It's hard to tell," I said, scanning my memory. "The last time his mother saw him was when she sent him out to pick up dinner on Thursday evening."

"I told them we bumped into him on East Capitol, but that's not true," Judy said, surprising me with her honesty. What was she up to?

"Why lie?" he said.

"I didn't trust them, and I wanted to see if they could tell if I was lying, if my story conflicted with what they knew, if they were confused."

"Smart," he said, lifting his eyebrows. "Did it?"

"Well, the queen bitch didn't like it."

"When *was* the last time you saw him?"

Judy's eyes met mine, requesting permission to tell him . . . what? Everything? Was this her new tactic: I'll show you mine if you show me yours?

Instead of signaling to her, I took over: "We went to our English teacher's—Miss Martins's—room after school hours. We wanted to ask her about an assignment." Although part of me wanted to tell him more, to just blurt it all out, I knew I couldn't. I didn't want him knowing that we'd broken into her apartment, that we were already up to our necks in this. He'd feel duty bound to protect us and that would lead him to inform Dad. Judy and I would be ordered to stay away from each other. We had to walk a fine line. "Cleve and Miss Martins were having a heated argument," I added. "We interrupted them, and Cleve ran away."

"Oh, interesting," Quincy said, but before he could ask another question, Iris arrived with the malts.

Judy's peak of whipped cream was already dissolving; the cherry had begun to sink into the white froth. She plucked it out, flashing her arms again, sucked off the cream, and ate it with a murmur of pleasure. She was *really* enjoying herself, and Quincy's eyes sparkled as he watched her. I wasn't sure if I was more annoyed at Judy for working Quincy or at Quincy for allowing her to.

"What happened to your arms?" he said to her. There it was. He was hooked.

Her gaze lingered on him, a touch sultry. "It happened when I was young. I don't remember." She waved it away.

"Oh," he said. "It looks like it hurt."

"Hmm," she said, plunging a straw into her malt.

He stared at his drink, embarrassed, it seemed. His hamburger arrived, the bun slick with melted butter and the beef patty oozing grease. "Thank you," he said to Iris, who smiled and was gone, and to us: "Is there anything else you can tell me?"

I considered telling him about the cabinet full of sleeping pills or even about the gray ghost that had followed Judy home, but that would set off too many alarm bells.

But before I could speak, Judy nudged me under the table and said, "Nothing more to report, but may I ask you something?" And I understood: this was a quid pro quo. We'd given him something, and now it's his turn.

"I'm not sure I'll be able to answer." He picked up his burger and took a sloppy bite.

"If they don't suspect family members, who do they suspect?"

He shook his head and swallowed. "Can't say."

"Come on."

"Sorry." He wiped ketchup from his cheek.

"Is it Adrian Bogdan?"

Quincy's face drained of blood. It *was* Bogdan. He looked away. Was he worried about being so easily read?

"I thought so," Judy said. "My parents would like it to be."

"That so?" he said.

"They think he killed their daughter, Jackie, my illustrious predecessor. Bart and Edith are still obsessed with seeing Bogdan prosecuted."

Quincy's eyebrows were parked high on his forehead. "How did they make the connection?"

"The writing on Cleve's arm," she said. "It was reported in the newspaper. Jackie had writing on her body, too. Did you know that?"

"I did." He took another bite.

Why hadn't she mentioned the writing on Jackie to me? We're supposed to be in this together, confidants. Was I being manipulated too? I shot her a look, but she ignored it.

"That detail shouldn't have made it into the newspaper," Quincy said. "It's not helpful, but at least they didn't report what it said."

"So, what did it say?" Judy said, cocking her head.

Quincy's eyes narrowed. "It's not information I'm privy to."

"But it's possible the murderer *is* the same person," I said, sitting back. I wanted distance from them: They were doing a dance with each other that I felt excluded from. Judy leading, Quincy following clumsily.

He blinked.

"Of course, it is," Judy said. "But it doesn't feel right, somehow." She sipped her malt. "But I bet the police think it is."

"Can't say," he said, but the quick shift of his eyes betrayed him.

"Both were kids," she said, leaning in and lowering her voice. Her eyes were wide and flashing. "Both were found in the Anacostia River, both were written on, and both were molested."

"*Okay*," Quincy said, holding his hand up. "I didn't come here to have you ruin my career. I've already given you too much. Let's talk about something else."

Although I wanted the information as much as Judy, I was relieved he was standing up to her. She'd been pulling his strings too easily.

"They were both sexually assaulted, right?" she said. "*Right?*"

He stared at her, his thin lips clamped together, his nose twitching. "You're not as smart as you think," he said. "Let it go. This isn't your problem. You should be talking about school or finding dates for homecoming, not murdered kids."

Judy crossed her arms, the scars blazing like red pen marks. "I've spent most of my life thinking about her, not to mention living in her angel-shaped shadow. It's all I know how to think about. I've been well trained."

"Sorry," he said, softening. Once again, she was tugging on the right string.

"What kind of person is Bogdan?" I said, trying a different approach. "Judy knows some things, but—"

"Why do you care?" Quincy glared at me, his eyes pleading: "Please, don't push it, Phil."

"If you won't tell us anything, fine. I understand," I said. "But we're going to figure it out. We're not scared to."

Quincy darkened with concern, but I knew he respected my sentiment. The sense of adventure we shared when we were young was still there. "Well," he said, after sipping his malt, "he grew up in Odessa, Ukraine, on the Black Sea. He had a horrific upbringing. According to Bogdan, his father was an abusive drunk and, in a fit of anger, killed his kid sister with an ax. He spent his teenage years in an orphanage and then joined the Red Army. He became disillusioned with Stalin during the Soviet famine and immigrated to America in '35. He worked the New York shipyards and eventually the Port Authority. In 1941, he moved to DC and began working at the Navy Yard as a boat mechanic. Before he was implicated in the murder of Jackie Peabody, his record was clean. In fact, the only reason he was implicated in her murder was because he'd been reported for loitering outside schools on three separate occasions. One of those schools, St. Timothy's, was Jackie's school."

"Tell her about Shirley Temple," Judy said.

"After a neighbor told them about seeing him with a young girl on the day of Jackie's murder, they got a warrant and searched his home, a houseboat on the Potomac. In his bedroom, he had plastered magazine and newsprint cutouts of Shirley Temple on the wall. I've seen the photos. Little Shirley, everywhere."

"The Good Ship Lollipop," Judy said, smirking.

"His boss at the Navy Yard vouched for his whereabouts the afternoon that Jackie disappeared. They had no hard evidence, so they stopped pursuing him."

"Bart and Edith were *very* unhappy about that," Judy said. "They launched their own campaign against him, unsuccessfully. They were—they *are*—still convinced he's guilty."

"From what I understand," he said, "they had a right to be upset. His boss George Shebold was his friend. They were drinking buddies. He could've lied for him. Clearly, Bogdan was a troubled man. I'm surprised the investigators didn't do more digging."

"Did they question him about his Shirley Temple hang up?" I asked. "That's bizarre."

"He said she reminded him of his sister. That's when they got his tragic childhood story."

"Jackie could look a bit like Temple," Judy said, "especially when Edith decided to torture her with a perm."

Judy's eyes fixed on something behind me, and her face drew tight: Ramona Carmichael was sashaying toward us, her chin tilted up and her dainty purse hanging from the crook of her arm. She was wearing a red gingham dress with a Kelly green sweater draped over her shoulders. Her lips were deep scarlet. As she approached, she nodded at us and held out her hand to Quincy. "How do you do?" she said. "I'm Ramona, a dear friend of these two." She was true to form.

"I'm Quincy, Philippa's first cousin," he said, smiling. He was taken in by her lacquered facade. I wanted to kick him under the table: "If you want to be a detective, cousin, you should be smart enough to see through her!"

"Are you visiting from out of town?" Ramona said.

"No, I live here. I'm a police officer."

"Oh!" she said with a little gasp. "So, I guess you know all about the classmate of ours, Cleveland Closs. What a sweet boy! I'm torn up over it."

She was laying it on thick.

"Sure you are," Judy said.

She turned to her. "It put things in perspective."

"Go away." Judy flicked her hand at her.

"I'm just being friendly," she said, wrinkling her brow. "I wanted to tell you that I forgive you for including me in your little prank on Mrs. Whitlow. I don't want this to be uncomfortable, so no hard feelings."

"I'm comfortable with hard feelings," Judy said.

Ramona scowled at her. "Philippa?" she said, looking my direction. "You're more . . . even tempered than she is. You understand what I'm saying. I just want to clear the air."

"Go away," I said. "Please."

"You too, Philippa! Well, I guess I should've expected that."

A spray of malt hit Ramona's dress, and she shrieked like she'd stepped on a snake. Quincy grimaced and offered her a napkin, which she snapped out of his hand and began using to dab the gingham furiously. Judy had sucked in the liquid through her straw and blown it out—a blunderbuss of sugar-milk.

Judy tapped me with her elbow and smiled.

Ramona seethed. I could see the hate twitching at the corners of her mouth. The first honest emotion she'd expressed. After she'd finished dabbing and fussing, she flung the napkin to the floor and vanished out the front of Horsfield's.

Quincy shook his head.

"What?" Judy said. "It's vanilla. It won't stain."

Quincy paid for his burger and malt and excused himself. We must've exhausted him. He didn't understand that someone blunt like Ramona requires a blunt response—an elbow to the ribs, a smack in the face, or a splatter of malt.

After he left, Judy pushed her empty glass to the side, turned to me, and said, "We learned a lot from him, don't you think?"

"About Bogdan?"

"No, I knew all of that."

I let out an exasperated huff. "Okay," I said, sinking in the booth. "Well, was there something else he said you didn't know?"

"Not a thing."

"Huh?"

"It's not what he *said* . . ." She smiled.

"Come on, Judy!" I sat up, as if to leave.

"He confirmed for us that the police think there's a connection between the murders. He didn't correct me when I brought up B and E's theory about a connection. I'm also willing to bet what was written on Cleve's body is what was scrawled on Jackie's." She lowered her head and whispered, "You see, I know what was written on Jackie's body."

"You do? How?" Not only hadn't she told me about the writing on Jackie, even after she knew about the inscription on Cleve, but she knew what it said. I remembered Sophie's warning: "She's bad news. I can see it, all around her, a backdrop of shadows." It's true, even though Judy can be bold and outspoken, nothing is upfront with her; she's always withholding and playing games. If I'm being honest, I enjoy those games sometimes—her wit, her cleverness—but other times, they feel designed to keep me at arm's length, dancing alone.

"B and E found out. They have connections. Friends in the mayor's office, that sort of thing. Several years ago, I overheard them talking about the case in Bart's study. They always return to the topic on her birthday or on the day she died or at Christmas or at Easter. Lots of tears and hand wringing. Anyway, it's not something they're *supposed* to know. They had to keep it a secret, or they'd screw up the case."

"So . . . what was written on her?" I asked, gripping the edge of the leather booth's slippery upholstery, worried that it might be something gruesome.

"In red nail polish—A-H-K-A," she said. "The second letter was a little blurry, so it could've been A-U-K-A or A-N-K-A. All uppercase letters. There might have been other letters that were washed away. Another word or even a longer word."

"What does it mean?" I said, a little relieved.

She shrugged.

"It could be an acronym," I said.

"B and E—and the police—thought it might be Anka, which is a diminutive of Anna in Russian, like Anya. Anna could be Bogdan's sister's name, but it's never been verified. If you ask me, it's not worth trying to figure it out. Besides, establishing a connection between murders isn't the most interesting thing we learned."

I glared at her. "You're being cryptic again."

Unfazed, she said, "Quincy told me, 'You're not as smart as you think,' when I asked him to confirm that Cleve was molested."

"So?"

"Well, that made me think he *wasn't* molested. Quincy was annoyed and wanted to prove me wrong. He has a terrible poker face. He should work on that if he wants to be a detective."

She was self-satisfied, but she was also right. Quincy needed to learn not to wear his thoughts on his face.

"It's how the two murders are different that's important," she said. "If Cleve wasn't molested, that's significant." She nudged me and raised her eyebrows. "See, we're getting somewhere."

"Do you think Cleve's murder is a copycat?" I said, plucking my straw out of my glass. "Or that Bogdan has an accomplice?"

"I don't know, but it's interesting." She breathed in. "That's all I know." She flicked her hand at me. "Scoot! I'm dying for a cigarette."

I slid across the smooth cracked leather of the booth, but before I stood, I paused and looked up into her eyes. "Why didn't you tell me about the writing on Jackie?" I wasn't going to let her out without an answer.

She gazed at me for a beat—I continued to twirl my sticky straw—then she cracked a weary smile. "B and E are a nightmare, but I don't want them to go to jail." Her eyes drifted across the room, past all the commotion. "I don't want to end up in foster care again." A tremor of sadness rolled through her. "You get it, right? I'm not eighteen yet."

I glanced at her scars. They looked like a child's unfinished draw-by-numbers. If you connected them, what would they reveal? Something sad? Something morbid? She caught me gawking and drew them in, trying to cover them with her hands.

"Seriously, scoot," she said. "I need a smoke."

JUDY, OCTOBER 30, 1948

For me, smoking has always been contemplative, not something you did out in the open on street corners or at bus stops. It's private, personal.

After Philippa peeled off to pee, I plunged into the cold air and sunshine, looking for a place to hide out and take a drag or two. I wandered into the alley behind Horsfield's, assuming she would sniff me out when she was finished.

In the stagnant, fried-food-tinted air of the alley, I caught a whiff of smoke—Chesterfields—and spotted Iris slouched against the outside wall of the restaurant, her elbow propped at her side, cigarette poised in her hand, and her mind miles away. "Want company?" I called, and she waved for me to join her.

She lifted her pack of Chesterfields from her apron to offer me one. "It's a nasty habit," she said, "but a necessary one." I retrieved one, and Iris lighted it with her tarnished brass lighter. "My father's," she said. "It brings me good luck."

I took a long drag and soaked in the stillness.

Iris leaned back against the grimy wall and into a bright bar of light. Something about her position, or perhaps how she contrasted with the dreary setting, helped me see past her frumpy, white-collared waitress get-up. Suddenly, there she was—a tall, lean woman with high cheekbones, a long angular nose, and flawless golden-brown skin. Her wavy curls had been gathered and pinned in place under her starched cap. Her bronze eyes caught the light, which exposed their depth, their shrewdness, as if they could penetrate any facade, any bullshit, with a well-aimed glance.

"That was quite a scene you made," she said, after blowing a cone of smoke to the sky. "I hope you didn't leave me a mess to clean up."

"Ramona is a twit."

"It's best to ignore girls like her. They're trouble."

"Don't you get tired of 'yes ma'am-ing' her and the other fools who come in?"

"You can't fight every fight. I need the job—and I was lucky to get this one. I have tuition to pay, and Mr. H pays well, and he doesn't put up a fuss if any of us want to eat at his place, although few do if you haven't noticed."

"Still, it's got to get old."

"Don't get me wrong. Sometimes I want to toss a malt in their pretty faces." She mimed the gesture. "But the satisfaction isn't worth the cost. When you get a little older, you'll understand. The best revenge I can serve up is to go to medical school, get my degree, and do what God—or whoever—sent me here to do."

I took another drag.

Iris never talks about having a boyfriend or men at all. She rarely chitchats about the mundane, like work or the weather or movies. She's always going on about the news, railing against "separate but equal," and the absurdity of Jim Crow. She often expresses her admiration for Thurgood Marshall and the NAACP. She mentions the future a lot—her hope for a better society, her plans. "Listen," she told me once, leaning over Horsfield's counter so customers couldn't hear her, "The world is always whispering to us: 'Sit down, dear. Shut up, sweetie. Look pretty, honey, and maybe a good churchgoing man will want to marry you.' To hell with that, I say."

Iris studied me, flicked ash off her cigarette, and said, "So, who was that with you and Miss Strawberry?" Iris called Philippa "Miss Strawberry" because of her hair color and her *Seventeen* magazine perkiness.

"Philippa's cousin. Quincy. A police officer."

"Hmm."

"A classmate of ours was murdered."

"I read about it. The Closs boy. He liked chocolate malts, no whipped cream. He was dumped in the river, right?"

"Philippa and I—we're trying to figure out what's going on. It might even have something to do with our English teacher."

Iris raised her eyebrows and then flung her butt to the pavement and ground it out with the sole of her shoe. "Be careful," she said, "the

Closses are influential. They own that hardware store chain, and they're big Republicans. Not friends to the Negros. They won't like you snooping in their business. My father worked for Cleve Closs, Sr."

I stubbed out my cigarette.

"Do you trust Miss Strawberry?"

"Yes. Why?"

"She seems nervous—like a lot of the other white girls."

"Like me?"

"You know what I mean." She squared herself with me, her eyes kind, soft. "You're different."

"She's just . . . jittery."

"Hmm," Iris said. "Be careful all the same."

At the entrance to the alley, I spotted Philippa. The bright sun from the street cast her in silhouette, and traffic swished behind her. She spun this way then that, her skirt flaring and falling, flaring and falling. She was looking for me. I let her search, enjoying her desperation, her huffiness. "Down here!" I shouted finally, and she squinted into the alley like it was a portal to an alternate reality.

"Back to work," Iris said, reaching for the door to Horsfield's.

PHILIPPA, OCTOBER 30, 1948

Where had she gone? Why abandon me? I wanted to kill her. The fear she was playing games with me had wormed its way in again. When at last I heard her calling from the alley, I flipped up the collar of my jacket. She deserved a cold shoulder. She ignored the gesture and slipped her arm through mine—and like that, I felt settled again. I was going to say something sharp, but her hand in mine—its firm soothing grip—obliterated the need. Our stride was buoyant and syncopated, as if we'd been friends for ages, as if we might break into song. Golly, that would've been a sight! After pausing for a streetcar to clank by, we dashed across Pennsylvania Avenue and headed up 7th, falling in with a throng of commuters. The wind dragged its icy fingers through our hair, and Judy leaned even closer for warmth.

We passed by two men with "Dewey or Don't We" buttons on their lapels. Judy sneered, "Dewey canvassers. What does that asshole stand for? Status quo." Then louder, in the direction of the men: "You might well be Dixiecrats! Dewey's dried up! He's not going to win!"

It's unlikely Truman will win next Tuesday. That's what everyone says, at least. I don't pretend to care much about politics, which, of course, irks Judy. Regardless, there was something thrilling about hearing her blast the canvassers. Suddenly, I wanted Truman to win, if just to please her.

We saw a homeless woman with feverish, bloodshot eyes squatting on the stoop of a burger joint named, rather depressingly, Uncle Sam's. Judy stopped, scooped change out of her pocket, and handed it to the woman, who smiled and said, "God bless you." Dad always warned me against giving beggars cash. "It rarely does them good," he said. "Let social programs take care of them." As we walked on, I said, "She's just going to use your money for booze."

"So what? I would, too," she replied.

At the end of the block, Judy yanked me through the door of Somerset's Bookstore. The front desk was unattended, and the store was packed with books, shelved in tall, mismatched bookcases with surplus volumes stacked precariously on top, little Towers of Pisa threatening to topple. At some crucial nexus, I imagined, there was a single book, some great linchpin novel, like *Moby-Dick* or *War and Peace*, that if removed, would cause a cataclysmic domino effect, bringing the entire store to the ground in a cloud of dust.

Judy glanced around, settled on a direction, and pulled me into one of the canyons of books. We plunged through the life sciences, history, fiction, and the pulps. I even caught the titles of a few Kane novels: *The Gemini Case, Seeing Red,* and *Cry of the Dead.*

Despite its grimy windows and tattered awning, Somerset's had beck-oned to me before, but I'd never gone inside. In San Fran, I used to spend entire afternoons in the North Beach used bookstores. I'd pick up an old novel, flip through its yellowed pages—as I often still do my mother's books—smell the old ink and musty paper and fantasize about who'd owned it before. Did she like it? Did she stay up reading it all night? Or did she give up and set it aside? Or did it change her? Does she still think about it? Occasionally I'd come across notes scrawled in the margins or on the inside of the cover, and I'd invent a story about its owner, usually some assertive and free-spirited version of my mother. It made me feel closer to her, as if she were there, dreaming along with me.

At the back of the store, a black velvet curtain hung over a narrow door. Judy peeked through the thick drape. "Come on," she said. "No one is here."

"Where are we going?" I asked, but I knew.

Judy slipped in, but I stalled, letting the curtain fall back in place. I knew rooms like these existed, but I'd never dared to go in before. During a slumber party several years ago, one of the girls dangled her father's 1945 pin-up calendar in front of us. We all huddled around its glossy pages, gawking and giggling like morons. All the models were contorted in impossible poses. Their backs were arched, butts cocked, and toes pointed down as if they had been broken and reassembled to create the right look. Their faces gaped with surprise and delight. They seemed somehow both humiliated and thrilled you'd just stumbled on them in the dressing room or the bathroom or the kitchen or on the sidewalk half-undressed. Sure they were. But I couldn't lie. As each month fluttered past, my heart quickened a little more.

Judy poked her head out and grabbed my arm. I resisted, but behind me, the doorbell clattered. Her grip tightened, and I feared being spotted loitering by the smut room, so I let her pull me in. Rows of out-facing books and magazines wrapped in brown paper lined the walls of the cramped, windowless room. I imagined what they concealed: Oiled men and slippery women moaning and writhing and thrusting against one another, their eyes rolling back in their heads. My face flushed, and I felt a little sick. Judy picked up a magazine, slid the paper off, and began flipping through it. "Jesus," she said and flashed it at me. There it was: an erect penis in full color, veiny and greased, and a naked woman gripping it like a microphone. My eyes fell across her forced smile, her neck, her breasts, her crouching shape, and I felt a rush of sadness for her. The doorbell jangled, and I gasped. Judy closed the magazine and began replacing the brown paper, unfazed, it seemed, by the thought of a lurking customer. My heart was in my throat. I didn't want to be caught. God, how would I ever explain this to Dad?

I went to the curtain and peeked through it. Fifteen feet from me, a tall man in a fedora was browsing in the aisle. I withdrew and began gesturing to Judy.

Ignoring me, she said, "*This* is a book we should read," holding out *Lady Chatterley's Lover*. "It's been banned in the US since the twenties. This copy must be black market."

I shushed her, pointed, and mouthed, "A man."

She rolled her eyes and shoved me aside for a look. After a minute, she spun and said in a shrill whisper, "That's *him*! The gray ghost."

"What?" I looked again, parting the thick drape with a trembling hand. The man's face was in profile, shaded by his dove gray fedora. He wore a well-cut charcoal suit, and his black oxfords gleamed. I turned to Judy. "Are you sure?"

"I recognize his suit—and the hat."

"He's tall and looks . . . strong."

Judy paced the room, tucking *Lady Chatterley* into her sweater. I would've objected, but I was too distracted, too afraid. Why was he here? How long had he been following us?

"We'll either have to wait or make a run for it," Judy said.

"If he's following us, he's not going away," I said. "Anyway, can you imagine the headline: 'Teenage Girls Attacked in Dirty Book Room!' Read all about it!"

"Okay," Judy said, making eye contact. "We'll have to rush past him. On three, we make for the door." She breathed in, her face puckering like a tennis player about to serve. "Are you ready?"

"Wait!" I said, clutching the flesh of her upper arm, digging my nails in.

"One," she said.

She yanked her arm away but gave me an encouraging nod.

"No, no—" I begged.

She grabbed my wrist.

"Two."

Her grip tightened.

"Three!"

She flung the curtain open like a big flap of a wing, and we hurtled forward toward the bright pane of glass in the front door, the goal, the gateway to freedom. As we rushed past the ghost, Judy jabbed him with an elbow. He fell forward, crushing the brim of his hat against the shelf and swiping several books with his flailing arm. As they hit the floor, I thought about the linchpin novel—*Great Expectations*? *Anna Karenina*?—about its thick spine, about its fluttering pages, about its musty odor, about how easily everything could come tumbling down. That's when the gray ghost's cologne hit me, the heavy metallic scent I knew from Miss Martins's apartment. It was the same man!

We ran north on 7th, and then southeast toward Lincoln Park on North Carolina. The ghost was following us. We dodged pedestrians, servicemen, and even delivery men carrying a large rectangular mirror, its surface catching us, flushed and panicked, in a brief tableau. We barreled through traffic at a red light, chrome bumpers glinting, horns blaring, and stony faces gazing over their steering wheels. The wind was still up, stirring leaves into little tornadoes. Everything seemed to be spinning—and the man was still pursuing us, but lagging, his hand now on his fedora so it wouldn't fly off. Once in the park, we broke into a full sprint, Judy now clutching *Lady Chatterley* in her hand.

Once we bounded across East Capitol and stumbled onto Tennessee Avenue, we slowed down. I couldn't see our pursuer. Perhaps he was held up by traffic on the other side of the park? We tore up the front steps into Judy's house, locked the door behind us, and fell against each other, gasping, chests aching, legs burning. Judy tucked the filched book into her sweater and said, "Come on."

JUDY, OCTOBER 30, 1948

We leaned over the raised cornice on the top of Hill Estates, searching for the gray ghost. We spotted him standing near the statue of Lincoln, his fedora twitching back and forth. He was bewildered, then resigned, then gone, swept away in a group of sightseers.

I retrieved a matchbook and my pack of Chesterfields from the chimney while Philippa slid below the top edge of the cornice, shielding herself from the wind. I sat beside her, my back against the cold bricks. I cupped a match and lit my cigarette. Philippa edged over to me, the outside of her upper arm pressing against me. I recoiled a little. I didn't like her so close. It was confining, suffocating. But she didn't move away; in fact, she scooted closer. Although I was annoyed, I let her warmth fend off the chill spreading through me. I took a drag on the cigarette and absorbed the soothing smoke. I offered it to her, and she snatched it out of my fingers without hesitation.

"He's the man I saw in Miss Martins's apartment," she said, letting the smoke drift from her lips. "He's the one."

"How do you know?" I said, my jitters abating as the nicotine did its job.

"His cologne."

"Lots of men could have the same cologne. Bart douses himself with Seaforth to cover up the alcohol fumes. I've smelled it on other men. Drunks too." I reclaimed the cigarette and took a puff.

"This smell, it's distinctive. Perfume changes when you put it on. It mingles with your scent. It was the same man." Her expression clouded over, and her brow wrinkled.

"Are you okay?"

"No," she said, glossy-eyed. "He was on top of Miss Martins, crushing her, and she was gesturing to me, wanting me to help. It must've been what happened, and I did nothing. I just ran." She wiped her runny nose with her sleeve. "The gray ghost knows about me, about us. I bet he found *Love's Last Move* and forced Miss Martins to tell him who I was. And now he's coming after us."

So, it seemed, Philippa had decided that what she'd witnessed was rape. I wasn't there. I don't know what she really saw. But our minds are like mazes with many blind corners and dead ends, and memory is like a string that is supposed to lead you out, but sometimes it crosses and tangles and leads you in deeper. Hell, I can't even remember why I have scars on my arms. Maybe Philippa was shocked to see Miss M with a man. Perhaps she needs to believe she was attacked. She's a bit of a ninny when it comes to sex. She even broke into a goddamn sweat at Somerset's.

After taking another pull, I said, "You're positive the man you saw was forcing himself on Miss M?"

"Yes, something happened to her. She changed."

"If he's the same man, if he attacked her, then he wants to hurt us, or at least scare us, but I wonder why he followed me the other day. I mean, wouldn't he go after you? You borrowed the book."

She shifted even closer, pressing her arm to my arm, her leg to my leg. I was aware of her rough wool coat, her smooth nylon stockings, her crushed velvet Mary Janes, and even her soft, wind-tangled hair as it brushed against my shoulder. At first, I resisted these little details, these quiet fireworks popping, but then I gave in. I scanned the curve of her breasts, the gentle slope of her neck, and even the bean-shape of her small ears hung with small silver hoops. I breathed in her flowery perfume, which was similar to Miss M's, detecting a hint of sweat underneath. The images from Somerset's backroom rose up, rustling behind their brown paper wrappers like insects caught in a bag. My body tensed. I'd never felt this way about a girl—or if I'm being honest, a boy. Sex isn't all that if you ask me. I wasn't sure what it was that I was feeling.

"Are you sure you couldn't have misread the situation at Miss M's?" I said, fidgeting with my coat sleeves, ordering my feelings to retreat.

"I know what I saw," she said, brushing a strand of hair from her cheek.

My cigarette suddenly became ashy and sour, so I tossed it. "Maybe Miss M liked it that way, like a character in one of her shitty pulp novels."

"No! Jesus."

"Maybe we should've told your cousin more." I didn't believe that, though.

"About the ghost?"

"About what you saw at Miss M's," I said, studying my fingers, noting a chipped nail.

"We also didn't tell him everything about our visit to the Closses, not even Elaine Closs's menagerie of pills."

"Slow down. It's not a good thing to show all your cards," I said, trying to curb her impulse to run to Quincy and blurt everything. "But, yeah, maybe if we'd shared more, we might've learned more."

Philippa shifted, rubbing her leg against mine, setting me off again, making me itchy and uncomfortable.

"We need to find Miss M," I said, shoving my body away from the wall, relieved to put space between us.

"She has to answer our questions now," she said, holding her hand out for me to pull her up.

PHILIPPA, OCTOBER 30, 1948

Why did she do it? Why drag me into Somerset's dirty book room and shove smut under my nose? At first, it felt like a punch in the gut: "Here, Philippa, see how ugly the world is! I've seen it all. Now you need to see it, to get me."

But now, I don't know.

Sure, the image was crass, but the sadness in the woman's eyes tugged on something in me. Since I can remember, I've been curious about other girls. They always seem to possess some secret knowledge, something I missed along the way, perhaps something my mother would've whispered to me. Over time, my yearning became wondering. I wanted to know what it'd be like to run my hand over their arms and down their legs as if they were my arms and legs. I wanted to see what they saw in the mirror. I wanted to feel the air in their lungs. All this, because I don't feel like one of them. Sure, I can give my hair the right amount of wave and curl, apply lipstick with deft strokes, and wear a rotating array of pastels, but I'm playing pretend. I'm a fraud. Perhaps there are other girls who feel like they've arrived at the party late and don't get the inside jokes. Maybe Judy's one? Although she seems to get all the jokes.

The smutty photo also picked up the thread of a particular memory, which now that I'm alone in my room, I can pull on. Two summers ago, at Camp Bothin, I met a girl named Thea Ray from Sacramento. She was pals with the sporty girls, the golfers, and the archers. For the most part, they let the bookish ones, like me, be. Toward the end of the summer, after the barriers between the social groups had dissolved, a result of living in close quarters, a group of girls went on a candy-fueled tickle attack. They called it the Battle of Midriff. Can you believe it? Groan. Anyway, in a fit of giggles and blond curls, Thea pinned me to my cot, dug her fingers into my sides, and pressed her body against mine, giving me a peck on the lips that lingered a beat too long. She was trying to get a rise out of me and embarrass me. But her kiss branded me and burned for weeks. In my mind, the peck grew into a longer, deeper kiss. It lasted for ages, our clothing gauze-thin and sweat-damp between us, our lips, breasts, stomachs, and limbs melting together. It took pure willpower to drive her away, like kicking the Spanish flu. Even now, I can still smell her, the funk of her sweat, like a mixture of tennis balls and athletic tape.

This is the first time I've written about it, afraid that putting it down would've sealed my fate. Thea tore something open inside of me, wiped her lips, and was gone—all in the name of "good fun." Not writing about it made little difference. When Judy flashed that photo at me, the dormant Thea, the Thea I'd driven into hibernation, woke up, yawned, stretched, and dug her nails into my insides.

Judy is always treating me like I was born yesterday, endlessly horrified by my apparent naivete. I wonder: Is she just another eye-roller, sniggering behind my back? Did she lure me into the dirty book room to torture me? Is she another Thea?

Like me, she's worked hard to cultivate her look: the angular cheeks, the chopped black hair, the elliptical eyes. But it's a barrier. She reminds me of a Klimt portrait that I once lingered on in a massive art history textbook. In the painting, this dark-haired woman, Adele something, is emerging from a geometrical gold-leaf background. She's in motion but still trapped somehow, like an anesthetized butterfly. I loved it and was unsettled by it. Judy is like that woman. It's like she's flattened against a plate of sun-drenched glass, bits of her seeping through the cracks, two dimensions trying to become three, like when she froze at Sophie's cellar door or when she's struggling to remember her childhood. If she's not like Thea, then maybe, just maybe, she's the antidote to Thea.

❧

PHILIPPA, OCTOBER 31, 1948

Bonnie cooked a pork roast, rosemary potatoes, twice-cooked green beans, baked fresh rolls, and served pumpkin pie for Sunday lunch. She didn't usually go overboard, but Quincy was coming, so she dusted off the fine china and expanded the menu. Although the conversation veered toward Cleve several times, Bonnie and Dad guided it away, fearing, I can only guess, that it might be too morbid for me. Quincy and I made knowing eyes at each other. I even dared an eye roll. Afterward, I asked Dad if I could show him my room.

After a cursory tour, I plopped down on my bed, grabbed Mr. Fred from my pillow, and held his scrawny body close to me. Quincy picked up the photo of my mother and studied it. After a moment, I said, "Any news about Cleve?"

He smiled, but it was guarded. "Nothing." He wasn't going to share.

"Okay," I said. "I get it. We rushed you at Horsfield's. I don't want you to lose your job."

His eyes lifted, and he placed the frame back on the dresser. "That friend of yours, she thinks she's very clever."

"She *is*," I said sharply and thought, "She's extracted information from you, information you still don't realize you shared." But I could tell he was bewildered by her. He wasn't alone.

"You know," she said. "She felt bad about how she behaved at Horsfield's."

He grimaced. "I guess you know Sophie's not a fan."

"She doesn't really know her."

"Do you?"

Did I? Well, I was beginning to, and I wasn't going to let Quincy underestimate her. "She's had a hard time. The Peabodys treat her like a cheap imitation of their dead daughter."

A smile crept onto his lips and said, "Maybe I'm being unfair."

"You think?"

"You have a big heart, Phil." He sat at the other end of my bed, putting his elbows on his knees. He hunched, breathed deeply, and ran his fingers through his thick black hair. He seemed weary. I took Mr. Fred, his limp body still curled in my lap, and propped him on his shoulder.

"Who's this?" he said, catching him before he tumbled off.

"Monsieur Fred."

He held him up, regarded him, and demanded, "What *are* you?"

"A bear-otter mix. Or a weasel. No one knows. His past is shrouded in mystery."

He sat Fred on his knee, my mother's carnelian locket still buried deep in his stuffing, a kind of transplanted heart, and said, "He's a blue blood. He has those regal cheekbones, that stately nose. His inheritance is out there waiting for him."

"Use your razor-sharp detective skills and help him claim his birthright," I said with forced gusto. "It could be a rags-to-riches story."

"He does look like he could use a little food."

"Bonnie feeds him a whole honeyed ham every night, but he never grows an inch!"

"She would, wouldn't she?" He laughed, then grew quiet, turning something over in his mind. "You know," he said softly, "they're bringing Bogdan in." He tucked Mr. Fred beside him. "He doesn't have an alibi for the Closs kid's time of death, and they found a 1947 Eastern High School yearbook in his trash. Cleve's photo had been circled. Bogdan circled other photos, too. Girls *and* boys. But you didn't hear that from me."

"Was Judy circled?" I said, thinking of the gray ghost. I've never seen Bogdan, so he could be the man who followed us from Somerset's. Of course, Judy would have recognized him. Unless he'd changed in some way.

"No, she wasn't. I'm sure of that."

"They have it wrong," I said to Quincy. "I'm sure of it."

"Maybe," he said, "but the yearbook is significant. It's got his fingerprints on it. The dockmaster saw it when he was dumping his garbage."

"The dockmaster?"

He stood. "Please, don't tell anyone I told you." A worry line creased his forehead. "I can trust you, can't I? Like old times." That's when it occurred to me that *I* was the one with sway, not Judy and her bizarre manipulations. He remembered the adventurous little girl in me or perhaps his own daring spirit. When we were kids, we would sneak out of Sophie's and go swimming in the river. We'd do things we were forbidden to do, like swing on vines across creek beds and crawl into caves. I was grateful he still trusted me. After all, he was taking a serious risk. So, I decided to trust him in return and said, "We didn't tell you everything we discovered when we visited the Closses'."

"Okay?" he said, raising his dark eyebrows.

"I don't know if these things are important, but Cleve's mother had a cabinet full of medications."

He didn't seem surprised. "What kind?"

"There were lots of sleeping pills and syrups, according to Judy."

"Did she mention any types? Veronal, perhaps?"

"What's Veronal?"

"A barbiturate. A sleeping aid."

I stared at him, searching for a tell, the slightest twitch of a muscle, but he remained still. He'd been working on his poker face. "Is it poisonous?" I said.

"It can be, in large doses."

"Was it what killed Cleve?"

He smiled grimly. "No."

"What killed him then?"

"Can't say."

He was withdrawing. "Come on, Quincy."

"Really, I can't," he said, waving his hand and moving away. "The coroner is having trouble determining the cause of death."

"So, he wasn't strangled like Jackie?"

"I'm not saying."

"I told *you* something."

"Okay." He gave me a wary look and rubbed his chin. "But you can't tell this to anyone else, especially Judy."

"Cross my heart."

"Well, they think he drowned, but it's hard to tell whether the water entered his lungs before or after death. It's almost impossible to determine. Although there's definitely river water in him, they also found traces of a cleaner, something like Bon Ami."

"Did he drown somewhere else?" I said.

Quincy shrugged, and before I could ask another question, I heard Bonnie calling from the bottom of the stairs.

As I think it over, it seems probable *and* impossible that Bogdan killed Cleve. Probable, because of the evidence: the mysterious word scrawled on Jackie and, I assume, on Cleve; his lack of an alibi; his creepy fascination with Shirley Temple; and now the yearbook. Impossible, because I know that there's a connection between what I saw in Miss Martins's apartment and Cleve's murder. I can feel it in my gut. Of course, I don't know what that connection is. Why would Bogdan lust after a grown woman if he had a fixation on young girls? Don't psychos have a pattern, like Jack the Ripper? For that matter, why would he kill a seventeen-year-old boy? And why would he drown him somewhere else and then dump him in the river? Nothing is adding up.

PHILIPPA, OCTOBER 31, 1948

When I arrived at the Peabodys' annual Halloween soirée, Edith answered the door in a long black gown and a black beaded beak-nosed mask. "Hello, my dear," she said, "and who are you supposed to be?"

I'd braided my hair into two loose pigtails and suited up in a blue gingham dress, baby blue socks that I dug out of the bottom of my dresser, and Mary Janes with glued-on red sequins. Mr. Fred was stuffed in a basket hanging from the crook of my arm. "Dorothy," I said.

"Oh!" Edith laughed, which surprised me. "I'm a Poe poem! Can you tell me which one?" Her eyes were warm and flashing with enthusiasm. I knew the answer but was too stunned by her amiability to blurt it out, so I stood there, mute.

"'The Raven,' my dear," she said with good-natured impatience. "Well, I suppose you're looking for Judy. She's upstairs dilly-dallying, of course."

I was woefully unprepared to navigate the party, but Judy had demanded that I come: "It's always a goddamn nightmare," she said. "It's your sworn duty as my friend to run defense—or at least be a distraction." As soon as I entered the front parlor, it was like stepping into another world. Draped with crepe streamers, the room was saturated with eerie candlelight. Here and there, hurricane lamps flickered and papier-mâché jack-o'-lanterns grinned and howled. A mixture of cinnamon and eau de toilette and linseed oil spiced the air, and all the wood surfaces were polished to a mirrorlike shine. The Peabodys had pushed the chairs against the walls, and on a round table in the center of the room, they had displayed an assortment of hors d'oeuvres, including a platter of caramel apples, nut-encrusted cheese balls, pumpkin–and–cream cheese petit fours, and an impressive crystal punchbowl containing fragrant cider. "Happy Halloween" in big block letters hung limply over the fireplace on the far wall.

It was early, so there were only a few guests present: an ancient Lucifer with a red pitchfork, a scrawny Roman soldier in tin foil armor, and a fat skeleton. They chatted together in the far corner, each sipping punch from dainty glassware, like some sort of perverse triumvirate. The hired waiters drifted around the room in black tie, adjusting flowers and fluffing pillows. Nestled on a divan near me, a fairy, not much older than I am, flirted with a cowboy in a ten-gallon hat. She smiled at me and mouthed, "Dorothy" and "Cute." I turned away, overwhelmed. It was all a little too absurd and macabre, and I had no idea what I was supposed to do, so I made a beeline for the stairs.

When I knocked on Judy's bedroom door, a black cat answered. "I hope you don't have an allergic reaction," she said, swatting me with her paw. She was wearing a tight black sweater, black slacks, and black velvet cat ears. Her lips were dark purple, her eye shadow a smoky smear.

I pretended to sneeze. "I thought you hated cats."

"I love irony more than I hate cats."

"I promise not to drop a brick on you."

"Or a sandbag?"

"Or a sandbag."

"Well, then I promise not to claw your eyes out." She showed her claws. She had painted her fingernails black as well. "Let's go downstairs and critique costumes. Loudly."

She grabbed my hand, and we descended into the thickening crowd. We skirted the fringes of the parlor, living room, and dining room. If anyone approached us, Judy hissed and swatted at them, committed to her costume. The guests laughed nervously or smiled politely and walked on, giving her a wide berth on their next pass through the room. After a while, we became aware of our unique vantage point: the partygoers' costumes, which were meant to obscure their identities, or enhance their best qualities, or a combination of the two, unwittingly amplified their vulnerabilities and quirks.

"Philippa, I ask you, why is Attila the Hun wearing socks?" Judy flung out in a full stage whisper.

"Dear me." I nodded. "Joan of Arc shouldn't have cleavage."

"She should be burned at the stake for that costume."

"Coming as President Truman is a cop-out. That's *not* a costume."

"That one over there. Is he in a prison outfit?"

"No, he's a Communist."

"And Lana Turner—she's looking a little plump, don't you think? Sometimes wishful thinking isn't enough, dear."

"The one with the horse head and the elephant ears—what is he sup- posed to be? A Chimera?"

"Bipartisan."

"Oh, it's a donkey."

To us, they all became sycophants and neurotics, wannabes and never- could-bes. We were encased in a bubble, floating above them. We had their numbers.

Eventually, Bart made an entrance as a Minuteman, musket in hand, brass buttons glowing, brown wig lopsided, and reeking of booze. Judy wouldn't go near him, and Edith took his arm and guided him to a chair. While he sat sipping a cup of punch (spiked, no doubt), Edith darted around the parlor dipping in and out of conversation. Her favorite topic was Bogdan's arrest. Like me, Judy thought the police had it all wrong, but Edith was delighted with the turn of events. She told guests, "At long last, they're on the right track!" and "It only took another murder for them to wake up," and "I don't think they'd question him if they didn't have hard evidence." From behind sequined masks and fussy wigs and silly clown faces, the guests murmured about the inadequacies of the police and justice for Jackie. At one point, Judy leaned in and whispered, "I'd love to crack that punchbowl over Edith's head."

Finally, we retreated upstairs, grabbing Roosevelt on our way. After depositing the dog on her bed, Judy went to her record collection, selected several LPs, and dropped one onto her player. As Chopin's "Nocturne in E Minor" floated out from the speaker, she plucked off her cat ears and tossed them across the room. She curled up with Rosie and gave him a belly rub. I slung my basket and Mr. Fred to the side, flopped on the window seat, and pulled my legs under me, soothed by the warmth from the nearby radiator. My Dorothy outfit was too skimpy for this time of year.

Scooping up Rosie and drawing her close, Judy looked at me, her eyes shiny and deep like polished marbles, and said, "There are things I remember that never happened to me."

"What?" It was a startling thing to say. "That doesn't make sense."

"It does, and it doesn't."

A little exasperated, I said, "Is this a riddle?"

She glared at me. "It's my life."

"Okay," I said, hugging my bare arms, "so explain it to me."

JUDY, OCTOBER 31, 1948

As soon as I said it, I felt like a total fool: "There are things I remember that never happened to me." Philippa gaped at me like I was as doped up as Elaine Closs. I wiped the wetness from my eyes. My thoughts were spreading in all directions like scampering mice: Why was I blurting this out now? Did I trust Philippa with it? It would feel so good to tell someone! Something in me—a tactical impulse—drew in all the scattering thoughts, and breathing out, I said, "I remember when Bart and Edith came to visit me at Crestwood for the first time." I paused, taking in Philippa's gingham jumper, her pigtails, and her makeshift ruby red slippers. The absurdity of her costume—of me divulging all this while she was dressed as god-damn Dorothy—calmed me. "I was on the floor, playing with a doll, and Edith kneeled and placed her hands on the sides of my shoulders and said, 'My darling little girl. You're perfect. It's like you're ours already.' I didn't know what to say. I didn't know I was being adopted. Her expression was odd but full of something. Love, maybe? I don't know." Philippa listened quietly, her eyes flickering, taking it all in without judgment. I was suddenly thankful for that, for her. "Within a few weeks," I went on, "they had adopted me, and I was no longer Judy X. I was Judy Peabody. We went shopping, and I got more dresses than I ever imagined I'd own. They were frilly and hideous, but they were new, and they were mine. Edith told Bart they were 'what Jackie liked' and 'wouldn't she have looked the little princess in them.' I wasn't sure who Jackie was, but at the time, it seemed like a good thing."

"Okay," Philippa said, adjusting her thin cotton dress over her knees, "but I don't understand what this has to do with your misremembering things."

"I'm getting to it," I said, a little prickly. Rosie slipped through my hands and leaped from the bed. "First, you have to understand what they did to me."

Laughter swelled from downstairs, cutting through the dreamy Chopin. "For a short time," I said, hesitating, afraid to go on. I didn't want her to think I was totally nuts. I had to go on. I'd committed to telling her. I wanted her to know. I flexed my jaw muscles, and blood swelled in my temples. "You see, after I was adopted, I . . . "

"Yes?"

"I-I began to believe I was Jackie."

Philippa didn't move or speak, but her silvery eyes grew wide.

"Edith began dressing me like Jackie and calling me Jackie and talking about things we'd done last year at Christmas time or during summer vacation at Cape May," I said, forcing it out quickly. "She'd say something like, 'Jackie, darling, do you remember the time we went to the Smithsonian and saw dinosaur bones?' and then she'd order me to sit beside her, and we'd flip the pages of her photo album. She'd point to a picture of Jackie standing beside a triceratops and say, 'There you are. What a cute little hat you have on!' She even avoided calling me by name around her social circle, as if somehow, they wouldn't notice I wasn't Jackie. I was baffled at first. I mean, what the hell. But with time, I started to believe her. Maybe, it was me. Maybe I'd forgotten about the triceratops and the cute little hat. Eventually, I began to buy it: I was the girl in the photo. Of course, I was. Sure."

"Weren't you furious?" Philippa said, leaning in, engrossed. I couldn't believe she hadn't run from the room screaming yet.

"It was easier to believe it than fight it. I started rewriting my past, blotting out the old memories and replacing them with Jackie's. Besides, she'd had a much better childhood. I even started to add on to her memories. Her face would light up when I would pick up a memory she'd laid down and develop it, expand it, find its core—'Do you recall your sixth birthday picnic at Rock Creek Park?' or 'Oh, remember seeing *The Wizard of Oz* at the Uptown?'" Philippa glanced down at her costume, startled, it seemed, to remember she still had it on. "I'd feign recognition and say, 'I sure do! That was so much fun! Remember the cake shaped like a music box with the little ballerina in its center? Remember the ruby slippers? Remember the Wicked Witch of the West?' I could make up ridiculous things, just bullshit, and she was happy to play along. I'd watch as color would rise through her pasty face. It felt like I was giving her something, relieving her grief a bit. I guess I was trying to love her."

Philippa's shoulders drooped and her braided ponytails slipped over her shoulders. "That's so sad," she said, and I could tell she meant it, but I could also tell she didn't know what else to say. Jesus, what could you say?

I went on: "Then Bart caught wind of it. Between his martinis and highballs, he ordered Edith to go for a rest cure and straighten herself out. While she was away, he tried to explain what had happened to Jackie. I was only eleven, so it took me a while to get it. What the hell did I know? The worst of it, though—" A big wet ball of emotion swelled up in me, and I breathed in, trying to keep it together. I wasn't going to start blubbering. "I can't remember who I was before all the fucking lies."

Philippa didn't move; she just sat there, stroking one of her pigtails. I looked away, wiping the dampness from the corners of my eyes. Chopin wavered in the air between us, as if sprinkled there like shimmery black dust.

Breaking the silence, she said, "What do you remember before being adopted?"

I was glad to have a question to answer: "Crestwood, of course. Its sickly green walls. Its lawn. The boxwood hedges. Some faces, women's faces. There was another place too . . ." I fell back against my pillows, wanting to sink deep into them, hoping they might muffle my mind. "I don't remember things that happened. I don't remember events. I have dreams, but I'm not sure what they mean. Some of them are too bizarre to be real—and then there's the one about the cats." My stomach cramped, and I folded over, grunting softly. The impossible smell of damp earth wafted into my nostrils, and a chill ran head to toe. Goddamn cats. Jesus Christ.

"Are you okay?" she said, uncurling her legs and sitting up.

"Yes, yes," I said, holding my arm out. "It's just too many pumpkin-and-cream-cheese petit fours." I stared at the molding on the ceiling, willing away the pain and the tears; it was becoming difficult to keep it all tamped down. "Fuck B and E," I said, biting my lip. "Fuck Jackie, too." I didn't want Philippa to see me like that—so raw. But maybe she needed to. After all, we're both jigsaw puzzles with missing pieces. My childhood is full of holes, and she never knew her mother. Maybe we need to see each other's gaps. If we can identify their shapes, we'll know what pieces to look for.

Philippa stood, came to me, and bellyflopped across the end of the bed, her homemade ruby slippers scissoring the air above her, shedding sequins. "You know," I said, feeling calmer, "I used to stand in front of the mirror and try to imagine what my parents were like. Did dear ol' Dad give me his swarthy looks? Did Mother Dear give me her thin waist and long, tapered fingers? I imagined them being Italian aristocrats. Or Texas oil moguls. Or jet-set adventurers who hiked Mount Everest and paddled the Amazon." I felt Philippa's eyes on me, soaking it all in. "Or maybe they were just average. A milkman and a seamstress. A store clerk and a housekeeper. Or maybe they were the victims of a robbery gone wrong or a horrible accident—something tabloid-ready and gruesome: 'Mr. and Mrs. Jack Nightingale, of the esteemed Earnshaw-Nightingales, died in a tragic hot air balloon crash. They plummeted two thousand feet into the Potomac and were never heard from again!'" I said in my best news announcer voice.

Philippa stretched her hand across the bedspread. I reached back, feeling the tips of her fingers and the smooth polish on her fingernails, but I couldn't meet her eyes. I feared her pity. It would crush me. I shoved those memories from my mind, withdrew my hand, and hugged a pillow to me. "I'm not going to let B and E get away with celebrating because they think they got their man," I said, looking at her. She was clear-eyed and somber, no trace of pity. Thank God. "Bogdan didn't kill Cleve. I know it."

"Of course not!" she said, rising to her elbows. A shadow of a thought crossed her face, and she said, "Listen, I have to tell you something—"

There was a rap on the door. It swung open, and Edith swooped in, now with her Raven mask off. "Dears," she said like she'd just chimed fine crystal for a speech. "Why are you hiding out up here? The party is just warming up."

I studied the sheen of her black dress, the hard line of her lips, her plucked eyebrows, her over-powdered cheeks, and her proud Roman beak. She was trampling on our private moment, and I had no patience for it. I wanted to lash out, to drive her away, but I was unsure how Philippa would react, so I held back, but just barely. "No thanks," I said flatly. "We're fine here."

"Don't be a sourpuss," she chirped, crossing to the bed. "Philippa isn't a mope like you. Are you, Philippa?"

Philippa, now on her feet, shrugged helplessly. I felt protective of her. I didn't want Edith to get into her head.

Edith turned to me, and we locked eyes. For a split second, I saw a glimmer of something there, as if she was trying to grasp my mood—or even consider my point of view. Imagine! Then, I remembered her reaching down to me when we first met in Crestwood and running her manicured nail along my chin. "You're perfect," she cooed, "a perfect little girl." Anger thumped in my chest, and in a modulated tone, I slowly spelled, "A-H-K-A." Her eyes flickered, and she gave me an odd look, like a cat might to a strange noise. She'd had a realization, but she wasn't going to acknowledge it—or even me. She looked as if she were about to float out the door and melt back into her party. So, feeling bold and, to be honest, vengeful, I said, "A-H-K-A," again, giving each letter a crisp pop. Each letter bit into her, and with each bite, she became more alarmed. This time she couldn't slip out, wrapping herself in gauzy denial. "AHKA," I said again, pronouncing it as a word, an evocation, a necromancer's spell, conjuring Jackie back from the dead. The little bow-festooned vampire was now in the room with us. "I know all about it," I said. "AHKA. Anka. Anna. Whatever it is."

Edith cocked her head, and the black feathers sprouting from her collar twitched. "How did you find out about—?" She caught herself, not wanting to reveal too much to Philippa, I assumed. "You're babbling like an idiot." She laughed, waving it away, her eyes damp. "Philippa, can you please tell me what's wrong with her? I don't see how you can tolerate her. She's strange and ghoulish and disruptive. She wants to destroy my good mood!" Her voice was high and brittle.

"Bogdan didn't do it," I said, locking in on my target. "Crazed killers choose victims with similar characteristics. Cleve and Jackie were like night and day."

"You don't know that," Edith said, sniffing at me. "Since when are you an expert?"

"Why wait all these years, then choose a victim who wasn't your type?"

"The police have solved it. Just let it be."

"So now you trust the police?"

"Judith," she snapped, and then in a tighter, hotter voice, she said, "you have no idea what your father and I have been through. How could you?"

Philippa remained motionless, her arms crossed, and her shoulders drawn up. She looked like she wanted to click her ruby slippers three times.

"Cleve wasn't molested," I said, hopping up from the bed and tossing the pillow to the side. "The police know it, and we found out." I approached her, gazing into her bronze irises, feeling razor-sharp. "He wasn't fucked like Jackie."

Her face contorted and flushed bright red. "Don't you—!" she seethed. "Don't you dare. It's awful to think . . . just awful . . . my God . . ." Her eyes burned with tears. She trembled, unable to speak. Suddenly she cried out and left, slamming the bedroom door so hard it popped open again. The murmur from the party seeped in. Philippa walked to the door and closed it. The Chopin had ended, the crackle of the turntable filling the airless room.

CHAPTER FIVE

As I thumb through the past hundred and fifty pages or so, I notice a theme emerging: THE ABSENT MOTHER. That's what we had in common, the fertile soil for our bond to grow. If I'm honest—the sort of honesty that comes with a few martinis and a cigarette or two (or three)—it's mothers, or our lack of them, that spurred our misdeeds. We might be the angel and the harpy or Leopold and Loeb, but we were both born from ghostly mothers, phantom ladies who drifted along the battlements of our childhoods. We couldn't be raised by a wisp of smoke at the end of a long corridor or a faint shadow in a high tower. We were left empty, desiring.

Maybe it's not their absence that's the problem, but the presence of another kind of materfamilias: THE INEFFECTUAL MOTHER. Poor Edith Peabody couldn't find her way out of her grief, so tethered she was to Jackie's memory, and Bonnie couldn't find her way out of the kitchen, so wedded she was to the frying pan, and, let's face it,

Elaine Closs was no mother of the year—which is putting it lightly. In the grip of pharmaceuticals and her abiding despair, she couldn't find her way out of a medicine cabinet. Of course, that may have been the idea. Anyway, none of them did much nurturing—well, not much that was of use. Bonnie tried, and Edith tried in all the wrong ways, and Elaine—she was beyond trying.

I would be remiss if I didn't mention yet another species of mother stalking her way through these pages: THE MONSTER MOTHER. A literary favorite. Think of the deformed child-eating Lamia from Greek myth or Grendel's Dane-devouring mother from that cornerstone of English literature, Beowulf. Our monstrous mother is the inestimable Moira Closs, chinchilla cape swaying, bright eyes glaring, teeth gnashing. A controlling bitch of a woman. A Lady Macbeth with steely sanity and a penchant for unscrupulous self-preservation. Of course, I can easily—and with delight—point to her for the source of all our woes. But even monster mothers make better mothers than ghost mothers—they love fiercely. At the end of the day, I admired her. She knew what she was about, and she loved her son.

Since we're on the topic of parents, let's have a word about the fathers, shall we? Frankly, they're kind of a blur; they melt together. If I concentrate hard, though, I can make them out, like tiny points on a continuum. Carl Watson was the upstanding, tight-lipped, morally righteous sort, terrified of his own flaws. Bart Peabody was always dissolving into the background, trying to be 3-D, but allowing alcohol to dilute him like watercolor paint. And Cleve's father—well, he stands out a bit brighter and sharper, like a polished dagger wielded in the night. He's there, then gone, the depth of the wound he caused uncertain; the blood is still seeping.

Of course, all of this is excuse-making. (Dear Reader, I can hear you saying it now!) We could endlessly blame our mothers and fathers for our behavior, but they're like the masks we wear to avoid seeing

ourselves clearly. Eventually, you have to take that mask off and
say: "That's me. I am what I am. I did what I did. No more excuses.
No more fathers. No more mothers."

❦

PHILIPPA, NOVEMBER 1, 1948

After school today, Judy wanted to "stick a pin" in each of the pieces of
information we'd collected so far to decide what our next move should be.
So, once again, we climbed out of her bathroom window and up the fire
escape. Still afraid to make the leap to Hill Estates, I crossed on the board.
"Aargh, matey," Judy said, "it's always the plank for you!"

She fished a bag of M&M's out of her sweater, ripped it open, and
popped a few pieces in her mouth. "There are three crimes—Jackie's murder.
Cleve's murder. And the attack on Miss Martins," she said, holding the bag
of candy out to me. I took several. In addition to smoking like a fiend, she
had a sweet tooth. "Let's lay out what we know about each."

"Okay," I said, slipping a pen and a notebook out of my lapel pocket. If I had
to juggle clues, I might as well take notes. I didn't see how any of it fit together,
and it was beginning to bewilder me. "Let's start with Miss Martins."

"Hmm," Judy said, mulling it over. "On October twentieth, you walk in
on a man having sex with—or maybe even attacking—Miss M. We now
know the man is the gray ghost, because he wears that awful cologne, and
he's been following us. While you're there, you drop your book, which
either Miss M, or this man, or both of them find. Miss M is absent from
school the next day. We search her apartment and find her smashed pin.
Later, we walk in on her fighting with Cleve."

"That's right." I gestured to her for more M&M's.

"Then, Cleve disappears."

I sucked on the chocolaty pebbles and scribbled a few notes. "So, we're moving on to Cleve?"

"They run together," Judy said, inhaling deeply. "There must be a connection."

"Meanwhile, the gray ghost—I really want to stop calling him that," I said. "It sounds like a bad detective novel: *Ghoul in the Gray Hat* by Ray Kane. 'He comes for you by night. He comes for you by day. He's the Man in Gray!'"

"No longer a Kane fan?"

"Moving on," I said, wagging my pen at her. "The gray ghost starts following you and then both of us."

"Why?" Judy said, popping more M&M's.

"What do you mean?"

"Why is he following us? What does he want?"

"I don't know," I said, turning my attention to the bright patch of sun on the chimney across from us and the high wispy clouds overhead. Coming back to earth, I added, "Maybe he thinks I could identify him as Miss Martins's attacker." The thought chilled me as I spoke it, and suddenly I was so glad to be on the roof with Judy, hovering above everything, gobbling M&M's, safe for now.

"That makes sense." She crumpled up the empty M&M's bag and tossed it over the roof. She walked over to the chimney and forced a few low-set bricks loose. She produced a small flask. "Want some?" she said. "I filched this from Bart's stash. It's gin."

"Ew. No."

"Suit yourself." She took a swig. "Okay, on to Cleve."

"I'll do him," I said. "Although he's always been the sulky sort, over the past few weeks, his anger at Miss Martins has been escalating." I jotted notes while I spoke. "Then he runs us down on the sidewalk, and I clobber him with an iron railing. On the twenty-first, he and Miss Martins have it out. He calls her a whore and storms out of her classroom. The weekend passes, and his body is found washed up at the edge of the Anacostia. One of the witnesses mentions writing on his arm, which is most likely AHKA, but we need to verify that." A thought flashed through my mind, and I gasped. "I forgot to tell you something! I was going to, but then Edith came in and it slipped my mind."

Judy stared at me, her eyes urging, "Get on with it!"

Although I felt a twinge of guilt about breaking my word to Quincy, I explained to her that he'd told me that it was difficult to determine precisely what had killed Cleve, but that most likely, he had drowned. He wasn't strangled like Jackie. I also told her about the traces of Bon Ami in his lungs and that Quincy had asked me if we'd discovered any Veronal in the Closses' drug stockpile.

"Wow, Quincy *was* chatty," she said, clearly pleased. "Hmm . . . I wonder about the Veronal. Maybe he was drugged and then drowned in a bathtub or pool. That would explain the Bon Ami. Then later, he could've been dumped in the river."

"He also told me why they arrested Bogdan," I said.

"The yearbook, I know. The police told Bart and Edith." She squinted at me and twisted her lips in thought. "I'm beginning to think the Closses had something to do with his death, don't you?"

"Cleve wasn't happy at home. His father was gone a lot, and his mother—I don't know, you saw her." That day on the steps of Eastern High rushed back to me: Cleve bent over his biology textbook, blond hair catching the light. At that moment, I liked something about him. Perhaps his vulnerability—or his status as a fellow outcast.

"The queen bitch, the grandmother," Judy said, after taking another swig of gin. "She knows something, I'm sure of it. And what about Cleve's dad? We need to meet him and size him up."

"Slow down. We're not done yet," I said. "Jackie has something to do with this." Feeling bold, I gestured for her to hand me the flask. I took a whiff, winced, and drank from it. It burned like acid and soured my stomach. "Yuck, that tastes like rancid Christmas trees."

"Bogdan didn't kill Cleve," Judy said firmly. "Maybe he killed Jackie, but he did have an alibi for her murder. The only thing that connects them, other than the Anacostia River, is the writing on their bodies."

"What about the yearbook?"

"It just implicates him but doesn't connect the two murders. Besides, it sounds too convenient, don't you think?"

I glanced over my notes. "How do we go about checking what was written on Cleve? We need to know that for sure."

Judy capped her flask. "The witnesses that found the body."

"Rody James and Linda Wells?"

"That's how."

Back inside, we located Bart and Edith's phone directory, grabbed the phone in the Peabodys' main hall, and hunkered down in the powder room. It was as far as the line would stretch. We searched for the names. We didn't find a Linda Wells, but we did find three Roderick Jameses.

Doing my best impression of Torchy Blane—the swift-talking journalist from *Torchy Gets Her Man*, *Fly-Away Baby*, and *Smart Blonde*, all movies I'd adored when I was little—I impersonated a *Post* reporter. With the receiver between us, we rang the first Rody. No one was home. The second Rody—he went by Rory—growled about clogging the party line and hung up. Finally, the third Rody answered. After I explained that I was calling for a follow-up interview, he said, "Well, I don't have anything new to add. I'm still reeling from the whole experience."

"Our follow-up article will go more in-depth, make use of the human angle," I said, having no idea what "the human angle" might be.

Judy rolled her eyes.

After soliciting some background information from him, I asked, "Would you mind describing the scene again? We want to see it from your perspective."

"Okay, okay," Rody said. "Well, let me think. Linda and me, we'd prepared a Sunday picnic. We decided to go down by the Sousa Bridge. It's not far from my apartment on Kentucky Avenue. Linda, who lives in Cincinnati, was visiting me—we're engaged, you see."

"Congratulations," I said.

Judy glared at me and gestured for me to hurry up.

"Anyway," he said, "we'd just finished eating—we'd set up a nice little spread, but we had to bundle up in the blanket to keep warm. It was a cool day. That's when Linda pointed over my shoulder and said, 'What's that?' I stood for a closer look. I thought he was debris from a boat or something. But there he was, thirty or forty feet from us, floating facedown in an inch or two of water, his body stuck in the silt. He was stripped to the waist, and I could see he had something written on him." He paused. "But the cops don't want me gabbing about that."

"It's okay, Mr. James," I said, trying to balance being at once amiable and authoritative. My mind was racing. How do I get him to spill the beans? So, I decided to use one of Judy's tricks: "We already know that AHKA was written on his arm."

"Oh, I'm glad the police are sharing information with you. It seems important."

Confirmation! I gave Judy a thumbs-up. "Thank you so much for your time, Mr. James. Look for the article in the next few weeks."

"Is that all you need?"

"Yes sir, you've been extraordinarily helpful."

"I hope they catch the guy who did it."

I hung up.

So, it *was* true: Jackie and Cleve had the same word written on them. Judy was frustrated by the news, but not daunted. "We need to find out more about the yearbook. Bogdan's boat is moored on the Washington Channel near the Tidal Basin. I overheard B and E talking about it. That's our next step. After school tomorrow, we'll go."

On my way home, the weather began changing again, becoming gray and chilly. The trees' limbs were showing through the leaves like lines of ink on washed silk. The shift in the weather or the swig of gin or the phone call—or all of it—had brought on a spidery headache. Rody's description of Cleve's body lingered, and even now, still won't go away. To be honest, it satisfied a morbid curiosity in me, but I feel ashamed of that urge. Although Cleve was no friend—he'd tried to run us down after all—I didn't want that horror to happen to him. I saw Elaine Closs's unfocused eyes, her uncertain voice, her broken bearing. That was what devastating grief looks like, but I didn't feel it then, and I don't feel it now. When Blake Le Beux committed suicide, I felt nothing, too—or no, that's not true: I was awestruck, like he'd done something fearless and remarkable. Maybe that's how I feel about Cleve's murder: there's daring in it.

JUDY, NOVEMBER 2, 1948

Dewey has it in the bag. Damn. I wish I were old enough to vote. Truman, who's something of a reformed racist, seems to care about civil rights, about Iris's rights and Alice from Crestwood's rights. The buzz is exciting—but damn the polls!

Anyway, after school, Philippa and I waded through the Election Day pandemonium and caught the streetcar on Pennsylvania Avenue and rode it down Independence Avenue to the marina. By the time we arrived, a storm was rolling in. Uneven raindrops splattered the streetcar's windows, and the sky was tarnished blue-black. When we stepped out, I popped open my old umbrella, and we walked down to the maze of boats, most of which were leisure cruisers and motorboats covered with white tarps for the winter. A fishy odor wafted through the air.

We wandered the empty docks, hoping Bogdan's houseboat would show itself. I thought I might remember it from a newspaper photo. We were sure it'd be shabby and not moored with the swankier boats. At the end of a long floating dock, we stopped. Before us was a box on rusty pontoons. Its decaying wood siding was slimy and marred with mold. Its small deck was in disarray: a few overturned chairs, thick rope in a messy knot, a cluster of rusty fishing gaffs, and other trash. Maybe the aftermath of a police search. It had a large sliding door, slightly ajar, and on the starboard side, there were a few fogged-over portholes. A rickety ladder led to the roof, which served as a secondary deck. A single folding chair was still up there, overlooking the river. I took a step forward and noticed a magazine stuck to the damp boards of the lower deck, its few dry pages flapping in the breeze. The photo of a smiling face fluttered by—Shirley Temple.

I called out: "Anybody home?"

No reply.

No one was in sight, so I collapsed my umbrella and hopped on board. The boat shifted with my weight and clanged gently against the pylons. Philippa followed me. The sliding door had been pried open. The odor of stale beer and sour rags hit me as we entered. Yellow light from the dock lamps shined through bent, half-raised venetian blinds on the port side. In the dull glow, the furnishings were shapeless, shadowy creatures lying in wait. My pulse surged, and Philippa grabbed my upper arm and squeezed it. I dug a lighter out of my sweater's pocket and flipped it on with my thumb. The room flared to life.

It was obvious that the police had rummaged through the boat, which I would guess hadn't been particularly tidy to begin with. Candy wrappers and beer bottles and food cartons lay on almost every surface. Dirty plates and glasses had been tossed in the sink of the small galley, and all of its cabinets were unlatched and spilling their contents. I separated myself from Philippa's grip. "I don't know what we're looking for," I said, "but let's nose around."

After a few minutes of searching, I opened the small icebox under the counter and gagged. The stench of spoiled cheese or milk billowed out.

Philippa tucked her nose in the crook of her arm. As I was about to shut the door, she saw writing on the greasy brown parcel paper wrapped around the offending food. I bent down and used my thumb and forefinger to extract it from the shelf. I held up my lighter, and Philippa came closer, her elbow still raised across her face like *The Shadow*. It was difficult to make out, but it had Bogdan's name and address on it, as well as postage and a postmark dated five days ago.

"Who mails cheese?" Philippa said, her voice muffled.

"I don't think that's what was originally in this," I said, "and it has no return address." I shoved it back into the icebox and closed the door.

In the backroom, we discovered a narrow bed, stripped of its sheets, and a small beat-up dresser with its drawers open, revealing a tangle of clothes. Beside it was a guitar with broken strings, propped up on end, and a pile of crinkled sheet music. Behind the headboard, the infamous Shirley Temple collage bloomed like a perverse flower. Bogdan had pieced together faded and stained fan photos, magazine shots, ad campaigns, and movie flyers—*Curly Top, Bright Eyes, Heidi, Dimples*—with thick layers of yellowing tape. Little Shirley was everywhere, beaming out, her face flickering in the flame from the lighter.

"*Dimples*? Really?" I muttered with disgust.

Above his stained pillow, at the origin point of the Shirley explosion, was another photo. It was a blurry picture of a lean teenage boy, perhaps fifteen or sixteen, sitting on a bench in a stone-paved public square of some sort, somewhere foreign, perhaps the Ukraine. He was wearing suspenders and a duckbill cap. His eyes were knowing, but wrong somehow, like they belonged to an older man. Beside him, in the crook of his arm, was a pretty blond girl of six or seven in a sackcloth dress. Both were smiling. "Is that him as a boy?" I said. "And his sister?"

I carefully peeled the photo from the wall to avoid ripping the fragile paper. On the back, it said, "Адриан и Анна, 1918." I took a summer course at Edith's insistence a year ago—"We'll be dealing a lot with the

Soviets soon, so you should be prepared, my dear!"—but I didn't retain much. "Анна" was most likely Anna. Bogdan's first name was Adrian, and the girl in the photo must be the sister who was murdered, Anna, or, in the diminutive, Anka. Philippa, ever prepared, wielded her notepad and pen. She wrote down the inscription, and I fixed the photo back in place.

Standing back from the Shirley Temple collage with all those perky kiss-blowing Shirleys staring at me, I couldn't decide what it meant: Was it a disgusting pervert's fantasy or a grieving brother's tribute to his dead sister? Whatever it was, it was alarming.

Footsteps were approaching. I snapped my lighter closed. We crept to the front room and saw a pair of legs pass by on the pier. I held my breath.

"Let's go," I said, exhaling. "We have one more stop."

Outside, it was dark, and fat raindrops were pelting the Potomac, sending a shimmer across the black water. I shielded us with the umbrella, and we made our way to the dock master's office beside the main gate. A light was on. I tapped on the door.

A voice said, "Yep, come in."

The cramped office was decorated with grimy paintings of ships and seascapes, and stale cigar smoke floated in the air. A man with a wiry yellowed beard and a murky expression regarded us from behind his desk, which was strewn with papers, ledgers, maps, and other nautical bric-a-brac. He was wearing a dirty captain's cap, a placard on his desk said, "Capt. Gabriel Lamb," and behind him, crooked on the wall, hung a pinup calendar. I immediately didn't like him. "Are you the dock master?" I said.

"That's right. Who's asking?"

"Friends of Cleveland Closs," I said.

"That right? I'm sorry about that business." He shook his head. "I kinda liked Bogdan. In a way, he was the dock's mascot. You just never know about people." His expression darkened. "Why are you two down here?"

"Are you the one who found the yearbook?" I asked, not buying Captain Lamb's breeziness.

"How do you know about that?"

"You took it from Mr. Bogdan's trash," I said matter-of-factly.

"Correct."

"Why were you rifling through his garbage?"

Philippa shifted next to me, clutching her elbows. Clearly, my questions were making her nervous, but I couldn't stop. In for a penny!

"Why do you care?" he asked.

"Is that something dock masters usually do? Go through the garbage?"

"Get out of here." He waved us away.

"Were you looking for something?"

He stood. He was tall, at least six-foot-two, and he had a distended gut that strained his soiled shirt and pushed his buttons out, which seemed like they might pop off at any moment. "The damn thing had Adrian's fingerprints all over it."

"You're lying," I said, stepping toward him, emboldened.

"Get out!" he said, throwing daggers with his eyes. "Now!"

I glared back at him and said, "Let's go."

The wind was whipping across the marina, dragging sheets of water with it. I fussed with the umbrella, which kept buckling in the gusts, and Philippa pulled her coat around her. In the slip closest to the office was a motorboat called *The Crawdad Express*.

"What's a crawdad?" Philippa said.

"It's a crayfish."

"A crustacean, right?"

My instinct kicked in: "Didn't Cleve say something to you about a boat?"

"He said he liked going out on the Potomac in the boat," she said.

"A specific boat? Like his family owns a boat?"

"His mother also mentioned it."

I really wanted to go home. I was shivering, and my shoes were soaked through. But this detail nagged me. Down the steps from us, a deckhand was furiously trying to cover a motorboat with a tarp. Most likely, it was his legs we'd seen before. "Wait here," I said.

"Really?" Philippa said, wiping the rain from her cheeks.

Ignoring her, I descended to the dock again, struggling to hold on to the umbrella. The Potomac gurgled and frothed against the pylons.

"Excuse me," I said.

The man looked up. His face was streaked with water, his peacoat was drenched, and his scarf was a soggy snake around his neck. He was only a little older than us, maybe in his early twenties. "This isn't the best time," he said, stating the obvious.

"Could you tell me where the Closses' boat is?"

"Whose?"

"The Closses'."

"It's in slip . . ." He caught himself. "Well, I suppose I shouldn't give that information out. Sorry, I need to cover two more boats before the storm gets worse." He began to turn away.

"Wait."

He gave me a withering look, and I smiled at him sweetly and batted my eyelashes as best I could in the rain. "I was just wondering if you've seen anything unusual going on around here?"

"You mean, besides you asking me questions?" He smirked.

"Forget it," I said, waved my hand, and turned away.

"Okay, okay. I'll tell you if you let me buy you a cup of coffee after my shift."

"Tell me first," I said, rolling my eyes on the inside.

He hesitated, and I looked up at the rain impatiently. "The houseboat over there—" he nodded toward Bogdan's boat—"it's like a revolving door. First the police, then these guys in suits, looking like they just stepped out of a James Cagney movie. Whatever that chump did, lots of folks are interested. That's all I have."

"Thanks," I said, winked at him, and walked away.

"Hey, where should I meet you?" he called after me.

"Have a nice life," I said.

I learned two things: Someone else was interested in Bogdan, and the Closses moored their boat at the same marina. There weren't many marinas in town. I doubted that it was a coincidence. But what did that mean? Did it connect Bogdan to Cleve's death? Then, like that, it clicked. I knew why the yearbook was significant, and it wasn't for the reasons the police thought.

I grabbed Philippa's hand and said, "I'm hungry. Let's drop by the Closses' for milk and cookies."

PHILIPPA, NOVEMBER 2, 1948

The bell made a tinny, distant sound, and anxiety rolled through me. In the streetcar, we'd run through the major questions we wanted to ask. Judy had her proverbial guns out, twirling them, ready to take aim, but I wasn't prepared. I wasn't even sure this was the best approach.

The door squeaked open, and Elaine Closs craned toward us, clutching its edge. Her moist green eyes peered out from her pasty face, blinking and roving over us. Her long eyelashes had trapped crumbs of mascara like a spiderweb does gnats. "Hello," she said, slurring a bit. "And who are you?" A button midway down on her housedress had been neglected, revealing a slice of pale flesh as she leaned toward us. She was clearly doped up.

"We've met before," Judy said. "We're Cleve's friends from school."

"Oh, yes," she said, smiling dreamily at me. "His English classmates." She nodded at Judy. "You— Did the jam come out of your blouse?"

She was confused.

"Moira's goddamn cookies," Elaine said and giggled a little.

"Yes," I said. "It's as good as new. Right, Judy?"

"Well, I'm glad," Elaine said, giving her free hand a little flutter.

A man's voice from behind her called out: "Who's there, Elaine?" His tone was terse and impatient.

"You should go," Elaine said, grabbing the door and beginning to close it. Her eyes shimmered in the light from the entryway sconces. So green, like jadeite stones.

"Who is this?" the man said, emerging out of the shadowy hall. He was tall, broad-shouldered, in his early forties, and handsome, but in a hard, sculpted way. He had dusty blond hair, neatly parted and slicked across his scalp, and a prominent chin like Robert Mitchum's. I recognized him from his photo; he was Cleve's dad, but of course, much older than in the photo.

He took Elaine by the wrist and guided her away from the door, supporting her with his other arm. It was a calculated, expert gesture, as if he were her doctor, and she his patient. When he returned, he said, "What can I do for you?" and smiled, his teeth flashing full and bright.

"We're Philippa and Judy," I said. "Friends of Cleve's."

His tanned face had a polished sheen, which was striking even as it hovered between puzzlement and concern. "Ah, yes, my mother told me about you," he said, straining to be upbeat. His starched collar was unbuttoned, and his necktie, forest green with little red shamrocks, hung loosely around his thick, ropy neck.

"We'd like to talk to you about Cleve, if you don't mind," I said, trying to be careful with my words. We didn't want to rush him with questions, or he'd slam the door in our faces.

His square brow creased. It seemed like he was trying to read us and craft his responses accordingly. It made me uncomfortable. "Come in," he said at last.

I smiled politely, and we entered. The hall was hot and dry. The warm air from the furnace rushed across my ankles. We shrugged off our damp coats, which Cleve's mother, who had wandered close again, took from us and hung on the coat rack beside the door. She drifted back down the passageway, running her hand over the textured wallpaper, tracing its pine-apple design with a roaming finger. I thought of the quotation she'd said to me: "Love is a thing ever filled with anxious fear." Was she describing herself or someone else? I wasn't sure.

Mr. Closs stepped back and gestured for us to go ahead of him. As I passed him, I caught a whiff of his cologne, but it wasn't until I was in the parlor that its distinctive metallic odor registered in my soggy brain: "Oh my God, it's him!" I thought. "The gray ghost! Miss Martins's attacker!" I didn't know what to do: Should I scream? Should I run? Or should I accuse him? Or should I stay calm? My heart was galloping. Thump, thump, thump. Sweat beaded on my forehead and my breath shallowed. But I couldn't fall apart, not now. We still needed the information that we'd come for.

He motioned for us to sit on the sofa, the dreary landscape hanging above us like our own little black cloud. He positioned himself across from us in a wingback chair. Looming nearby, the grandfather clock counted out the weak pulse of the house—or was it my heartbeat? As discreetly as possible, I wiped the sweat from my forehead. The radio babbled in the background, first a commercial jingle and then some jazz standard. Mr. Closs leaned forward with his elbows on his knees, revealing his muscular forearms. He asked us a question, some pleasantry, but I only grasped that he was speaking, not what he said. I was speechless. But Judy answered him. He smiled and said something else.

I scanned his face as if it would reveal some answer for why he'd hurt Miss Martins. Or why he'd chase us across town. Did he want to hurt us? Rape us? Kill us? My curiosity was battling with my fear, but not winning. Crowded with sprays of lilies and clusters of white roses, the parlor was suffocating; the condolence bouquets were cloying, even mocking. This man was dangerous. We were in his parlor because he wanted something from us. He wanted to know if we could identify him, if we knew he was our pursuer or a rapist or even a killer.

"He liked going out on the boat," Judy said. "He told us about all those Sundays on the Potomac and the Anacostia." She was embellishing, using small talk to break down his defenses, but she didn't know who he really was.

He offered us a gleaming smile, but his eyes were too still, too fixed. He was a bad actor. "Look, girls," he said in a crisp tone. "Why are you here? It's not to discuss Cleveland's nautical interests."

I glanced at Judy, who read my distress, her eyes like tiny black mirrors.

"You're right," Judy said in a strange, bright voice. "We wanted to tell you about something we figured out. You see, Adrian Bogdan didn't kill Cleve."

"Don't say?" he asked with amusement.

She regarded him, then spoke slowly: "The yearbook—that damning piece of evidence—is worthless. It's a fraud." His eyes opened wide. So did mine. "Bogdan didn't steal it. It was mailed to him. We have the parcel paper it was wrapped in." A lie. We'd left the smelly paper wrapped around that nasty piece of spoiled cheese. "He received it, opened it, and being the sad and confused man he is, he threw it out, thinking it was a cruel joke or maybe even a threat. Someone instructed and probably paid the dock master to dig through the trash, find it, and turn him in. Like that, you have an incriminating yearbook covered with Bogdan's fingerprints. It's smart because it's simple. Except that Capt. Lamb Chop is a bad liar. I mean, who decides to rummage through garbage on a whim?"

As she launched her theory at him, his face shifted from incredulous to smug to somber. His liquid blue irises seemed to drain out and pool between them. His lips moved like he might confess, like the weight of his misdeeds was just too much, and he needed to get it all off his chest—but instead, he beamed: "Wow!" He slapped his knee. "What a story! Sounds solid. Have you shared it with the police?" He was making fun of us.

"Of course," she said, her confidence unfaltering. "That's where we came from." She was ensuring our safety, and I was thankful.

"Who'd you talk to?"

Judy blinked. "Leo Paulson."

I had no idea who Leo Paulson was, but his name made Mr. Closs flinch.

A contemporary jazz tune with whiny alto sax and plinking piano intruded on their little battle of wills. Elaine, the source of the shift in volume, swayed across the room in a frantic and clumsy dance. In her left hand, she held a small circular needlepoint, stabbed through with a needle. As her arms swung around, a thread trailed behind her like a wisp of cobweb. "Don't you just love it?" she gasped. "The bird is the best. Tweet, tweet." As Elaine flapped her arms doing "the bird"—whatever that was—I caught a glimpse of the needlepoint, but all I saw was a red-orange shape. Was it "the bird"? I couldn't tell, but what was clear was that Elaine was out of it, even more than before. If Mr. Closs had viciously attacked Miss Martins, he may have hurt Elaine, too. Was she drugged to keep her quiet? That would explain her behavior.

He stood, taking Elaine by her arm. "The girls are leaving."

She dropped her needlepoint. "Oh," she mumbled, then with unexpected petulance, "Let me go!" and pulled away from him.

As I rose, I picked up the frame, glancing at the design. It wasn't a type of bird after all—it was some sort of leaping animal, perhaps a tiger or some kind of big cat. I handed it back to Elaine, and the woman's eyes brightened. "Thank you," she said meekly, murmuring as an afterthought, "Tyger Tyger, burning bright . . ." Wasn't that from one of Miss Martins's favorite Blake poems? But the thought vanished when Elaine jolted me back to the overly flowered parlor, commenting, "You're such a nice girl. I'm glad you were Cleve's friend." I ached for her and wanted to say something kind, but nothing came, so I smiled.

"They're leaving." Mr. Closs scowled. "Right now."

She raised her hand to my cheek. "I hope you'll come to the funeral this Saturday," she said. She glanced at Judy but didn't extend the invitation to her.

JUDY, NOVEMBER 2, 1948

As soon as we were in the Closses' parlor, Philippa turned sheet-white, began perspiring, and started giving me big eyes. She'd recognized him. Closs was the man in Miss M's apartment. The gray ghost. Of course he was—and probably worse! And we were getting somewhere until Elaine, high as a kite, cranked up the music and began careening around the room, babbling about a bird or something. Was it for show? A distraction? Then, she invited Philippa to Cleve's funeral, but not me. She made a point of it. What was that about?

Shaking it off, I focused on my next question for Closs: "Did Cleve know something about our teacher, Miss M? Do you have some connection to her? Is that what all this is about?"

Philippa snapped her head around.

Elaine clutched her needlepoint to her chest.

Closs stepped toward me, looming, his prominent eyebrows and Cro-Magnon forehead jutting out. "It's time to go."

"And what about this?" I said sharply, snatching Miss M's art deco moon pin out of my pocket. "We found it in her apartment, smashed. She wore it at school all the time. Was it something you gave her?"

Elaine recoiled, and Closs grabbed me above the elbows, his eyes locked on mine, and jerked me toward him. He was strong, and for the first time, I was scared of him. He stared at me for a beat, eyes trembling, and growled, "Go!"

Elaine croaked, "Howard!"

"I'm not asking again," he shouted, spit flying. His fingers dug into my upper arms, and he began dragging me toward the door. I bared my teeth, flung my arms around like a maniac—maybe crazy is catching—kicked his shins, and tore away. Flushed and panting, we circled each other like wild animals at an impasse. The hyper piano and blazing sax roared along like a stampede about to level us. His features narrowed like he was trying to concentrate, to impress a feeling on me, or send a telepathic message. I tried to read him. Was he angry? Afraid? Desperate? Sad? Whatever it was, it wasn't coming through, and I didn't know what to do, so I just stood there.

Philippa's hand was in mine, gripping me, tugging at me. She was pleading, "Let's go! Let's go!" I didn't move at first. Closs's eyes were glassy, brimming, and a tear streaked down his cheek. A tear! What the hell? Bewildered and light-headed, I gave in and allowed myself to be pulled out of the room. Philippa tore our coats, hats, and scarves off the rack, and we flew out the front door.

PHILIPPA, NOVEMBER 2, 1948

Judy flung open the window and gulped in the icy air, and I flopped in the chair beside her bed. As my mind slowed its spinning, my eyes fell on the miniature sheep, shepherds, and shepherdesses that floated across the room's misty-green wallpaper. Clearly Edith's decorating choice. Above Judy's headboard, a shepherdess with blond curls reclined on a log, dreamily staring out. She was repeated across the walls every four feet or so, but this one was different, which I'm sure is why I noticed her. Judy had filled in her big blue eyes with black pen, transforming them into gaping holes. Commentary, I'm sure. On her dresser, continuing the pastoral theme, a ceramic shepherd and shepherdess surveyed the green carpet. As I studied them, I noticed they'd been broken in several places; the shepherdess's arm extended out at an odd angle grasping a missing crook, and a fissure along the neck of the shepherd gave away his past trauma. I imagined Judy smashing them, and Edith dutifully, even desperately, sticking them back together. If you removed Rosie's dingy dog bed, the line of postcards and knickknacks on the fireplace mantle, the record collection and player, and the stack of novels at her bed side, the room revealed its original purpose: a nursery. And its intended occupant, Jackie. Despite all her fury, it seemed like Judy had only put a slight dent in Edith's delusion.

Judy shut the window, stretched out on the window seat, and said, "So, Closs is the gray ghost."

"That cologne! He must bathe in the stuff."

"You should've seen the look on your face." She dropped her mouth open, doing an exaggerated version of me, and smirked. "You looked like you had seen a real ghost."

I still felt wobbly from the ordeal. "I didn't know what to do. Fight or flight?"

"What about Elaine Closs? Is she a dope fiend or what?"

"If you were married to that—to *him*—you'd take anything you could get your hands on."

She sighed. "I'd just shove him in front of a streetcar."

I didn't doubt she'd try.

Judy studied her feet, which she'd propped up on the window's molding. "I get why he might force himself on Miss M. He's just a jilted lover or a crazed sex addict or something conspicuous like that. But I don't get why he'd kill his own son. What's the motive?"

While Judy pondered the question, picking at a loose thread on her sweater, I thought about Miss Martins before her ordeal, about our conversations, about what college I might go to, about literary last names, and even sordid boons. I remembered the dreamy lilt of her voice, her graceful gestures, her beauty, particularly when she was still reading or grading at her desk, the light pouring in from the tall classroom windows. She could've been a mentor to me, someone like my mother, someone who understood me. We have to find her.

"Everything keeps taking us back to Miss Martins and her spat with Cleve," I said, ending the lull. "She knows something."

Judy twisted toward me, a wedge of straight black hair falling across her dark cheek. "If she does, she's in danger. Now that Closs knows that we know he's connected to her he'll go after her. I shouldn't have shown him the pin. That was damn stupid. Once he discovers that I didn't tell my theory about Bogdan to Paulson, he'll . . . stalk . . . us again."

"Who is Paulson?" I asked.

"The lead detective on Jackie's case. He's also been consulted on Cleve's case. I overheard Bart and Edith talking about him."

"Mentioning him was quick thinking."

Looking up through her bangs, she smiled. "Howard—no, How*weirdo* Closs never looked guiltier."

My stomach growled. "It's dinnertime," I said, standing up. "I should go."

"B and E are in the kitchen, so just slip out the front," Judy said, getting to her feet. "Tomorrow, we find Miss M."

I let myself out of the room, but stopped at the top of the staircase. Edith was in the hall below, wrapped in a dark shawl, standing in front of Jackie's portrait and a fresh spray of lilies. She hadn't seen me approach, so she remained motionless, staring at the display. She must've just arranged the flowers. My first impulse was to dash back to the room, but something about catching her in a private moment, the strange doubleness of staring at someone staring at something else, made me linger. She lifted her hand to her mouth and held it there. As if participating in a psychic relay, I felt a rush of sadness, too. It was a horrific thing that had happened to Jackie and to her.

I was aware of Judy beside me.

As if she had a sixth sense, Edith looked up and frowned. "Girls, come here at once."

Judy groaned, and we went downstairs.

The well-oiled antiques that had been shoved to the edges of the parlor for the party had been returned to their original positions as if a fussy poltergeist had tidied up. Flames flickered in the fireplace, throwing faint shadows across the walls. Bart was slumped in his chair, a tumbler of whiskey dangling between thumb and forefinger. He was a weary prize-fighter against the ropes, struggling to stay vertical.

"Sit," Edith said, pointing at a dainty settee. "We need to chat." She walked behind Bart, gripping the back of his chair. Against her high cheekbones and up-tilted chin, the shifting light from the fireplace gave her a diabolical cast. Gone was the heartbroken mother. In her place, another woman, intense, shield out and sword drawn.

Judy refused to move. I didn't know whether to sit or stand, so in solidarity, I remained standing.

Bart sipped his whiskey. "You shouldn't have done that, either of you," he said gloomily. "You've upset a lot of people."

"What'd we do?" Judy said, puffing out a bit.

"You harassed the Closses," Edith said, placing her hand below her onyx choker. "You spewed absurd accusations at them. Jesus, how could you be so insensitive?"

Bart raised his eyebrows as if to echo the question.

"How did you find out?" Judy said, keeping her voice even.

"They rang just a few minutes ago," Bart said. "They know who you are, of course. They know about Jackie's case." The ice cube in his glass clinked.

"Mr. Closs is a bad man!" I blurted, immediately embarrassed. "It's obvious."

"Don't waste your breath," Judy said. "They won't listen. They've decided Bogdan is their man. That's the story that works for them, so they'll stick to it."

"Tell me," Edith challenged, holding her chin up, "Why are you so sure he's innocent? What's your proof?"

"He was framed for Cleve's murder," Judy said with the slightest tremor. "I can't prove it, but I know it. Closs sent him that yearbook and paid the dock master to 'discover' it."

"Let me get this right," Bart said, his small eyes becoming incredulous slits. "You're suggesting that he killed his own son and framed Bogdan for it?"

Judy didn't move.

"Ha!" Edith scoffed, waving her hand at us. "So, you expect us to believe that . . . what? He used Jackie's case to cover up his son's murder? That's absurd. So much time has passed. And how would he have known about the undisclosed evidence? Explain that to me. Hmm?"

It's a good point. I'll give her that. Linking Cleve's murder to Jackie's is an effective way to shift the police's focus away from him, but of all the possible crimes, why choose *hers*? And how did he know what was written on her body? It's a stretch. It makes more sense that Bogdan did both. After all, he's the one with the nutty tribute to Shirley Temple. But what about Mr. Closs's reaction to us; he seemed so unnerved, so guilty. And we know he attacked Miss Martins.

Moving out from behind Bart's chair, Edith continued: "Bogdan has been *officially* charged. We'll be attending his arraignment tomorrow."

Judy locked eyes on her, the muscles in her jaw rippling. She was furious, but also frightened. I thought about Edith's repairing of the smashed shepherd and shepherdess and, I imagine, insisting that they remain in Judy's room. There they stood, guardians at the shrine to Jackie. Judy hadn't won that battle, had she?

"Cleveland's funeral is on Saturday, and Bart and I will be going to pay our respects. Judy, we want you to go and apologize to the Closses. Philippa, we'd like you to do the same. We haven't contacted your father and stepmother, but if you refuse, we'll be forced to. It's the right thing to do. We believe you are big enough to admit when you're wrong. Isn't that right, husband?"

"Yes," he said, stymieing a yawn.

"Fuck you," Judy growled. "Fuck both of you."

Bart snapped to and rose from his chair.

Judy's dark eyes blazed. "I refuse to apologize to that evil goon—"

Edith stepped forward, and in a single fluid movement, as if practiced many times like a tennis swing, slapped Judy. "What were we thinking?" she snarled, her complexion bright and indignant, and her lips trembling. "Why did we bring this . . . this castaway into our lives? We gave her the best of homes, all the privileges of our social station, access to a world she never would've had otherwise, but she's thankless. She hasn't healed us, Bart! She's worse than no daughter at all!"

"Listen, Edie," Bart said, his jowly face drooping. "You don't mean that." He reached out to touch her, and she swatted his hand away.

"I do," she said coldly. The quiet mournfulness that I observed from the top of the stairs had melted into cruelty.

Judy stared at the floor, the vehemence knocked out of her. I wanted to rush her out of the room, to console her, to hold her, but she'd surrounded herself with what felt like an impenetrable bubble. All of her railing against B and E, and her declarations of a post–eighteenth birthday transformation and name change seemed in peril. The Peabodys had real power over her. She needed them, their wealth.

She looked up and, in a low simmer, said, "Maybe Jackie deserved to die." Her voice cracked, as if as she said it, she knew it was a mistake. "Maybe *you* deserved me." Her desire to inflict pain had overridden her need for self-preservation. I imagined her flinging the shepherd lamp across her room or scratching out the shepherdess's eyeballs, converting her into a symbolic witness: "Look at the horrors I have to put up with. Look at what I have to do to survive." Now, I'm that witness.

Edith was speechless, and Bart bowed his head. The parlor's floor seemed to be shattering like ice, about to plunge us all into a frigid river. Dazed, I searched for something to say, some salve for her wounds, but nothing came. Judy walked away, and after looking at the Peabodys accusatorially, I followed her upstairs to her room.

JUDY, NOVEMBER 2, 1948

When Philippa knocked on my door, I didn't respond. I couldn't face her. I collapsed on my bed and curled into a tight ball. "What happened to the Peabody girl?" they'd ask. "She imploded, and a black hole opened in her bedroom. Tragic, really."

I was a goddamn mess. My cheek stung, sure, but it was that whole bit about "the privileges" of her "social station" that sliced through my gut. She'd said things like that to me before—and there's truth to it, I know—but saying it in front of Philippa, that was cruel. Any modicum of sympathy that I had dredged up for the woman now seems perverse.

Money or no, when I turn eighteen, I'm leaving this house and changing my name. Miss M was right: "Nightingale" has a nice ring. "Introducing Miss Judith Nightingale. Judy to her friends. J. Nightingale to you." J. Nightingale is a professional woman's name, a real go-getter. She's the sort that might work in publishing in New York, or open a rare books store in Chicago, or deal in art in Mexico City. She'll wear smart outfits, black tams, sunglasses, and gloves up to her elbows. Or perhaps she'll live differently, more hand-to-mouth, but with a zest for exotic experiences. She'll book passage on an ocean liner and loaf on the Continent, picking up odd jobs, but enmeshing herself in the art scene, edging her way into café society, whatever that looks like these days. She won't depend on anyone. She'll just tap her cigarette, sip her gin, and appraise the world as it drifts by.

PHILIPPA, NOVEMBER 2, 1948

Since Judy didn't respond to my knocking, I slowly opened her door. She was lying with her back to me, twisted into herself. I moved around the bed. Her head was resting on her arm. Her eyes—those shiny pinpoints—were now soft and bleary. She refused to acknowledge me. Her protective bubble was sealed tight around her. I felt terrible for her, but I feared that if I said the wrong thing, I might make it worse. I didn't want to cause her more pain. As I started to pivot away, she shifted, uncurled her body, and said, "Don't go."

I breathed out and sat on the edge of the bed. The bubble had lifted, but I didn't want to trigger it again. For a moment, we listened to the soft creaks in the room and the sound of traffic, then she slid her fingers over to me and scooped up my hand. She turned it over and studied the contours of my palm. "You're going to have a long life," she said, more to herself. "Two husbands, five kids, ten dogs, a house in Chevy Chase. *Boring.*"

"You read lifelines, do you?" I said.

"Not a bit," she said and released my hand. Her eyes glazed over.

"What Edith did, it was vicious," I said, stumbling, trying to wedge a metaphorical foot in her descending protective shell. Suddenly, she looked at me, full-on, her eyes alert. She bent toward me, her face inches from mine, her breath on my skin. Everything in me was prickling and alive, like a moth scratching out of its cocoon. I wanted her to kiss me, but her eyes flicked away.

JUDY, NOVEMBER 2, 1948

When she said that—"What Edith did, it was vicious"—she bent toward me, resting her hand on my upper arm, leaning in. She didn't pity me. She admired me, and through that admiration, like an open window, I saw who she was. Her flipped strawberry curls, her creamy freckled skin, her naturally pink lips, and those slate-gray eyes—all those girlish qualities that annoyed me—were radiant, transformed. They glowed, not in and of themselves, but because underneath them was something hard and bright and true: her belief in me. I leaned into her, our faces inches away, but before I could kiss her, my body tensed. I didn't know what to do. I looked away, then I gazed right at her, and whispered, "I hate Jackie. I fucking hate her."

PHILIPPA, NOVEMBER 2, 1948

As she said it, my mouth collapsed into hers, our noses bumping. At first, nothing happened. Was it a chaste touching of lips? Then something in us dissolved, and we sank into a deep kiss. That horrible feverishness I'd felt for Thea Ray summers ago rushed in and, with it, the smut from Somerset's. I imagined pushing back Judy's collar and tracing her pale clavicle with my fingers. I wanted to reach under her blouse and cup her breasts, feeling her nipples graze my palms. I wanted to run my hand over her shoulders and down her arms, registering every scar, connecting them like I was plotting constellations. As I pressed close to her, the fantasy clawed its way out, wanting to be real.

JUDY, NOVEMBER 2, 1948

As Philippa pushed deeper into me, I returned the kiss, drunk, elated—but then my mind snagged me and began reeling me back. Where was this going? What's next? Tugging at each other's waistbands and necklines? Unbuttoning our blouses and unhooking our bras? Flattening flesh against flesh? Feeling each other up? Breaking the tension? No, it was too much. It was too fast, too new. I needed her to believe in me as I am: Judy Peabody becoming Judy Nightingale. If we continued, the alchemy of our relationship would change. We'd become something different to one another—or even something impossible: Two girls in love with one another. How would that work? So, I sank away from her as gently as I could, wrapping my sweater across my body and shifting back into the mound of pillows.

She was deflated, but not destroyed.

"You must be—" she said. "I can go."

I nodded, and she touched her lips absentmindedly.

Before she opened the door to leave, she turned and, with absolute conviction, said, "I hate Jackie, too. For you."

PHILIPPA, NOVEMBER 2, 1948

I don't know what happens next. I'm not sure if that's a good thing or a horrible thing. Does Judy hate me? Or love me? Is she frightened? Or inspired? What is she thinking now? Writing this feels dangerous and thrilling, like transcribing black magic, something I could be burned at the stake for. Imagine if Dad or Bonnie read this! But I need to record it, to know that it happened, even if seconds later, I might tear it up and light it on fire.

JUDY, NOVEMBER 3, 1948

The entire city was buzzing today. The election results came in, and it had a perfect twist ending. Truman defeated Dewey, even though the *Chicago Daily Tribune* blasted out a humiliating headline claiming the opposite. On our drive to the arraignment, a group of revelers haloed in a mist of booze, spilled in front of the cab waving Truman campaign posters. Edith tutted with dismay, which is pretty rich considering Bart's love affair with gin. Or maybe she was just peeved because her candidate didn't win.

Journalists swarmed us as we stepped out, so I was relieved when we made it to the courtroom, which was calmer, just the murmur of people finding their seats. B and E were dressed to the nines: Bart in his best tweed suit, with a black and chartreuse diamond-patterned tie, and Edith with a fox-collared hunting jacket and felt hat reminiscent of a tricorn, sending a message to the accused: "You've put up quite a chase, but now you're caught!" I wore a simple black sweater and skirt and pinned my bangs to the side. Edith and I still hadn't spoken, deciding that weaponized silence was a more effective way of waging war. Bart stayed out of it; he was too focused on drying out and putting on his best face in the midst of this public ordeal.

Down the aisle, Howard Closs and his mother Moira sat side by side. Elaine was absent, perhaps too hysterical—or drugged—to attend. Both wearing black, they also were dressed to make a statement. A long black feather swayed and bobbed above Moira's toque. Closs's broad shoulders formed a dark square in an otherwise bright room. I still couldn't shake the look he'd given me, especially the tear. He's guilty. I know it, but I don't know how—or why.

A door opened. Adrian Bogdan, flanked by uniformed guards, was escorted in. Heads spun around, and the room murmured with excitement. In the back row, however, two men in dark suits—one gaunt, the other thick-necked—remained unmoved, silent. Who were they? My attention then flitted to Bogdan's lawyer, who stood to greet his client. He was a slight, cocky middle-aged man with a scrap of golden-brown hair and a very expensive suit. Bogdan can't even afford a proper house. How can he shell out for this guy? The man of the hour was surprisingly handsome—a narrow, clean-shaven face; well-oiled dark hair; full lips; and jewel-like blue eyes—not the scruffy, bearded tramp I'd seen in photos. He wore a crisp, sapphire blue suit, which was so blue it was like he wanted it to scream, "I'm innocent! Really, I am!" None of this fit in with his squalid houseboat.

The judge entered, and everyone rose. The upsweep of all the bodies thrilled me. The Honorable Warford J. Humblehold, a name ripped from the pages of Dickens, was presiding, and he looked the part: exaggerated waistline, bald head, bushy mustache, and sharp little eyes. All he needed was a pipe.

The room simmered with anticipation. Everyone wanted to know how Bogdan would plead. Of course, B and E wanted a guilty plea. It would mean the beginning of the end of their nightmare. I wanted it over, too. Jackie is haunting all of us, her little lily-white hands around our throats, squeezing with all her might. Although they'd never say so, B and E want her gone as well. I recalled Philippa's parting remark to me, "I hate Jackie, too. For you." There it was, that gorgeous loyalty. Despite my doubts, I would've kissed her again just for that. I wished she could've come with me; we could've compared notes.

Bogdan didn't plead guilty. Of course. For one, he isn't guilty, and for another, the yearbook is weak evidence. B and E are fooling themselves. What I wasn't prepared for, though, was the sound of his voice—a smug, soulless purr. As he was escorted from the courtroom, he smiled, exposing his stained and ravaged teeth, shattering his looks.

CHAPTER SIX

To prepare for what comes next, for where all this is headed, we need to review some not-so-distant history, so bear with me, dear reader. If you recall, in April 1948, Truman signs the Marshall Plan providing economic assistance to Western Europe to slow the spread of Communism. We extend a hand to the Soviet Union, but they slap it away, fearing our meddling could cost them the Eastern Bloc. In June, the Soviet Union obstructs access to sections of Western-occupied Berlin. The Berlin Blockade is one of the first major events of the Cold War.

Well before Berlin, the FBI had been boosting its counterintelligence, anticipating Soviet probes into government agencies and, in particular, the Manhattan Project. In August, Whittaker Chambers, an editor at Time *magazine and ex-Communist, points his big Red finger at Alger Hiss, a former State Department administrator, during testimony before the House Committee on Un-American*

Activities, or HUAC. J. Edgar Hoover, director of the FBI and an anti-Communist zealot, plays puppeteer from backstage. Hiss refutes Whittaker's allegations, but he's labeled a Commie traitor all the same. The Red Scare of the 1950s has begun. Fun times.

What the hell does this have to do with two high school girls?

Fear was in the air. Truman's desegregation of the armed forces had churned up reactionary sentiments. Black men were being beaten with greater frequency. Black women were being belittled, threatened. Paul Robeson created the American Crusade Against Lynching and was investigated by the FBI for ties to Communism. J. Edgar was more interested in using counterintelligence to expose Communists, some dangerous, most benign, than neutralizing very real homegrown violent racists. Iris told us stories of sit-ins turning violent, about heightened intolerance, a palpable hostility present in daily exchanges. It was necessary for progress, she said, but the anxiety was there, on both sides. Likewise, Communism had been branded a creeping evil, a phantom infestation, or so some politicians wanted the public to believe. Unfortunately, there was just enough truth to it to fuel the fear—and several political careers.

It swirled around us, this fear, and whether you knew it or not, it seeped into your pores. Of course, it wasn't just the zeitgeist. It was closer to us than we could've known.

PHILIPPA, NOVEMBER 6, 1948

I wanted to scream. My blue wool dress was itching me, my stockings were slouching, and my size-too-small pumps on loan from Judy were crushing my feet. I clenched my teeth, doing my best to hide my agony. As a distraction, I studied the small group gathering around the excavated plot. Many of the mourners who had attended the funeral service, including a cluster of police, Principal Green, and other teachers from Eastern High, weren't there. Bundled in coats and hats against the nippy weather, it was just the essential players, except Miss Martins, who hadn't appeared yet. Judy was sure she would. Her sense of decorum was too strong.

Led by Mr. Closs, the pallbearers transported the polished cherry coffin from the hearse up the slope of Prospect Hill Cemetery. Cleve's father remained stone-faced, staring at nothing, his lips clamped shut. Elaine and the older Mrs. Closs looked on, gripping each other's hands but standing at a distance from one another, forming a V with their arms. Elaine sniffled and swayed, seeming on the verge of collapse, but never quite caving in. Moira, in contrast, held herself still and erect, resplendent in her shimmering mink and sculpted felt hat swathed with black lace. She knew how to dress for a funeral.

Once the graveside service had commenced, my shoes shrank a size—or at least that's how it felt—and my heels began sinking in the damp sod. The pain in my calves crept into my thighs. As we droned through another hymn, I prayed to God for it to be over.

Judy elbowed me, but I didn't look at her. She hadn't mentioned our kiss. It was like it had never happened. I wasn't sure what to think. Perhaps she didn't know what to say, or maybe she didn't want to say anything, or perhaps she thought nothing needed to be said. I wanted to talk about it, place it in some context, assign it meaning. Was it a brief diversion or a major turning point? I wanted it either packed away or thoroughly analyzed. Judy wasn't having either. She nudged me again, and I glanced at her. She gestured with her chin toward a figure lurking behind a tree down the hill from us. I squinted. It was Miss Martins.

"Come on, it's our chance," she whispered to me and began backing away. Only a few feet from us, Edith glared, her upper lip flat against her teeth, resisting her urge to snap. Aware of Judy's movement, Bart shifted toward us but stopped. Like Edith, he seemed wary of causing a scene. I froze. If I went with Judy, Edith would tell Dad and get me in serious trouble, but I desperately wanted to talk to Miss Martins. I glanced at the Peabodys again, giving them my best "I'm sorry" eyes and a bit of a shrug, then I stepped back. As Judy would say, "Damn the consequences."

We hurried, dodging the tombstones and grave markers, squishing on the damp grass and stirring up little clods of dark soil with our heels. Once we reached the gravel road, we followed it down the hill. A long scraggly boxwood hedge concealed us, allowing us to sneak up on her. We were twenty feet from her when she spotted us. She jumped with surprise and began vigorously waving us away. Even in her exasperation, she was still beautiful; wisps of blond hair had escaped her hat and were shimmering in the light. As we closed in, her slim pink lips narrowed, and in a shrill whisper, she said, "Leave me alone!" but we ignored her. I didn't understand her intense reaction; we weren't contagious. We needed to speak to her, so we weren't going to be put off. She was the only person who could answer our questions. She shook her head and started to flee down the hill. Judy kicked off her shoes, so I did too, relieved to be free from those miserable husks.

We followed her down the narrow lane, out of the stone-pillared cemetery gate, and to her silver Plymouth, sparkling in the bright sun on North Capitol Street. Traffic whooshed by, a contrast to the muffled peace of Prospect Hill. She snatched her keys out of her purse and fumbled them. They fell under the Plymouth's bumper. She cursed. I'd never heard her do that. She had to talk to us now. She lowered her shoulders and said, "Why are you doing this?"

"We know what happened," Judy said, her chest heaving, "to you."

"I saw what he did to you," I said, not thinking it through. "And, and . . ."

Miss Martins was trembling out of exasperation or fear. I wasn't sure which. "You don't know what you saw, Philippa," she said, the sides of her mouth creasing with worry and the muscles in her jaw twitching subtly. "Leave the Closses alone—and me, too."

Finding her breath, Judy asked, "What were you and Cleve arguing about the other night in your classroom? Why was he so angry?"

Miss Martins regarded her for a moment, her irritation mellowing, becoming something else. Resolve? Clarity? Despite the dash down the hill, she still looked smart in her tight black suit. The golden silk scarf that bubbled up like honey from her neckline cast a faint glow across her cheeks and into her eyes. "None of it matters," she said, looking at Judy, then me, and then again at Judy, her eyes softening. "What's important is that you, *both* of you, promise me you'll stay away from the Closses."

"No," Judy said, crossing her arms, refusing to be swayed by Miss Martins's charm. "Not unless you tell us about Cleve and his father—and what they have to do with you."

An enigmatic smile crept into Miss Martins's lips: At first, it was guarded, even sad, but it melted into something like amusement or even appreciation. "You are excellent students," she said, her tone buttery and light, her poetry recitation voice. "Both of you. I hope you continue to read and write with gusto."

"Tell us what happened!" Judy said, prickling with desperation.

She tenderly placed her hands on the sides of Judy's arms and leaned toward her, the wind toying with a strand of her hair. "You, my dear, are brilliant, but you mustn't be ruled by your anger. The most horrific stories in Greek mythology end with the transformation of a character into a tree or bird or even a constellation. Whatever makes you miserable, transform it, and let it go."

"What does that mean?" Judy said, pulling away. "That's not advice."

"The wisest advice often feels like it's spoken in code. Don't be impatient. Sit with it. Life, like great art, is always asking a question: 'Was it a vision, or a waking dream? Fled is that music: Do I wake or sleep?'"

The Keats line was like a feather being drawn across the back of my neck. She often conjured a similar magic in English class, but this time chills ran through me. Maybe my kiss with Judy or even my memories of Thea made me more susceptible, but I was absolutely mesmerized by her beauty, her manner. It was an elusive attraction, not physical—ethereal, like staring at a gorgeous sunset or a work of art and wondering, "How could this be? How was this made?" I wanted to penetrate the mystery. I wanted to understand how she worked, so I could be her. As I write this, I still do.

Unfazed, Judy remained motionless.

Miss Martins noticed me shiver. Did she know I was smitten? "I'm going to be like the nightingale," she said, winking at me, "and say 'Adieu! adieu!' to you. You must do the same to me. Okay?"

Judy scowled, still unmoved by her aura.

"Philippa," Miss Martins said, her eyes on me, "watch out for Judy. Treat her like a good sister would. Be there for her, protect her."

I nodded.

Judy came to life and snarled, "You haven't answered our questions."

"You don't need answers. You need each other," she said, unwavering. They regarded each other for a tense moment. "Enough!" she said, throwing her hand up. "I need to go before the service ends." She reached down beside the car's front tire and plucked the keys off of the pavement. As if waiting for this opportunity, Judy grabbed the damaged moon pin from her pocket and, as Miss Martins rose, dangled it in front of her.

She blanched. "That's not . . . Where did you get it?"

"Your apartment," Judy said.

Her mouth fell open. "How did you—?"

"We broke in, looking for you. We wanted to know what happened to you."

"You shouldn't have done that." She took the pin and examined it as if it were a delicate pressed flower and said, "This meant something once." She turned it over, the damaged waning moon flashing. Somehow it shaded her entire mood. A deep sadness seemed to well up in her, a muted echo of the fear and confusion Cleve's threats had caused. "Throw it away," she said, foisting it back into Judy's hand as if she feared its lethal spell. "Destroy it." She unlocked the car and swung the heavy door wide. "Judy," she said, her silken timbre stripped away, "The Closses, me—none of us will do you any good. Believe me." She sighed. "It's dangerous for you." She studied each of us. "For both of you." She slid in and closed the door.

JUDY, NOVEMBER 6, 1948

We drove up a steep drive through a screen of turning leaves. At the top, Moira Closs's triple-gabled manor house monstrosity, a spoil of the Capitol City Hardware franchise, revealed itself. It reminded me why I hate Chevy Chase. The neighborhood's display of wealth isn't even glitzy or glamorous; it's tailored, zipped up, and hedged in—the old-line veneer of power, or at least, of those who seek it.

We parked and followed clusters of mourners into the house through a large wooden door stamped with an oversized iron knocker. We funneled into an Elizabethan-themed main hall lined with dark mahogany paneling, a coffered ceiling, a massive brass chandelier, and a reproduction of an oil painting of Queen Elizabeth I set catty-corner from a gilded portrait of Andrew Jackson and various American Indian artifacts in shadow boxes. All of it was designed to send a message: The Closses are patrons of art, preservers of history, and proprietors of status. American nobility. Whatever.

Philippa whispered, "It's like we're entering a horrible fairy tale."

"So, where's the evil queen?" I replied.

We moved through the house and into a cavernous solarium, humming with chatter and stuffy with body heat. Snippets of conversation floated around us—criticisms of the *Chicago Tribune*'s botched election headline, disappointment over Truman's win, murmurs about Bogdan's arraignment, admiration of the Closses' stiff upper lips, and praise for

Moira's "brave choice" of white calla lilies over chrysanthemums at the funeral. How courageous.

In the corner, a tall man with thinning hair and caterpillar eyebrows was holding court—or perhaps preaching to the choir. "We're already under attack from the inside," he said in a vibrant and patronizing voice. "It will get worse before it gets better. HUAC is doing good work." His audience leaned in, rapt. "We must look for weak places in our government agencies. Persons of feeble moral constitution who can be easily manipulated. Take, for instance, the homosexuals . . . "

Hearing enough, we moved on.

Multiple platters of canapés and other hors d'oeuvres radiated out from a polished silver punch bowl on a table in the center of the room. I was starving and needed a jolt of energy before approaching the Closses and miming an apology. Philippa and I made up plates, ladled out frothy orange punch, and hid behind a gigantic potted fern to wolf down the food.

As we ate, I spotted a man sitting in a wingback chair in the living room, which opened onto the solarium through wide French doors. He reminded me of a pug or even Rosie—nose crushed, eyes darting, ears bat-like. I felt a sudden stab of déjà vu. Recalling the conversation about HUAC I'd overheard, the party must've been lousy with politicians and Washingtonian elites, so I wondered if that's why he struck a chord. And like that—bingo!—I knew who he was: the Director of the FBI. J. Edgar Hoover. Seriously. He was much smaller and slighter than he appeared in the newsreels. I nudged Philippa and nodded in his direction. She just shrugged.

After making the rounds to say hello to common acquaintances of the Closses, B and E hunted us down. "It's time," Edith said. "You need to get in line and tell Howard and Elaine how very sorry you are, and it better sound sincere."

The receiving line began at the far end of the room. Shaded by a massive White Bird of Paradise, Howard and Elaine seemed guarded by the plant's paddle-like leaves, as if it were ready to animate and gobble up anyone who might offend them.

"Judy, you must do this," Edith said, screeching with desperation. In silhouette against the solarium's condensation-coated walls, the Closses' heads were bobbing like pigeons, their shoulders tightening and loosening with each handshake. Oddly, Moira Closs wasn't there. "Philippa, you too," Edith added. "If you don't, I'll tell your father about your little adventure at the graveside service. Both of you have pushed us to the limit."

I glared at Edith and bit into my last salmon and cream cheese canapé.

"Do it!" she snapped.

A bevy of guests glanced in our direction.

From behind us, mink and hat removed, Moira materialized, as if out of a cloud of L'Air du Temps. Her makeup was fresh, expertly applied: arching eyebrows, lined red lips, a velvety sheen of powder, which smoothed her wrinkles into gentle character lines. Her deep blue eyes were uncanny, as if she'd harvested them from a younger woman.

"There you are!" she purred. "Judith and Philippa, I'm so glad you've come. My son and daughter-in-law will be touched."

"I'm so sorry for you and your family," Bart said.

She nodded. "We've both lost that which is most precious to us." Her eyes gleamed with wetness. "Both you and Edith are such an inspiration, a model for how to see through this fog and understand . . . well, whatever we're supposed to understand from this, if there's any meaning at all," she said, bringing her hand to her throat. Her pear-cut diamond ring winked at us.

Moved, Edith touched the woman on the elbow.

Moira flinched, then smiled apologetically.

So much of what Moira presented was polished artifice, but there was something in her expression: a trace of conflicting emotions? Sorrow? Horror? Rage? It was hard to say how she truly felt about her grandson's death. Was Cleve the apple of her eye, or merely a fact, the heir apparent, a necessary vehicle for advancing the Closs name?

"Girls," she said, "could you help me with something?" She looked at B and E. "Do you mind if I steal them for a minute?"

"Of course not," Edith said.

I glanced at Philippa, who seemed curious and willing, so we followed her. The three of us passed through a large kitchen and into an oak-paneled study lined with books and more exotic collectibles. The air was thick with the odor of musty leather. Moira gestured to a low-slung leather couch. A portrait of a grim man in thick-framed eyeglasses and symmetrically parted hair peered down from above the flickering fireplace. Mr. Closs Sr., Moira's late husband? We sat, and she stood in front of us, her black crepe de chine dress swaying against her legs. For a long moment, she studied us. I didn't know what the hell was going on.

"So," she said, in a businesslike manner, "look at you, a couple of Nancy Drews. You need more finesse, dears. My son is a sensitive man. Barging in and questioning Halo and Elaine like they were responsible for my grandson's death was crude and rather cruel, don't you think?"

"Halo?" I said.

"As a boy, he had mounds of fleecy golden hair, so I said he looked like he was wearing a halo. The nickname stuck."

I laughed. The irony was too rich.

And like that, Moira popped like a balloon. She dropped her gracious hostess facade, descended on me, and took me by the chin, squeezing it firmly. "You!" she snarled, baring her tobacco-stained teeth. "Don't be so superior, you little bitch. You don't understand a damn thing about him or me or any of us. You have no idea what we're going through. What we've been through!" I froze, blindsided. Moira's protuberant eyes seemed huge and hungry, but they also exposed her. Had we frightened her? Were we closer to the truth than we thought? Although I was shaken, a part of me swelled with pride. I tried to pull away from her grip, but she pinched tighter, the purple veins on her hand bulging. "I know all about you," she snarled, stepping close to the border of unhinged. "I know more about you than your parents do. I know more about you than you know about yourself."

She released me, stepping back, her eyes cooling like blue flames running out of gas. I had no idea what she meant, but I was convinced it was true. "I know more about you than you know about yourself," crashed through my skull. What did she know? Why tell me now? This way? "Whether you understand it or not, I'm dangerous to you. If I'm dangerous to you, I'm certainly dangerous to your friend here." She shook her finger at Philippa, who was horrified by her outburst and shrank back, nearly in tears. My swirling brain snapped into focus. Fuck her for threatening Philippa. I wanted to scream or attack her with a fireplace poker, or even grab Philippa and dash. But instead, I just sat there, my rage and my astonishment at odds. As I write this, they still burn.

"This is what will happen," Moira said, throwing her shoulders back. "We're going to go out there. You're going to tell your parents you apologized to me, and I promised to relate your heartfelt apology to my son and daughter-in-law. Then you're going to go home and not bother us, any of us, again."

Emboldened, Philippa shot up from the couch: "How do you expect us to ignore what your son did to Miss Martins?"

I liked her this way: strawberry curls bouncing, cheeks flushed, gray eyes bright like flash bulbs. There it was: the barb under all her girly trappings, that steely core of hers.

Moira didn't flinch. She studied her, shifting her weight from leg to leg under her rippling dress. "What your Miss Martins has done to our family far outweighs what my son has done to her," she said, tilting her chin up. "You have no idea."

"I witnessed it," Philippa spat. "I saw what he did to her."

Tension rippled through Moira's powdered jaw. She looked as if she were preparing to roar, but instead, she cocked her head and, like that, was back in supreme hostess mode. "Okay, dears, off you go."

PHILIPPA, NOVEMBER 7, 1948

I spotted Judy sitting on the edge of Hill Estates, her legs dangling, staring at the narrow alley four stories below, zapped of her usual confidence. She'd already laid out the plank for me. But instead of crossing, I plopped down with the ten-foot gap between us, hung my legs over the edge, and faced her, a warm current of garbage-scented air flowing up between us.

For a time, we didn't speak, then Judy raised her head. Her bangs were flat and low over her eyes. Her face was still and dark. I expected her to begin with our little tête-à-tête with Moira. She had to have her theories. Instead, she said, "You know those little scars all over my arms?"

"What?" I thought. "Wait. Where's this going?"

She paused, her attention seeming to stray. "I think I know what made them."

"Okay?" I said, keeping my voice level.

"Last night, a dream looped through my head like I had a fever." She took a deep breath. "In it, I'm in this dark, musty place. There's light, but it's only faint. It's coming from those horizontal slotted windows like the ones in bunkers. I can't see the shadowy corners of the room. Then I hear this horrible noise. It's that howl feral cats make, but it's louder like there's a lot of them. It's relentless. Deafening. I try to run away from it, from them, but each time that I try, the sound gets louder and closer. I can't breathe, and I panic, and I trip over something—that's when I'd wake up. Every time. Eventually, I stopped trying to sleep."

"What do you think it means?" I asked, wondering why it was coming up now.

"It was so real," she added, picking at a loose bit of tar paper roofing. "To be honest, it didn't feel like a dream."

"You think it actually happened?" I asked and thought about what that MBBS girl said months ago in the cafeteria, my first introduction to Judy: "She kills stray cats. Drops bricks on them for fun." Was this connected to that somehow? I glanced down at the strip of grimy black pavement below, cluttered with trash cans. The impact of a brick on a cat from this height wouldn't be a pretty picture, and Judy's aim would need to be impeccable. It was like a word problem from third period physics: If a brick is falling for 2.5 seconds, what will its final velocity be when it smashes a cat?

Judy flicked the tar paper into the alley. It fluttered out of sight. "I don't know."

I rose, walked across the plank, and sat beside her. "Is it coming back to you because . . . well, because of what happened yesterday? Sophie says that dreams are fragments of the past reordered to tell us something about the future. But who knows?"

She didn't answer me.

"Maybe Miss Martins is right," I said. "We don't need answers. We should just stay away. Maybe we should listen to her." I remembered what she told me to do about Judy: "Treat her like a good sister would. Be there for her, protect her."

"I thought about what she told me," Judy said as she continued to fiddle with the roof's edge, tearing off little strips. "That I shouldn't be ruled by my anger and then some bullshit about Greek myths. But this damn thing—whatever it is—has hold of *me*, not the other way around. How can I let go of something that's latched on to me?" I sensed the anxiety vibrating through her. "And the Closses, they know what it is. Moira practically said it. B and E, too. We're all part of this." She looked at me. "You, too."

"What do you think Moira meant when she said that what Miss Martins did to them was far worse than what Halo did to her?" Of all the details from yesterday, this was the one that I most wanted to hash out. I couldn't imagine what Miss Martins had supposedly done.

"She knows that her son attacked Miss M," Judy said, the eager investigator surfacing a little from her gloom. "But I don't know what Miss M could've done to them. I'm sure it was justified."

"I guess we're going to find out what it was," I said, leaning toward her, closing the space between us.

"Yes," she said softly. "We're going to find out everything."

I rested my head on her shoulder, her bob tickling my cheek, and slipped my hand in hers. I wanted her to know that I was with her, that I accepted her, crazy dream and all. We'd get to the bottom of this, the two of us. We looked at the scatter of chimneys, the cloud-streaked sky, and the seagulls that had strayed too far inland as they caught an updraft. Everything felt still and perfect like we were staking a claim for ourselves in this spinning world. We were untouchable, and everything happening around us were just frames in a movie reel.

As we held hands, I thought about my classmates in San Fran, who had sniggered about men who went with men and women with women. Queers and dykes. For some, it's a dire and incurable ailment. They're institutionalized for life. I wondered if I'd be strapped to a bed and given shock treatment one day? Would a grim psychiatrist in a starched white lab coat hover over me with a syringe, ready to neutralize my feelings? Oh, I couldn't imagine it. Besides, if it did happen, that wouldn't be the worst of it. If Dad found out, it'd destroy him. He'd kick me to the curb.

No, I decided right then, I'm not like those poor, desperate people. As it is with others like me, these feelings are a passing affliction, a hiccup in our maturity, cured by time. My heart will change. My feelings for Thea, Miss Martins, and even Judy will fade. Each of them will be as they ought to be in relation to me—a fleeting acquaintance, a beloved teacher, and a best friend, accordingly. But, I thought, this brief aberration, this wrinkle in time, why not enjoy it while it lasts? Why turn away from it when, within months, it will turn away from me?

So, I leaned into Judy, her spicy, sweaty odor surrounding me. The same mysterious energy that she'd emanated on that first day in the cafeteria sank into me, and I wasn't afraid of anything—not judgmental kids, not the white-coated doctors, not even Dad. Suddenly, nothing mattered except Judy. I squeezed her fingers and lightly grazed the side of her neck with my nose, sucking in her smell, hoping she would meet my lips with a kiss.

Instead, she leaned back. "Fuck, Philippa," she said, disentangling herself. "I don't know why you'd do that *now*."

"Oh, I'm sorry."

"I need to think." She stood and brushed off her backside.

"So sorry. I—" I lurched forward, and the alley rushed up to me. There, between the trash cans and debris, churned a sea of yawling, flea-infested cats, like the horror from Judy's dream. A muscular spasm shot through me, and I grabbed the roof's edge. I wasn't sure whether I was gathering energy to fling myself off or hold myself in place.

"Watch it!" Judy grabbed my shoulder, and that's what I needed to begin to breathe and move back from the edge. When I looked again, the cats were gone—if they'd even been there in the first place.

PHILIPPA, NOVEMBER 9, 1948

After dinner on Sunday, Sarah Yolland phoned us with bad news. Sophie fell and fractured her arm. Poor Sophie! She'll be okay, and she's already home from the hospital and on the mend. Thank God. Sarah found her sprawled on the bathroom floor, unconscious, with the bathtub overflowing. She must've fainted while drawing her bath. She's been reacting poorly to her cancer treatments, having dizzy spells and endless nausea. We drove up today to check on her, despite my missing school.

When Sarah showed us into Sophie's drafty east-facing room, soft light was pouring in. When I saw her, I knew that I couldn't fall apart. It would be unfair. She was unexpectedly cheerful and propped up on a mountain of pillows. Her right arm was in a plaster cast, which rested awkwardly on a stack of small cushions. Her hair was teased, and makeup had been applied, perhaps to cover up bruising from the fall. Sarah's doing, I'm sure.

"Well, I guess I have to break my arm to get you to visit me," she said. "What will it be next? A leg?" The quiver in her voice thwarted the delivery of her joke. I took a deep breath, keeping those tears in check, and went to her. As I began to hug her, Sophie winced. She was too tender, too fragile for an embrace. "Oh, I'm sorry!" I said, horrified.

"Sophie," her father said and smiled. "You're looking spry."

"Thank you, Carl," she said.

"Poor thing," Bonnie said. "You certainly have been through an ordeal."

"I'm still quite strong. I'll heal with time."

But that wasn't true. On the drive, Dad had told me that her cancer was advancing. Although he didn't want to trouble me, he said, I should know that Sophie may not make it through the New Year. I bawled, and Bonnie held me, running her hand through my hair. I felt so small, so helpless. I had the slightest inkling that, if anyone would, Sophie would understand my feelings about Judy or, at least, the intensity of our friendship. After all, she and Sarah had a close and lasting bond—not to say that it was a romantic relationship, but perhaps, she would have some insight. Or maybe that's why she told me to stay away from her, in which case, I'd just get more of the same. Vague prognostications are useless to me.

After the five of us chatted about the hospital, doctors' recommendations, her cancer treatments, the house's upkeep, the weather, and even

Thanksgiving plans, Dad, Bonnie, and Sarah excused themselves, giving me time with her.

"Come, Philippa," she said, "sit over here, beside me."

After sweeping a stray gray hair from her cheek, I climbed on the bed and leaned against one of the posters. I looked at her, lingering a bit, a mist of tears forming. In a bright voice, as if to ward off my sadness, she said, "Read to me." I wiped the dampness away. "I want to hear your voice. What about one of your mother's favorites?"

"Whatever you want."

"I have *Great Expectations*." She gestured toward a bookshelf across the room. "I've wanted to reread it. It's been so long. Your mother and I, we'd read to each other. She had a wonderful reading style. She could do the voices so well. She could have been an actress."

"You know," I said, rising to retrieve the novel, "I want to study literature and be a writer."

"Your mother would be so proud."

I remembered the book's distinctive brown leather spine with gold lettering. "Dad thinks it's impractical. I can tell."

She chuckled. "Oh, ignore him. He thinks being impractical is a bad thing. But it isn't. Sometimes being alive is impractical, but we do it anyway."

I smiled.

"Promise me to be a little impractical in your life."

"I promise," I said, pulling myself up on the bed again. I flipped to the first chapter and began. Pip, the main character, explains he's named Pip because he couldn't pronounce his family name, Pirrip, or his Christian name, Philip, as a child, and then he says:

> As I never saw my father or my mother, and never saw any like-
> ness of either of them (for their days were long before the days

of photographs), my first fancies regarding what they were like were unreasonably derived from their tombstones.

I stopped and looked up. "How Pip feels about his parents," I said, "that's how I feel about my mother sometimes. Like I'm just interpreting a tombstone and getting it wrong or incomplete."

"Your mother was a wonderful person," she said. "You have the right idea about her."

The oak branches just outside the window were swaying in a breeze and drew my attention. "But most adults aren't who they seem to be."

I could feel her eyes on me. "Are you okay, dear?"

"It's nothing."

"It's not nothing." Her voice shifted down a register. "Remember, I can sense things."

"Judy," I said. "She's like Pip, too. She doesn't know who her parents are—or were. She doesn't even have gravestones to go by."

Sophie scowled. "I'd hoped you'd moved on from her."

"You have it wrong about her," I said, trying to suppress my irritation. I didn't want to quarrel. "Judy's not dangerous. Not really."

"She *is*," she said, deadly serious. "I've known creatures like her. Move on. Find new friends."

I couldn't imagine dropping Judy and—what? Sip soda and quote Bible passages with Ramona? I wanted to ask Sophie why she hated Judy so much, but I feared the answer. Did she sense that Judy had touched on something deeper in me? Was that what she meant by dangerous? "Please, you don't understand—"

"Drop her. Promise me."

I didn't know what to say, but I couldn't make that promise, and I was annoyed that I was being asked to. I'd tried to call Judy to tell her about Sophie's fall before I left DC, but what I really wanted to talk about was why she'd pushed me away. It had stung—it still stings—and it had felt like a turning point, but a turning point to what? Had she rejected me? Judged me?

So, I lied to my aunt: "I'll look for other friends."

After an hour of reading, she became drowsy and needed to rest, so I left her. To kill time, I wandered the house, stopping at the panel in the dining room that leads to the cellar, the vestige of the underground railroad I'd shown Judy. I popped it open and peered in at the musty gloom. I recalled her refusing to go down its narrow stairs. Why had she reacted that way? Perhaps it was the memory she had about the cats? Maybe it'd happened in a cellar.

JUDY, NOVEMBER 8, 1948

Philippa is miffed at me, but I don't care.

Right after I told her about the dream and the cats—the fucking cats—she tried to kiss me and then nearly nosedived four stories. I had to keep her from falling. What does she want from me? To be my lesbian lover? Sure, I feel something for her, something about the two of us, but . . . Jesus. It's not like I don't have enough weighing on me. Moira's threat most of all: "I know more about you than you know about yourself." Whatever that means? And now, after saving her life, Philippa has disappeared. I've searched for her everywhere. She wasn't at school, and she wasn't at home.

Needing someone to talk to, I waited for Iris to get off work at Horsfield's. It was almost 9:00 P.M. when she stepped out of the alley entrance and said, "You been out here long?" I was leaning against the wall, flicking my lighter, and soaking up the unseasonably warm night.

"One of my two friends has vanished," I said. "I get mean if I don't have someone to annoy."

"Where's Miss Strawberry?" she asked.

"I don't know. She's upset. I'm getting the silent treatment."

Iris gazed at me with her large skeptical brown eyes. Despite her kitchen-heat frizzed hair, she looked shower-fresh, her face tawny in the streetlight. "Well," she said with a weary huff, "you can walk me to my bus, I guess."

As we strolled, I noticed that her long arms and legs moved as if each motion was in sync with a dreamy tune in her head. I wondered if her unshakable poise was a result of her professional training. Doctors, especially surgeons, need cool dispositions and dancer-like control over their bodies, right? Poking around in somebody's guts is a tricky business. She'll make a great surgeon if she's allowed to be one. It's not going to be easy.

After a block or so, fearing we'd be at her bus stop too soon, I started yammering. I told her that I was adopted, that I didn't remember much of my early childhood, but that I was beginning to. I showed her the scars on my arms. She guided me over to a lighted window display at a women's boutique. A gown-laden mannequin, who had more blood surging through her veins than Moira Closs, gazed down at us. "They look like cat claws," Iris said, holding my arms and turning them over in the sickly glow, "not that I'm an expert, but they should've healed. These scars mean that they were infected. You must've tangled with some pretty nasty cats."

I shivered; I felt like someone was watching us. I glanced around. Was it Halo lurking again? I scanned the street, but didn't see anyone. "I don't know," I said, sliding my sleeves down.

"What does Miss Strawberry think of all this?"

"Not much. She'd rather focus on Cleve's murder."

"Are you guys still harping on about that?"

"Moira Closs threatened us, and she has a mysterious grudge against Miss M."

"Jesus, girl." She wagged her finger at me. "My father told me that Mr. Closs—the dead boy's grandfather—was a tyrant." I remembered the grim, owl-eyed portrait over the fireplace in Moira's study. "He told me a story about a time when workers, both Negro men, had parked a Capitol City Hardware delivery truck in Adams Morgan on a steep grade. The truck's brakes gave way, crushing one of them to death and breaking the other's legs—and Mr. Closs threw a fit, screaming stupid nigger this and stupid nigger that, and instead of offering support for the dead man's family, accused the men of incompetence. Once the living man recovered, his wages were garnished to pay for the repairs. The Closses, they don't play fair, my friend." She started walking again. "So, tell Miss Strawberry to turn on her pretty little heels and head in another direction."

I smiled. "Everyone keeps telling us to turn around."

Her eyes grew wide. "Well, listen to them."

"Moira might know something about me, about who I really am."

She regarded me, her big eyes softening. "You are who you are," she said, lowering her chin and lifting her eyebrows. "It doesn't matter who you were. Don't get too wrapped up in the past. It's more important who you become."

I appreciated her directness and her kindness. Right then, I needed to feel like someone was watching out for me. And yes, I heard what she said, but I didn't agree—and still don't. All of us are what we remember. It's not what happened to us that makes us who we are; it's what we remember about what happened to us. Maybe Philippa's aunt was right: Memories, like dreams, are guideposts pointing us to the future. If I don't find a way to fill in the gap of my childhood, that blank space will continue to draw me into the shadows. No past, no future. Philippa is the only one who understands that emptiness.

I waited with Iris at the bus stop. We chatted about the election. She was thrilled, although she didn't especially trust Truman. I told her about seeing J. Edgar Hoover at the Closses and asked what she thought of him. She called him "an arch-racist with a Napoleon complex." After the small talk died out, we smoked together in silence. Once the bus scooped her up, I walked home, wanting to call Philippa, but it was too late to ring her.

PHILIPPA, NOVEMBER 10, 1948

As I entered school this morning, Judy caught me by the arm, groaned, "Where have you been?" and told me to meet her after school. When we rendezvoused, she commanded me to follow her. I understood where we were headed: Sousa Bridge, where Cleve's body was discovered. The journey was unlikely to yield much new information, but it was necessary to make all the same. We trudged down 17th Street, and I walked a step or two behind her, feeling detached from her, having flashes back to our romp through Harper Cemetery, playing at being Catherine and Heathcliff.

It was an overcast and humid day for November, so I shrugged off my sweater and draped it over my arm. For a while, we didn't speak, and I studied Congressional Cemetery on the right, its headstones, obelisks, and statues mocking the houses on the other side: "When you die, at least you won't have far to go." I thought of Aunt Sophie—about her illness and my frustration with her: She was *so* fixed in her dislike of Judy. Then, my annoyance with my friend rose up: Wasn't she the slightest bit curious about where I'd been? Did she care? Before I could follow that train of thought, she broke her silence and said, "I've had that goddamn dream three nights in a row."

"About the cats?"

"What else?" She kept looking ahead as if she were watching her dream projected on an invisible screen. "Every time, it becomes clearer. Last night, I woke up, and the skin on my arms stung like a thousand little paper cuts." She shoved up her sleeve. Her scars seemed raw as if recently irritated by rough wool or nervous scratching. When I was a girl, I surprised Sophie's cat while he was eating. He ripped into my forearm, but my wounds didn't scar. "I could hear their yawling and feel them swatting me as I kicked them away. I could smell cat piss." Her voice wavered; it was real for her.

"Is it happening in a cellar?" I asked.

A trace of relief fell over her face. She seemed grateful that I understood some part of what she was telling me. "That's why the light is faint and comes from above," she said. "I'm remembering ground-level windows, like in Miss Martins's apartment. How did you know?"

"Your reaction to Sophie's cellar was . . . visceral."

"I hate going below ground level. It's like being buried alive." Judy nodded toward the cemetery. "Why would anyone want to be dropped in a hole and covered with dirt and bird shit? I want a Viking's funeral. Plop me on a pyre and send me out to sea."

"What were you doing in a cellar?"

"I don't know. It must've been when I was really young."

"Was it at Crestwood?"

"I don't know," she said with a touch of desperation. "I'm not sure what to do. I need your help, I guess."

She seemed to have transformed from a confident avenger to . . . what? An introspective and self-interested sad sack? I just couldn't dredge up sympathy for her. I wasn't in the mind to. She hadn't even asked me what I'd been up to for the last few days, and I was still waiting for an apology for her rebuffing me on the roof. But like after our first kiss, she seemed uninterested in talking about it, like it hadn't happened at all. It made me crazy, as if I'd just imagined the whole thing. If the first time hadn't been life-changing, then the brush off shouldn't be heartbreaking. Right? But that first kiss *was* life-changing or something *like* life-changing—and her rejection stung. So, in a snide tone, I said, "Well, I guess I'm not getting the cold shoulder anymore."

Judy rolled her eyes. *Not* the right response.

"You pushed me away," I said, not hiding my anger. "It hurt."

Judy stopped and turned to me. Her expression wasn't biting, as I antici-pated. Her big, sinkhole eyes wandered over my face trying to decipher me. What was she thinking? Was she going to shove me away again? "Look," she said, "you don't have to help. I understand. It's just that these dreams are happening for a reason. What Miss Martins said to me on Saturday set them off—no, it's not *what* she said, it's *how* she said it."

She was too preoccupied with herself to see me—but what could I do? So, resigned, I said, "What do you mean?"

"There was something in her voice, like I was especially important to her."

"We *are* her favorite students."

"Come on, that's not it. And then Moira: 'I know more about you than you know about yourself.' What does that mean?"

"She's trying to scare us."

"No, you don't get it," Judy snapped, shook her head, and started off down the sidewalk. Miss Martins and Moira Closs had sunk their claws into her. I wondered if I should be worried.

After following 17th Street and crossing several lanes of traffic, we were on the bridge, leaning against the tall railing, peering through its slats at the murky green water and the mess of weeds and shoreline silt. My eyes fell on a large white object, partially concealed by feathery grass. It was obviously debris, a piece of a cardboard box, but for a moment, I saw it as Cleve's bare torso, pale in the sunshine with the word written on him in bright red: "AHKA." Neither of us knew the body's exact location, so there wasn't much to learn from studying the scene, other than the eerie contrast between the whirring traffic behind us and Anacostia's peaceful shore. Something extraordinary and horrible had washed up there, but today it was business as usual. I glanced at Judy's profile. Her hands were gripping the metal slats, and she had a far-off look, not, it seemed, taking in the scenery or even thinking about the murder. Something had entered her expression in the place of anger: Sadness? Relief? Even wonder? Without turning to me, as if she knew I was waiting for her to speak, she said, "What if . . ." She pulled on the slats and swung back a little. "What if Miss M is my mother?"

I knew it was impossible—or at least highly improbable—that our English teacher was her long-lost birth mother. Of course, I understood why her mind would go there. Who could blame her? She'd been through a lot, and Miss Martins was a sort of mother figure to us. Still, it frustrated me. She'd banished the brash, cynical Judy and, in her place, inserted a sentimental little girl, pining for her mother. I missed her barbed wit, her daring. I needed the Judy who stood up to the Closses, who fought with Bart and Edith, who spat malt all over Ramona and humiliated Roy Barnes—the Judy who might have bombed cats with bricks. I could forgive her for being cruel, but this new Judy was inexcusable.

"I don't know," I said, shaking my head. "It seems . . . farfetched."

She glared at me. "I'm sure of it."

"So, *why* do you need my help?" I said, letting my exasperation bleed through.

"Over the years, Bart and Edith have refused to tell me who my birth parents are. I've asked many times, but they tell me that I shouldn't know for my own good. During one of these talks, Bart, who was sloshed, warned me to leave his desk alone. I hadn't said a thing about his desk, but in the soaked sponge he calls a mind, he must've thought I had. That was a year ago. The point is that something is hidden in there. I didn't want to know what it was until now, until I thought my mother could be more than a deadbeat or wino."

"And you want me to help search for it?" I liked *this* Judy much better.

"I read in *True Crime* magazine about how to pick a lock with bobby pins. I need you to stand watch. If B and E catch me, and there's nothing in the desk, it could ruin our chances to look at other places."

I didn't want to get in even more trouble with Judy's parents. If we keep snooping, Dad will find out, and he'll drive a wedge between us. But with Judy back in the saddle, it didn't seem to matter. She'd make anyone feel invincible. "Okay," I said. "Let's do it."

❦

Mr. Peabody kept his study door locked at all times. Because of its location at the end of a poorly lit corridor at the back of the house, it served as his hideaway, according to Judy. It was his refuge from Edith, from reality.

With *True Crime* and two bobby pins, Judy unlocked the door and opened it. I peered in. A colossal mahogany desk dominated the room. The walls were cluttered with oppressive hunting scenes. Glossy cracked varnish spread across them like old spiderwebs. A small, worn leather couch, Bart's napping spot, stretched under a line of half-shuttered windows. The peppery odor of pipe smoke lingered. Judy waved me away: "Go, stand guard."

Per her orders, I stationed myself at the entrance to the corridor, just under the main staircase, to keep an eye on the front door. If Bart or Edith came home, I would dash down the hall and alert her. If we had to, we could escape from the study into the kitchen through a servant's door that was catty-corner to the study. The kitchen has access to the alley in the rear—a clear escape route.

I waited, obsessively tracing the ornate plaster molding on the ceiling with my eyes. Then—a door squeaked somewhere behind me, followed by footfalls and distant murmurs. Wait, behind me? I crept a step or two down the corridor toward the cracked study door, light spilling out from around its edges. Someone—or several someones—were in the kitchen. They must've come in from the alley. The Peabodys rarely used the back entrance. Judy had noted this several times when she had sneaked me in to avoid painful small talk with Bart and Edith.

I tiptoed to the study but didn't know how to signal to Judy without drawing attention to myself. After all, the kitchen door was just a few feet away. Through its thin wood, I recognized a male voice—Mr. Peabody.

"Thank you," he said warmly. "That will help us put it behind us. It's been a long road."

"Well, for your sake, I'm glad of it," the woman said, her voice familiar, its tone like polished brass. "But if Judy harasses Elaine and my son again, I won't use my influence to help you." Moira Closs!

"You've been good to us," he said. "I'm sorry for her behavior. I'd never want her to hurt you or your family, especially after what you've been through."

"I know you're doing your best with her. Sons are easier to manage than daughters. I'll grant you that. But you *must* be strict, Barton."

Judy swung open the study door with a clumsy bang, and the voices stopped. She was holding a document of some sort. She was pale and swayed unsteadily, as if she'd just been knocked off balance. Acting quickly, I shoved her back inside, hoping for another escape route. I managed to squeak out: "They came in from the alley. They heard us—" Then Bart and Moira were there on the threshold, glowering.

"My office is out of bounds!" Bart said, his sweaty brow furrowing. "Why do you think you can just disregard—"

In a delayed reaction, Judy attempted to conceal the document in her sweater pocket that was already stuffed with her rolled-up *True Crime* magazine. Bart stepped forward, caught her wrist, and ripped the papers from her. He glanced at them, then stuffed them into his pocket. "You shouldn't be in here," he said, his voice lower, but still shaken. "You shouldn't be going through my things."

Both Moira and Mr. Peabody were still wearing their outdoor coats. Moira coolly observed the commotion from above her fur collar.

Judy was seething, but she wasn't speaking up. Something in her demeanor lacked force. What had she discovered? What was that document?

Moira stepped forward and placed her gloved hands on the sides of Judy's arms as if about to embrace her. The leather of her gloves stretched and crackled as her fingers bit into Judy's flesh. A faint smile, if you could call it that, crept into her lips. She released her and brought her palms together. "Barton," she said with delight, "you know what she needs—an environment that encourages structure and discipline. I know of some wonderful all-girls schools. Madeira. Foxcroft. Agnes March. I even know a few headmistresses socially. I'd be happy to make introductions."

He turned to me, a twinge of distress in his eyes. "What do you think, Philippa? You'd go away if your father saw it fit to send you, wouldn't you?"

I blurted out, "He'd never do that." I didn't want Judy to be taken away, and besides, she'd *loathe* boarding school.

"Well," Moira said, disappointed by my response, "these schools shape girls into women and keep them out of trouble." She looked at Bart. "Act now, before she ends up pregnant or a dope fiend, or worse, dead. The big city is a dangerous place for young women." Another threat.

Bart gave a meek smile. He ordered Judy to go to her room, and Moira guided me out, resting her gloved hand in the small of my back, like an adder waiting to strike. When we were in the alley behind the Peabodys', she slid her hand away and said, "Your father is a lawyer. A JAG, right?"

"Yes," I muttered.

"I would so like to meet him—and your stepmother, too. Bonnie, is it? I hear they're good people. I'm always willing to widen my social circle for *good* people."

A chill cascaded through me.

"You're a sensible girl," she said as we parted. "Make sure Judy stays far away from me for her sake—and for yours."

When Bonnie first moved in, I fantasized that my mother hadn't died. In my eleven-year-old brain, I imagined that she might've developed amnesia from the trauma of childbirth and wandered out of the hospital in a daze. The doctors, embarrassed they had lost a patient, showed Dad another woman's body (as if he wouldn't know the difference!). After she'd recovered from her amnesia—it took many years—she'd come looking for Dad and me and would appear on our doorstep one day. We'd have a tearful reunion between father, mother, and child, and Dad would send Bonnie packing. It was a ridiculous idea, and I'm pretty sure that I stole it from a radio show. But it helped me, at least for a time.

As I walked home from the Peabodys', I wondered if Judy's conviction that Miss Martins was her mother was a bit like my melodramatic daydream—a strong wish, but not grounded in reality. If it was true for some crazy reason, it couldn't be a coincidence. Our teacher would've sought out Judy, but why hover so close and not say anything? Then, I thought of Moira, the imperial queen bitch, and her threats. This is about more than lost mothers, abandoned children, and grieving grandmothers. There's something more at stake—perhaps a cover-up of a murder?

When I came in, the phone was ringing. Bonnie, who was busy tending a pot on the stove—beef stew of some sort—picked it up and handed it to me. "Don't be long," she whispered. "Dinner will be ready soon."

"Hello," I said, pulling off my coat and wedging the receiver between my shoulder and chin.

"Why didn't you warn me?" Judy growled.

"You didn't tell me they might come in from the alley," I said, not restraining my irritation. "I *couldn't* warn you. There wasn't time." I didn't want Bonnie to catch wind of my anger, so I kept my voice low. Nothing would send me over the edge faster than nosy questions from my stepmother.

Judy sighed but didn't say anything.

Impatient, I said, "Well, dinner's almost ready. I should go."

Still nothing.

"Goodbye."

"Wait!" Judy said. "Just wait, goddamn it."

"Okay?"

"I found *it*—or at least some of it. The documentation of my adoption from Crestwood. It's what Bart snatched from me. It was a cinch to break into his desk."

"So? What did you learn?"

"I skimmed the pages. I didn't have much time." She paused for a beat or two. "My mother's name is Charlene Peters. My birth name is Judith Peters. It said nothing about Christine Martins. Nothing about any foster parents." She exhaled heavily. "Fuck."

I wasn't going to be petty and tell her, "I told you so." I thought about my own mother, about her photograph, her one eye not covered by her hat's brim, smiling out at me, fixed forever like that in time. "At least you have a name. That's more than you had before, right? We'll find her."

CHAPTER SEVEN

It's a strange endeavor to humanize your arch enemy, someone who brought about such suffering to you and the people you love. It's even stranger to humanize that enemy posthumously. After all, the winners write history, and it usually behooves them to cast their enemies as despicable villains, right? At some point, though, if you're ever going to gain an understanding of why things happened the way they happened—or even how they might yet happen—it's necessary to give your nemesis some texture.

Moira Closs died in 1954 but it wasn't until a few years ago that I decided that I'd failed to understand her. I came across an article on her in the Washington Star. *The focus, of course, was her death: Was it an act of random violence or cold-blooded murder? Well, that's a story for another time. But in its early paragraphs, it detailed her background, of which I knew only fragments. She'd been born Moira Lutz in Bluefield, West Virginia, the daughter of a butcher. Hardly*

*glamorous beginnings. She married a coal miner named Randal Pat-
terson when she was eighteen. She soon became restless and wanted
something more for herself, spending days at the library devouring
every book she could, especially biographies and autobiographies of
famous political figures, from Roman emperors to Civil War gen-
erals. She educated herself on ambition and cunning.*

*When Randal died in a mining accident, smashed flat by tons of
rock, she grieved, but not for long. She wanted to transform herself
and get the hell out of the mountains, so she moved to DC, shook
her Appalachian accent, and entered the secretarial pool, spending her
evenings socializing. One night in 1910, she met Cleveland Closs Sr.
outside of the Cosmos Club, where he was a member. He was taken
with her beauty.*

*Originally from eastern Pennsylvania, he had moved to DC to
attend Georgetown and remained, using his family money to begin
what would become Capitol City Hardware. By all accounts, the
couple was in love. Soon they married and had their towheaded son,
Howard. Her pregnancy was difficult, and although she would try
for another child, Halo would be her first and last.*

*In 1928, when Halo was twenty years old, Cleveland died suddenly
of an aneurysm, an inherited anomaly. Although distraught, Moira
didn't miss a beat. She seized control of Capitol City Hardware and
managed it through the lean years of the Depression. To keep the
company in the black, she inserted herself into Washington society
and became adept at rubbing elbows with prominent politicos, like
J. Edgar Hoover. She took her husband's company and transformed
it into the regional gold standard for high-end appliances.*

The gilded first part of the article was meant as a preamble to
Moira's "tragic end," its scribe squeezing as much pathos out of the
story as he could. However, it suggested something about her that I
hadn't considered before: She was self-realized. She was a modern

woman, calling her own shots and succeeding. I also began to under-
stand her as a mother, a mother who would want to protect her child
no matter what he did. I understand the desire to protect someone you
love, no matter the consequences. In that respect, we aren't all that
different.

No, I'll never forgive her for what she did. Why should I? But can
one really continue to hate a vanquished enemy?

I don't know.

JUDY, NOVEMBER 13, 1948

I have no words.

It's too much, too horrible.

I'm not sure I can write this now.

All I can think about is that famous pre-Raphaelite painting of drowned
Ophelia, her glittering dress fanning out among the reeds and algae, hands
open to the sky, jewel-toned flowers floating away from her hand, her face
impossible to pin down: tortured, serene, lifeless, as if struck dead the
moment she opened her mouth to speak.

JUDY, NOVEMBER 13, 1948

I can't sleep, so here goes. Maybe writing it down will help.

I was a fool to think Miss M was my mother, but it felt right. It still does. I
have no interest in finding the Peters woman. I don't want to discover that
she's spectacularly average or washed up or worse—the monster who fed

me to the goddamn cats. Today, in need of a distraction, Philippa and I, in true Calvin McKey fashion, decided to stake out the Closs townhouse and follow whoever stepped out of the front door first. A blunt approach, but what did we have to lose?

We bundled up in coats and wide-brimmed hats—the weather has turned cold again—grabbed a leash and Rosie and skulked in a small public garden down the block from the Closses'. Around ten o'clock, Halo left the house, dressed in a gray plaid jacket, navy tie, and dark blue hat. He bought a paper at the newsstand on Pennsylvania Avenue and entered Tune Inn, a local hole-in-the-wall breakfast spot. From across the busy street, we watched him take a seat in the front window and unfold his paper. It was boring as hell. We didn't know what we were looking for. It wasn't like he was going to run into the middle of Pennsylvania Avenue and declare his guilt. We entertained ourselves by petting Rosie and pacing the block. About an hour later, he folded his paper and stood. When he exited, he crossed the street, headed in our direction. We faced the stationery store and pretended to window shop, our reflections distorted in the old leaded glass. He passed by, oblivious. That's when we realized that two men, both in dull gray suits and equally dull fedoras, were following him. One was tall and bony, and loomed scarecrow-like over the other one, who was squat, muscular, and strode like an angry penguin. They seemed vaguely familiar.

Halo made several stops—the barbershop, the drug store, and the corner market—before heading toward the house on A Street, freshly shaven and holding a paper bag of groceries and prescriptions. It was early afternoon, and his invisible entourage was still patiently trailing him. However, Philippa was beginning to give out, moaning about being hungry. As Halo made a sharp left into an alley—a shortcut to A Street, she supposed—the two men sped up and surrounded him. I handed Rosie's leash to Philippa and told her to wait at the end of the block. I inched to the corner of the row house, creeping as close as I could, but still out of earshot. The scarecrow stood behind Halo, walling him in, and the other man spoke to him with a frothing, ferret-like intensity. Halo looked distraught and said something like, "leave her" or "let her." Then the talker laughed and slapped Halo on the shoulder, but the gesture wasn't jolly. Suddenly, I realized where I'd seen them before: Bogdan's arraignment, sitting at the back of the courtroom. Who the hell were they?

Then, they were gone, having vanished around the corner.

For a few minutes, Halo stood in the alley, grasping his bag, crinkling its paper, eyes wide and troubled. He began walking toward me, and I retreated, finding cover behind a parked car. I waved to Philippa, who was milling around with Rosie, and we followed Halo several blocks to a streetcar stop. While he waited, he removed the bottle he'd picked up at the pharmacy—Veronal, perhaps?—and dumped the full grocery bag in a waste can. He caught the next streetcar. I flagged down a cab, and Philippa scooped up Rosie.

Halo's destination was the Daphne Arms Women's Hotel, an eight-story art deco building of pink granite, streamlined chrome, and silvery glass on Meridian Hill. With few trees or shrubs around it, it blazed against the cloudless afternoon sky. My gut told me that this was where Miss M was living. So, why was Halo here? Was it a result of his conversation with the scarecrow and the penguin? Who were they after all? G-men? Mobsters? I paid the cabby, and we spilled out on the sidewalk.

After tethering Rosie to the handrail outside the entrance, I pushed through the rotating door with Philippa trailing me. Halo was nowhere to be seen. A plump woman in horn-rimmed reading glasses and a floral seafoam green smock lowered her *Photoplay*.

"Hello," Philippa said, brightly. "We're wondering if you saw a man pass through here."

She frowned, the rosacea on her cheeks flaring. "Not a soul."

That wasn't true. "He was just here," I said. "We saw him come in."

"You're mistaken."

Under the edge of the woman's *Photoplay*, I spotted a twenty-dollar bill. "Look, we know you're lying. Can you tell us where he was going?"

"Like I said, nobody was here." She sniffed and set her jaw.

Philippa leaned in. "We know he passed through that door"—she pointed—"four or five minutes ago."

"Like I said, you're mistaken. No men allowed. I would've seen him. For Christ's sake, I can smell 'em." She stuck her nose in the air and sucked in her nostrils. "So, if you don't mind . . ." She raised her magazine, creating a partition between us. Rita Hayworth, wrapped in red, beamed up from its cover. Its headline read, "Who Are Hollywood's Dangerous Women?"

Trying a different approach, I said, "Does a Miss Christine Martins live here?"

"Can't give out that information."

Philippa was losing her patience; her arms were crossed.

"How much?" I said, digging in the pocket of my dress.

A smile crept into the woman's face. "How much you got?"

"Five dollars." I had twelve, but I wasn't going to give her all my money.

"How much does your friend got?" the woman grunted.

Philippa glared at me. "I'm not giving her a cent." She turned to the woman: "Look, our teacher, Miss Martins, could be in danger. Please tell us where she's living."

"If you care so much, why don't you know?"

Philippa gripped the edge of the chest-high desk and leaned toward the woman: "Do you want to be responsible for something terrible? Do you want to lose your job?"

The woman chuckled. "You're a feisty little bird, aren't you?"

"Tell us where she is!" she yelled, batting a glass cardholder off the desk. It hit the ground behind the woman and shattered. Daphne Arms information cards scattered everywhere. It startled me, but I was thrilled: I'd never seen Philippa do something like that.

"Okay, okay," the woman said. "No need to get violent. Five dollars will do it."

I tossed the wadded-up bill at her, and the woman flipped through her directory, running her yellowed fingernail down a list of names. "Apartment 508," she said, and we hurried to the elevators, our shoes squeaking on the buffed linoleum. As we waited for the car to descend, I noticed a sign written in swooping cursive tacked to a bulletin board: "Remember, ladies, gentlemen are only permitted in the lobby and in the 'beau' parlors. The halls, living quarters, and sunbathing deck are off limits! Please honor the house rules."

"Too many fucking rules," I said, nodding toward it.

The elevator dinged, and two women in pencil skirts, tailored blazers, and tams stepped out, trailing a mist of strong fragrances—lemon oil, sandalwood, gardenia, musk. One said to the other, "O'Rally's has the best cocktails! Their scotch sours go down like lemonade." They flitted past us, and I said to Philippa: "Sieves for brains."

The elevator took us swiftly to the fifth floor, and we stepped out into a long hallway with hectic red and gold deco wallpaper and a bright geometric carpet. The automatic doors closed behind us, and we stood together, motionless, staring at the dizzying vortex of color. Cigarette smoke lingered, but no one was in sight, and the hall was quiet. Most of the women were out, enjoying the day. Neither of us wanted to make the first move. If Miss M was in danger, so were we. If Halo's visit was unplanned, maybe he didn't mean harm. But who could tell?

Apartment 508 was two suites from the end of the corridor. I rapped on the door. "Hello? Miss Martins?" I called out. No response. I tried the knob; it was open.

The dayroom had a series of broad windows hung with sun-filtering sheers. The furnishings were modern and spare, the upholstery all pastel colors. Just inside the door, a chrome-countered efficiency kitchen gleamed. To its left, a glass-topped breakfast table held two china mugs, one of which was overturned. The light brown liquid it had contained now spread across the glass and dripped on the parquet floor, causing faint splattering noises. There were also two metal chairs: one pulled out at an angle and the other overturned, its back on the floor. Nothing seemed to belong to Miss M.

"Hello?" Philippa said. "Anyone home?"

Silence.

I ventured in, pausing at the overturned chair. I leaned toward the table and sniffed the liquid. Sweet and a touch bitter. Maybe cocoa or Ovaltine? I scanned the kitchenette, selected a large butcher knife from the drying rack, and grasped it tightly in front of me. I checked in with Philippa. She gave me wide, frightened eyes.

We moved into the next room, the bedroom. Ceiling-to-floor forest green curtains had been drawn over the windows, emitting only slivers of bright sunlight. The two dim bedside lamps failed to chase the shadows from the room's nooks and corners. Someone had torn the coverlet from the bed, balled it up, and tossed it carelessly to the side with the pillows. Only the bottom sheet remained—a stark eyesore in the middle of the room. On a lacquered vanity trimmed with green ruffles, Miss M's jewelry chest spilled a strand of pearls and tangle of necklaces. Philippa inspected it, holding up the knot of chains, before returning them to the box.

"What's going on?" she said, looking at me, her face bunched with worry. "Something isn't right. Shouldn't we go?" My heart was pounding. Without answering her, I continued to search, the knife trembling in front of me, cutting little circles in the air.

I noticed wet spots on the carpet near the bathroom. I stepped through its threshold. A small, high window beamed light into the mirror above the sink, giving the rose petal pink room a cloying glow. A thin glaze of water coated the floor, and the frilly shower curtain for the inset tub was cinched back and damp along its bottom edge. Faint lilac perfume swirled in the air.

Someone had draped a white bedsheet over the tub, and water had soaked through it, revealing the contours of a face and shoulders underneath. Poking out from the shroud, two fingers were frozen in a strange, beckoning articulation. Above the body, in contrast to the wall color, written crudely with lipstick was AHKA.

I couldn't move. I couldn't breathe. Philippa muttered something, but it was garbled, broken. I wanted to reply, to gasp, to scream, but nothing came. Something shifted in me, and I began sinking into the floor, its checkered tiles quicksand. I needed help; I needed a lifeline before my head went under. I felt a tug on my sleeve and flinched violently. "Fuck! Don't touch me!" I snapped, lowering my knife, which I was still holding in front of me like a sword.

As if guiding my actions from outside myself, like being my own puppeteer, I approached the body. I picked up a corner of the sopping sheet and peeled it back. Beneath it, Miss M was fully dressed and crammed in the tub like a doll in a toy crib. Her elbows were wedged at her sides, forcing her forearms out at unnatural angles. Her right hand seemed to be frozen midgesture as if she'd been summoning a taxi or a waiter when she was struck down. Her smooth skin, although still flushed, was marred by dissolving makeup, eye shadow, and liner. Her blond curls fell across her forehead in loose, damp strands. Her warm gray eyes, eyes that had smiled at me and read my heart many times, glowed dimly through filmy white slits. Her mouth gaped like drowned Ophelia, emptied of its poetry. Around her neck, the killer had twisted a dark green tie flecked with little scarlet shamrocks. Between the silk flaps at its back, sewn into the tip lining, the image of a swimsuit-clad pin-up girl peeped out. Her sexy smirk, a sick taunt.

I touched her forearm, hoping that, like Prince Charming, I could reverse this terrible spell. She seemed so vacant I expected her skin to be icy, but it was warm. I recoiled. The contents of my stomach slid into my throat, but no vomit came up, just scorching acid.

"She's dead?" Philippa asked.

"Yes," I said.

"What do we do?"

"I don't . . . I don't know."

"This is, is . . . Oh Jesus."

"Yes, it is." I glanced at Philippa and saw Miss M's empty face transposed on hers. I gasped, felt my stomach churn, and looked away.

Philippa took my hand. "Should we go?" she said, pulling me back from Miss M's body.

"Yes, yes," I said. "Right now."

PHILIPPA, NOVEMBER 13, 1948

Before Judy removed the sheet, I willed Miss Martins's body to be unreal, a prop in our little drama. I was sure she would look like a marble figure in repose—or an ethereal corpse from a Hollywood movie, draped just so for aesthetic appeal.

Of course, I was horribly wrong.

It was absurd, like walking into your living room one day and finding a gorilla or an army tank. How did it get there? Who brought it? What terrible force was behind it? It couldn't be reckoned with. It *refused* to be understood.

As I'm writing this, I still can't picture her. It's a blank in my mind's eye.

When I took Judy's hand and moved her away from the body, sorrow began rolling toward me like an enormous wave. Before it crashed over me, we launched into action, racing out of the bathroom, through the gloomy bedroom, past the overturned chair and spilled hot chocolate, over the loops and flourishes of the hall carpet, and into the elevator, which took centuries to descend, the floors ticking off like the countdown to an atomic blast. We squeaked across the lobby, past the unattended front desk, and out into the sun. Judy grabbed Rosie and held him close, despite his whimpers. We crossed 16th Street, ran down the hill to U Street, and scrambled onboard the next streetcar.

After we plopped into our seats, I had the sudden urge to smash something, something that would shatter in thousands of pieces. I wanted to break the calm of the streetcar ride, the hum of its motor, the clank of its wheels, the murmur of the other riders. Most of all, I wanted Judy to stop smothering poor Rosie, to look at me, and say something. Anything.

But none of that happened. Instead, I leaned against the streetcar window and thought of Aunt Sophie—just a flash of her kind face—and burst into tears.

JUDY, NOVEMBER 13, 1948

As the streetcar trembled down Florida Avenue, I clawed my way out of my dark hole, a shadowy place in my memory filled with yawling cats and musty cellars and now Miss M. As I surfaced, I imagined her below me, standing in a dank corner, her neck contorted, her jaw slack, and her eyes barely open, just the whites showing. I wanted to stay with her, reassure her, but I couldn't. Rosie was squirming in my lap, licking my fingers. Philippa was sniffling beside me, needing me. I reached out and took her hand and squeezed it, and let it go. She looked at me, wiping the tears off her cheeks. We were silent. What was there to say? Within twenty-four hours, I'd lost Miss M twice: first as my mother and then all together. At least Philippa wasn't trying to console me.

She exhaled and said, "I can't believe it. I just—"

"Believe it."

"Was it Halo?"

"Who else?"

"Are you sure? He would've had to act fast. He only had about ten minutes on us."

"Her killer was someone she knew," I said, failing to disguise my impatience. "The door to the apartment was unlocked, but not damaged. It was him."

"I know, but still, he would've had to strangle her, drag her into the bathroom, fill up the bathtub, turn off the water, write AHKA on the wall, and leave before we got there. Oh, and why strip the bed? Just for the sheet?"

"I don't want to talk about it," I said, not in the right frame of mind to play detective.

But she kept on: "And why write that? Bogdan is still locked up. Right? Why try to frame a man who couldn't possibly have done it?"

"Philippa," I groaned, but she had a good point. Of course, there's no accounting for psychos. "It's not about framing him. He's just fucking crazy."

"If he's so crazy, why did he go through the trouble of framing Bogdan with the yearbook?" she said, undaunted. "Why frame him then unframe him? It doesn't make sense."

I was trying to listen to her and not lash out. I wanted to knock each of the points down, just to shut her up, but I couldn't focus. Blood was pounding in my brain. I knew Halo was responsible. My gut wasn't wrong. Perhaps Miss M had known something, perhaps she could've implicated him in Cleve's murder. "Jesus, you saw him raping her," I said. "You saw it!"

Rosie snorted, and a woman across the aisle flashed us a stern look. I rubbed Rosie's head, letting his soft ears slip through my fingers. Maybe Philippa was right, I thought. Maybe it wasn't cut and dried. Then, like that, I remembered something: "The tie around her neck," I said, "it was the same one Halo was wearing when we first met him. Green with little red shamrocks."

"You're right," Philippa said. "But—" and she stopped herself and glanced out the window at the townhouses and storefronts drifting past us and didn't say anything else.

When we reached our stop, we stepped out of the streetcar and into the chilly dusk. I set Rosie down and let him piss on a nearby tree.

"I want to catch him before he does the same thing to us," I said. "I want him to pay."

Philippa nodded, her eyes avoiding mine.

"Don't tell your parents what we saw. We need time to make a plan." I touched her shoulder lightly, a little skittish of her. "Be careful. Okay?"

She looked at me, and I took in her blue-gray eyes, wisps of her mussed hair floating in the breeze. For a moment, something about her—perhaps that mix of gentleness and tenacity, a hint of her implacable core underneath—reminded me of Miss M, the thought of which suddenly became unbearable. "He was wearing blue today," she said, stepping away from me. "He didn't have on that stupid tie. Why not use the one he was wearing to . . . to strangle her? Especially if it was on the spur of the moment?"

I didn't have a good answer. I didn't have an answer at all.

PHILIPPA, NOVEMBER 14, 1948

When Dad, Bonnie, and I returned from church today, Quincy was sitting on our stoop, flipping through the morning paper. He stood when he saw us, folded the pages over, and said, "I'm sorry to surprise you." Inside, he eased into telling us what I already knew. As he spoke, a new wrinkle bunched on his forehead, and his dimples, prickly with stubble, disappeared and twitched into life again whenever he edged toward a difficult bit of the story. This boyishness made me want to reassure him, to tell him that I had seen her, that it was so much worse than anything he could say to me now. When he finally came to the point—"Your teacher, Christine Martins, has been murdered"—I forgot to react. Bonnie and Dad stared at me for several seconds before I took my cue, forced out a melodramatic sob, and fled upstairs.

In my room, I took a deep breath, but before I could collect myself, there was a knock on the door. Quincy peeked in. "You okay, Phil?"

"No," I said and dropped on my bed in a spineless flop, sinking my face into my pillow. I'm an atrocious actor, so I didn't want him to see that I wasn't crying. The horror of seeing Miss Martins refused to settle in. It was still too foreign, too impossible.

He sat beside me. For a minute, he didn't say anything, then he spoke. "Phil, you've got to tell your dad that you've been snooping around. Whoever killed Cleve and Jackie also killed Christine Martins. It isn't Bogdan, at least not Bogdan alone. You could be in danger."

I surfaced from my pillow and debated blurting it all out. I wanted to tell him that we'd seen Halo enter the Daphne Arms, we'd seen Miss Martins's body, we'd seen AHKA written in bloodred lipstick. I wanted to tell him about the connection between Halo and Miss Martins. I wanted to explain Judy's theory about the yearbook. The clues darted through me like flecks of goldfish in a murky pond, refusing to coalesce. No, I couldn't tell Quincy. Not yet. Besides, the clues belonged to us. We should be the ones to act on them.

"I'll tell Dad," I lied. "I promise."

"We'll figure things out." He put his arm around me, and I leaned into him. "I'm sure of it." The faint musk of his cologne made me wince and think about Halo, about his mean good looks, about his body flung over Miss Martins on her bed. Maybe he was a killer, maybe he wasn't, but I know what I saw: He violated her, and he had to pay for it.

Judy met me at the door and gestured frantically for me to come in. "The police are going to release Bogdan," she whispered. "B and E are in the kitchen. It's not pretty. They've been on the phone all morning, but it's not doing any good."

I slid out of my coat and draped it over my arm. Cigarette smoke hung in the air, which was odd. Edith usually forbade smoking. A cluster of fresh calla lilies had been arranged on either side of Jackie's photo. Judy closed the door, held a finger to her lips, and pointed toward the stairs.

Before we could cross the foyer, Edith was marching down the hall and calling out, "Who's there? Who is it?" Wedged between her fingers, a butt smoldered, trailing a ribbon of smoke. When she spotted me, she groaned, "Philippa, are you *ever* at home? Your parents must wonder where you are? How do you pacify their curiosity?" She squinted at me. "Do tell me." She'd pinned up her hair sloppily, and her face was stretched tight and raw as if she'd scrubbed it with a rough sponge. Her dark purple dress was bunched at the waist and crooked on her shoulders. Bogdan's release was taking its toll. I might've been sympathetic had I not been under attack. With a little edge, I said, "They trust me, I guess."

"Aren't they fools!" she squawked.

I looked to Judy, who took a half-step forward, and her eyes narrowed, taking aim. "Stop it," she snapped at Edith, drawing back her shoulders, which caused her loose sweater to slip down her arms and expose her clavicle, a bright ridge of olive skin. Dark energy coiled between them, ready to spring. I wanted to leave. But I couldn't back down now, especially in front of Judy.

Edith seemed briefly unsettled, then scoffed. "Go home. Now is *not* the time."

"Don't tell her what to do," Judy said, making a fist, cocking her right arm, and thrusting her chest out. Her small breasts rose in distinct ridges under her cream-colored camisole, her skin seemed to deepen a shade darker, and her bangs fell over her forehead like spider legs. She was beautiful in a weary and ferocious way. Despite the distance between us, I swooned with admiration. Sure, I still wanted her to apologize for rejecting my kiss, but I don't think she's going to. Doing so, would make it real—*us* real. It stings, but it doesn't change how I feel about her, how I adore her.

"Philippa, dear," Edith said with a condescending air. "You must have some sense of what we're going through. It's not a good time for you to be here." She began to turn away.

"I want her here," Judy said, tightening her fist.

Edith swiveled back. "I'll ring her father if she doesn't go."

"No, you won't," Judy flung at her. "It's an empty threat."

Edith chewed on this, then spat back: "We made such a mistake with you." She planted her hands on her hips. "We doted when we should've disciplined. We tried to mold you into something better than you were. We gave you everything. I should've known: Disposition is in the blood. Biology is fate. If you came from nothing, you were bound to be nothing. I'm shooing Philippa away because it's better for her. Why should she suffer, too?"

"I don't feel that way," I said, horrified.

"Then you're a fool," Edith said with surprising earnestness. Edith was scared of Judy—or at least afraid that she couldn't control her. I considered their confrontation over Bogdan at the Halloween party. Edith and Judy were in a constant tug of war over the past. In Edith's version, Judy was a willful and ungrateful student, unable to be tutored in the ways of becoming her daughter in the mold of erstwhile Jackie. In Judy's version, Edith offered her comfort and wealth, sure, but not freedom. She was Edith's plaything, a Jackie doll.

During Edith's tirade, she had come gradually to life like Pygmalion's Galatea, alabaster becoming flesh, flecks of jet becoming pupils, shards of ivory becoming teeth. Her joints seemed to creak and activate. Her face and neck muscles flexed. Heat rose through her, and perspiration formed on the ridge of her nose and her upper lip. She gave off a familiar spicy odor. She took another step, but instead of boiling over with rage—which I was bracing for—she just blinked.

"Please—" I said, but she shot me a look, and I stammered.

"She's right," Judy said. "You should go."

Edith seemed puzzled.

I shook my head; I wasn't going to budge.

"Okay," she said and strode past Edith to Jackie's photo. From between the sprays of calla lilies, she snatched it up, the little girl's inscrutable expression flashing briefly, and brought it down on the corner of the table. Glass shattered, and with it, the full magnitude of her rage broke through. She gritted her teeth, and the sinewy contours of her forearms bulged. She slammed the fancy frame into the wood again, scoring the table and ripping the photo. Its leather back popped off and hit the floor with a clunk. She held it up again, perhaps to take a swipe at the lilies, but Edith grabbed her arm and wrenched it hard. Judy cried out and dropped the mangled frame.

Casting her extinguished butt aside, Edith knelt to pick up the torn and crumpled photo. She held it as if it were little Jackie herself. "How could you?" she murmured as she stood. "It's the only one I have. I'll never be able to replace it." Tears were streaming down her cheeks. "How could you be so, so vicious? How could you?"

Judy didn't respond. She'd made her point.

PHILIPPA, NOVEMBER 15, 1948

It's nearly 1:00 A.M., and I can't sleep. I've been up for over an hour. Exhausted, I went to bed early, and then at 11:30, I woke up with my heart pounding. Propped up at the foot of my bed, Mr. Fred glared back at me, his eyes glinting in the shadows. I didn't like it, so I grabbed him and squeezed him. My mother's locket slithered through his stuffing and strained against his faux fur, and I remembered Judy's question: "What's the worst thing you've done and never gotten in trouble for?" Considering everything we'd experienced, sewing the locket inside Fred seemed childish. I tossed him to the side and whipped back the coverlet.

I padded downstairs, working out the kinks in my stiff legs. Dad was still sitting at the kitchen table, paying bills.

"Nightmare?" he said, looking over his reading glasses. "You want to talk about it?"

"Not really."

"Are you okay?" he inquired, removing his glasses.

His shirt collar was unbuttoned, and his tie was off and slung over the back of his chair. His handsome face was grooved and weary, but softer. It was too late in the evening for his usual formality. Lately, I've been steering clear of him, but tonight he seemed relaxed, even open, and I needed someone to talk to. It was too terrifying to tell him what we'd witnessed, though.

My first instinct was to ask him to retell the story of how he met my mother, about their blind date mix-up, about how they hadn't liked each other at first, but later ended up bumping into each other at a cocktail party and hitting it off. About how, once they fell in love, it had been certain and clear, like the diamond on her engagement ring. About how the wedding was a rush job at Harpers Ferry, just immediate family, but lovely, on a crisp and bright spring day. But as soon as the thought popped into my head, I saw instead the shape of Miss Martins' face pressed against the underside of the wet sheet. An echo of my bad dream. Not a wedding veil, but a winding-cloth. The contours of her face contorted; it seemed like she wasn't so much dead as in the process of being formed out of a viscous white substance. I teetered, gripping the edge of a kitchen chair to steady myself. The sheet melted away, leaving a woman's face I'd never seen, a blurry composite of Miss Martins and my mother.

"Are you okay?" Dad asked, beginning to stand.

"Yeah," I said, waving the image away. "Just a bit tired, I guess. There's so much to think about, and now Mrs. Peabody and Judy are . . ." I said, regretting my choice of topic. "At odds."

"What happened?"

"The Peabodys were upset about Bogdan being released from custody, so when I got there, Mrs. Peabody lashed out . . . at me."

"She did?"

"And Judy got angry, *very* angry, and they had a quarrel—well, it was more than a quarrel."

"What happened?"

"I don't want you to get the wrong idea." I bit my lip.

"Tell me," he said, stern again.

"Judy smashed a photo of Jackie."

He raised his eyebrows. "Really?"

"You should've heard what Mrs. Peabody said to her. That they'd made a mistake in adopting her. It was so evil."

He shifted his weight back, the caning in his chair creaking, and said nothing.

I turned to the refrigerator and rummaged through it. I located the milk and a leftover piece of sweet potato pie. I poured the milk in a saucepan and began to heat it up. It was my childhood antidote for nightmares.

Breaking the silence, he said, "You need to take a big step back from them."

An angry lump rose in my throat, but instead of snapping at him, I said, "Judy needs me. Especially now."

"You're not helping them. The Peabodys need to work things out on their own, and you need to focus on school and being a normal teenager."

"What does that mean?" I said, allowing my temper to crest a little. "Is that something you aspire to be? A *normal* father? A *normal* lawyer? A *normal* husband?"

He winced. "I don't know," he said, shaking his head. "All I know is Judy is changing you, and not for the best."

A thin layer of skim had formed on the milk. An image of Miss Martins under her soaked shroud rose up again, and I quickly stirred the simmering liquid. I removed the saucepan from the burner and switched off the gas. "You've been listening to Sophie."

His eyes were steady, penetrating.

I tipped the saucepan, pouring the hot, frothy liquid into a celadon mug. I held it close to my lips and took in the rich odor of the milk. "I won't promise to stay away from her."

He looked like he might become cross. "The Peabodys are grieving." His expression loosened. "They thought their daughter's murderer was going to be locked up, and that hope was yanked out from under them. Grief can make anyone, even the most self-composed person, act out of character."

"Mrs. Peabody wasn't acting out of character."

"Maybe, but do you know her well enough to say?"

I sipped my milk, set it down, and slid the pie closer. After plucking a fork from the drying rack, I sank it into the dense filling.

"Are you going to offer me some?" he said and wiggled his eyebrows.

I scooped up a bite, held my hand under it, and delivered it to his mouth, smearing a little on his cheek, like he'd always done to me. He ate it and wiped his face with a napkin.

"Sit down," he said, nodding to the chair across from him. "I want to tell you something—something I should've told you before."

"Okay."

I picked up the piece of pie from the counter and came to the table.

"As you know," he began in a subdued tone, "your mother's death was a difficult time for me. The hardest in my life. Harder than the war. If it hadn't been for you, I'm not sure I would've made it out of my grief—or my guilt."

What did he mean by "guilt"? I wasn't sure I wanted to know.

"You see, having children for me was important, and your mother . . ." A thorn of some memory was digging into him. "Well, she didn't want children. Not at first, anyway. But I was young, and I couldn't understand that. It shocked me, and I was angry. I told her that not having children was odd, that people would talk. Eventually, she gave in, and you came along."

He scanned his checkbook and the stack of bills as if they were memories he couldn't quite piece together. I didn't know how to process this news—I still don't. It stings that my mother didn't want children, didn't want *me*. I existed because of *him*, because of his persistence. As I sat there pushing around the pie with my fork, I felt a shift in my heart, a step away from her, that impossible dream, and a step toward him, something sturdier, something real. I wanted to say something to him, but his expression was closed off, tangled, and he was struggling to form words. The lawyer! Then, instantly, I understood what he was trying to tell me. I said, "Do you blame yourself for her death?"

An intense tug of war played out on his face. I'd never seen him this way, so fraught, so vulnerable. It irritated me, then angered me, but my fury was brief. As I write this now, something else has bloomed in its ashes. What, though? Gratitude? For him? For his honesty? I don't know.

"You fixing milk like that," he said. "It reminds me of her. What she'd do when she was sleepless."

I stood, went to him, and gave him a sideways hug. I was glad that he'd told me about my mother, but I didn't want to linger too long. He felt prickly, electrified. What he told me drew me closer to him but also made him more foreign to me. He's no longer just my dad, but a flawed husband and a guilty lover. He let down his guard, but that's not always a good thing. No one wants to see their parents in their underwear.

He patted my forearm and whispered, "I don't want anything to happen to you. Promise me you'll stay away from Judy and her family."

I released him without a response.

JUDY, NOVEMBER 15, 1948

My room is a dead girl's tomb.

Sure, I'm here in bits and pieces. In the rickety stand below my record player, I sorted my singles and albums alphabetically: Debussy, Ellington, Fitzgerald, Parker, Piaf, and Satie, etc. Next to my bed, I sprouted a stack of novels, gradually growing like a literary stalagmite: *Lady Chatterley's Lover*, *A Puzzle for Fiends*, *Wuthering Heights*, *Miss Lonelyhearts*, *The Gemini Case*, *Nightmare Alley*, and *The Razor's Edge*. On the fireplace mantel, I displayed bric-a-brac from national monuments, souvenirs from beach vacations, and postcards of creepy portraits by Dalí, Magritte, and Modigliani. Much to Edith's dismay, I tacked sketches of bizarre art class still lifes and tracings of fashion ads from *Charm* and *Glamour* over my desk. Under the bed, wrapped in a dirty baby blanket, I hid my scrapbook, sliding it out late at night and pasting in personal keepsakes, newspaper clippings, drawings, and my thoughts.

But the room itself, with its fringe, molding, and girly colors, was designed as a backdrop for Jackie, and her presence is still stronger than mine. I'll always be an inferior substitute. The saccharine to the dead girl's sugar. The chicory to her coffee. The Sears catalog to her couture boutique. I'm glad—no, thrilled—that I destroyed her stupid fucking photo. I'm over the moon that Edith is now downstairs, sweeping up the glass. I hope she cuts herself.

Someone's at the door—

Bart just left, and I'm—I don't know what I am.

If it wasn't enough of a blow to discover that Miss M isn't my mother, any vestige of her, any glimmer of my silly fantasy has been ripped from me.

You see, I know the truth: I'm a big nothing, a zero girl. I'm from nothing and headed toward nothing.

When he opened the door, Bart braced himself as if he might need to duck. Did he really think I was going to hurl something at him? He stepped in and shut it behind him. His wide patterned tie was loose, his shirt was in need of ironing, and his blazer hung from his shoulders like a damp rag. He reeked of bourbon, but if his steady movements were proof of anything, he wasn't smashed. Perhaps he was just warming up. He smiled at me and wandered over to the window, took in the street below, and said, "I know you're angry."

"Wow, you're brilliant," I said.

"Your mother can be cruel."

"She's not my mother."

His gaze was unfocused, and his eyes were wet. Over the years, he'd been kinder to me than Edith had been—and more in touch with reality. After all, he was the one who popped Edith's balloon and sent her off to "convalesce." Since then, he has hovered beside her, becoming more see-through the more he drank. I couldn't hate him, but I didn't want to be around him. His self-loathing spread like a fog, engulfing whoever was nearby in its sour haze.

"I know she's not your mother," he said, "and I know she hasn't been a particularly good mother at times, but you've wanted for nothing." He pointed at the ceiling, the roof over my head.

"I'd rather live in a box than this mausoleum."

He moved a few paces toward me, inches from the edge of my bed. "Look," he said, "there's something I should tell you. Maybe I should've told you this before. Edith had a younger sister, a kid sister named Olive, who died during the 1916 polio epidemic in New York City. It was devastating for her, and shortly after, she went for a rest cure. Her trip to the Greenbrier after Jackie's death wasn't her first time. I know she comes across as confident, even overbearing, but she's fragile."

I glared at him: "Where did I come from?" I didn't want to hear about Auntie Olive, whoever that was, or Edith's crack-up.

"What do you mean? Crestwood?"

"I mean, who are my real parents? Who's my real mother?"

"We don't know. You were left at the—"

"No, you know. Who's Charlene Peters?"

He stood a little straighter and sighed. "You read more of those papers than I thought. Okay, she's your mother."

"Yes, but who *is* she?"

He studied me grimly. I expected to detect anger in his face or some feeble attempt to show authority, but instead, I saw pity. It's a terrible look, vicious and devastating. "I'm sorry," he said, "but she was a victim, you understand."

I scooted back an inch or two. I didn't understand.

"She was taken advantage of by a man and couldn't care for the child. She gave you up for adoption."

His curly brown hair lay flat on his head, glued down with oil, and his cheeks, pocked with evidence from his teenage blemishes, were pale and lifeless as a lunar landscape.

"What are you saying?" I glared at him in complete disbelief.

"She was, ah—"

"She was raped?" I hated that he made me finish his sentence.

"If you want to put it that way. Yes."

"And I'm the result?"

He stared at me, blankly. My thoughts were careening around the room. Why was he telling me this now? I wished Philippa were there. I really needed her.

"Edith doesn't—"

"Shut up," I snapped. I didn't want to hear his voice. It felt violent to me, invasive. "I'm a mistake that keeps getting in everyone's way." I stared at him, burning him with my eyes. "No wonder Edith treats me like I'm subhuman."

He dropped his head, but I couldn't tell if he actually felt bad or if it was put on.

"So," I said bitterly, "that's why you didn't want me digging in your papers."

He nodded but avoided eye contact.

"And you never met her?" I asked.

"It was all done through Crestwood."

The bald spot on the crown of his head was exposed, and I imagined splitting it like a sack of grain.

"Believe me. Our intentions were—"

"Get out." I didn't care what his intentions were.

"Judy."

"Get. Out."

He dropped his shoulders and lurched away. I imagined Philippa stepping forward and, strawberry curls swaying, hurling a question at Bart, startled by her own gall. So, before he reached the door, I channeled her and asked, "What's your relationship with Moira Closs?"

He let go of the doorknob. "We're friends."

"What kind of friends?"

"Old friends."

"Don't you think it's odd that two 'old friends' have children who die in similar ways?"

He lifted his eyes to meet mine. "It's horrible."

"What does she know?"

His limp expression sputtered to life. "Stay away from her, from all of the Closses. Promise me." Recently "Beware the Closses!" has become the mantra of everyone in my life.

"What does she know?" I repeated more heatedly.

Gloom hooded his face. He was loyal to her, to that bitch.

"Tell me."

He left silently, closing the door behind him with a muted click.

Feeling the full force of this news, I gasped, and hot tears welled up. I clutched my mouth and screamed into my palm. I caught the bedcover in my hands and wrung it, forcing my pain into it. I hated being lied to. I was glad Philippa wasn't there to see me like that, so blown over.

"There are three sisters," Miss M had told me, "Clotho spins the thread of life, Lachesis directs it, and Atropos cuts it. Gods and men submitted to them." I've been struck down by Atropos, and now I'm in Lachesis's grip. Where is my thread going to lead?

PHILIPPA, NOVEMBER 17, 1948

It's been two days, and Judy hasn't been to school. I've tried calling her several times, but nobody has picked up. So, despite Dad's and Quincy's warnings, I went to the Peabodys. Before I approached the front door, I lingered by the gate. The house's buttercream icing stucco, ornate Juliet balcony, and crown molding struck me as flimsy, like the recycled and jerry-rigged backdrop of a high school musical. I felt like I could give it a nudge, and the whole thing would topple over. I've become more sensitive to the fragility of facades.

I made my way to the door and knocked. No one answered, so I tried again, this time banging the brass knocker. It echoed through the house. I waited a little longer and turned away. I was almost at the gate when a voice behind me said, "Hello?"

I spun and saw Bart Peabody. He was leaning forward, steadying himself against the out-swung door, holding a glass decanter half-full of a caramel-colored liquid and an empty tumbler. "Philippa," he said, slurring his words. "How?—*What* are you doing here?"

"I'm returning a book," I said, lying. On my way out, I'd grabbed *Brideshead Revisited* from my shelf to serve as a cover for my visit. "Is Judy in?"

"No," he said. "Edith and—they're out getting their hair done."

Judy must've been forced into it. What a nightmare!

I held out the book as I neared him. He shrugged and said, "Don't have enough hands. Come in." His face was flushed, and his eyes were soft and unfocused.

Edith's calla lilies still dominated the table in the foyer, but instead of the ornate frame that Judy had destroyed, there was a smaller, more modest frame for Jackie. The marks on the table had been blotted out with stain. Edith wouldn't be daunted. Jackie was her religion.

"Drop the book there," he said, closing the door and lurching forward to recover his balance. It was 4:00 P.M., and he was three sheets to the wind.

I felt a little bad for him. I set the novel beside Jackie's photo and said, "Well, I should be going."

"What's it about?"

"The book?"

"What else?" he said, smiling. "Is it about second marriages? *Brides*head *Re*visited?"

"Huh?"

"Exciting stuff, I'm sure," he said with a chuckle. "Or maybe it's about returning to feminine purity." He snickered, then stopped himself, seeming to realize that what he'd said was inappropriate.

"My dad is expecting me," I said, stepping toward the door.

"Wait," he said, slipping between me and the exit. "I have no one to talk to. The girls, they're getting their dos done. Dos. Done. Donest. Ha!" His breath reeked of whiskey, and underneath it, I detected something sour, perhaps halitosis. The liquid in his decanter sloshed and, in a stray beam of sunlight, glistened like amber.

"I don't have much time. He's waiting—" I said.

"Shhh!" he said and waved his empty tumbler at me. "I know you're lying. You just want to run away from the sad drunk. Well, okay. I'll let you go." He stepped to the side. "The women come and go . . . come and go talking of Michelangelo. Isn't that from something?"

I smiled, but not warmly. He was putting me on edge.

"My poor little girl," he went on. "We should've been there for her, you know, but that's all over now." He raised his glass to his lips, found it empty, and frowned. "It's never over, is it? Never. Jackie and then Judy. Poor Judy. You know, she rose out of Jackie like a phoenix from the ashes. But this bird, the Judy-bird, she has burned feathers—and a terrible temper." He leaned in and poked my shoulder, the tumbler dangling between his thumb and pinky. His breath was unbearably ripe. "Did you know the fairy godmother brought us little baby Jackie—Judy, I mean. She wasn't a replacement. She was a *placement*." He continued, his voice lowering, "But fate, it laughs, and laughs hard." He swayed, his gaze falling on something behind me. "Judy was justified in smashing Jackie, although I wish she hadn't done a number on the table. To tell you the truth, I've wanted to smash her too. Many times." He smiled, but it quickly vanished. "Don't tell Edith. Oh, God, don't tell her." He belched and surprised himself. "Excuse me."

"I should go," I said, nodding toward the door.

"Fine," he said. "The girls come and go."

As I walked home, Bart's babble wormed its way in. He'd said that Judy was a placement, not a replacement. Whatever that meant. He'd also mentioned that a "fairy godmother" had brought her to them. Could that be Moira? I remembered what she told Judy: "I know you better than you know yourself." When I was eavesdropping on Bart and her while Judy was searching his study, he said to her, "You've been good to us." Perhaps there's something deeper between them, and that something is Judy. But why use the word "placement"? Had Judy been unwanted from the beginning? Were the Peabodys upholding part of a deal by taking her? That couldn't be the case. It didn't fit with Edith's obsession with her early on, all the daydreaming and the fake memories.

As I passed through Lincoln Park, I paused at the Emancipation Memorial and stared into Lincoln's shadowy bronze face. "I understand what being shackled is all about," Judy remarked the day I met her. And she's right; she does. She's bound to Jackie and to the mystery of her childhood. The Peabodys are also tethered to the dead girl, to her murder and her murderer. That's what Bart hates. Not Jackie, but the memory of her, like a rope tangled around his feet, keeping him from moving on. Maybe that's how my father feels, stuck between the death of my mother and me.

I wonder if he regrets pressuring her to have me. Does it ever hurt him to be with me, to look at me?

I wanted Lincoln to unfreeze and impart some wisdom. As I was about to tear my eyes away, I noticed something that I'd overlooked: The liberated slave is gripping the links to his own severed chain. Is he clutching them because he's newly in control of his destiny? Or is he squeezing them out of rage? After all, the manacles are still around his wrists, and he's still kneeling. "Have you really freed me?" his blank eyes seem to ask. "Or is this just another trick?"

CHAPTER EIGHT

We were avid cineastes. At first, we bonded over films we'd seen separately. Then, we began grabbing matinees together at the Penn or trekking down to the National Theatre for a double feature. Philippa was initially leery of crime dramas, refusing to admit her attraction to them. With Miss Martins's permission (by way of the Ray Kane novels) and Judy's enthusiasm for that species of film, she shrugged off her snobbery and sank into them, their shadowy cinematography, their twisty plots, their viciousness, their fatalism. So often, they were films about outsiders, and those outsiders—the luckless detectives, the hapless petty crooks, the cheaters, the swindlers, and of course, the femmes fatales—almost always were punished, such were the restrictions of the Hays Code.

But it didn't matter. We would fall in love with these characters, especially the femmes fatales, even when they were at their most despicable—Kathie Moffat in Out of the Past *or Kitty Collins in*

The Killers *or Nancy Fuller in* The Locket. *That wasn't by acci-dent. The directors crafted them to be loved, luxuriated in, and cast away. But we'd rewrite the endings. We'd un–Hays Code the plots. In our versions, these women would escape, reinvent themselves, and find financial independence. They would crossover from their respective storylines, meeting up in a tropical location, sipping dai-quiris and soaking their sore feet in a turquoise sea. We'd sentence the "good girls," the chaste love interests, always glittering and intangible on screen, to a truly horrible fate: they would wind up married and lonely, darning stockings and changing diapers.*

I don't think we understood these characters—or rather, we only understood their relationship to the world and the world's disap-proval of them. Still, we didn't understand their relationship to one another. They guarded and wielded their secrets. It was their source of power. In the original movies, it's often why they were punished or even killed. In our versions, it's how they leveraged the means for their escape. But a kept secret isolates you. These women had no hope of finding each other, no means of connecting. They would always be alone.

If only we'd understood that sooner.

❧

PHILIPPA, NOVEMBER 22, 1948

I can't sleep. I haven't been able to sleep since it all happened. Every moment flashes and spins like a kaleidoscope—or more like a collide-o-scope. I shift between panic and horror and grief and another more peculiar feeling—a sense of awe, I think. You see, it's not the violence or the nightmare that followed that surprised me; it's the strange beauty of keeping a secret about it. That's why I haven't slept. The secret burns too brightly. That's why I have to write all of this down. Once I do, I'll be able to dim the light and get some rest.

So, where do I begin?

Horsfield's, I guess. Quincy called the house and asked me to meet him for breakfast. He sounded distant, even a tad fatherly. With still no word from Judy, I was happy to meet up. I needed someone to talk to. When I arrived at the counter, Iris was telling him that she'd observed a dissection in the medical program at Howard: "I wasn't fazed by it. You wear a different hat, you know, and it's okay." She poured his coffee. "Like I do here—which is why I shouldn't be discussing dead bodies." She spotted me. "Looks like your date's here."

Quincy spun around wearing a somber expression. I slid onto the stool and ordered two eggs over easy, toast, and an orange juice. He'd already placed his order. For a few minutes, we chatted about the surprise twist in the presidential election, the birth of Prince Charles, the Redskins–Detroit Lions game at Griffith last weekend, and *Sorry, Wrong Number*, which Quincy had seen the night before. "Maybe if you watch more movies about crime, Phil, you'll feel less compelled to star in your own crime story."

I rolled my eyes.

He cleared his throat. "So, the Peabodys spoke with my boss, Paulson, and told him about the negative influence you're having on Judy, especially how you're encouraging her to pry into Jackie's and Cleve's cases."

"What! I couldn't influence Judy to eat eggs for breakfast."

He smiled and took a sip of coffee. "I know, but you can't deny that you're meddling. *Both* of you."

I lingered on our funhouse reflections in the chrome behind the counter. I missed Judy so much. She could think on her feet; she'd know what to say.

"Although he doesn't know the extent of it," he continued, "your father asked me to talk to you about your friendship with her. He thinks she's no good." I turned to him, and his dark eyes narrowed. "And, well, I agree."

I glared back, straight on and unblinking. "Everyone thinks that. The Peabodys. The Closses. Sophie. The kids at school. She's an easy target. Her hair, her clothes, her way—but she's not what you think. She's not playing at being rebellious. She just knows who she is."

"Maybe you're right," he said, retreating, "but it doesn't change that your interference has become an official police matter. You have to back off."

Iris arrived with OJ and silverware. I picked up the juice and drank it in big gulps. As I set it down, the thin napkin in my lap drifted to the floor. As I reached for it, my reflection in the chrome became sharp; all my twisted parts coalesced. It was a sign. I knew what I needed to do. I righted myself and said, "I know things that could be useful to the police—and to you."

He raised his eyebrows.

I told him about walking in on Halo Closs and Miss Martins, about our snooping at the marina, and about how we think Halo attempted to frame Bogdan with the yearbook. I touched on Moira's threatening us after the funeral and explained that Moira's connection to the Peabodys might have something to do with Judy's adoption. But I didn't mention Charlene Peters; I felt protective of Judy. Of course, I didn't tell him about finding Miss Martins's body. I didn't want to talk about it, and besides, it would've spooked him. "We're in danger, I know. I'm not stupid," I said. "But even if we back off, we'll still be in danger. Halo Closs is responsible for this. We know it."

When I said "we," I meant Judy. I still wasn't sure she was right. It didn't add up, and that bothered me. Yes, he was there. Yes, he had a motive. But how did he do it so fast? And why would he unframe Bogdan?

"Jesus, Phil," Quincy said, shaking his head, causing his dark bangs to fall across his forehead boyishly. "Maybe you're the one who should be the police officer."

"Maybe," I said and smiled.

Iris arrived with eggs and toast. "Here you go," she said and winked at me, which made me think of Miss Martins. Iris possessed that same self-respect, poise, and intelligence. It was amazing that she, a Negro woman, was in medical school. She wouldn't have to sling milkshakes and pie much longer. Emboldened by her fearlessness, I said to Quincy: "You understand why we can't leave it alone."

"You'll end up dead like your teacher and the Closs boy," he said. "You have to take it seriously."

I tilted my head. "Are you saying they died the same way?"

"Come on, Phil. I'm not telling you," he said gloomily.

"Most likely, Cleve was drowned," I said. "He had traces of Bon Ami in his lungs, right?"

"Yes."

"Could he have been drowned in a tub and later dumped in the river?"

He perked up. "That's a good theory."

So, both murders might have happened in bathtubs. AHKA connected them. Halo Closs connected them. What else? Who else?

As Quincy drank his coffee and started in on his food, I visualized Miss Martins's suite at the Daphne Arms: There were the two mugs, one clean and the other toppled and drained of cocoa or Ovaltine. There were the tangled contents of the jewel box. There was her stripped bed. There was the sheet draped over her body. There was Miss Martins, clothed, in the tub. Clothed. I played it backward and forward like a filmstrip, and as I did, I began to understand it: Miss Martins collapsed while she drank her cocoa. Drugged perhaps. Halo, or whoever it was, tore the sheet from her mattress so he could roll her body on it and slide it from the dayroom to the bathroom with ease. I'd learned this technique in first-aid training at school. We'd assumed the sheet was symbolic, but maybe it was practical. He then hoisted her into the tub, ran the water, and started to drown her, but she woke up.

Perhaps she hadn't consumed enough of the drug, or the water roused her, so in a panic, he took his tie off and strangled her to finish the job—except of course, he wasn't wearing *that* tie.

As I picked at my eggs, I remembered that Halo had kept the medicine bottle he purchased at the pharmacy before dumping his groceries and heading to Miss Martins's apartment. I looked at Quincy and asked, "Were both Cleve and Miss Martins poisoned *before* they were killed?"

He stopped midchew.

"Was it with Veronal?"

His eyes, blaring like megaphones, confirmed it.

"I knew it!"

"Settle down," he said, wiping his mouth. "Cleve consumed a large dose of it, enough to put him out for a long time, but it wasn't what killed him. The coroner thinks he drowned, but like I told you, it's difficult to determine. He hasn't confirmed Veronal for Christine Martins, but it's the same MO."

"She was strangled, right?" I blurted, then bit my lip. What was I thinking?! I didn't want him to know that I'd been at the crime scene.

"Why would you think that?"

I had to think fast, think like Judy: "Jackie was strangled, wasn't she? I just thought . . . "

"Your Miss Martins wasn't strangled. That's for sure. She probably drowned like Cleve." He frowned and stabbed his fork at an egg, yolk oozing out. "You got it out of me. Satisfied?"

My mind was galloping. So, Halo, or whoever, hadn't finished her off with the shamrock tie. Then, why was it there, around her neck?

"I'm going to tell your father everything. I have to." Quincy said, checking my face, bracing for my reaction.

"I know," I said, and thought to myself: That's why I have to act now.

❧

I gave the Peabodys' knocker three hard swings. Footsteps approached, and the door opened. Edith was herself again—hair set and sculpted, dress pristine, earrings dangling, and makeup like the glaze on a cake. Before I could ask for Judy, before I could lie that I'd come bearing homework, before I could try any angle at all, she said, "Go away."

"*Please*," I said, placing my foot across the threshold so she couldn't slam the door. "Let me talk to Judy. Just for a minute."

"We told the police about you," she said. "You're pressuring her into dangerous situations. You're a bad influence."

I smirked. I couldn't help it.

Edith lifted her chin. "She may be strange and sullen, but she's never been a troublemaker."

That was a one-eighty! I wanted to say: "What about Roy Barnes? Or the trick we'd played on Ramona and Mrs. Whitlow? Or our clash with Cleve?" Judy lived for trouble, and days ago, Edith would've agreed with me. I couldn't figure her out. Either she was lying and trying to scapegoat me, or it was too terrifying for her to believe that Judy would never be a suitable replacement for Jackie. Then, I had another thought, which was perhaps the most frightening of all: that Judy and Edith had made amends, that Judy had capitulated. After all, she went to the beauty parlor with her.

"You don't know her at all," I said, barely concealing my fury.

"I'll let Detective Paulson and your father know what you're up to," she said, advancing, closing in on me. I lost my footing and braced myself against the doorframe. Edith's face was near mine; her breath was cigarette-tinged, and white hairs on her upper lip were alert like little antennae. I swayed, still not having regained my balance. In a low growl, she said, "Do you know the pain you've caused?"

She gave me a little shove and slammed the door. The knocker bounced.

❧

JUDY, NOVEMBER 22, 1948

I was in my room, listening to Charlie Parker's "Chasin' the Bird," hoping the alto sax's muffled squeak would thread together my shifting thoughts, when I heard the front door knocker slamming.

I went to my window: it was Philippa, but I didn't move.

This week, I had spent an afternoon with Edith shopping, getting a trim, and eating ice cream. I'm not sure why I didn't kick and scream my way out of it. I was—*I am*—flattened by Bart's news about my origin story: child of a rape victim! It zapped my will, made me pliable. So, I played along, letting her drag me through Woody's and to the beauty parlor and lunch at the Occidental. I'll give it up to B and E; I punched hard by smashing Jackie's photo, but they punched back twice as hard. I should be furious, but I don't have the energy to be. I'm down for the count, I guess, and on the verge of being . . . what? Compliant? Ha! The odd thing, though, is that I didn't completely hate letting go. For an afternoon, I was a pleaser, their Jackie—or some idea of who their Jackie might've been. Occasionally, Edith would smile at me, and there was an authentic glimmer of affection in her eyes.

As I listened to her bitch at Philippa, I knew that she was doing it for me. Testing me. Had I actually changed? Was I Jackie now?—which of course, would mean rejecting Philippa. In a flash, I saw the allure of melting into Jackie's mold. It's insane, but right then, it seemed as if it might be like falling asleep. As I began to resist its draw, I felt a strange overwhelming sadness for Edith, that she'd do that to another human to feed her sorrow. But as I stood and shook it off, I couldn't be angry at her. It was too pathetic.

I wouldn't choose her. I would *never* choose her. I would choose Philippa every time. Besides, we had work to do. Both Cleve's and Miss M's killer was out there and, Philippa's doubts aside, Halo was our chief suspect. I couldn't let Edith cloud my focus.

PHILIPPA, NOVEMBER 22, 1948

I channeled PI Calvin McKey and decided to pursue the truth on my own. Really, I didn't have a choice. When Quincy alerted Dad, he'd ground me. I needed to ask the Closses questions and gauge their responses. Before going over, I swung by the house and, as a precaution, slipped one of Bonnie's steak knives into one of my coat's cavernous side pockets.

"Yes?" Elaine Closs said, opening the door as I climbed the steps. She must've spotted me on the sidewalk.

"Hello," I said, steadying my voice.

"You shouldn't be here." She was alert and dry-eyed. Her crisp mint green blouse was wrinkle-free, and the sharp pleats of her dark blue dress had been painstakingly ironed.

"Do you have a minute?" I asked, smiling. "Then I'll leave you alone. I promise."

As she considered my request, she tried to maintain a neutral expression, but the veins in her temples popped, and her facial muscles twitched like they were being plucked by an angry guitarist. At last, she sighed and said, "Well, I suppose you can come in for a few." She turned from the door, and over her shoulder, she said, "Would you like some refreshments? I'm famished." She always seemed ready for a snack. Perhaps her drug habit makes her perpetually hungry.

"No, I'm okay," I said, running my finger over the handle of the knife. "Be brave," I told myself. "Be brave."

"If you're here, you might as well," she said. "Have a seat in the parlor." She vanished down the hall.

I closed the front door behind me, leaving it unlocked. If I needed to, I wanted to be able to make a fast escape. In the parlor, I waited at the U-shaped window seat. The hazy pink glow that had filled the room before was gone. The red leaves that had filtered the light had fallen. However, the spray of cobweb-laced roses still moldered in the fireplace, the storm still threatened the rolling plains in the painting above the sofa, and the grandfather clock still menaced the room, its gears grinding seconds into dust. It was like the inside of a nightmarish snow globe. This place—it must have been horrible for Cleve. Maybe if I'd known him better, I could've helped him; I could've found a way past his anger.

China clattered in the kitchen, and I touched the handle of the knife again. It was becoming a talisman of my determination, of my nerve. I wondered if it was Elaine, not Halo, who had served Miss Martins the drugged cocoa. Could she have done something like that? But why? Or could Moira have done it? But again, why? Neither woman had a motivation for killing Cleve or Miss Martins, and of course, they didn't strangle and violate Jackie. Although his motive for murdering Miss Martins was convincing—he'd already attacked her once—Halo wouldn't have killed his own son, would he? He might've used Jackie's murder as an excuse to pin Cleve's death on Bogdan, but he had no reason to kill her, unless of course, as Judy thought, he was a crazed sexual pervert. Were there other suspects? Bart and Edith? After all, they were involved with the Closses somehow, but that was beyond me. Like the grim Victorian knickknacks scattered around the room, the clues to the murders—the water-related methods of dispatching victims; the cryptic inscription; the presence of Veronal in Cleve and, I supposed, Miss Martins; the damaged crescent moon pin; the damning yearbook; the shamrock tie around her neck—pointed toward something. But what?

Tearing me away from my thoughts, Elaine was suddenly hovering over me. She placed a tray on the table between us, on which she had arranged a small plate of petite muffins and gumdrop-topped Empire biscuits, a silver teapot, and two cups and saucers. After fussily adjusting herself on the cushion across from me, she poured tea for us, dropping a cookie on each of the saucers. "Do you take sugar or cream?" she said.

I held up my hand. "Neither. Thank you."

"Tea is better with plenty of cream, but suit yourself." She scooted a cup toward me, its side decorated with an intricately enameled blue jay. "Now," she said, depositing cream and a sugar cube in her own cup, "what did you want to ask me?"

I didn't know where to start. After an uncomfortable pause, I said, "You've heard about Christine Martins?"

"Yes," she said, her bottom lip trembling. "Awful. Just awful. The police are saying it's the same man who killed my . . ." She glanced down at her lap, plucked a stray hair or something from it, and brushed it clean. When she looked up, she said, "Why haven't you taken off your coat?"

"Oh," I said, "I wasn't planning on staying long." I wanted to keep my protection near me. "Did you know Miss Martins well?" I said.

After taking a sip of tea, she said, "As Cleveland's teacher. We've covered this territory before." A muscle trembled at the edge of her mouth. "She was some help to him, I believe. Lord knows, he wasn't good at his compositions. But you know that, too."

"You're good friends with the Peabodys, right?" I decided to steer clear of Cleve.

Elaine seemed confused. "No, we don't know them. Not really. We only recently met because of the similarities between Cleve's and Jackie's deaths. We have too much in common now."

"But Cleve's grandmother knows them well. At least, I thought . . . "

"They know each other socially, but not well, not close friends." Her eyes sharpened. "How did you get that impression?"

I didn't believe her. She wasn't a good liar.

"Why aren't you drinking your tea?" she said. "It'll get cold."

I studied the steaming amber liquid. It had come from the same pot as Elaine's, but still. The cup could've been laced with poison before she added the tea. I had to make a move, or she would become suspicious. I lifted the dainty china to my lips, sticking out my pinky to maximize control, and pretended to sip, a tactic I could only use once or twice.

"You and Judy Peabody are fast friends," Elaine said. "Yes?"

"That's right," I said, settling my cup back in its saucer.

"The way you are together," she said. "So alive and full of energy. You can tell. Just a pair. Like sisters."

"We are, I guess."

Elaine smiled, her eyes glinted. "That's wonderful. Sisters—of blood or in spirit—can be a beautiful thing. A perfect thing." Without warning, a pall dropped over her features. She leaned toward me and, in an empty, toneless voice, said, "Be a good sister. Don't keep secrets from her. They spread like a disease. They eat you up from the inside."

Her eyes darted up, her jaw fell open, and blood drained from her cheeks. A shadow shifted on the carpet, and I whipped around and gasped. Halo was charging toward us, his muscular arm driving down. He yelled something unintelligible and slammed his fist into the table, sending the teapot, cups, sugar, cream, platter, and edibles to the floor with a crash. I cried out, and Elaine yelped like a wild animal, shot to her feet, and gripped her chest as if to keep her heart from popping out. I sprung up, tripped over the bottom edge of the window seat's molding, and hit the carpet hard, smashing a saucer and several cookies. Ignoring the pain, I rolled over, sat up, and scooted frantically away, my back colliding with the wall. I snatched the knife from my pocket and held it in front of me with both hands.

Halo spun again, his handsome, thuggish face scrawled with panic. As I slid up the wall, he stepped toward me, arms open, palms out, chest heaving. His red and white polka-dotted tie swayed like a pendulum. The pinup girl from the tie around Miss Martins's neck flashed in my mind, and I thought, "Why'd he leave it behind? Why do that?" It didn't matter. The monster was closing in.

"What *is* this?" he gasped, spittle showering me. "What are you doing here?"

"Having tea," Elaine whimpered from the corner, her eyes darting back and forth in a frenzy.

"Shut up!" he said over his shoulder.

"Stay away!" I screamed, the knife zigzagging in front of me. My confidence was shot. Some Calvin McKey I'd make.

He took a step toward me. "Why are you here?" he asked again, his voice dropping a register. "You shouldn't be here." His eyes were wet and startlingly bright.

"Howard, please," Elaine muttered.

"Back off!" I said, jabbing the knife at the space between us.

He edged closer. Seven feet. Six and a half feet. His square-jawed face was waxy and coated with a sheen of sweat. A sour boozy odor seeped from his pores. Feeling helpless, I continued to flick the blade at the air in front of him. He put his hands up but crept closer. Six feet. Five feet. Four and a half feet. He was near enough to lunge and wrap his big hands around my throat. "Give me the knife," he said, gesturing to me. "You don't want to hurt me." Sure, I thought. Suddenly, he took a swipe at my outstretched arms, trying to catch me by the wrists. I ducked and thrust the blade at him, striking his left thigh. The tip penetrated his wool trousers. He cried, "Damn!" and pulled away, and the knife fell to the floor.

Then, as if the house had cracked open and had begun to cave in, the massive grandfather clock to my left heaved forward. Its chimes clashed loudly, chaotically, and its weights struck the inside of its walnut casing. Time seemed to be folding in on itself. Only feet away, Halo sprang into action and caught it, his knees straining under the weight. He struggled with its top-heavy bulk, grunting through his teeth. "Jesus!" he moaned, "Help me!" But as soon as he uttered it, he lost his grip, and time sped up: The clock hit a wingback chair hard, gonged, splintered, and tumbled to the floor, a heap of broken panels, glass shards, dials, and gears.

Elaine palmed the sides of her head as if the noise were melting her brain. That's when I saw Judy, the author of the mayhem. "Come on!" she shouted. I glanced at Halo, who was applying pressure to his wound and breathing hoarsely. Everything was blurry and about to go sideways. I didn't want to pass out. "Come on!" she yelled again. "What are you waiting for?"

But I couldn't steady myself. The floor was bending away from me, and the ceiling was folding down over us. I took a step and nearly collapsed. Judy seized my hand and tugged me, stumbling, out the door.

JUDY, NOVEMBER 22, 1948

When I heard the commotion downstairs—a thump, breaking glass, a cry—I snapped Charlene Peters's journal closed. A man's voice, Halo's voice, bellowed, "What is this? What are you doing here?" I shoved the book into my coat, filing away a sentence or two, unable to process the rest. I rushed out of Cleve's room and to the top of the stairs, which minutes before, I'd crept up.

After Philippa's confrontation with Edith, I'd followed her, suspecting that she was headed to the Closses'. I didn't want her to go alone. I was a block away when I watched her follow Elaine inside. "Jesus Christ," I thought, "she can't be serious!" When I approached the door, I was surprised to find it sprung from its latch. When I nudged it open, Elaine was walking down the hall to the back of the house, away from the parlor where, most likely, Philippa was waiting. No one else was in sight. My first impulse was to join Philippa, but I didn't want to cause a scene and miss my chance to snoop upstairs. The opportunity wouldn't present itself again.

After popping into a bathroom and a guest bedroom, I located Cleve's room at the end of the hall. The off-white walls were hung with boring seascapes and an architectural sketch of a Capitol City Hardware building. In an old bookcase, he'd stacked textbooks, adventure novels, and back issues of *Boys' Life*. His baby blue bedspread was tucked in at the sides; a quarter would've bounced on its surface. His large dresser, which reeked of furniture polish, was free of knickknacks, other than a blurry photo of him on *The Crawdad Express*, smiling, holding a fish. I rummaged through the dresser, which was full of fastidiously folded clothes. I peeked in his closet, which also was spookily neat. Everything felt tidied up, scoured. As I turned from the closet, I spotted his red backpack under the edge of the bed. It was *always* with him. I remember him swinging it at me from his bike like a flail. The clash still stings a bit—and I still don't understand why he was so furious.

I unbuckled its flap and searched inside. Unlike his room—but much like his desk at school—its contents were a jumble of loose papers, pencils, notebooks, and even a broken compass. At its bottom, dusty with pencil shavings, was the reddish-brown journal he'd had out on his desk the day Miss M ordered him out of class. I opened it. Written on the inside flap was "Charlene Peters: 1928 to ____" in neat handwriting that reminded me of my own. What the hell was Cleve doing with my birth mother's diary? What's the connection? I couldn't make sense of it, but I knew it was significant. I let a few pages fall through my fingers, stopping on a random page dated February 21, 1929, and a name jumped off the page: Halo Closs.

PHILIPPA, NOVEMBER 22, 1948

Halo roared after us: "Stop, damn it! Just stop!" We glanced back. He was on the stoop, blood blooming across his pant leg. I steadied myself against Judy, still woozy. "We've got to go," Judy said in my ear. "Can you move? Can you run? You've got to." I wanted to throw up, my stomach was somersaulting, but a voice clicked on in my head: "Don't be a weakling. Be brave. Go!" As Halo started toward us, Judy tugged on me again, and the sidewalk lurched and began sliding underneath us. Somehow my feet were carrying me forward.

Undaunted, Halo pursued us, his leg slowing him only slightly. The sky was strewn with fast-moving rain clouds, and a breeze blew at our backs.

We dashed by pedestrians on A Street and bolted in front of traffic on 8th. Cars blared their horns. We flew past Eastern Market, North Carolina Avenue Methodist Church, and the Carolina Theater. We hurtled ourselves across two busy lanes on East Capitol, coming close to being clipped by a streetcar. Pedestrians barked, "Watch it! What's the idea! Stupid fucking kids!"

We were about to cross to Tennessee Avenue when Judy stopped. She put her hands on her knees and caught her breath. "We have to split up," she said. "You go down Twelfth and lead him up the fire escape to the top of Hill Estates. I'll go around the other way."

"What?!"

"And use the plank. It's important."

Judy glanced over my shoulder. "Wait here, let him see you, then do what I said."

"No! Why would we do something like that? It's crazy."

"So we have the upper hand."

"I'm not doing it. No way."

Judy touched the side of my arm and locked eyes with me. "You stuck a knife in his leg," she said, still breathing hard. "You can do this."

I pulled away. "We need to find a safe place to hide, not lure him to us!"

"We have to end this," she said. "Do it for me." She took off before I could hold on to her, before I could demand that we think it through. We needed to step back from the chaos and construct a reasonable plan. Halo spotted me from the edge of the park. I couldn't believe what Judy was asking me to do, but what choice did I have? I had to go.

When I reached the fire escape, I jerked down the counterweighted ladder. It groaned and hit the ground with a clang. Thirty yards away, Halo appeared and began stumbling through the rear access alley toward me. His large frame lurched forward, as hulking and disheveled as Frankenstein's monster. With his adrenaline up, he would rip me in two if he caught me. I focused on the iron rungs and started climbing. The sky had darkened to a slate gray, and the breeze had stirred into a wind. Droplets of cold rain pecked at my cheeks. The flaky metal bit into my palms, but I ignored it. I had to make it to Hill Estates for Judy's sake, for both of us. As I ascended through the shaky, noisy, labyrinthine structure, I chanted to myself: "Be brave, Phil. Be brave."

When I emerged onto the roof's open expanse, the wind whipped through my hair, tossing startling spurts of rain in my face. Halo was at the bottom of the second story. Climbing the ladder with a wounded leg had slowed him, but he was undaunted, his muscular arms hoisting his body up with ease. He kept calling out: "Talk to me! Judy? Philippa? Stop running away!" I thought of my tarot reading, especially the Devil card. Here he was, Halo Closs, the Devil himself, the cat-faced creature with twisted horns, leathery wings, and vulture's claws, crawling through metal bars toward me. What was the word Sophie used? Depraved. He was a depraved man, a vampire, draining the life out of everyone he knew.

I bolted toward Hill Estates, dodging the chimneys, lightning rods, towering furnace vents, and almost jumped to the other building. It would've been my first trans-alley leap. But my fear of thwarting Judy's plan—not to mention being unable to make the jump—stopped me. I hastily dragged the plank to the raised edge of the roof and slid the bridge over the gap. The board was eight inches wide and an inch thick and not usually much of a challenge to navigate, but I'd never crossed it in the wind and rain—nor under so much stress. I didn't want Halo to catch up to me while I was on it, but I also didn't want to hurry and stumble. So, I advanced cautiously, stiffly, all the while terrified I wasn't moving fast enough. I had the urge to glance over my shoulder, but I was afraid it would shift my weight, and I'd lose my balance. My nerves buzzed, and the plank seemed made of rubber under my feet. A burst of wind slapped me with the pungent odor of garbage, and a glass bottle clattered below. Out of the corner of my eye, I glimpsed a stray cat flit between trash cans and vanish under a dingy awning.

I reached the end of the board, hopped off, and spun. Halo was ten feet or so from the opposite edge. "Philippa," he said, "I just want to talk!" I didn't believe him, not for a second. He hobbled forward, his shoulders rising and falling as he gulped air. His hair was damp with rain and sweat, and his left pant leg was soaked with blood.

Behind him, four roofs away, Judy had just popped up from the fire escape.

"You don't understand," he said breathlessly.

"Don't come any closer," I said, taking a step back.

"You're always running away," he said, as he stepped up and balanced on the board. It creaked and bowed with his weight. "I'm not going to hurt you or Judy."

I didn't know what to do. Every muscle in my body was drawn tight, my throat was bone dry, and blood whooshed in my ears. If he made it to Hill Estates, I'd be trapped. I'd be done for.

He took his first step and peered down, scowling.

Judy was three roofs away.

Frantically, I glanced around, hoping a solution would present itself. Nothing. Doing the only thing I could do, I lifted my knee and rested the sole of my scuffed-up Mary Jane on the end of the plank.

"What, what are you doing?" he stammered, and his face, which I could see clearly now, startled me. Its handsomeness was masklike, concealing something darker, unfathomable. What I'd taken for rage earlier now seemed like pain or confusion or even sadness.

Still, I feared him, so I ground my sole against the rough edge of the plank. Bits of wood splintered off. "Don't come any closer."

He stepped forward again, now in the middle of the bridge. The rain had flattened his thick blond hair and trailed through his chiseled features.

Judy was two roofs away.

He held out his arms like a tightrope walker. His muscular, top-heavy frame wasn't to his advantage. He wavered, then steadied himself. The board bowed even deeper, a slight parabola. Stained with rain and sweat, his tie drooped crookedly from his neck, a doe-eyed pinup probably lurking on its flip side.

He took another step, his legs wobbly. I didn't know what to do. Tension thrummed in my abdomen, along my thigh, in my calf, and in the arch of my foot. Why wasn't he listening to me? As much as I was afraid of him, I was afraid for him, too. I wanted to scream: "Go back! Turn around!"

Judy was a roof away, lithe and intense, like a greyhound charging the finish line.

Cleve's wounded and furious face rose up in my mind, followed by Jackie's broken picture and Edith's tears and Miss Martins's bathtub tomb and Halo's thrusting buttocks. Under the pressure of the images, a staccato of questions burst from me: "Why did you kill Cleve? And Jackie? And why—" The words caught in my throat. "Why did you rape and kill Christine Martins?"

His silvery blue gaze retreated. "I didn't kill any of them—and I'd never hurt Christine that way," he said, his face draining of anger. "I loved her. I'm chasing you and Judy because I need to know what to believe." His eyes flickered with anguish. "I want to know if she's my daughter."

"Your daughter?" I said, dumbstruck.

"I think, I think so."

Judy was nearly there.

"And her mother?" I asked. "Miss Martins?"

He nodded, sorrow working the muscles in his jaw.

My stomach twisted, churning its contents.

Miss Martins's slender arm appeared in my mind's eye, reaching out to me, her palm cupping the light from her bedside lamp—but that wasn't what she was doing, was it? She hadn't been asking for my help; she hadn't been beckoning to me. She didn't want him off of her. They were in love, and I was a blundering intruder, a stupid schoolgirl returning a book!

Judy was there, her foot slamming into the other end of the bridge. The board vibrated under my shoe, and Halo's eyes flipped like shiny quarters.

His mouth gaped.

His arms shot out.

His knees broke.

Like a great dying bird, he flapped and screamed and pivoted away from me, the weight of his shoulders drawing him over—then, pure noise, white and terrible, inside and out.

He hit the alley with a dull cracking thud.

The board pursued him with a punctuated *thunk*, followed by the din of trash can lids.

Judy yelled at me: "Philippa! Come on! Wake up!" She was hopping up and down and waving her arms. I wasn't sure what I was waking up from, but I shook my head to get the blood flowing. "You've got to hurry!" she said. "We don't know who heard that." I staggered over to the crumbling chimney, where she hid her cigarettes, and slouched against it. "Philippa," she said, keeping her voice low, "you have to run and jump." She was right. There was no other way down. My head spun, and I dropped to my knees and fell forward, bracing myself.

I didn't know what to do. I was in no state to make the jump. With a bit more urging, I found my feet and walked cautiously to the edge. The rain was coming down harder, soaking everything. I peered over, and in the dim alley, I saw Halo's mangled body and the plank at an angle next to him. He lay face up, legs parted and knees bent, one arm twisted underneath him, one arm outstretched. His tie was flipped up over his face absurdly, its blank interior covering part of his horrible expression. I stepped back. "I can't do this."

"You have to. It's not hard. I do it all the time."

I stared at her: Now shorter, Judy's black bob was slick against her bony head. Edith hadn't been able to force a new hairdo on her. Her loose button-up sweater hung wide from her shoulders. Her saturated camisole drooped away from her neck, exposing her clavicle and a slender pink bra strap. She was so beautiful and mad, so terribly mad. Why hadn't I seen it before? I searched her eyes for recognition of what she'd just done, for a trace of remorse, but I only detected a heightened, feverish focus. I wanted to reach across the chasm and shake her and kiss her and shake her again.

"Come on, Philippa!" she said. "Just run and, about a foot away from the edge, jump. You'll make it."

I bent down and unfastened the straps on my Mary Janes, slid them off, and tossed them to the other roof. I backed away about twenty feet, took a deep breath, and sprinted. Every instinct told me to abort, to go back, to think it through, to recalibrate, but with the rain lashing my face, I rushed past the doubt, launched into the air, flew over the gap as if I'd grown wings, and landed on my feet, stumbling only a little.

Before I could fully recover, Judy threw my shoes to me and said, "We need to make sure he's dead."

I followed her down the fire escape in bare feet, the rusting metal tearing at my soft soles. A tetanus nightmare. At the bottom, I insisted that Judy stop, so I could put on my shoes. She frowned, glanced around nervously, and said, "Wait here." I watched as she disappeared around the corner and into the alley beside Hill Estates.

The rain was coming down in waves now, so I sheltered behind a dumpster situated under an overhang. I brushed off my feet, rubbed my arches, and strapped on my shoes. After a minute or two, Judy reappeared. She was walking briskly, but not in a panic. I flagged her down, and as she neared me, she said, "I know what we're going to tell the police. I've worked it out."

I'm fairly sure that Judy didn't overhear Halo's revelation. She seemed too focused and too unaffected. Of course, she can be frustratingly unreadable; she's made an art of it. She's hot and then cold, leaning in for a kiss one day and shoving you away the next. You never know where you stand, or if she even still wants you around. One thing is clear, though. She was crushed when she discovered her birth mother wasn't Miss Martins. If Halo knew the truth, if he were her father and Miss Martins, not the Peters woman, were her mother, the irony would be stark, a dagger in her heart.

I haven't decided to tell her that secret, or if it's even the right thing to do.

Before we alerted the police, we worked out the details of our story. It wasn't difficult. After all, most of it was true. Detective Paulson, a handsome, soft-spoken man about Dad's age, and the slim, somewhat effeminate Detective Kipps, the lead investigator on Cleve's and Miss Martins's cases, questioned us in separate rooms at the Peabodys' for over two hours. I repeated everything that I'd told Quincy (who, it surprised me, wasn't there) and then I told them something that I'd withheld—that we had followed Halo to the Daphne Arms, that he had bribed the desk clerk, and that shortly after that, we found the body. Paulson and Kipps blinked calmly at this news but said nothing.

When Paulson asked me why I went to the Closses', I explained that I wanted to confront Halo. I knew he was Miss Martins's attacker and suspected that he might have murdered her, Cleve, and even Jackie. "It was foolish," I said, "but I wanted to prove he was the one—or disprove it. If he was, I wanted justice for Miss Martins and the others." Judy had advised me to say the last part.

I told them that Halo had barged in and attacked Elaine and me while we were chatting, and Judy had come to my rescue. Before the police arrived, Judy had told me that, when she heard the commotion, she'd leapt into action, rushed downstairs, and kicked a shim out from under the clock, destabilizing it. Using the wall for leverage, she'd tilted the bulky piece of furniture in Halo's direction. I described how Halo chased us to the top of Hill Estates and, in attempting to cross on the plank, fell. "The board could hold us," I said, "but not a man like him."

After I'd run through the story three times, Detective Kipps asked me *why* Closs was chasing us. In my mind, Halo's face warped from earnestness to horror and back again, looping like a filmstrip. I wasn't sure how to answer Kipps's question, even for myself. Had he been telling the truth about his relationship to Miss Martins? About who Judy was? Perhaps, but what difference did it make? He was dead. I could still feel the sensation of the plank trembling under my shoe, and my sole biting into the wood. Maybe he had been trying to find a way to explain himself to us, even if his attempts were blundering. Or perhaps he did want to shut us up or even kill us. What mattered now was protecting Judy, so I lied to Kipps: "I saw him attacking Miss Martins in her old apartment, forcing himself on her. He was a sex pervert, one of those maniacs who enjoy that sort of thing. He was going to kill us. I'm sure of it." This seemed to satisfy them, but it made me uneasy; it felt like a line from a B movie. If they asked Judy, she'd tell them the same thing, but she'd come closer to actually believing it.

Dad and Bonnie, who sat with me while I was questioned, ushered me from the house under a large, rain-pelted umbrella to the Chrysler. During the short drive home, neither Bonnie nor Dad spoke, but I knew what was coming: They would insist I end my friendship with Judy and stay away from the Peabodys. It would be a firm, absolute statement uttered by Dad with Bonnie hovering over his shoulder, poised to swoop in and offer a sympathetic smile and a plate of cookies.

The drum of the windshield wipers soothed me, and the knot in my stomach began to release. Exhaustion rolled through me, and I closed my eyes. Would I tell Judy about Halo's last words? I wondered. What if I didn't? God, what if I didn't want to? After all, Judy kept things from me. She orchestrated little manipulations here and there. Most of all, she concealed her feelings from me—and was still holding back. No, I won't share my secret. Not yet.

When we pulled up, someone in a gray raincoat was standing on our stoop. As I scooted across the damp seat and into the downpour, I saw who it was: Quincy. His shoulders were forward and low, and he wasn't covering himself from the weather. Without asking, I knew that something terrible had happened. Dad tried to hold his umbrella over me, but I ran out ahead of him. My cousin's face, as always, betrayed his feelings: Sophie was dead.

CHAPTER NINE

*I'm sure you're wondering: Well, now what? The villain has been
vanquished (maybe), and Judy's true parentage has been revealed.
But look at all those pages. Please tell me that it's not just one long
denouement!*

*Of course not. Philippa and Judy, the white hat and the black bob,
have secrets, and secrets, as I explained, are a girl's best friend . . .
and worst enemy.*

*Halo's fall bonded us—a secret we shared—but Judy wasn't ready
to tell Philippa about Charlene's journal, about what she'd gleaned
from that random page, and Philippa, well, she liked having a secret
of her own. It's hard to blame her.*

*You're probably getting frustrated with me. I understand, I do.
We're over three-quarters of the way through this memoir, this diary
collage, this true-crime exposé, this novel, this . . . whatever you
want to call it, and I still haven't told you who I am.*

The truth is that, after all these years, it doesn't matter.

But I get it. You want to know. Soon. I promise.

Until then, I want you to reflect on something: What is it like to be lied to? To be on the outside of a secret, peeping over the edge of a window on your tiptoes, wondering at the darkness? Is it dangerous? Maybe. Is it hurtful? Sometimes. Is it entertaining? Hmm. Does it matter?

That I'll answer unequivocally: Yes, it always matters.

I wonder if you agree.

JUDY, NOVEMBER 22, 1948

After the police left, we gathered in the kitchen. For a long time, we were silent, and rain splattered against the windows. Edith began chopping carrots and onions for dinner, and Bart sipped his brandy and stared into space. The news that Halo Closs had raped and killed Miss M and, most likely, committed the other crimes, especially Jackie's murder, was settling in. For Bart, it might be hard to swallow. If I read his body language right the other day, he's closer to Moira than he lets on, perhaps she's even an old flame. And Edith, she'd been so focused on Bogdan, so righteously convinced of his guilt, that I know she's a wreck. To have bet so much on the wrong horse is humiliating.

"We should go away," Bart said, swirling his glass. "We'll go somewhere warm for the holidays."

Edith turned from her preparations, lay down her knife, and walked behind him, resting a hand on his shoulder. Her eyes were distant but not unkind. "That's a wonderful idea," she said with little enthusiasm. "We could go to Miami."

"No," he said, perking up. "A tour of the Caribbean. Do it up right?"

Edith smiled. "And then, after the New Year, Judy will go to boarding school."

I glared at her, and she looked away, saying, "I should finish this stew. We all need something hearty to eat."

"Don't send me away," I said, pleading to Edith's back and then to Bart, who sat across from me at the breakfast table. A flash of life without Philippa shot through me. As ridiculous as it sounds, until that second, I didn't believe we'd be separated. "You have Jackie's killer," I said, my voice emitting a frantic squeak. "There's space here for me now."

Bart stared at his snifter. "I know it seems harsh, but it's not a punishment. It's for your own good."

Philippa is the only person who understands me. The *only* one! I respect Iris, of course, but Philippa and I, we're meant to be together, two halves of the same heart, two heads of the same monster. Sure, on the surface we're different, but underneath we're the same. We can't be pulled apart. It would be fatal surgery. Neither of us would survive—and why should we be separated? It's Moira's nasty scheming, and B and E's morose blundering. Heat rose through me, and I blasted back at them: "First, you tell me that my mother—my real mother—was raped and that I was, I was the . . ." I grabbed the sides of the table. "And now you're fucking abandoning me."

Bart turned his chin up and sniffed. I was getting to him. "Look," he said, "it's just for a semester. You'll be an adult next September. You'll be free to do whatever you want. You can find a fine young man. Go to college. You can make a life for yourself. We'll support you financially, but you can't stay here. We can't have it, either of us. I'm sorry."

"That bitch Moira. This is her idea!" I remembered her telling Bart that I needed "an environment that encourages structure and discipline." "Why in the hell would you listen to her after everything that's happened?" I said, nearly boiling over.

Edith stepped forward and forced a smile. "Moira has been good to us. She didn't know what her son was capable of. We can't punish her for her son's evil deeds, can we?"

I couldn't believe what I was hearing, then a lightbulb went on. I finally understood something about B and E. Because Bogdan worked with his hands, because he was a boat mechanic, he was an acceptable choice for the role of super-evil murderous sexual pervert. This new revelation threw a wrench in their bone-deep snobbery. "Yes, okay, fine." I imagined them telling themselves. "Halo was bad but surely he was an exception to the rule. One bad seed."

"Besides," Bart said, "Moira has been so helpful. She's used her connections in the local government and the police to keep Jackie's case alive. She didn't know, she couldn't know, that she was working to uncover the truth about her son. And now, although I wish it hadn't happened this way—and hadn't happened to you and Philippa—her son is dead. She's devastated, and for us, this chapter is closing."

B and E's bizarre defense of Moira chilled me, but I didn't have the energy to fight them, so I hung my head and studied the scars on my arms. I needed to see Philippa, to lay out all the pieces, to make a plan, to be near her. That's when I first thought of it as a possibility: Could Halo be my father?

At that point, I'd only had a brief glance at Charlene's journal. In an entry from 1929, I'd read these lines: "I met this handsome fellow—Howard 'Halo' Closs—and we hit it off. He's tall and wide-shouldered and charming. He's the center of his social circle—not my usual type, but that made it even more exciting." Because I jumped to Philippa's rescue, I didn't have time to read more, and there hadn't been time since.

As I sat across from Bart, I thought it over: If Charlene and Halo had met in 1929, then I could be their daughter. The timeline worked. Perhaps he was her rapist, and she, his victim. Or perhaps that was a big lie, too. Maybe they were lovers, not victim and villain. In my rush to protect Philippa from Halo's thrashing, I hadn't stopped to consider whether or not he was "our man." In the moment, his behavior seemed to prove his guilt.

I ran my fingers over my scars. The questions Philippa had pelted at me after we discovered Miss M rose up, as if summoned by my gesture: Why would Halo unframe Bogdan? Why would he do something so damning to himself? I didn't know, and she was right: the shamrock tie didn't make sense. If the crime was committed impulsively, a reaction to something the goons in the gray suits told him, wouldn't he have used his own tie or, hell, his hands? He was strong enough. For that matter, what did the scarecrow and penguin tell him? How were they involved?

I rolled back through the scene at Daphne Arms: Miss M submerged and shrouded, AHKA written in lipstick, and the pinup tie around her neck. The arch of the recessed bathtub resembled a miniature proscenium stage, and we were the audience. It was designed to free Bogdan and implicate Halo. But designed by whom?

I lifted my chin and studied the side of Bart's face, his botchy skin, the acne pockmarks. He seemed unwilling to look at me. Perhaps he was ashamed. What was the nature of his "friendship" with Moira? At the reception, Moira had told me that what Miss M had done to her family far outweighed what Halo had done to Miss M. So, what had she done?

As the questions whirled through my head, I knew that I needed answers. "I'm not hungry," I said and stood.

Bart didn't respond. Edith kept chopping.

During my mad dash to the roof to stop Halo, I'd wedged Charlene's journal behind the bathtub before climbing out the window. It was time to read it.

PHILIPPA, NOVEMBER 24, 1948

The past few days have floated by at a distance. Sophie's funeral and her graveside service at Harper Cemetery were tasteful, a credit to Dad's and Sarah Yolland's quick planning, but they seemed to have little to do with Sophie. But no ceremony or speech or song would've been good enough. I am too shattered. When Quincy first told me that she had collapsed and tumbled down a flight of stairs, I flopped into his arms. It was a physical reaction—a sudden contortion of my internal organs, my breaking point.

I've regained my cool now. Well, mostly. The grief still comes in waves, but the thickest gloom has lifted. Tomorrow is Thanksgiving, and out-of-town family are congregating for a big meal. This evening, though, the house was quiet.

After an early dinner, I found Quincy building a fire in the living room. For a while, we sat on Sophie's creaky antique sofa and watched the flames crackle as dusk fell. In the semidark of the room, Quincy's face appeared dim and closed off in the firelight, but no less handsome. He held a tumbler, which every few minutes, he would agitate and drink.

"May I have some of that?" I said.

He looked at me incredulously and smiled. "Okay," he said, "but it's whiskey. You're not going to like it."

When I sipped it, I winced, but it was better than Judy's nasty gin. It warmed my throat and chest and eased the tension in my neck.

"Did you know Mom wanted me to have children?" he said. "Lots of them. She wanted grandchildren to spoil."

There was a heavy pause while I studied the shadows playing across my aunt's antique bric-a-brac. I didn't want to talk about her. I didn't want to fall apart again.

"I'd like to be a father, you know," he added. "I'm suited for it."

"Do you have a girlfriend?"

"No. Not exactly."

"What does 'not exactly' mean?" I said.

He smirked.

"Hmm," I said. "I hope she's a nice girl, someone I'll get along with."
When I was little, I thought I'd be jealous of Quincy's first serious sweet-
heart. Other than Dad, he's the most important man in my life, and in every
way, he's the sort of man I *should* marry. But I have no desire to marry or
have children or bake cakes or whatever wives and mothers are supposed
to do. I want to be a teacher like Miss Martins, or maybe a writer like
Ray Kane. And I don't want to spend time with anyone other than Judy.
Through this entire ordeal, she has fluttered in my periphery. I wonder what
she's doing. Is she thinking of me?

He raised his eyebrows. "Do I need your approval?"

"Of course!" I said and held my hand out for his whiskey. He gave it to
me, and I took an aggressive swallow.

"Easy does it," he said, laughing.

The burn hit my stomach and spread through me. I let it sink in, my eyes
tearing. Then I asked, "Have you heard anything?" I relinquished the glass.

"You mean about Closs?"

I didn't say anything.

"I have. Case closed. Well, nearly closed."

"Really?"

"When they broke the news of his death to his wife, she fell apart, and
when they told her they suspected him of the murders, she had quite a
story to tell."

I didn't want to pressure him for the details, so I focused on the fire and
watched the heat swell in the glowing logs and the smoke drift up the flue.

"Don't you wanna know?" he said, giving me a sarcastic side-glance.

"You know I do."

He studied me a moment. "Can I trust you not to blab this to Judy?"

"Yes," I said, knowing it was a lie. "I promise."

He smiled faintly and sipped his whiskey. "Okay. So, Closs's wife tells Kipps that the mister was a maniac, that he'd force himself on her and other women all the time. She tells him that, when she finally confronted him about it, he attempted to poison her milk with an overdose of Veronal—her sleeping aid, if you remember. But that night, she broke her pattern; she had an upset stomach and didn't drink her milk. But her son did—two glasses! Closs came home late and was surprised to find his wife still alive and his son dead. He threatened her and demanded that she help him wrap up the body and carry it to his car. She doesn't know why Cleve was shirtless, or why Closs dumped him in the river, or why he had writing on him."

"Wow," I said. "But I thought Cleve drowned—and didn't he have traces of Bon Ami in his lungs?"

"Yes, and yes. Kipps and Paulson aren't sure what happened, but they think the Closses took him for dead when he was just unconscious—it's happened before—and he drowned in the river after Closs dumped him." I thought of Cleve sinking below the waves, eyes shooting open, gasping for air but only getting the Anacostia. "But it could've been that Closs needed to finish the deed and drowned him at home before dumping him. You didn't hear either theory from me."

"And the Bon Ami?"

He shrugged. "Police work is like drawing a constellation. You have a few guiding stars like you do clues, but you have to use your imagination to make Orion look like Orion or Ares like Ares."

"What about Miss Martins?"

"They think he killed her to silence her. After all, based on what you witnessed, she was most likely his last 'conquest.'"

"And Jackie Peabody?"

"They're less sure about that, but the nature of the crime, that she was violated, points to him as a strong possibility. Also, as you know, all three crimes are linked by that word, whatever it means."

I slumped back on the sofa, returning to my doubts about Halo, to the puzzled look on his face before Judy sent him four stories to his death. "Why would Halo scrawl AHKA over Miss Martins's body? Why would he strangle her with his own tie, a tie he wasn't even wearing, and leave it behind? He was undermining his scapegoat and implicating himself."

"Maybe he *was* a lunatic and more committed to his MO than protecting his alibi. Psychotics often become more reckless as the victims stack up."

"Why not kill Elaine, then?"

"That would've pointed all the suspicion right at him. He wasn't *that* insane."

"I guess." Had I misread Halo's expression before his plunge? Had I been so shocked by what he said that I'd convinced myself he wasn't a villain?

A log shifted in the fireplace, followed by a burst of sparks. Quincy rose, picked up the iron tongs, adjusted the charred wood, and stoked the flames. When he finished, he returned to the sofa and said, "I'm glad you and Uncle Carl are here. I'm glad I don't have to go through all this alone."

"I miss her so much," I said and scooted close to him, resting my head on his shoulder, feeling tears welling up. I needed his reassuring warmth. Unlike Judy, whose physical presence stirred me, he soothed me.

"That reminds me," he said, reaching inside the pocket of his suit. "She told me to give these to you." In his hand was Sophie's worn deck of tarot cards. "She said you'll need them."

I took them gingerly, aware of their power, shuddering at the Devil card inside, the vampire, the depraved child. Once again, I remembered Sophie's warning about Judy: "All around her, there's a backdrop of shadows."

❦

PHILIPPA, NOVEMBER 28, 1948

Quincy is staying in Harpers Ferry another week. He's preparing the house to go on the market, which is breaking my heart all over again. It's really the only place I've called home. I hope he'll change his mind—or at least delay the process.

This afternoon we piled into the car and headed back to DC. Just outside the city, Dad caught my eyes in the rearview mirror and, in a tentative tone, said, "This has been an extraordinary week, Philippa, a when-it-rains-it-pours stretch. So, I hate to ask this of you now, but you need to end your friendship with Judy."

Although I knew it was coming, it still felt as brutal as a backhanded slap.

Bonnie chimed in, her voice fluttery, "Mr. Peabody rang us before we left. They're taking Judy on a whirlwind trip to the Caribbean for several weeks. Can you imagine? After Christmas, she'll be going to boarding school at Agnes March." As Bonnie droned on, I didn't cry. I couldn't feel anything but deep vibrating anger, as if my spine had been struck with a tuning fork. I glared at Dad in the rearview, and he patted Bonnie's knee, his universal signal for "Thank you, dear, but that's enough." I hunkered down and pretended to sleep.

As soon as we arrived, I went to my room and flopped. After a few minutes, there was a knock at my door. Dad entered holding a small parcel wrapped in brown paper. He smiled, but I couldn't bring myself to return the gesture. "This came for you." I snatched the package from him and closed the door.

It had no return address. I tore at it and threw the paper aside. It was *Love's Last Move*. So strange. Was it some sort of parting gift? I flipped it open. Inside the cover, written very neatly in Miss Martins's delicate hand, was a note:

> To Philippa, so that'll you'll remember me, as a friend, as a mentor, as a mother of sorts.

I wish I had said goodbye properly, but I wouldn't have been able to find the words.

Promise me, you'll always stay close to Judy.
    Love, C

Then below it, a quotation:

From her own mouth no way of speaking's found.
But all our wants by wit may be supply'd,
And art makes up, what fortune has deny'd.
                                    —Ovid, *Metamorphoses*, Book VI

PHILIPPA, NOVEMBER 29, 1948

I've kept my secret from Judy to protect her, but now, I might spill it. To be honest, it wasn't just to spare her, although I'm sure that learning you dropped your father four stories won't come as welcome news. No, I've clung to it to create a level playing field. I want to know why she draws me close one moment and pushes me away the next. I want to know who we are to one another. Friends? Or something more? I've been telling myself: If she shows me her heart, I'll show her the truth. But now, we have more to worry about. Moira and our parents want to rip us apart, to destroy our friendship, our love for one another. I want to tell her my secret, so it will become *our* secret, and it will fortify us against them.

But I had trouble finding her. No one answered the Peabodys' front door, and she wasn't in school. It was too soon for Bart and Edith to have shipped her off. God, she'll hate the beach with all its preening sunbathers, tacky palm trees, and the blistering sun! We're alike that way. We see no romance in paradise; we like back alleys and blustery skies.

Mrs. Blandish didn't even call her name in English. I overheard Ramona Carmichael whispering to Jake Wallace behind me: "I hear Judy Peapod is going to reform school. I can't say I'm surprised. Good riddance, if you ask me." I swung around to set her straight, but before I could, she winced, clearly frightened of me, which shocked me. I'm a bad girl now, it seems. I've come a long way since my San Fran days. Anyway, I glared at her, aware of my power, and aimed as much enmity toward her as I could muster. The MBBS queen blinked, and the blood drained from her face. It felt good.

I slipped *Love's Last Move* out of my bag and covertly opened it on my lap. I scanned the Ovid quotation again. At first, I'd assumed it meant that Miss Martins struggled to find a way to say goodbye, that the words just wouldn't come, that from her "mouth no way of speaking's found," but if that's the case, then what did the last two lines mean: "But all our wants by wit may be supply'd, and art makes up, what fortune has deny'd"?

I closed it and gazed at the dramatic green lettering of the title and of Kane's name, at the curl of smoke from the revolver's muzzle, and at the scatter of rose petals evocative of spilled blood. I remembered Miss Martins saying, "Would you like to borrow it? It has a wonderful twist."

And it struck me: Perhaps it's *all* a clue—the book, the inscription, the quotation. She's trying to tell me something without outright saying it. She was testing me. If I read the Ovid line with a different emphasis, it made more sense: "From *her own* mouth no way of speaking's found." If not *her* mouth, then perhaps another's?

I needed to go to the library, and then I had to find Judy.

JUDY, NOVEMBER 29, 1948

I see the appeal of tarot readings, tea leaf divinations, and even astrology. They're about reading an interpretation into a preexisting pattern, like a puzzle with more than one solution, but at least the clues are limited, man-ageable. So, what about my shitty life? It's a scatter of infinite fragments, spread across my memory like too many tea leaves or the vast Milky Way. It's evidence of something, sure, but what? What story does it tell?

Then, the day comes when you begin to see a pattern, even if it's a few trembling stars that suggest a shape in the night sky, and you get so excited, so delirious, that you don't stop to think that, instead of clarity, the future may hold only greater confusion. You don't stop to consider that one open door might lead to an entire passageway of closed doors with big question marks scrawled across them. You have no idea how to feel, and how to place yourself in the world. In this new state, you don't know what your next move will be. It might be something that terrifies you.

Today was that day for me.

PHILIPPA, NOVEMBER 29, 1948

At the 14th Street crosswalk, a voice called out, "Philippa!" I whipped around. Judy was rushing toward me. She wore a bulky black coat and had a dark felt tam pulled down over her ears. "Jesus," she said, her breath visible in the chilly air. "You walk fast!"

"I almost gave up on you," I said. "I thought you'd left town."

"In a week," she said and groaned. "We'll be making a complete tour of the Caribbean: Cuba, Jamaica, Puerto Rico. I'm calling it the Sunburn Tour. I'm sure I'll peel a layer of skin off before I get home."

"Sounds like a blast," I said flatly.

"It should be a goddamn nightmare. Fuck B and E."

Her profanity was the first thing I'd heard in the past few days that made me feel normal again. The traffic had halted, so I started up East Capitol, our familiar route. "Were you following me from school?"

"B and E think I'm downtown at Woody's buying bathing suits."

"I can't imagine you in a bathing suit."

"Can't you?" She smiled and wiggled her eyebrows, her way of saying: "You've imagined me in far less, haven't you?"

Anger shot through me: Days before she was going to vanish from my life, she was teasing me! I drew back, afraid of being suckered in again. I was sick of her toying with my feelings. But as I was about to tell her to go to hell, fear rippled through her face—not fear of me but of something else. Losing me, maybe? It was a chink in her smooth armor, a brief glimpse of her soft underbelly. It disarmed me. So, instead of lashing out, I listed toward her as if she'd just given the invisible string wrapped around my heart a firm tug. I wanted to touch her, kiss her. Being separated seemed unimaginable, cataclysmic, like surgically severing conjoined twins. I thought about my secret, about how it could bind us to one another, keep us whole, but I didn't know how to tell her.

She seemed to notice my whiplashing emotions and, in a defeated tone, said, "I don't know what I'm saying." She hung her head. "I wish you could go with me. We could coat our bodies in zinc oxide, hide under big umbrellas, and read *Lady Chatterley's Lover* to one another. That would be almost tolerable." A smile crept onto her lips, and she poked me. "Well, if you practiced your reading voice first."

I murmured, "We'd have an outrageous time," and my heart seesawed again. I didn't want to fantasize about being together. It was too impossible, too painful. I commanded myself to move forward, to stamp out any base urges and, especially, sentimental impulses. I couldn't live that lifestyle anyway. Be what? A lesbian? Live like a bohemian? No, I needed to be realistic—a fortress of self-possession! Perhaps I even needed to be ruthless, the bad girl Ramona Carmichael thought I was. My secret could be a weapon. It has the potential to bring us together, but if I sharpened it, if I delivered it with contempt, if I drove home that Judy had mercilessly murdered her own father, it could sheer us apart, cleanly. I would be safe.

I breathed in, the cold air biting my lungs, and prepared to unleash what I knew. "Judy . . ." I said and stumbled, unsure how to make the sharp edge of it land right. She bumped my shoulder. I shivered, and she grabbed my hand. Her warm dark eyes took me in, dazzling me for a moment. "I'll miss you," she said. "I need you. You know, underneath it all, we're the same person."

My first impulse was to pull away. She seemed to sense it and leaned toward me. In my ear, softly, she said, "I—I love you. I do."

I jerked away. What was she doing? Why *say* something like that? What does it even mean? I darted across East Capitol to Lincoln Park. She followed me, snagging my coat sleeve and forcing me to stop. I spun on the sidewalk and stepped back, wedging space between us. I wanted her to explain herself. When you say something like that, when you put that out there, you better know what it means. The consequences are too great. Judy never likes to pin things down, and this time was no different. She just looked at me, openly, unguarded, inviting me in but with no direction. I needed her to be demonstrative, to illustrate "I love you," to paint a picture of what that meant for us. Jesus, did she even know? Did I? The sun caught her face, and her skin brightened from an olive hue to a gold luster. Her eyes gleamed. Then, shockingly, she smiled. It was like having your pet suddenly speak to you. I didn't know what to do. I couldn't look away. She was beaming her heart at me. It was a swirling vortex of hope, fear, anger, and pain, and I was mesmerized. I wanted to step toward her, to touch her, to kiss her, but something deep in me—that creeping doubt—was latched to my leg like a bear trap. Would she leave me like Miss Martins, Sophie, or even my mother? What horrors were in store for me by loving her?

She sensed my reservation. The glitter in her eyes darkened and a wrinkle formed in her brow. "Well, I'll go," she said. "Have a nice life."

She walked past me and crossed the street. As she did, that invisible string between us pulled taut and tugged me out of my bear trap.

"Yes!" I thought, "I accept your invitation, your love, whatever that means—whatever we make it mean!" My body lurched and trembled, and I shouted, "Wait! Just wait!" and began running toward her.

She stopped. "What?" she said, her face stony. No more talking pet.

I couldn't tell her what was banging around in my head, and she wasn't going to cough up her innermost thoughts—but I didn't want her to go. I couldn't let her go. Minutes before, I'd almost told her about Halo and Miss Martins, but I wasn't giving up my secret yet. Telling her now might backfire, and frankly, she hadn't earned it. I'd keep it a little longer. Perhaps I'd use it to pry apart that chink in her armor. Or maybe I'd just nurture it, cherishing its mystery. I don't know. What I did know was that the idea of letting her go was impossible to imagine. Thinking on my feet, and knowing I had to do something to lure her in, I said, "Do you know anything about Ovid?"

"No," she said, squinting. "Why?"

"It may be the key to Cleve's and Miss Martins's murders."

JUDY, NOVEMBER 29, 1948

"I did research in the library during lunch," Philippa said, after we'd found a bench and scrunched close, "and here's how the myth goes..." Her warmth next to me was reassuring. The contents of Charlene's journal were still ricocheting through me. What I'd discovered was staggering, life-altering. After I'd finished it, I had to find Philippa, or I was going to blow apart like a miniature atomic bomb. She's the only person who's never lied to me, who's never kicked me to the curb, who can keep me together. I wasn't prepared to tell her about it. It would change how she saw me. But I wanted to be close to her, to try to make it clear how I felt about her.

"So, this Procne woman is married to Tereus, the King of Thrace," she began, gesticulating as she spoke. "She's missing her sister, Philomela, who she hasn't seen in ages and who still lives with their father, the king of Athens. She asks Tereus to sail to Athens and fetch her for a visit. Tereus agrees. When he first sees charming, gorgeous Philomela, he gets hot and bothered. On the boat back to Thrace, he becomes so lustful, so obsessed, that he detours to a cabin nearby where he locks her up and violates her."

"Jesus."

"Oh, wait. There's so much more. When he tells her not to say anything, she says, 'No way, buddy! I'm telling my father and my sister. You're done for.' Fuming with rage, he grabs her tongue with tongs and cuts it off. Because that's easy to do."

I wagged my tongue, trying to escape the invisible tongs.

Philippa raised an eyebrow.

"So, he leaves her," she continued. "Since she can't speak, she weaves a coded message into a tapestry and has it secretly sent to her sister, who by this time, thinks she's dead. Once she receives it, Procne, full of righteous rage, rescues Philomela and decides the best way to get revenge on her husband is to . . ." She paused for dramatic effect.

"It's cold," I said, watching a stray snowflake float by.

" . . . To kill her son, Itys, Tereus's child. She slits his throat, boils him, and serves him to her husband for dinner."

"Yum."

"Once Tereus has snacked on Itys, the sisters present him with Itys's severed head and tell him who he's eaten. Obviously, that pushes him over the edge. He picks up his sword and goes after them—and then, poof, all three turn into birds. A nightingale, a swallow, and a hoopoe."

"A nightingale."

"The name you want to be called."

I remembered my chat with Miss M: "Judy Finch? That's better, right? Or wait, I have it. Nightingale, like the poem!" That's who I was to her, a nightingale, a horror transformed. "Which bird is which character?"

"Tereus is always the hoopoe, but different versions of the myth mix up who's the nightingale and who's the swallow."

"So, why is this important?"

Philippa hoisted her satchel on her lap, and after struggling with its straps, she produced *Love's Last Move*. "Miss Martins sent this to me. Look at the inside flap."

I opened it and scanned the inscription. "Do you think this is a message?"

"Well, it led me to Ovid."

"But all our wants by wit may be supply'd," I read out loud, "and art makes up, what fortune has deny'd." I knew what it meant. I also knew where it was going to lead and what would be discovered there. Charlene's journal, through a twist of fate, made me a fortune teller, a soothsayer. In its pages, I'd seen the shimmer of Clotho's threads, like spiderwebs in the dew. I wasn't going to tell Philippa the truth, but I'd nudge her. "The 'wit' is her sending you this clue," I said. "Circumstances had made it impossible for her to tell the truth, but 'art'—*The Metamorphoses*, in this case—is her way of communicating."

"Just like Philomela in the story."

I closed the book and turned it over in my hand. "This Ovid tale, it's about sisters. Miss M told you to treat me like a sister."

A light clicked on in Philippa's mind; I saw the glitter in her metal-gray eyes. "Before Halo stormed in and chased us," she said, "Elaine said something about sisters, too. She wanted me to promise to be a good sister to you."

"There's also a rape in Ovid's tale," I said.

"And a tyrant," she said.

"And a murdered son."

She clapped her hands. "I know who did it, and I think I know why."

She didn't know the half of it.

PHILIPPA, NOVEMBER 29, 1948

Elaine greeted us with a smile. "Well, here you are," she said, gesturing for us to come in. "I wondered when you would show up. Hang your coats beside the door." That wasn't the welcome we were expecting. Neither of us took off our coats.

On our way there, we ran through strategies for how to talk our way in. Our smartest approach, Judy thought, was to offer our condolences for Halo's death and to apologize for our part in it. Elaine wasn't torn up over it; after all, she'd characterized him as a bloodthirsty maniac to the police. But we didn't want to spook her. If we played dumb, she might be more willing to let us linger. That this plan now seemed unnecessary was unsettling.

In the parlor, she waved us toward the usual spot by the window. "Have a seat, girls," she said brightly, her eyes darting between us. "I'm afraid I won't be able to offer you tea or cocoa," she said, shrugging. "Moira would be shocked at my manners, wouldn't she? Would a glass of warm malted milk do?"

Her lipstick was brilliant red, the red of geraniums, and her busy canary yellow dress, out of keeping for the season, fit her snugly, straining at her bust and hips. She seemed like a flower trying to bloom in a freeze. Still trying to execute our plan, I blurted, "We're so sorry about Mr. Closs," and fumbling, added, "About the accident."

Her geranium lips froze, and her eyes fluttered like little camera shutters. She just stared, her gaze straining, communicating something—fear? Pain? Anger?

"Warm milk sounds fantastic," Judy said, ending the awkwardness.

"Wonderful!" she said, bringing her hands together, fingertips tapping lightly. She whirled around, dropping her arms to her sides and cocking her wrists as if she were walking the runway at one of Woody's fashion previews. She paused at the radio console, switching it on. A jazz tune slid into the room, listless and sad. She hurried on into the kitchen, her lurid yellow dress flashing behind her.

Judy whispered, "She's nuts." She looked around. "I'll be back in a minute. I have a hunch about something."

"What?! You're leaving me?" I whispered.

She ignored me and crept across the room, peered into the shadowy hall, glanced back, her black eyes wide and reassuring, and disappeared.

I settled in at the window. The parlor's rug was littered with glass, splinters, and small metal parts—screws, washers, dials, and gears—debris from the grandfather clock, which now lay facedown in front of the fireplace like a coffin at a wake, dragged there, I imagined, to get it out of the way. No one had bothered to clean. Even the painting above the couch was crooked, its murky landscape straining at its borders as if, at any moment, it might split the frame and spill out on the floor. The only object that emitted any life was the radio, which continued to coo melancholy jazz. Beyond that, only the scrapings of silver and china in the kitchen. As I waited, my heartbeat quickened. Had we made a terrible mistake? How would we get Elaine to incriminate herself? After all, we were only operating on a hunch.

Judy dashed back in and scooted beside me on the window seat seconds before Elaine emerged from the kitchen. On her tray, our hostess carried a chrome pitcher, a familiar display of shortbread cookies, and three large ceramic mugs. "Well," she said, setting it on the small table between us, scored with a deep gouge from our skirmish with Halo. "Here we go." She delivered a stream of warm milk into the mugs, smiling up at us after each pour. Her hair was in a tight bun, pulling at her temples. Falling short of her jawline, her orangish makeup lay like snow across the contours of her face. Rather than the expected chalky sweet smell of malt, the pungent odor of ammonia wafted up, making me wince. I now understood: When Halo smashed up the tea service, he wasn't attacking me, he was thwarting her attempt to poison me. I glared at Judy, who glared back. She'd smelled it too. "Oh my God," I thought, "what are we going to do?" I wanted to grab her hand and run.

"Now then," Elaine said, positioning herself across from us, "what should we chat about?"

From the pocket of her coat, Judy fished out two objects. The first item was the damaged moon pin. "This one we asked you and your husband about," she said. "We found it in Miss M's apartment." The second was its unscathed replica. "This one," she said, holding it up, "I swiped from your jewelry box while you were in the kitchen."

I was baffled. That's what she was doing upstairs?

Conflicted emotions rippled across Elaine's face: first irritation, then panic—and finally, cutting through it all, she beamed preposterously. What Judy had just shown her could've been a new dress pattern from McCall's or a friend's wedding announcement. "Now, girls," she said, "I went through the trouble of making you a refreshment. Drink up. I insist."

"Why do you have a pin exactly like Miss M's?" Judy asked.

Elaine continued smiling. "Not *exactly* the same. She wore the waxing moon, and I wore the waning moon. Our father gave them to us."

My hunch was right: they *were* sisters!

Judy turned the intact piece of jewelry over in her hand.

"The direction of the pin on the back tells you how it should be worn, going from left to right," I said, taking it from her. "Otherwise, it'd be impossible to notice the difference between them. They're mirror images." I held it over my left lapel. "This is the one Miss Martins wore."

"It's the waxing moon," Judy said. "The smashed pin is the waning moon."

It didn't make sense. Why did we find Elaine's pin in Miss Martins's apartment?

"When I shoved it in your husband's face, you knew it was yours," Judy said to her. "And when you went to the Daphne Arms to kill your sister, you rummaged through her jewelry box and took her pin to replace the one you lost, protecting you against any questions its absence might raise."

Elaine's smile clicked off like a light. Her brow darkened. Then, she said, "You're right, Judy. Is that what you want me to say? Should I also add that it was a memento?"

I said to Judy, "How did you know?"

Out of her pocket, Judy extracted a reddish-brown leather journal, placing it on the table as if it were a rare artifact. "I took this from Cleve's backpack while your husband was plowing through teatime," she said deliberately. "It's your sister's diary. She mentions the day your father gave you and your sister the pins. Christmas 1927." To me, she said, "Miss M's real name is Charlene Peters." Her eyes lit up; she was enjoying herself. Looking back at Elaine, she said, "Your maiden name is Peters. You're her younger sister by two years."

Once the initial shock faded, anger flooded in. Sure, I wanted to know how it all fit together, but first, I wanted to know why Judy had kept the diary from me. Why didn't she tell me that Charlene and Miss Martins were the same person? That her mother was Miss Martins? I'd puzzled over the cryptic inscription in *Love's Last Move,* and I'd babbled on about Ovid, when in her coat, she had the key to our teacher's life. What other precious tidbits were buried in those pages? She had to know that Halo was her father. No need to share that news! My secret was obsolete, useless. Was she thumbing her nose at me? Making fun of me?

Elaine pantomimed astonishment: "Cleveland had it under *this* roof?" But I didn't buy it. She seemed to be playacting.

"How did he get it?" I snapped.

"He probably stole it from Miss M's desk at school," Judy replied and glanced at me, registering my anger. "But I don't know."

"What he must've thought," Elaine said, shaking her head in the pretense of concern. "Poor boy. He must've hated her as much as I did. He should've told me. It might have made a difference. I might have . . ." Like a mechanical toy, she seemed to wind down, becoming eerily still.

Judy also remained motionless, but she was alert, eyes drifting over Elaine and the mugs of lethal milk. She was planning her next move, but what that was, I had no idea.

The radio switched to another jazz tune, something harsher, rawer, marring the stillness. It triggered something in me, and I spoke: "Before

Mr. Closs crashed through our tea, Mrs. Closs, you told me to be a good sister, that secrets between sisters spread like a disease." Judy shifted uneasily beside me, perhaps the parallel had struck a chord. "You were talking about you and Miss Martins, weren't you?"

She blinked as if I'd just blown dust in her eyes. "Call me, Elaine. *Please.*"

"You killed Cleve and framed Halo for that reason, didn't you?" I said, leaning forward. "It's like the myth, isn't it? Cleve is Itys and Halo is Tereus, and you—who are you? Procne? Or Philomela?"

Her tight-stretched veneer seemed to tear a little, then suddenly rip wide: "Well, you *are* smart girls!" She emitted a single bitter "Ha!" and attempted to force her face back in place, but her eyes grew hot and damp. "Oh, I'm not sure how to explain . . ." She touched the back of her hand to her quivering lips. "You see, my husband, like Tereus, he . . ." She struggled to find the words. The geranium gloss was now smudged along her upper lip. Briefly, I had the bizarre impulse to reach over and wipe it clean. "He forced himself . . . on me." She sniffed and looked at me, her eyes watery green and shot through with an unnatural light. "You saw *me* that evening in my sister's apartment, not my sister. You walked in on my husband attacking me"—her voice cracked—"and, and you did nothing. You just stood there, gawking in wonder."

I saw Halo on top of Miss Martins, his hat cocked back, his belt snaking, his hips thrusting ridiculously. As the vision surfaced, new details bubbled up: the sheen of sweat on his buttocks, his heavy, impassioned grunts, the funk of his body odor, the smell of lilac perfume. But that lovely hand—its palm cupping the light, its fingers beckoning to me—belonged to this hateful woman, who now wanted my sympathy, who might, in some way, deserve my sympathy. It was impossible to hold all of it in my head. I felt dizzy. I couldn't tidy it up; I couldn't fix it in place. A sharp pang of shame shot through me. Suddenly, I understood. I didn't try to stop Halo because I didn't *want* to stop him. I wanted Miss Martins to be reaching out, to be groping for me, to need me. I wanted her to be wounded by him, to hate him, and to turn to me. Under Elaine's mad gaze, I could admit it.

"Why would he do something like that?" Judy said, simmering. "Why . . . why rape you?"

"To finish me off."

"What do you mean?"

"He came looking for Charlene, and he found me. I was there to confront my sister, to tell her to quit carrying on with my husband, to tell her to leave us alone. To leave *you* alone, Judy. But no one was home. I'd swiped Halo's key, so I let myself in. I'd find out later that she was delayed at school, meeting with the principal about my son's behavior. Of all things! So, I snooped. I sampled her perfume, I listened to music on her radio, and I tried on a dress or two. After so many years, I wanted to know who she was. The Charlene I grew up with wouldn't hang a scarf over her lampshade like a whore. That must've been when I lost my pin. I don't know who damaged it, perhaps my husband when he was—" As if sprinkled with fairy dust, she tittered. "Oh, I just realized something! I'm wearing one of her dresses now. I took it that night." She turned a shoulder toward us and, modeling, touched her hand to her throat. "Lovely, isn't it?"

The yellow fabric strained at the seams and clashed with her skin tone. It might've been striking on Miss Martins, but on her, it was appalling, like a corpse walking in its burial clothes.

"When Halo arrived, he flew into a fury," she continued, settling back in her seat. "He grabbed her dress, this dress, and tried to rip it off me. We struggled, and I knocked over the flowers that he'd brought her. Such a considerate man." Her pupils narrowed, her irises becoming bold and birdlike. "He called me sick and pathetic. I screamed, looked him dead in the eye, and told him everything. I told him about you." She gave Judy a condescending frown—or was it an attempt to show concern? "About who you *really* are. I don't think he believed me, but all the same, it sent him over the edge. He tried to push me away, but I snagged him by his jacket collar and pulled him on top of me. On the bed, I kissed him, I clawed at him, I did whatever I could to reverse what I'd told him, to keep him there, to bring him back to me. He hissed at me and told me he hated me and then, to prove it, he . . ." The memory of it pierced her—her chest bowed slightly inward, her shoulders bunched together, her green eyes shook. "I didn't fight him. It sounds ridiculous, I know, but I still wanted him. I loved him. I did. But then, in the midst of all that, it changed—like how lightning can reduce a tree to a cinder in a flash—and I saw who he was. I saw who my sister was, too. I knew what I had to do; I had to become Procne. I wanted to whittle him down to nothing, take him apart grain by grain until there was nothing left."

We didn't respond. A smooth clarinet warbled from the radio and slithered between Elaine and us. With an awful sinking feeling, I realized something: "*You* sent me *Love's Last Move*," I said to her. "You wrote the inscription and the quotation. It makes sense now. Miss Martins wouldn't have chosen such a horrific myth."

Her eyes lingered on Judy, squinting at her, appraising her, and shifted to me. Smiling, she said, "You're wrong about that: she knew the story well. She mentioned it to me when we were having our last cup of cocoa, didn't she? That's just what happened. As she was beginning to feel the effect of the Veronal and drifting off, her eyelids drooping, she called me . . . 'Procne. Sad, vengeful Procne.' Her words. We studied the classics at Mary Todd, so I knew the allusion, mind you. But I can't take full credit. You understand, Philippa. *Full* credit. I inscribed the novel, doing my best imitation of her handwriting. We have similar longhand, trained by the same witch of a schoolmistress. If I sent it to you, I knew you'd find your way back here." She gasped melodramatically. "Oh my, your milk must be getting cold!"

"What about Cleve?" Judy asked, pushing her mug away. "What happened to him?"

Elaine shook her head as if fending off grief, although I wasn't sure I believed it. I couldn't tell which emotions were real, which were artificial, and which were a soup of the two. "He had his hot cocoa like he always did, and I tucked him in." She dropped her chin, revealing her pale scalp underneath her thinning hair.

"Like Miss M," Judy said, "once he was unconscious, you dragged him on a sheet to the bathroom, dumped him in the tub, and filled it with water."

"I wanted him to go . . . peacefully." She looked up, and a tear slid down her face, streaking her powder. To me, she said, "My sister too."

"But how did Cleve get into the river?" Judy asked, her tone clinical. "And why did you write AHKA on him? What does it mean?"

"I didn't do it," she said, shaking her head in despair. "When Halo came home, I showed him Cleveland. I told him how it was *his* fault, how it was on *his* shoulders, and how he should've loved me, his wife, not my sister. He threw me against a wall and nearly killed me, but when he simmered down, he realized he'd lose everything—his inheritance, the house, the meager allowance Moira uses to string us along, and of course, my sister. So, he called up his mother, the puppet master, and explained everything to her, and she was furious—I heard her screeching over the phone—but she knew what to do, as she always does. He demanded I find some nail polish, an old bottle—a color I didn't use anymore—and give it to him. Then he told me to take a dose of Veronal and go to bed. My head ached horribly, so I obeyed. I learned later that Moira had instructed him to implicate that Bogdan man."

Cleve's anger—his hatred of Miss Martins, his violent outbursts—seemed pointless. Pathetic, really. His actual enemy was at home, serving him cocoa and kissing him good night. If I'd only tried some other angle with him, found some way in, maybe I could've helped— No, he would've never allowed it. I know that. All the same, he deserved to grow up.

"So, your husband took him on your boat, removed his shirt, wrote on him, and dumped him," Judy said.

"To do such a thing, to mar him in such a way." She bit her geranium red lip against more tears.

"How did Moira know about AHKA?" I said.

"I don't know, but Cleveland's death had nothing to do with the Peabody girl."

As we were questioning Elaine, Judy's expression had been growing more intense. Her features had become predatory, like a beast with its ears flat against its skull, stalking its prey. "What did the two goons in suits have to do with this?" she asked, glancing at me.

Elaine seemed perplexed. "What do you mean?"

"One is tall and skinny, and the other walks like a penguin."

"Oh!" Elaine said, clearing her throat, "the men from the FBI. They dropped in after that Bogdan fellow was arraigned, didn't they?" Her gaze fixed on Judy. "Halo was out on errands. He was buying more sleep aids to keep me doped up—or maybe to kill me. Who knows? I'd dumped the entire cabinet down the drain the night before, except for a bottle of Veronal, which I hid away." I remembered Halo tossing his groceries in the trash after his confrontation with the men but keeping the prescription that he'd picked up at the drug store. "While he was out for the morning, I'd paid my last visit to my sister," she continued, again seeming proud of her scheming. "When the FBI showed up, I thought they'd found her and were calling to arrest my husband. Of course, I hoped they hadn't come for me after the trouble I went through to stage the scene and write that ridiculous word—whatever the hell it means—above Charlene. But that wasn't the case." A mischievous, childlike glint danced in her eyes. "All I had to do was talk about my husband's 'violent tendencies' and they bit. Besides, his and Moira's attempt to frame Bogdan was ill-conceived. Judy, you saw through it immediately, didn't you?" She gave Judy a warm smile, flecks of lipstick stuck to her teeth. "When I'm not being plied with sleeping potions, I have a sharp mind. Like both of you."

I didn't understand why the FBI were involved in a local murder case. I wasn't sure I believed it. "Why again were the FBI visiting you?"

She glared at me like I was an idiot: "Who cares?" She swayed and a smile flickered across her lips. "As you know, the police discovered that Halo had been spotted at the Daphne by the desk clerk and you—that clinched it. They didn't even think to ask the clerk if she'd seen me, or anyone else, for that matter."

"What did the FBI say to your husband that spurred him to race to the Daphne?" I said. "It's like they sent him there on purpose."

Elaine shrugged. Clearly, she wasn't interested.

Judy asked, "How did you find Miss M?"

"One day, when Moira wasn't watchdogging me, and my medicine had worn off, I followed my husband. I knew he'd go to her, and I *knew* he was going to run away with her."

"And how did you kill her?" Judy pushed. Her eyes were black slits.

Elaine hesitated, seemingly frightened of Judy or, perhaps, of how she would react to what she was about to say. "When I returned for my final visit, I explained to the clerk, some lazy slattern, that I'd forgotten my sister's apartment number. She wouldn't budge, so I bribed her." She looked at me, avoiding Judy's gaze, as if it might turn her into stone. "I buzzed Charlene, begged to see her, and told her that Halo was lying to her. She let me in, and I explained that her beloved had killed Cleve by accident, that he intended to kill me, the story I'd tell the police. She didn't believe me, but it didn't matter. She'd already had her cocoa."

As she spoke, her veil of domesticity dropped back into place—or was it apathy? Now, she seemed more the smug Junior Leaguer than the distraught psychotic. Even the music from the radio seemed to shift, becoming jingly and jaunty.

It was appalling, it was grotesque, but I'd begun to understand it and even sympathize with her. After all, to a degree, I was responsible. I could've helped her. I could've screamed that night in Miss Martins's apartment. I could've hit Halo with something. I could've interrupted the dominoes that led her to madness. No, that wasn't true; it had started long before then and ran much deeper. What I did or didn't do wasn't going to change it. But I hate that I didn't try, if for no other reason than I thought she was Miss Martins and that, in some dark corner of my heart, I wanted it to happen.

Something still nagged me, though. What had Elaine told Halo that night about Judy? Why would that push him over the edge and prompt him to attack her? She'd told Judy: "I told him about you—about who you *really* are." What did that mean?

Elaine flashed a smile. "Seriously, you two, are you going to drink this milk or eat some shortbread cookies? I baked them myself."

JUDY, NOVEMBER 29, 1948

Philippa was furious with me for not telling her about Miss M's journal. I read her expression immediately. I wanted to tell her. I did. But it wasn't time yet. I didn't know how to put it into words, my new truth, the facts about who I am. It'd just come out as gibberish. But I didn't want that bitch Elaine to spill the truth, so I seized her mug and stood. Maybe I could distract her. "Why haven't you had a sip?" I said to her, looking down at her and holding out the toxic liquid, wafting the fumes under her nose.

"Guests first," she said, waving it away. "It's only polite."

"I insist," I said, thrusting it at her, the pale fluid sloshing over its brim.

We regarded each other, her eyes digging into me, trying to excavate some secret knowledge—or maybe just predict my next move. A big band tune spun idiotically in the background like a troop of whirling Busby Berkeley dancers. Elaine emitted a deep sigh, dropped her shoulders, and took the mug from me, cupping it as if to absorb its warmth.

Then, I understood: She'd passed the baton. She was granting me permission to complete the story. She wasn't going to tell Philippa everything. "You see," I said to my friend, walking over to the radio, "many years ago, Halo and Charlene—she would later change her name to Christine Martins—met and fell in love, but Charlene, she got sick of Halo." I switched off the radio. "He was always a lady's man, always screwing other girls. Society girls. Government girls. Whores. You name it." I returned to the window seat.

"That's right," Elaine chimed in, still coddling the mug.

"And Miss M, she kicked him to the curb and left town. But then poor, sad little Elaine came along."

Interrupting, Elaine sneered: "Halo was distraught. He loved my sister, but like many young men, he was red-blooded. So yes, we started up. I was his second choice, but I didn't care. We were in love . . . for a time." She smirked. "Judy, you know what that feels like—living in someone else's shadow, being the stand-in, a simulacrum."

"You got engaged," I said, wresting control of the story. "Then you broke it off and went away, too."

"My sister recorded all the big moments in her diary, didn't she?" She lowered the mug to the table but kept her fingers on it, tracing its rim. "She'd ignore her little book for months, years even, but when a momentous occasion arose, when she needed to process something, she'd lay it all out. That's Charlene for you—always wanting to be historical, to have the last word. Well, here I am, and the last word is mine."

"Why did you go away?" I said, leaning toward her.

"To help my sister with her baby"—her eyes flashed—"with you."

I took in her marred makeup, bleeding eyeliner, and smeared lips. She was sly, dealing in half-truths. She wanted me to preserve the lie, but I refused to keep it fully intact. I had to unload some of it, or it'd crush me. "It's the other way around. Your sister helped you with your baby."

"I don't understand," Philippa said. "What do you mean?"

I sank my gaze into Elaine: "*She* had a baby, not Miss M."

"Cleve?" Philippa asked.

"He came a year later."

"I don't . . . ?"

She wasn't getting it, and I needed her to, or I'd blow apart. "She had *me*, Philippa!"

I'd learned the truth from Charlene's journal, but it still felt horribly raw. I wanted to scream, to tear at Elaine, to tear at myself. Instead, I tamped down all that chaos and tethered it to my heart like a gnashing dog. This woman, this murderer, was my mother—my mother! I'd been so sure Miss M was the one, so sure, but no, first, it was Charlene Peters. Then Bart, ever the blunderer, spun a story that she was raped and that—surprise!—I was the result. Thank you, Bart! Then, as if that wasn't enough, as if I was being forced to run a gauntlet of shame and woe, the veil was pulled back and—surprise again!—Charlene and Miss M were one in the same. "So sorry, Judy, Miss M is dead, stuffed in a fucking tub!" It was bitter news: a revelation with no future, nothing to act on. Of course, none of that could've prepared me for the journal.

"This woman," Philippa said, gaping, "is your mother?"

Elaine massaged her right temple, as if she were a character from the dramatis personae of a Victorian melodrama. I expected her to complain of a terrible headache, swoon, and collapse on the floor. Most likely, it was an attempt to elicit sympathy from Philippa. I wanted to snatch up the milk and pour it down her throat.

"Does this mean that . . ." Philippa added with a touch of wonder, "that Cleve was your half brother?"

Elaine's eyes shot wide open. They were tear-glazed and blazing with anxiety: "Are you going to tell Philippa everything?" they seemed to be asking me. "Are you sure you want to do that?"

She had deserted me; she had no right to ask anything of me. I wanted to tell the entire truth, to blurt it out, especially because it would humiliate

her, because she feared it. As we regarded each other, I spotted something sinister dart through her eyes. Under her fear, there was a haughty,
self-destructive impulse—an impulse I'd felt keenly in myself. She was
daring me to pull the trigger, to detonate all of us with the truth. But I
wouldn't do that to Philippa. Ever.

"You see," I said to Philippa, gripping the edge of the rickety table,
"she was upset when she discovered she was pregnant. She didn't want
to take care of me. She didn't want the responsibility, she didn't want to
answer all the questions, so she followed Miss M to New York City and
asked Miss M to claim me as hers."

Elaine broke in, murmuring: "I was weak. So, so weak—"

"Shut up!" I snapped, heading off her dramatics. Philippa jumped a
little. "You don't get to tell this part of it! It's not yours to tell."

Elaine flushed bright red and dropped her chin like an admonished
child.

"She was going to take care of me," I addressed Philippa, still fuming.
My anger was all that was keeping me together. "Wouldn't that have been
something? But she ran on hard times and needed the cash, so she went
to the Closses and told Halo that he'd knocked her up and that I was his.
Moira caught wind of it. She didn't like having her son 'blackmailed'—that's
what she called it—so she threatened Miss M and forced her to give me up
for adoption." Philippa scooted to the edge of the window seat. I looked
at Elaine, measuring her expression, wondering about her breaking point,
and slowly stood. "Miss M even tried to force you to take responsibility
for me, but you claimed that you were too 'emotionally fragile.' So, I went
into the system. Moira was on the board at Crestwood, so of course, it
was handled with the utmost discretion. Anyway, it freed you to renew
your engagement with Halo and, once married, have Cleve, who I guess
you weren't too 'emotionally fragile' to raise. After years in and out of
Crestwood and foster families, where I got these"—I stretched out my
arms, displaying my scars as the evidence of the damage those years had

done—"Jackie Peabody was murdered, and Moira saw an opportunity. She pulled strings and had me placed with B and E, keeping me, the liability, close." I glanced down at Philippa. "You know what's funny," I said to her. "Crestwood recorded my birthday incorrectly—or maybe fudged it on purpose to hide my identity even more. I'm actually eighteen. I can change my name now."

Grimacing sympathetically, Philippa rose and took my hand. Its touch was reassuring, even calming. Cool resolve cut through my thrumming anger. Clarity amid chaos. Even though I'd bungled telling her that I loved her, and even though we were staring down my nightmare of a mother, I knew that she loved me.

With her face still tilted forward, Elaine said, "A year or so ago, my sister moved back to town with a new name." She slowly lifted her chin. Frizzed strands of hair had slipped from her bun. "She wanted to be in your life, Judy, so she got a job at Eastern High. At first, she didn't want you to know who she was. She wanted to observe you from afar, but that changed, and then she made a point of bumping into Halo—"

"Not true," I said, taking a step toward her, dragging Philippa with me. I hadn't let go of her. "She wasn't planning it. *He* bumped into her. "

Elaine glared at me defiantly, trembling: "The worthless creep couldn't help himself, and the two of them, they started up again with no regard for me, for what I was feeling." Her voice clawed its way out of her throat. "Then he told me that he wanted to leave me for her, his 'old flame,' and that he wanted to embrace you as his daughter!" Her eyes bulged with rage. "I lost my goddamn mind, and Cleve, he overheard it all, which is why he must've stole Charlene's journal and why he hated you, Judy." She wiped her nose with the back of her hand. "I'd remained silent as Halo plowed his way through woman after woman. I'd tolerated his bitch of a mother. I understood I was just another one of his many women, another notch on the post. Other than being the mother of his son, I meant nothing to him. I never had! I knew what I had to do. I had to break free of it, of marriage and mother-hood." She covered her mouth in horror.

My pin-balling anger had subsided. Instead, something cleaner and sharper clicked into place. I picked up the mug in front of Elaine and said, "Drink it."

She reached out for it but drew back. Through her damp eyes, a knowing look emerged—perhaps an acknowledgment of her fate or maybe a touch of guilt for failing me. Who knows? I didn't care.

"Drink it," I demanded. "Drink it, or we'll make you."

Elaine rose and smoothed out her yellow dress. She looked first at Philippa and then at me. "Are you going to tell her everything?" she said to me, the light behind her eyes shifting. Was it a threat? Her irises seemed to expand like twin black holes, drawing me into their madness. Philippa squeezed my hand and whispered emphatically, "Let's go."

"Can I tell you something?" Elaine said, a smile creeping into her lips. "I'm glad you found Charlene. I'm glad you'll remember her in the bathtub that way. I'm glad it was *you*."

Fury shot through me, but I didn't move. Philippa's grip still anchored me, whetting my anger like a knife.

Elaine ran her tongue along her upper lip, exposing its soft underside. She straightened her back and shook her shoulders lightly. A smile flickered in her lips and fell away. As she rose to her feet, she scooped up the mug, a drop or two of the white liquid splattering on the table.

"I was going to drink it all along," she said, sighing with faux exaspera-tion. "If only I could've convinced you two to join me."

She brought it to her lips, tilted it up, and drank deeply, allowing the rivulets to pour over her chin and down her neck, soaking the collar of her dress. I held my breath, shocked that she'd done it. She lurched for-ward and dropped the mug, unwittingly kicking it across the room. We leaped back, startled. She clutched her throat and retched, her eyes wild and darting. Pink foam bubbled up at the corners of her mouth. A twitch of sympathy broke through me, and I took a step forward but stopped; I wasn't going to help her. She toppled backward toward the window seat, her shoulder smacking a pane of glass and cracking it from corner to corner. She groaned, and deep in her chest, a gurgle responded. She retched again, and her tongue protruded, a string of bloody saliva oozing from it. She whimpered, fell to the carpet on her hands and knees, and vomited.

I stared at her, unable to move.

Philippa staggered backward, releasing me. Elaine crawled toward me, collapsing a few feet away, her groan muffled by the carpet. She was pathetic, helpless. It made sense that she was my mother. In her I saw my rage, my ugliness, and my pain. There it all was, melting into the floor. Her hand shot out and gripped my ankle, as if she wanted to drag me to hell with her. But I didn't flinch. My heart had cooled; everything was clear. I took a step back, and the manacle of her hand fell away.

CHAPTER TEN

Ick! I know. But that's what happened. Elaine guzzled a lye solution, hence the ammonia-like odor. Apparently, she'd tossed out her Veronal, fearing it might implicate her in Cleve's and Charlene Peters's deaths, so she improvised. Her mind wasn't an ordered place.

I understand her better today than I did back then. I understand her fury, and I understand the importance of a melodramatic gesture. From the beginning of time, when women did or said something that challenged men, they called them "crazy" or "overwrought" or "emotional." It's 1963, and little has changed. Marilyn Monroe ended it last year. This February, Sylvia Plath. Both deaths were, perhaps, melodramatic gestures.

But they—we—aren't crazy or too emotional; that's just what the men think they're seeing, or more to the point, not seeing. The melodrama wouldn't be necessary if selfish fools like Halo weren't impossible to reach through the usual avenues of communication. No, men spark us to behave as we sometimes do. Without Tereus's vicious attack on Philomela, there would be no maimings, no murders, no cannibalism. Elaine's rage spun out of control, but you have to ask, why was it there to begin with? What seeded the storm?

Well, I've certainly embraced melodrama. Perhaps that's why I now write pulpy detective fiction à la Ray Kane. I've been churning out novels for about six years. Surely, you've stumbled across my paperbacks on a rack in the drug store or at the newsstand at the corner. Including this experiment, there are four novels under the pen name Abigail Knightley: The Longest Hallway, Flower of Death, Mother's Milk, *and* Seeing Double. *I began writing them after I moved back to DC. I've made a little money over time. Enough to get by. Of course, you understand, a pen name was a necessity.*

PHILIPPA, NOVEMBER 30, 1948

Judy and I were questioned in separate rooms. Shaken and drained, I gazed into Kipps's and Paulson's grim expressions and imparted everything that I'd learned about Cleve's and Miss Martins's murders—except that Elaine was Judy's mother, a detail Judy insisted that I withhold, and the existence of the diary, which we planned to retrieve later from its hiding place behind a bush across the street. To explain the pieces of the puzzle Judy lifted from its pages—the moon pins, in particular—I claimed that we'd deduced them through careful observation, that our sleuthing powers had been honed by our giddy infatuation with the PI Calvin McKey novels. Kipps and Paulson frowned skeptically but seemed to accept it as plausible.

After the interrogation, my parents escorted me home, both of them baffled, aloof, and unable to articulate disapproval or even words of comfort. We attempted small talk at dinner, but it was fragmented and elliptical. Mostly I listened to the scraping of flatware against dishes. Elaine Closs guzzling her milky poison continued to flicker through my mind. When it ignited in her, she seemed shocked, as if she was surprised that she'd done it, or perhaps, that Judy had induced her to do it. It all seemed unreal.

Minutes ago, Dad came to my room and asked me if I was okay. I told him yes, but he didn't believe me and reached out his hand to touch my arm. "Just go," I thought, "Please." He took a step back and said, "You scare me, Phil."

"I do?" I said.

"Detective Kipps rang while you were taking your bath. Elaine Closs didn't die, but the poison burned her mouth, throat, and stomach. She'll never speak again or, for that matter, chew solid food. It was a horrible thing she did to herself—and you saw it happen."

Fate was being cruel. Clearly, she drank it to kill herself, not just maim. The pain had to be excruciating, but she believed relief was just on the other side. My stomach churned. Had we caused this? We wanted justice, not torture. I looked at my lap, not wanting Dad to detect my guilt. "I'm fine," I said. "*Really.*"

"You're so unfazed," he said, crossing his arms. "You must be upset." He sounded as if he wanted me to explain myself, as if by not breaking into tearful sobs, I was confirming my "bad girl" status.

"I need time. It's shock, I guess." I softened my voice, understanding that he needed that from me. But it irritated me: Why can't I be okay? The situation was horrific, but it wasn't like Elaine was a saint; she'd killed her son and Miss Martins and had wanted to kill us.

He searched my face. "I wish . . ." he said. "I don't know who you are anymore."

I forced a smile. "Of course, you do."

He raised his eyebrows. "Well," he said, reaching for the doorknob, "if you have trouble sleeping, I could heat up—" He caught himself.

"My warm milk days are over," I said.

"I suppose so," he said gloomily.

When Paulson asked me what we'd said to Elaine before she poisoned herself, I told him that I was too distraught to remember, which of course was a lie. He was fishing for something to incriminate us—or at least explain us—but I wasn't going to bite. He also asked what Judy was doing while I was on the phone with the operator. I shrugged and told him that I didn't know, that I was focused on getting help. But I remembered. Judy just stood there, staring at her mother as she crawled across the floor, vomiting and bleeding, her garish yellow dress dragging behind her like wilted plumage. What was running through her mind? Hatred? Disgust? Moral righteousness? Even pleasure? God knows. She makes a mystery of herself. It's one of the things I love about her. Maybe it's *why* I love her. But will the secrets ever end? What did Elaine mean when she asked her if she was going to tell me everything? What is *everything*?

PHILIPPA, DECEMBER 5, 1948

After days of keeping me cooped up, Dad and Bonnie let down their guard. I slipped on my coat, scarf, and cap, and snuck out the front door. As I walked through the quiet Saturday streets, snowflakes swirled around me, light gusts sweeping them up before they touched the ground. In Lincoln Park, I passed the sixteenth president and the freed slave, and heard Judy's voice again: "Is he freeing him or making him beg for his freedom?" I made my way back to the Closses' town-house, lingered in front of it, taking in the now skeletal maple tree. I walked across the street to see if Judy hadn't returned to retrieve Miss Martins's diary. I wanted to read it. It was time. I rummaged through the bush, but nothing was there.

When I returned home, I shed my coat and scarf. Voices were coming from the parlor, a room Dad and Bonnie rarely used. One of the voices was my stepmother's, but the other? . . . I wasn't sure, so I crept closer, my winter coat and cap still slung over my arm. When I recognized her, I froze and became conscious of my breathing, of the potential for floorboards under my feet to creak. It was Moira Closs.

"What you've been through," Bonnie said, tut-tutting. "It must be so distressing."

"The universe has all its arrows pointed at me, it seems," Moira said, laughing hollowly. "Oh, I don't mean to be overly dramatic."

"It's understandable," Bonnie said. "May I offer you more coffee? Or a ham biscuit?"

"No, you're very kind."

"You're managing so well, though." I could tell by Bonnie's high squeaky timbre that she was straining to be conversational. I wondered if Moira detected her reticence.

"I'm doing my best. I just wish . . . Well, the police can be so help-less, you know. Not your nephew, of course, but so many of them. They still don't know why my daughter-in-law killed my grandson." Her voice cracked on cue. I imagined her dabbing her eyes with a hanky. "It's so difficult to talk about . . . and then what she did to herself was unspeak-able. And after all this mayhem, they don't even know who killed poor little Jackie Peabody. Mr. Bogdan has been cleared—Orpheus back from the dead, it seems!"

"Orpheus?"

"The myth."

"I'm sorry?"

"Orpheus goes to the underworld to retrieve his beautiful dead bride, Persephone."

"Eurydice," I thought, having recently had my refresher on Greek myth. Thank you, Elaine.

"Of course," Bonnie said, still baffled.

"He's a cat with nine lives," Moira said, dumbing it down. "Anyway, they've handed me a bunch of loose ends. Even the Peabodys have had to flee to the Caribbean for their own sanity. I may follow them."

"I know," Bonnie said, her voice dipping. "I'm afraid our Philippa might have a little something to do with that."

"Oh no," Moira said in a saccharine tone, "that's not the case. She's a good girl. If it hadn't been for her and Judy, I would never have known about Elaine."

She was lying. She was sinking her claws in.

"In fact, that's why I'm here."

"Yes?"

"I know this is a strange request, but I was hoping to speak with Philippa, just a word or two, to say thank you."

"I see."

"No, no, no!" I wanted to scream. "Bonnie, say no!"

"It would give me some solace. One less loose end to tie up."

I *had* to get out of there. I began backing away from the entrance to the parlor, but as I did, I bumped into the coat rack.

"Hello?" Bonnie said. "Is that you, Carl?"

I didn't know what to do. If I ran, I'd just have to do this some other time. Moira was the relentless sort. So, I draped my coat and scarf over a hook, noting Moira's glossy mink beside Bonnie's drab wool topcoat, and stepped into the room.

Both women rose when they saw me. Moira was in a dark blue wool suit with tortoiseshell buttons and velvet lapels. Her hair was swept up in an elegant coif, silvery and slick. Her earrings jangled as she offered me a bright, venomous smile.

"Where have you been?" Bonnie said timidly. "Your father went looking for you in the snow."

I gave Bonnie "not now" eyes.

"Philippa dear," Moira said, still smiling, her lips purplish and glossy. "I'm having a lovely chat with your stepmother. She's such a gracious host, but it's you whom I've come to see." She glanced at the pendulum clock on the wall and, to Bonnie, said, "Oh dear. I must be going! I have an early dinner date." A lie, and not a very good one. "Philippa, will you walk me out?" Bonnie was fiddling with the seam on her housedress. She seemed to sense that Moira was a viper, which oddly was comforting.

I shrugged back on my coat and, impersonating a polite young lady for Bonnie's sake, helped Moira on with her luxuriant knee-length fur and her orange poppy-print silk scarf.

Once out on the sidewalk, which was covered with a thin layer of snow, Moira turned to me, tilted her chin up, and said, "I should gut you and throw you in the city dump for what you and your friend did to my son." She grabbed me by the arm, digging her nails in through the wool, and drew me close. My adrenaline surged. She was surprisingly strong. "I know you killed him," she growled. Her face was stretched over her sharp-edged bones and brittle tissue. She was as fragile as papier-mâché, and decay was visible at the corners of her eyes, at the edges of her mouth, and in the purplish veins that crept up her neck. "You have no idea what you've done." She released me.

I rubbed my arm, seething but clearheaded. I knew what I needed to do. I wasn't going to let her threaten me. I felt Judy in me. Her righteousness. Her rage. "What does AHKA mean, the word you ordered your son to paint on Cleve—and how did you know it was written on Jackie?" We'd been searching for the connection, but even Elaine couldn't tell us. Moira knew the answer. I was sure of it.

She smiled and said nothing.

"Were you involved in Jackie's case from the beginning?"

She let out a derisive "Ha!" and added, "The Peabodys are old friends. I have lots of friends."

Thirty yards away, a black Cadillac started its engine and began to creep toward us.

Heat rose through me. "Tell me."

"No, dear, I won't. But let me ask you a question—"

Before she could, I said, "We have Miss Mart—Charlene Peters's diary." I wasn't intimidated by her. "I know what you did to her. I know about Judy." I wasn't sure if she knew that Judy was Elaine's child and not Miss Martins's; I didn't want to risk showing my hand.

"What do you mean 'we'?" she said, her eyebrows lifted.

I moved closer. "I know what it says." Bluffing.

She considered my statement, visibly rattled by its implications. The snowflakes collected on her mink like dandruff, making her seem shabby, moldering. "Elaine told me Judy has the diary," she said, unconvincingly blasé. "It was the first thing the pathetic bat jotted down in the hospital. 'Charlene's Diary. Judy.' So, what do you *really* know?"

It occurred to me that she had no idea what was in the diary either, so I continued to bluff: "It's enough to put you away for a long time." It was like a line from a Ray Kane novel. I knew I'd miscalculated.

"You're full of shit," she scoffed, waving her hand. "Besides, my important friends—well, you see, they'd believe Charlene's sad scrawlings as much as they believed my daughter-in-law's ravings. And even if they did believe them, they won't touch me."

I changed my approach: "Your son died thinking Judy was his daughter. He wanted to meet her—or don't you care?"

Moira's lips parted, and her posture drooped. I'd made the right move. She wasn't all stone. "He was a fool," she said, sadness lingering in the word "fool." I could tell she loved her son. After all, she'd gone to great lengths to protect him. Seeing a chink in her armor, I asked another question that had been nagging me: "All those years ago, when Charlene asked Halo for money for the baby, why didn't you just give it to her? Or insist she and Halo marry? Why take the baby from her?"

Her eyes flashed. "So, you haven't read the diary," she cooed triumphantly. "Certainly, Charlene would've written about that little episode. You don't know everything."

There it was again: Elaine asking Judy, "Are you going to tell her *everything*?" Desperate, I dropped the ruse and said, "What don't I know?" My voice squeaked. "*Tell* me."

Moira placed her finger over her lips. "Shhh!" she said. "I've got to go, but this isn't over." She started toward the Cadillac, which now was feet away, its motor purring. Icy snow tap-tapped its black metal finish. "You and I, your stepmother and your father, especially your father—we're all going to become good friends." The Caddy came to a full stop. A tall chauffeur in a black overcoat and trilby popped out and opened the back door. Moira took the door and spun around, her mink whirling in the snow. "As always, I enjoy welcoming new people into my circle," she said, lips quivering. "For the right people, there's always room."

I rushed to her, grabbing the edge of the door before she could get in: "Judy wasn't Charlene's child. She was *Elaine's*."

"Yes, I know," she said, trying to close the door.

"And Halo wasn't the father."

She sniffed. "I know that too."

She dropped into her seat. The chauffeur took the door, trying to squeeze me out, but I wedged myself between it and its frame. I'd come so far. "How do you know that?" I yelled. "Tell me!" The chauffeur's arm swept around my waist and lifted me up and away from the car. I landed on my feet, but stumbled backward, falling hard on my rear end in the middle of the sidewalk. Pain shot through me, and the cold snow burned my bare palms.

When I glanced up, I saw that, across from Moira, sat Judy, her face scrawled with concern. Why was she there? Moira slammed the door and said, "Goddammit," realizing what I'd seen. She rolled down the window and leaned out, her poppy scarf rippling in the breeze like a flame. I detected a flicker of admiration in her eyes. Perhaps my persistence had paid off. "Get her on her feet," she said to the chauffeur, who offered me his hand. As I took it, I gazed up into his face, which had been shaded by his hat. He wasn't a chauffeur at all. He was one of the two goons who had followed Halo into the alley, the rangy one that Judy had called "the scarecrow." "I was going to spare you," Moira said, "but now, you'll get what you asked for"—she sighed with contempt—"the truth."

The snow was falling steadily by the time we arrived at our destination: the Closs mansion. A thin crust coated the surface of the drive, making the Caddy's wheels spin on the steep incline before gripping the pavement. Dusk had receded, and light from the city burned at the edges of the trees. The Tudor home, with its three looming gables, chimney spitting smoke, and windows like lidless eyes, greeted us at the top like a monster patiently waiting for its dinner.

During our trip across town, at Moira's command, we remained silent. I sat beside the gaunt goon, whose unshakable focus on the road and refusal to acknowledge my presence made me increasingly uneasy. It didn't help that I'd glimpsed the grip of his pistol in his shoulder holster as he raised his arm to turn the steering wheel. Judy was behind me, inches from Moira, so we couldn't even exchange looks. What was Moira up to? Would she tell us the truth? Would she hurt us? My only consolation was that Bonnie knew who I was with, or, at least, could make a good guess.

The car rolled to a stop behind a black sedan, and Moira ordered us out. We crunched through the snow and into the entry hall, its dark paneling and coffered ceiling now veiled in shadows. It was quiet, save our footfalls and the ticking of a far-off clock. Glossy in the low light, the portrait of Queen Elizabeth seemed to arch her eyes at us: "You again? Fools."

"This way," Moira said, after yanking off her gloves and tossing her mink on a fussy accent chair. She strode past us, and we slid out of our coats and followed her.

Once again, we entered her oak-lined study, which gleamed eerily with firelight. Above the fireplace glowered the owl-eyed patriarch. Everywhere in this house, something was staring back at you. I shivered, almost expecting a secret panel to slide open to expose a Greek chorus on the other side: "The two girls, with fear and trepidation in their hearts, followed the cruel queen into her throne room, only to discover, they were not alone."

Indeed, we weren't alone.

"Here they are, Judy Peabody and Philippa Watson," Moira tossed out, cutting across the room to warm herself by the fire. "Hello there," a man said, rising from his chair. The fire lit up his face, making his black eyes shine and giving his blocky face the monolithic cast of an Easter Island statue. He was wide-shouldered, a little fat, and wore a dark, well-tailored three-piece suit, wine red tie and matching pocket handkerchief, and stank of cigarettes. My brain spun, trying to fit it all together. Who was he and why was Moira introducing us? Another spook perhaps? He had that aloof air, and his eyes parsed but revealed nothing. "I'm John," he said, offering his hand. His voice was warm, but it didn't match his crooked smile, which he put on like a hat. I shook his hand, but Judy remained still and said, "John what?" I sensed that she understood our situation better than I did, or perhaps she knew the danger we were in. He looked at her, his smile freezing, then vanishing. "You've met Agent Lott, I see," Three-piece John said, nodding to the rangy man, who now stood by the door, his trilby in hand. So, they *were* FBI agents—or government agents of some sort. Clearly, Three-piece was connected to the scarecrow and the other agent who had confronted Elaine and Halo. But how was he connected to Moira or Miss Martins or Cleve?

"So," Three-piece went on, "I hear you're fledgling detectives, seekers of justice in training. Or so Moira tells me."

Neither of us responded. Out of the corner of my eye, I spotted yet another man. His legs were jutting out of a shadowy nook off to the side of the paneled fireplace. Although I couldn't see his face, I could feel his eyes on us. The Greek chorus was chanting, "Beware, beware! Philippa, beware!"

"Girls," Moira said, turning to us, "have you forgotten how to make pleasant conversation?"

"Pleasant conversation?" Judy growled and stepped forward. I glimpsed her face. Perhaps it was the glow from the firelight, but she seemed—I don't know—sober, like she understood the score. A Calvin McKey look. How could she be so self-assured? Wasn't she afraid?

"Do you girls want to be FBI agents?" Three-piece said, flipping his smile on again. "It's not unheard of. Most women don't like that sort of work. They usually end up in the secretarial pool."

Ignoring him, Judy pointed to the man peering out from the nook and, in a low hostile tone, said, "Why is *he* here?" She'd been able to make him out, I guessed. A smoldering log popped and hissed.

"The question you should be asking," Moira said, "is why *you* are here."

Judy stuck out her jaw. "You want to frighten us."

"Yes, we do," Moira smirked. "It's for your own good."

"You've upset a lot of people," Three-piece said, doing a poor imitation of a father figure. "Put this tragedy behind you. Leave Moira alone. Go play detective somewhere else."

"We're not playing detective," I said, my hackles up.

"No, I guess you're not." He chuckled. "I like your spirit."

"You still haven't answered me," Judy said, seething.

Three-piece's face fell, almost as if she'd disappointed him. "Sit down," he said, nodding at the leather couch. Neither of us moved. "Sit," he commanded. "Now." I glanced over at the mystery man, hoping for a better look. A ribbon of light fell across his face igniting one intense blue eye, but still, I was at a loss. *Who* was he? And why was his presence unsettling Judy? We made our way to the couch. On the low coffee table in front of us lay a manila folder. "Go ahead," Three-piece said, waving his hand at the folder. "Take a look, Philippa." Moira stood by him, crossing her arms. Judy seemed more drawn to the lurker in the corner than the folder's contents. "It's a family album," he said. I flipped it open, and inside were a series of photos of Judy and Iris Baker strolling on the street. It was nighttime, but their faces were clear in the glow from a lighted window display. It looked like Iris was studying the scars on Judy's arms. "It's Judy and Iris," I said, baffled. "They're friends. *We're* friends. Is this a joke?"

"No joke," Moira said with a trace of pleasure. "Is it, Judy?"

I looked at Judy, whose attention was now fixed on the photos. Her face was slack with surprise—or wonder. She reached out and touched the edge of one of them.

"I don't get it," I said. "What do you mean this is a *family* album?"

"After you pelted accusations at Halo," Moira said to Judy, "I asked John to have one of his associates follow you. After all, he has a stake in the game. Mr. Lott spotted you with Iris Baker, took these photos. Iris, you see, is the daughter of Ellis and Alice Reynolds Baker. Alice Reynolds worked for Crestwood Children's Orphanage for many years, and she kept a good eye on you, which considering the circumstances, was a remarkably Christian thing to do."

I couldn't quite grasp what I was hearing. What does Iris have to do with this? And what "game" did Three-piece John have a stake in? Judy's eyes were activated, as if she, like me, was attempting to thread all of this together. I turned to Moira and her well-dressed FBI pal, trying to read their smug expressions. "I don't understand this," I said, exasperated.

"Of course, you don't," Moira said, almost sympathetically. "The only reason Charlene Peters—your beloved Miss Martins—took the child,

Judy here, from my daughter-in-law was because she wanted to use her to blackmail my son."

Miss Martins would've never blackmailed anyone. I knew that.

Moira registered my doubt. "That's when I realized you hadn't read her diary. She would've mentioned it."

"You don't know that."

"I don't, that's true. But the first time I set eyes on that child I knew something was wrong. Her complexion, her black eyes, her hair. No, she wasn't Halo's and Elaine's. Leo Paulson, an old fling of mine, had just made detective. Guess what he discovered . . . "

I shook my head.

"Elaine had been stepping out on my son and cavorting with Negros at some dive bar called Club Caverns. Apparently, she's a jazz enthusiast!" She flapped her hand in front of her like it was all just too much. "She met a man at the bar and had an affair. His name was Ellis Baker, a philanderer with a wife and daughter of his own, Alice and Iris."

Still stunned, I glanced at Judy, who didn't seem shocked by this news. "So," I said, "Iris is . . . is Judy's half-sister?"

"Hence the *family* album, dear." A smirk lurked on Moira's face.

"And Judy is—"

"A half-breed."

Judy shot up from her seat, bright with fury, but said nothing.

Moira lifted her chin. "You said you wanted the truth."

Was *this* what Judy had been keeping from me? Was it the "everything" that Elaine had mentioned? Had Judy discovered the truth in Charlene's diary? But why hide it from me? Either she was ashamed of it—which was possible but unlikely—or she thought I would reject her, which is what Moira was counting on.

I expected Judy to say something, but she just stood there, glaring. Her anger was visible, but distant, like flames behind glass. Moira regarded her and said, "Please, there's no need to make a scene." Judy blinked and lowered herself to the couch. Fumbling a bit, I attempted to defend Char-lene. "She wouldn't have used Judy to, to blackmail you. That's not who she was. We knew her."

"Well, it happened." Moira shrugged. "When I discovered the child wasn't hers, I didn't waste time in setting the baby on a new course in life. Elaine and Halo were re-engaged by that point, and I didn't want a scandal. I never told Halo the truth, but Elaine blurted it out a few months ago. At first, he believed her, but I convinced him she was lying, that she was trying to punish him, that he shouldn't listen to the ravings of a madwoman."

He'd believed her all right. It was the tipping point, why he snapped and attacked her. But he didn't at the end, or he wouldn't have pursued us—or maybe that's why he followed us. He was trying to decide who he believed.

"Anyway," Moira continued, sitting in the wingback chair across from Three-piece and crossing her legs, taking time to smooth her fine wool dress over her knee. "Ellis begged me to give the child to him, but I explained that she could pass. 'Wouldn't you want a life for her as a white woman instead of a Negro like yourself?' I asked him. He moaned and called me names, but he came around. His wife—the better part of that couple if you ask me—went to work at Crestwood to be close to her. I can't imagine why she'd want to watch over another woman's child, but there she was—your very own fairy godmother. Well, until she got a little too close for comfort, and we had her fired for stealing."

"What about Elaine?" I said, glancing at Judy, who sat straight-backed and still, head tilted forward a fraction. I didn't read shock or even anger on her face. Her eyes were roving, directed inward. "Didn't she care about the baby?"

"Elaine was as horrified by her indiscretion with Ellis Baker as I was," Moira went on. "Besides, if she had tried to find the child, I would have made her life miserable." Her upper lip twitched, and her eyes fell to her lap. "What I didn't count on was Charlene popping up again with a new name, and a desire to rekindle the flame with my son. I didn't count on

Halo being a fool, either. I underestimated how insane Elaine was—*is*."
She paused, distracted, perhaps by a flash of regret. "I imagine most of
the story—and perhaps more—is in the diary." She looked at me directly.
"That's why we're all here, to make sure we're crystal clear with each other."

Judy shifted her attention to Three-piece: "Why are you here?" He
adjusted the lapel on his suit and glanced at Moira, but before he could
speak, she added, "Because of him?" She nodded toward the shadow beside
the fireplace. There it was: the single eye twitching in a beam of light,
which now I realized was a reflection from the brass fireplace tools. The
mystery man leaned forward and slowly rose to his feet. At first, I didn't
realize who he was. The room was dim, and I'd only seen him in grainy
newspaper photos. As he approached, I saw that Adrian Bogdan was quite
handsome, in a swarthy way. But ruining the illusion, his body odor—the
stink of beer and sweat—wafted over me. He smiled, revealing a set of
rotten teeth. "Da," he said, "because of *me*."

Moira flinched almost imperceptibly. She was frightened of him.
"Adrian," she said as if she was admonishing him—and perhaps warning
us. How was he connected to her? Was there a final thread we'd failed to
pick up? He had to be furious with her, right? She and Halo had tried
to pin Cleve's murder on him—writing AHKA on Cleve's body and then
the stupid yearbook trick. What was the equalizer between them? The FBI?
"Meet Judy Peabody and her friend Philippa Watson," she said to Bogdan,
glancing at Three-piece, as if to implore him to step in. Bogdan squinted at
me, disinterested, then gazed down at Judy as she sat there frozen, his irises
preternaturally blue. He was only a couple of feet from her. With an eerie
calm, he reached out and took her by her chin, his large fingers gripping
the slope of her jaw, his grimy cuticles black crescent moons. "You don't
look much like a nigger," he said. The word stabbed through the room,
as ugly and corrupt as his teeth. Judy tried to pull away from him, but he
wouldn't release her. "The joke is on the Peabodys—and Jackie was such a
sweet little thing. White as snow."

Adrian Bogdan had killed Jackie. I had no doubt.

"That's enough, Bogdan," Three-piece said. "They get the idea. Don't you, girls?"

Judy yanked her chin away, and Bogdan reached for her again.

"Don't!" Moira barked, standing.

Behind us, the hammer of a gun clicked.

JUDY, DECEMBER 5, 1948

I leaned my head against the cab window and, through snowflakes, watched DC roll by—the National Gallery, the Capitol, the Senate. The light of the day was dying, and it was only 4:00 P.M. Edith had roped me into going downtown for another lunch date, followed by a trip to the passport agency. She's still determined to drag me through the Caribbean before they send me to Agnes March. The whole thing has a last meal air to it.

I lifted my head off the chilled glass. I studied her profile, her wave of auburn hair, her strong nose, the olive undertone of her skin. I see why Moira thought we were a good visual fit for one another. Stamped with the Peabody name, I'd be beyond scrutiny to casual observers unaware of the adoption. Of course, close friends and family would know, but the broader social circle wouldn't question it: "Oh, her complexion is so dark," they would say. "It must be the Georgiou coming out in her. That Mediterranean blood." Not wanting to linger on the unpleasant, they would forget, like Edith wanted them to, that Jackie had ever died. The names Judy and Jackie would blend into each other, becoming interchangeable. Moira probably thought she was doing me a favor. No wonder she resented my prying. It didn't matter. Charlene wrote it all down in her journal.

As a girl, I had stood in front of a mirror a thousand times, studying myself and fantasizing about my birth parents, but it had never occurred to me that I was mixed race. Not once. But there it was, in Charlene's fine hand: I'm the result of a fling, Elaine's and some Negro musician's error in judgment. Charlene never mentioned my father's name. Perhaps she didn't know it. Perhaps she thought that some things shouldn't be written down. Or perhaps she was too horrified by it. No, if she were, she wouldn't have sought me out, right? Why *did* she find me? A sense of responsibility? Guilt? I wish I could talk to her about it. I wish I could talk to the Miss M version of her. Maybe my teacher would offer words of wisdom. Hell, who am I kidding? What did she know about it? It's not like she would've learned about it reading Romantic poetry.

What I do know is that I have no direction. Just information. Don't get me wrong. I'm not embarrassed. That's why it's a secret, why Elaine, Halo, and Moira feared it, and maybe that's how I'm supposed to feel, but I don't. I do feel foolish. Foolish because the universe had been dropping hints, and I was too blind to see them. I've always believed Jim Crow was bullshit. It doesn't square with our country's war against fascism—or "the communist threat." How can we fight for freedom but deny it to each other? The logic is flawed. I've always known these things deep down. That's why Iris and I are friends.

The problem is that I'm the same person I was days ago, but I've ceased feeling like me. It's an invisible transformation. It's about me trying to change my idea of myself *to* myself. I look the same in the mirror, but I'm not white anymore, or not just white. And the Negro part of me ... What does that even mean? It's a sea of question marks. And tell me, how do I translate that for other people? It's not like losing weight or getting your hair dyed or taking a new name. You're new to yourself, but not to anyone else—well, until you say something. And I do want to say something. I want Philippa to know. But I have no doubt: it will level her. She may eventually understand, but it's too risky. If she rejects me, I don't know what I'll do. Shatter into pieces?

The taxi lurched to a stop behind a black Cadillac, jerking me out of my thoughts. We were home, and a man in a bulky coat and wide-brimmed hat was leaning against it, head bent forward. I stepped out of the cab and cold air bit into my lungs. My feet slipped slightly on the damp bricks. As I approached the man, he looked up. It was Agent Scarecrow. What was *he* doing here? He squinted at us but said nothing. Edith and I turned onto the path to the front door. On the stoop, Moira Closs was chatting with Bart, her long mink coat shimmering in the mellow snow-filtered light. He saw us and nodded grimly. Moira spun and beamed—her smile a gash and her eyes malevolent. "Judy," she trilled. "I've been looking for you. I promised your father that, before you departed for the sunny shores of St. Vincent, we'd have a little chat." Bart looked drained, helpless. I glanced back at Edith, who, to my surprise, seemed alarmed.

"We have so much to do, Moira," Edith said with false levity. "I don't think we can spare the time." She slipped her hand in mine, which startled me. I almost recoiled, but somehow (maybe it was the tenderness of her grip), I understood that she was trying to reassure me or lay some sort of claim to me. She didn't want me having this "little chat." That was clear. But I wanted to. What did the Evil Queen have to say to me? My curiosity was piqued. I still didn't know the origin or meaning of AHKA or who was responsible for Jackie's murder. Or, for that matter, my father's name.

"I need her for just an hour or so," Moira said. "You don't mind, do you? I'll bring her right back. I promise." She gave me an appraising look, like I was a ham she was estimating how long to boil.

Edith released my hand reluctantly, and the next thing I knew, I was in the Closs-mobile with Agent Scarecrow flashing his gun at me, a reminder to behave or I'd . . . what? Get a bullet? The FBI's no-frills parenting style. "We have a stop before we get to our destination," Moira said, no longer aggressively pleasant. "I want to know what Miss Watson knows. She may need an invitation to our little heart-to-heart."

In front of me, spread out on Moira's coffee table, were photos of Iris and me, the night I walked her to the bus and showed her my scars—a "family album" according to this FBI goon in a three-piece suit who called himself John and only John. He sat in his chair across from us, satisfied at his theatrical means of imparting this news. I could tell he enjoyed watching me trying to parse the truth. Moira was babbling on—unaware, I think—that I already knew much of what she was telling us. This was the "little chat" she told Edith she needed to have with me. "If you don't leave me alone," she seemed to be saying, "I'll tell the world what you really are." When she called me a half-breed, I wanted to tell her to go fuck herself, but instead, I just stood and said nothing, thoughts swirling.

All this time, my half sister had been in front of me, right across the counter at Horsfield's. The line between us, which ran hidden under the chrome counter, under all the malts and hamburgers, under the cigarette breaks, hummed inside me as if it had been violently plucked. Clotho's thread. I could feel, in a very physical way, the reality of what I'd learned about myself. It wasn't any clearer or any less confusing, but it was gaining density in my heart.

When Moira said, "That's why we're all here—to make sure we're crystal clear with each other," I understood why she was here and why I was here—she wanted Charlene's journal, which she'll never have. But what I didn't understand was why Adrian Bogdan and the FBI were here, or for that matter, Philippa. Moira could've threatened me one-on-one. Maybe she was worried that it wouldn't be enough. Of course, nothing would be enough. As we talked, Bogdan's silent presence seemed to radiate from his dark corner. No, there's more to this. I glared at Only-John's slash of a mouth and quick eyes and said, "Why are you here?" He fidgeted, and I added, "Because of him?" nodding to the creep breathing heavily in the shadows. Bogdan stood, revealing himself, and sauntered over to us, flashing his stalactite teeth. Only Philippa seemed surprised. "Da," he said, "because of *me*." I could hear the gears spinning in Philippa's brain. Mine were whirring fast, too.

Moira introduced us to Bogdan, unease with him rippling across her finely powdered face. After all, she and her son had framed him. That's when an idea slid into my mind: Moira wasn't friends with Only-John; she was working with him. Such things happened in the DC social scene. According to B and E, no one went to a cocktail party *just* for the cocktails. What if, somehow, they were *all* working together? It would explain why, in a moment of panic, she thought of Bogdan as a ready scapegoat, and how she had easy access to the information written on Jackie. But what were they working together on? Who were they to each other?

Bogdan leered at me, stepped forward, and grabbed my chin. He said, "You don't look much like a nigger." That word rocketed through me, stirring up shame I didn't know I had and pushing me out of myself. I felt its heat; its radiation; its ability to annihilate, but somehow—perhaps it's the way it flung me away from myself—it didn't have its intended effect. It gave me perspective, even clarity, which made me feel powerful. He wanted to belittle and demean me, to squash me, but it exposed him. Now, his guts were inside out. "The joke is on the Peabodys," he added with a chuckle. I gritted my teeth and tried to pull away, but his hand clamped tighter—I could feel the rough sandpaper-like surface of his fingers—and he hissed, "Jackie was such a sweet little thing. White as snow."

Only-John and Moira said something that I didn't catch. I glared back at Bogdan, trying to melt him with my gaze. His muscular face flexed and throbbed; his veins pulsed at his temples. His eyes pierced me with their aquamarine irises, and along the ridge of his nose bubbled oily blackheads. Without a doubt, I was staring at Jackie's murderer. His sinister aura wrapped around me as it had Jackie. Empathy for her—more than I've ever felt before or since—swelled up in me. It was unbearable to know that his face was the last thing she saw. I sensed her suffering, her terror.

He clenched his tartar-caked teeth. He wanted to kill me, and despite my energetic bitterness, my resolve, fear crept in.

Behind me, the scarecrow cocked his pistol.

Moira yelled, "Don't!" and flew to her feet.

The room froze in a bizarre tableau.

Bogdan released me and held up his hands, as if it was all no big deal, he was just playing around, the kidder.

Although I didn't see it, I sensed that the scarecrow had lowered his weapon. Bogdan's shoulders relaxed, and he dropped his hands.

Philippa tilted her chin, her blue-gray eyes catching mine—and a spark flew between us. Perhaps it was concern or righteous anger or even love. It was too quick, too subtle, to be sure, but it wasn't a rejection, it wasn't shame. I didn't know how she'd feel about my background, about who I was. Sure, she liked Iris, but Iris was the first Negro she'd ever befriended. What mattered at that moment, however, was that she was with me, not against me. I wasn't alone. She pivoted toward Bogdan and, in a classic Philippa move, blurted out rapid-fire questions: "What does AHKA mean? Why did you write it on Jackie?"

Always after the truth!

"It's not AHKA," he growled, and shifting into a Slavic accent, his Ukrainian origins showing, he said, "It's Эвридика. They mistook the и for an English H, and the first four letters of the Cyrillic washed off in the river. The joke's on Moira."

Moira was now behind her chair, clutching its back edge. Her eyes were darting nervously. Bogdan's behavior didn't seem to be part of the plan.

"Why did you write it on her?" Philippa said, undaunted.

"Her story isn't over." He seemed pleased by her question, as if, finally, someone had actually seen him. I didn't like it. At all. "I sent her to the underworld. Don't worry, I'll return to get her, like Orpheus did Eurydice, to save her from death, like the rest of them, the rest of Anna's friends." His voice was mild, even serene, the Slavic accent enriching its timbre.

"It's how I mark them, with the name of the original victim, Эвридика, beautiful Eurydice, bitten by the viper." The Shirley Temple memorial to his sister made sense now. Perhaps she was the original victim, his Eurydice, struck dead by his father—the original snake in the grass, so to speak.

"What do you mean, the rest of them?" Philippa said softly, not wanting to spook the beast. "How many?"

"As many who wanted to go," he said wistfully and turned to me and, as if it was my lucky day, said, "I'll send you there, too." His face lit up from inside, as if this thing he did—killing girls, his little Eurydices—brought meaning to his life. Although I'm sure my racial background sullied the purity of his precious ritual, he needed me—my banishment to the underworld—to fulfill him. Fear uncoiled inside me. It wasn't panic or adrenaline-ignited fight or flight. No, it was something else—perhaps it was being in awe of the enormity of the evil only feet from me.

Almost to herself, Philippa said, "The FBI, the Russian accent . . . I think I understand this." She seemed delighted by her discovery. We looked at each other. Her eyes flashed at me in an attempt to beam her epiphany into me like comic book telepathy, but I had no idea what she'd put together. I didn't see the connections between all of the people in that room, especially Bogdan and the FBI. What was I missing? Her expression dissolved into impatience, and begrudgingly, she said, "He's a *spy*."

I expected Only-John and the rest to laugh: "Oh, Philippa, you're such a silly little girl!" Instead, he sat up and placed his hands on his knees, worrying his kneecaps. His face was rigid and affectless. No one was denying it. Was it true? Were we in the midst of a spook party? Shit. So that's his stake in all of this. A cog in my mind ticked forward: "But Moira—she derailed everything by framing Bogdan."

"Her crime of convenience was a blunder," Philippa said, still focused on Only-John. "That's why, after interviewing Elaine Closs, your agents tricked Halo into going to the Daphne to incriminate himself?" She craned her neck back to address the scarecrow: "What did you say to him?"

He didn't respond; he just stared at her.

Moira's chin was cocked defiantly, but Only-John's eyes fluttered. He was annoyed. I'd hoped he'd explain himself or confirm our theory—or at least offer a glint of admiration. Fat chance. It didn't matter. The momentum of our deduction spurred me on: "Did your spooks tell Halo that Charlene was in danger? Is that why he moved so quickly?"

Still, nothing.

"But you knew she was already dead."

"Enough!" he snapped and stood from his seat. Despite his paunch and three-piece suit and tight little smile, he had a powerful presence. I'd struck a nerve. The scarecrow and the penguin must've seen through Elaine's act. Maybe she let them see through it. Moira must've been in serious trouble with the FBI's senior spooks for using Bogdan to cover up murder. Perhaps she caved under pressure and spilled her guts. Maybe they even told her that they were framing her son, that he was a necessary sacrifice. I wonder how she felt about that: her baby boy, the patsy for a crime his wife committed, a crime born out of bigotry.

Stepping out from behind the chair, she spoke: "I've done my part to make it right. My son is dead. Elaine is locked up." Then, to Only-John, her features narrowing as if taking aim: "Your precious resource, your child-murdering monster is out of control and has been for years." She pointed at Bogdan, jabbing the air between them. "If he hadn't murdered Jackie Peabody, none of us would be here, would we?"

"This isn't about you and your fucking cocktail parties and private parlor chats," Bogdan snarled, spittle flying. "This is about *me*."

"What is he . . . ?" Philippa said, then with more force, ". . . a resource for?"

"Information," Moira said with distaste.

"Information?" Philippa echoed.

I recalled a movie I'd seen several years ago at the Uptown. *The House on 92nd Street.* It's about a man who, because of his German heritage, is approached by the Nazis to spy on Americans. He goes to the FBI, and they enlist him as a double agent. Of course, Bogdan isn't a Nazi. He's Ukrainian. Maybe he's . . . What? A Communist? Or *was* a Commie?

Bogdan leered at us. His gemlike eyes danced in front of his oily skin. Chills ran through me—and I could feel Philippa shrink beside me. Then he smiled, and his ruined teeth, more than anything he could say, revealed the truth. "I'm the mythical boatman Charon transporting secret messages over the River Styx from the underworld to the land of the living, from my homeland to my new home. After all, the Soviet Union and this country pray to the same gods—Almighty Uranium and Supreme Plutonium. It's best to curry favor with these gods. They are tyrannical and absolute, just ask the Japanese."

He knew how to extend a metaphor.

"It's not worth the cost," Moira snapped, her shoulders sinking. "All those girls. Here, and in your country. Butchered."

"A moral conundrum, isn't it?" he said, encroaching on her, taunting her. "A few sweet girls or the lives of millions. It's not too much to ask, not really." He smiled again, flashing rot. "Besides, I'll bring all of them home one day, back from the dead, mothers and daughters reunited, brothers and sisters again arm in arm."

As I thought it, Philippa said it: "You're insane." She said it plainly, as if it was a statement the entire group could agree on, as if it was a fact—the sky is blue, the grass is green, Bogdan is fucking crazy. But we weren't in the realm of sanity. Moira's study was the anteroom to Bogdan's under-world, a space where government agencies protected child murderers in the name of national security. It was a shadowy place where moral logic didn't apply, nor did simple facts. That was Philippa's miscalculation, which is why, in a spasm of rage, Bogdan lurched forward and backhanded her. She cried out and toppled into me, her strawberry curls springing out of their shape and landing in my face, in my mouth. We crashed to the floor, knocking the coffee table over. The photos of Iris and me fanned out across the rug.

When someone strikes you, you don't know how you're going to react. I was startled, but my anger—all the frustration that I've carried over the years, the same fury I felt toward Elaine—seized me. Hitting Philippa *was* hitting me. As I write this, I can still taste the hair tonic from her curls—and I swear there's a mark on my cheek, as if he'd hit me. We aren't just friends or lovers; we're the same person, two sides of the same coin, *folie a deux*. But it wasn't madness; it was love. I felt it in my body—which is why, without thinking about it, I lunged at him, arms swinging wildly, only to be cut short, my forward momentum suspended. The scarecrow had gripped me by my waist, his fingers digging into my midriff. His long arms slid around me, pressing in on my stomach. My heart was slamming against my ribs. I wanted to beat and claw and smash Bogdan into nothing. I wanted to see him grow small. His handsome face, that savage symmetry, collapsed. His dazzling eyes retreated in their sockets, and his bottom lip drooped. He was frightened of me.

Still discombobulated, Philippa found her feet. She reached for me, tottering. Moira swept down on her, folding her winglike arms around her and holding her in place. Her gesture was sheltering, forming a protective cocoon. All the same, Philippa struggled, her face furrowed, her eyes bulging, glassy.

I continued to buck the scarecrow's grip, kicking at his shins and trying to twist away from him. In my periphery, I saw Only-John draw his pistol from his shoulder holster. "Jesus Christ," he spat, waving the barrel, "Stop it!" And with that, Bogdan backed away, and I ceased thrashing. The scarecrow released me, and I landed on my heels. Philippa slipped from Moira's embrace, and we took each other's hands, crushing close to one another. Her touch soothed me and quieted my mind. John looked at us, his intense eyes level, in control. "Girls," he said firmly, "so now you have an idea of the complexity of our situation—well, more than an idea. I don't want this to be a bigger fucking mess than it already is. You're going to leave and never speak about this again. Even to each other. If you do, I'll make it my pet project to destroy you and your families." He looked at the scarecrow and, shaking his shoulders to cast off the tension, said, "Agent Lott will drive you home."

PHILIPPA, DECEMBER 6, 1948

Other than throwing on our coats, we didn't let go of each other until we stepped out of Moira's door. Agent Lott was a few steps in front of us, and we knew (call it telepathy) what we were going to do the second our shoes crunched on the snow. We glared at each other, our hands broke apart, and we ran, plunging down the hillside. We weren't getting in the car with Lott. Neither of us believed he was going to drive us home. When we made our move, he spun around, but I didn't look back to see if he was pursuing us. We didn't have on the appropriate footwear for a dash through the snow—even in an inch of accumulation. The smooth soles of our flats offered no control, and the steep incline became perilous. Just beyond a line of pine trees, we landed on our rear ends and slid down the bank. The snowflakes stung our cheeks, and the icy slope burned the backs of our thighs. Somehow fate intervened, and we didn't collide with any tree trunks or rocky ledges. Like a carnival chute, we popped out on the curb. Judy stood quickly, offered me a hand, and we continued to run, our anxiety seeping out as we wove our way through the residential streets of Chevy Chase.

As our run became a walk, we drew close, interlocking our arms to stave off the chill. I thought of Moira's strange embrace after Bogdan had struck me. At first, it'd seemed cruel, like an attempt to keep me from saving Judy, who I was convinced Bogdan meant to harm, who I'm sure he *still* means to harm. But I became aware of something motherly in the way she was holding me. Not gentle, but not rough either. "Stop struggling, dear," she said in my ear, "I won't be able to protect you." Moira protect *me*? She was supposed to be threatening us, not protecting us—wasn't that the point of her introducing us to Three-piece and Bogdan? Maybe her threat was toothless or merely intended to scare—or maybe it had more bite than she'd intended.

After wandering the neighborhood, we found Wisconsin Avenue and hopped on the next streetcar regardless of its destination. We shook snow from our hair and inspected the damage to our clothes and bodies. I had no idea what I'd say to Dad and Bonnie—about the bruise on my face, my damaged dress, or where I'd been. I'd have to lie, but I was getting used to it. After we settled next to each other, Judy slipped her arm around me and whispered, "Jesus, Philippa." She gave a little, weary laugh and pulled me to her. I wanted her to know that I didn't care who her parents were, or for that matter, who her sister was. I was certain that she worried that it would change the way I saw her, but I was exhausted and couldn't call up the right words, so I just leaned my head on her shoulder and closed my eyes.

When I arrived home that night, Bonnie embraced me. She didn't ask me where I'd been or what happened. I'll give her credit; she seemed to understand it wasn't something I could talk about. Moira had made an indelible impression on her. She even permitted me to lie to Dad about my ruined dress and the mark on the side of my face ("I slipped in the snow. Ouch!"). I suppose she didn't want to him to know she'd left me alone with a viper—or maybe she just wanted to share a secret with me, reinforce our bond. Who knows?

Adults, it seems to me, think teenagers hide things from them to cultivate our private lives and stake out our individuality. That's not entirely true. Most of the time, we don't know what to tell them. We know we aren't who they think we are, and we suspect we aren't even who *we* think we are, because we aren't who we were a month ago, a day ago, a minute ago. We're too busy becoming something else, molting into something new, to know what that is. In that fragile limbo, so much can happen; so much can be discovered, so much can be destroyed.

I spent yesterday in bed, reading and watching the snow drift past my window, trying not to think. Judy phoned in the evening to tell me that Bart and Edith had moved up the timetable for their sojourn to the tropics. Moira had spooked them as well.

So, since school was canceled today due to snowfall, I flung on my boots and trudged over to Judy's house through the snow-speckled air and slushy streets, hoping to catch her before she departed. As I neared the house, I spotted a yellow-topped taxi idling in front with its trunk open and tailpipe spewing exhaust. I stopped a few houses down and waited for Edith, who had stepped out to greet the cab, to vanish back inside. Judy materialized and brought her valise to the driver. She was wearing her best coat, a tailored dark purple trench with onyx buttons, and a black-and-white checked tam. Rosie was on a short leash cinched around her opposite wrist. I whistled softly, and the dog perked up, saw me, and started toward me, towing Judy behind him down the shoveled sidewalk. As he neared, I kneeled and greeted him with coos and puppy talk, and his little pink tongue darted out for kisses.

"Have you come to save me?" she asked, and I rose to meet her. Her face was meticulously made-up: olive skin smooth, lips burgundy, eyeliner heavy but not excessive, a hint of rouge. The snowflakes trapped by her eyelashes weren't melting. She was beautiful.

"I was worried you'd already left."

"Soon," she said with a groan.

The dog jumped up and planted his paws on my thigh. He was wearing a tight red knit sweater and looked sharp.

"Rosie!" she snapped.

Puzzled, he dropped down and started sniffing a frozen leaf. We watched him as he followed a crack on the sidewalk, snowflakes dotting his black fur.

Yesterday, when I was trying hard not to think, the secret I'd kept from Judy continued to surface. Of course, Charlene's diary made the contents of the secret irrelevant, but I'd held on to it because I liked the way it made me feel, like I had a way to get to Judy. But we were beyond secret-keeping and petty manipulations. "I need to tell you something," I said.

She sniffed. "What?"

"I kept something from you, a secret."

A deep line formed in her brow. "Okay."

I shook my head. "It's something you know already—you figured it out on your own."

"What is it?" she said, still irritated.

I considered how all the contours and planes in her face, smooth and luminous in the overcast haze of the day, could easily collapse with distress. I couldn't bear to watch it happen. But I felt dutybound to be honest and ask for forgiveness, so I said, "It has to do with Halo's death." She gestured for me to continue. "Seconds before you jostled the board, he told me that he might be your father. Of course, you knew he wasn't—or soon figured it out—but I didn't know that, and I kept it from you. I was a little afraid of you and a little angry with you for keeping me at arm's length. It was wrong. I'm sorry."

I wasn't sure how she'd respond. At best, she'd show her disappointment with a barbed quip and let it go, knowing that the secret made no difference now. At worst, she'd feel utterly betrayed and turn her back on me. I crossed my arms, bracing myself for her reply. She cocked her head and said, "What do you mean 'jostled the board'?"

I blinked. "You shook the bridge with your foot," I said. "It's what sent Halo into the alley."

"I didn't touch it," she said flatly. "You did."

My gears locked up. I gawked at her. That couldn't be, I thought. She was pulling my leg. She *had* to be. "No . . ." I said, drawing out the word and smiling uneasily. "It was *you.*"

"What difference does it make?" She shrugged.

I stepped back and gazed at her from another angle as if gaining a new perspective would allow me to detect a tell in her and soothe the panic fluttering in my chest. "But it was *your* plan," I murmured. "It was *you.* I mean, of course, it was."

"Listen," she said. "It's okay. I would've done the same thing if I'd arrived there first, but I wasn't touching the plank when he fell. That's the truth."

I stared at her inscrutable face. A total deadpan. She was joking, trying to get a rise out of me. *This* was my punishment for having kept a secret from her. She'd swat it away as soon as she'd soaked up enough pleasure from my agony. "Of course, you did it," I said, emitting a jittery laugh. "I didn't put pressure on the board. I didn't have the—I don't have the—"

"Philippa," she said loudly and scowled. "I didn't touch it. He lurched toward you, and your foot was on the plank. It was you."

My entire body shook; it was impossible. I would've never done something like that, killed someone, sent a man to his death. "Maybe he fell—on his own, I mean."

"Maybe," she said, looking askance, "but seriously, what difference does it make?"

Exasperated and terrified, I blurted, "All the difference! I'm not a killer!"

She smiled a clever, pregnant smile: close-mouthed, chin cocked, eyes sparkling. She seemed smug, even superior, and then, ever so slightly, her expression shifted, and I detected something else in it: tenderness. "You think it makes you a better person," she said without judgment, "that it makes you better than me."

"No—just not a murderer."

She raised a skeptical eyebrow. "It's why you confessed your secret to me. Keeping it was a burden. You're just unburdening yourself." She mocked the sign of the cross, finishing with a flick of the wrist, more high fashion than Holy Ghost. "Consider yourself absolved, my child."

Maybe I jostled the board, but it wasn't on purpose. I don't know. In the moment before he fell, it's true, I'd learned a secret that left me reeling, not because of what it meant, but because it gave me leverage over Judy. I enjoyed having that power, but I wouldn't have killed for it. Maybe I nudged the board in a reflex reaction, a subconscious tremor. "He lost his balance," I said with a punch of certainty. "It couldn't have happened any other way."

"Whatever," she said, "but remember, he and his bitch of a mother sent me to live at Crestwood. If you'd driven a stake through his heart, I would've helped you hammer it in."

I'll never tell her that, seconds before he plunged to his death, he seemed truly earnest, that he wanted to confirm that she was his daughter. I'll also never tell her that, as he fell, I was immensely relieved. He was like a wall closing in, and then he was gone, an opening. "I don't want to think about him," I said, waving it away. "Let's think about Miss Martins. Remember the good times with her."

"Call her Charlene," she said, her gaze drifting away from me. "It's her real name." Darkness seeped into her mood, and her eyes strained as if she were staring at all the empty spaces in her childhood: her time at the orphanage, her foster parents, her ordeal with the cats, her adoption by the Peabodys, and her attempt to fit into Jackie's outline, a hole within a hole. And then Miss Martins, not a void, not a shadow, was snatched away from her, from *us*: a sinkhole opening under us. "When I return," she added, "I'm going to change my last name to Nightingale."

"It's a literary name," I said. "That's what Miss—Charlene told me."

Judy reached inside her coat and fished out a red leather-bound book, Charlene's diary. "No wonder Cleve was so angry at Charlene and at me," she said. "She broke up his family, and I was the reason she returned to DC. The day she kicked him out of class, he had this out on his desk. It was a threat." She sighed and handed it to me. "After I found it, I wanted to tell you about it. I wanted to tell you *everything*. But I was still thinking it through, trying to find the words."

"So, Cleve was your half brother."

"Apparently, I have half-siblings all over the place."

"Have you seen Iris?" I said, treading carefully on what I suspected was a tender subject. We hadn't discussed her since she had learned the truth.

"No," she said, still distant, "I'm not ready to. I need time."

It's impossible for me to imagine how she feels: One day Iris is your friend and the next she's your half sister. One day you're white and the next you're half Negro. How do you make sense of it? There were a few clues along the way, little impulses built into her machinery: Her persistent defiance of the norm, the black bob and the pearls. Her keenness for civil rights. Her affection for Iris. Her musings on the true meaning of the Emancipation Memorial—every time we gazed up into the freed slave's face, perhaps she was plucking an invisible chord in her heart. It all indicates something: a deep, buried need to be the thing that she actually is.

I studied the closed diary, wondering at what might be in its pages. It had the feel of a sacred text. In gilded lettering on its weathered cover, it could've read, "Herein are all the truths, all the mysteries, and all the answers to your questions." With my heart full and sad, I said, "Moira said that Charlene used you—the fact of you—to blackmail her," I looked at Judy. "But I don't believe it."

She offered me an ambiguous smile, took the journal from me, and leafed through it. "Here," she said, "read this." Before me, there was an entry from October 21, 1930, Washington, DC. Approximately a month after Judy's birth.

I reread "Ode to a Nightingale" today, and I thought of you, my little niece, my little nightingale—

> Away! away! for I will fly to thee,
>   Not charioted by Bacchus and his pards,
> But on the viewless wings of Poesy . . .

You've flown away from me now, and like Keats, I'll do my best to imagine what your life will be like, what you'll look like, what tune you'll sing. You're not mine, not exactly, but somehow, I must believe that, impossibly, you are, making my cruelty in giving you up even harsher. It's terrible, but necessary. I'll never know you, and you'll never know me, but I'll invent you, molded from what I remember and from my wishes for you. As I sit here, staring up at the trees, at the blue sky, at Lincoln's melancholy countenance, I'm creating you, will always be creating you, and you—somewhere out there—maybe one day you'll create me, the mother you didn't have, the aunt you never knew, filling that space in your heart.

Her presence, like her faint lilac perfume, floated up from the page. No, she didn't blackmail Moira. The woman who wrote those lines couldn't have used her niece as a bartering chip. Moira was being spiteful or, at the very least, cynical. As I reread the entry, it seemed like she was talking to me as my mother might have. What dreams did my mother have for me? How much had she invented me in months leading up to my birth? How much had I invented her over the years? I thought about her portrait, peering out at me from the top of my dresser at home, her white hat cocked, her inscrutable smile forever unchanged.

"May I read the rest of this?" I asked Judy.

She considered the request but said, "Not yet."

I wiped a few snowflakes from its pages, closed it, and handed it back to her.

Judy tucked it in her coat, and from a side pocket, she produced a small black velvet jewelry box. "Here's something I want you to have," she said. "I was going to mail it if I didn't see you." I took it and flipped it open. Inside was Elaine's crescent moon pin. "I told Edith it was mine and that I had accidentally stepped on it. She had it fixed. It's yours now."

I studied the sliver of moon. "Why do you think it was damaged?"

Judy shook her head. "I don't know."

"Maybe Charlene crushed it—a symbolic end to her sisterhood." Would it be bad luck? Sophie's warning against Judy rose up again: "All around her, there's a backdrop of shadows." But it was just a faint whisper.

"It's repaired now," Judy said. "I'll wear mine, and you'll wear yours. We're more sisters than Charlene and Elaine ever were."

I closed the box and slipped it in my pocket. "Thank you," I said and smiled. Judy touched my arm, and I returned the gesture, grasping her by the forearms, feeling the wet snow from her sleeve on my palms. The snow was falling steadily now; another storm was sweeping through tonight. She checked the street and bent toward me, her damp skin blotting out the spiraling snowflakes, and kissed me. It wasn't a deep kiss, but it was tender and lingering and changed everything. The thread that had drawn me to her that first day in the cafeteria was no longer outside of me, being pulled by some mysterious force, some fickle cosmic puppet master, or even Judy herself, but inside me, its end in my hand. Perhaps it was always there.

Edith called out: "Judy, we're leaving! Bring Rosie."

The dog heard his name and jerked the leash.

Edith was standing by the car with her hands propped on her hips. I wondered if she'd seen us kiss; I wondered what horrors were spinning through her head. Judy released me, and I felt a swift and sudden pang of sadness. It surged up from deep within me. I didn't want her to go. If she did, I felt certain that I'd never see her again, that my life after her would cease to make sense—that it might end all together. I reached for her, missing her arm and snatching instead her sleeve. "Don't go," I begged, exposing my desperation.

"I have to," she said, pulling away gently.

"I can't—I can't—" I said, shaking my head. "I'll miss you terribly."

"Don't worry," she said, her voice clear, resolute. "We'll find a way to be together."

"Okay," I said, tears pushing up through me.

"I'll try to find ridiculous postcards and send them to you. A new one from each stop. Colorized sunsets. Synchronized swimmers. Coconut bikinis!"

Edith called out: "Judy! It's time!" Rosie barked and yanked on her wrist again.

I threw my arms around her, held her tight. I smelled her body powder, the spicy odor of her hair. I soaked her in, hoping she'd leave traces of herself on my coat, in my hair, on my skin.

"You shouldn't be talking to her!" Edith snapped.

I released her and stared into her dark, gleaming eyes.

"Goodbye," she said, stepping back and waving. "Give those MBBS girls hell!"

I watched her spin and follow Rosie to the cab. I waited there for a minute, wondering what she sees when she gazes back at me. Does she see everything? My mother's ghost trailing me, guiding me at times and misleading me at others? Or my father's guilt, pulling me toward him and shoving me away? All my gaps, all my flaws, all my little savageries? No, she couldn't. There's so much I haven't told her, so much I've tucked away from myself. What *does* she see then? If not the entire picture, then perhaps the spaces between the fragments? An opportunity? Fissures she can grow into, fill up, and live in? Suddenly, I wanted to stop the taxi and tell her who I was, to let it out, the expansiveness of it, of me, but as soon as the impulse arose, I heard Sophie's warning, so faint now I knew it only by its rhythm, and I retreated, finding shelter again in my secret life. I gave a little wave toward the cab and turned away.

JUDY, JANUARY 4, 1949

I only had two days between the Sunburn Tour and the first day of spring semester classes at Agnes March. Philippa had been whisked away by her parents to the yet unsold house in Harpers Ferry for the holidays, surely a coordinated effort between B and E and the Watsons. So, arms peeling, cheeks sunburned, I pushed past my fear, and, in the short window of time I had, I confronted my half sister at Horsfield's after her shift last night.

When I told her everything I knew, she stared across the empty diner and said, "Well, damn," and shook her head. "I'm sorry you found out that way. That wasn't my intention." She gave me a hug, murmured another apology, and when we'd settled in our seats again, she said, "Your Miss M knew our father's name and put together that I was his first child. Since I was little, I knew I had a half-sibling, the fruit of a dark spell in Mama and Papa's marriage, but they didn't talk about it. It was forbidden." She swirled her malt with a long-handled spoon. "Then, one day, your fancy Miss M shows up at my place of employment—I was working the breakfast shift at this crummy diner on First Street—and told me your name and that you were, for all intents and purposes, a white girl." She took measure of me, perhaps gaging my reaction. My face muscles tightened. "Let's just say, I didn't handle it well. I let my folks have it." It hadn't occurred to me that she'd be upset by my skin color, and it unsettled me. Clearly, I wasn't the only one going through a paradigm shift. "They apologized and explained, and eventually, I simmered down. Curiosity got the better of me, and I followed you one day after school. You went to Horsfield's and plopped down at the bar by yourself. The other Eastern High kids steered clear of you. You seemed lonely, but somehow, a little, I don't know . . .

lofty." She smiled, her eyes lighting up, growing tender. "Call it sisterly instinct, but I knew I'd like you. I wasn't ready to walk up and introduce myself, though. Your Miss M warned me that it could be dangerous for me to reveal myself to you. She hadn't even done it herself, something about how carrying on with that Closs man complicated things." She looked me in the eye. "Forgive me for saying this, but she struck me as selfish—or maybe just careless." I bit my lip, not knowing what to say. "Anyway, when I saw a Help Wanted sign on Horsfield's door that day, I jumped at the chance."

I appreciated her candor, even if it was hard to hear. I felt like I'd found a solid piece of myself, something real. Without thinking it through, I asked her if I could meet my father and remeet Alice. I was hungry for more pieces of the puzzle. She leaned back against the counter and pursed her lips. Doubt crinkled the edges of her eyes. Then, reaching a decision of some sort, she asked, "Are you ready?" I nodded. She asked again, "Are you sure?" I said I was.

She told me to catch her after her morning shift, and she'd take me to her parents. The sun was out, and the air was crisp, almost electric. Horsfield's was still decorated for the holiday. Limp swags of tinsel hung along the inside frame of the window, and a plastic Santa waved from behind the plate glass. Emerging from the alley, Iris spotted me, gave a quick salute, dropped her butt and stamped it out.

"Hey there," she said, as she unhurriedly approached me. "Here we go," she added, winking at me.

"Here we go," I echoed, trying to conceal my trepidation.

As we walked to the streetcar, I watched her purposeful stride. She cut the air with her long body, demanding that the other pedestrians, many of whom were white, part the way for us. It was thrilling. As we crossed the street, she leaned in and asked again about my scars. I thought about those awful photos the FBI goons took and felt a surge of anger. Then, feeling freer, even bold, I told Iris about the cats and the cellar and that it had seemed more like a memory than a dream. She thought it over, giving it due consideration, and said that, with time, I'd remember more of it. She even offered to help me dig into it when I was ready. After all, her mother had worked at Crestwood for many years. I recalled Alice's sweet gifts: cookies, peanut brittle, and brown-sugary pound cake. I also remembered our chats, and how for a few minutes, here and there, I'd felt like I existed. It occurred to me: all that time, she'd never mentioned her last name.

At the stop, we hopped on 92 Northbound and changed cars at H Street. As we headed up Kenilworth Avenue, Iris asked again, "Are you sure you're ready for this?" The truth is: I had no idea. How do you know? Are you ever ready?

I shrugged and said nothing.

"Have you been struck mute?" she said, shaking her head.

Still, I didn't respond. How could I? I wasn't ready. There was no way to be ready. She gazed out the window at the passing row houses. As she had during our stroll down the sidewalk, she held her back straight and her chin up. Her thin wool coat was neat and clean, and her cotton gloves, still bluing white. She always maintains her bearing, her confidence, even while wearing street clothes or her ridiculous Horsfield's uniform. Usually, she made it look effortless, a seasoned ballerina executing a pirouette. But as I studied her, I detected weariness. Nothing anyone else would notice: a flex in her temple and a crinkle across her nose. Had I done something? Was I annoying her?

"This is all insane," I said. "But maybe it's the beginning of better times." I was shooting for cheerfulness, which isn't something that comes naturally.

She turned to me, her eyes frank, kind, and shining with intelligence. She wasn't irritated. It was something else. Sisterly concern? Love? She was really something. She was *exceptional*—a Negro woman with integrity, intelligence, and determination. That's what I could be, too.

"You and I," I said. "We're exceptions to the rule. We're different. Philippa, too." I couldn't forget her. "We could be anything."

A pall of seriousness fell over her. "I'm not an exception to anyone's rule." She added sharply, "Neither are you. Don't forget it."

I was confused, and she sensed it. "White folks always like to think of a successful Negro as an exception," she said. "Don't you see?" I didn't see. I couldn't see, which was scrawled across my forehead, I'm sure. "It's comfortable for them." Her eyes narrowed. "Maybe it's comfortable for you."

Shame rippled through me. She was right. I'd seen her that way, but not because I found it comfortable, but because I found it comforting. I was self-involved; I wanted to think of myself as an exception—as *exceptional*. That's what I looked for in Charlene, too. But clearly, Iris isn't an exception. She's self-made, not something molded by the gods or someone else's idea of her. She was always fighting for it—the respect she demanded at Horsfield's, at school, even walking down the street or sitting on the streetcar. All of it cost her; it drained her. That was the source of her weariness. She's not an exception. She's a possibility. If I'm not an exception, if I'm not Jackie's angel-shaped shadow, if I'm not Bart and Edith's sweet lily-white fantasy, then what am I? The result of a random collision, a bit of boozy sex between Elaine and Ellis, catalyzed by a mutual love of jazz. Was there possibility in that?

"I'll ask you one last time," Iris said, her chin lifting. "Are you ready for this?"

Her solemn face demanded my honesty, and it was the least I could give her. So, I said, "No, I'm not. Not at all."

She smiled, bumped my shoulder with hers, and said, "Well, too late. We're doing it anyway."

Once we arrived, we strolled down an oak-lined street with standalone homes. Purplish sky floated above the leafless canopy. We stopped at the second to last house on the left, a modest bungalow with a large well-appointed front porch, draped with still-lit Christmas lights.

We lingered on the sidewalk. Up a flight of concrete stairs and through the front door, I'd see Alice again, and for the first time, I'd meet my father, my *actual* father. Would the Alice of today match my memories of her? Would I see myself in Ellis? And afterward, standing before a mirror, would I see him in me? Would I conjure up bad memories for them? Or would I bring relief? Where was this getting us all? No telling. But what I did know was that, if I went inside, I'd be shedding the old idea of myself like an exoskeleton. I'd yearn for who I'd been, for what I'd made of myself, for what I'd shaped out of a few fractured memories and a reserve of imagination. The hardest part, of course, would be figuring out who I was going to be, not just to myself, but to the world.

As I teetered on my heels, the muffled swoon of jazz floated out of the house, loose and moody. It sounded like something that Charlene might have recommended, or Elaine would have swayed to in her gloomy living room. It was at once familiar and absolutely foreign. Was it a sign? And if so, was it a good omen or bad?

"Let's go in," Iris said, and I took my first step.

EPILOGUE

So, we return to the question: Whose story is this? Who am I? Do you have an answer yet? Have you guessed? I promised to tell you, I know.

But what if your question is the answer to a riddle, what if it goes like this:

If I told you that I was neither *girl, that might be true. We're no longer the girls you've just read about. We've changed over the years. There are more stories to tell, some of them beautiful, some of them ugly. Neither of us is a femme fatale or an ingénue. Perhaps we're a bit of both, as many women of our generation are, or maybe all women are. That's just prevarication, I know. We all change—all of us—but that doesn't mean we stop being ourselves, right?*

If I told you that I was both *girls, that also might be true. Unless you know one of us, your experience is limited to these pages, in which Philippa and Judy are, in essence, creations of one mind, my* mind. I pieced together meticulously kept journal entries, smoothing out and reconfiguring passages so the collage's seams aren't too visible, too frayed. I've appropriated artifacts from our lives, glued them together, and shaped the past. There's no built-in appraisal of my objectivity, no test for my rendering of the truth, unless my dear friend reaches out and supplies her opinion, her corrections, her account. I hope she does.

But I know that answer isn't going to satisfy you. It's the epistemological approach and much too slippery. Besides, damn it, you want a name, not some silly riddle!

Before I tell you, I want to suggest this: That withholding my identity as your kindly narrator freed you from making assumptions about me. You weren't judging me by my looks, whether it was the strawberry curls and saddle oxfords or the black bob and bulky sweaters. Or my tastes, whether it was for Wuthering Heights or for Lady Chatterley's Lover. Or the varying shades of my sexuality (although neither of us is a straight shooter, strictly speaking). Or finally, my race, whether I'm white or mixed or whatever. Remember, I told you that it was never that simple, never just black or white. My point is: Maybe, just maybe, for a few pages, you stopped thinking about me and just believed it.

Now, it's only fair that you have a name. I promised it, and I will deliver. I ask you, though, why is it important to you? Will it change everything or nothing? Do names have that power?

I've already given you a clue: My pen name, Abigail Knightley.

Look closely. Got it? I know you're no dummy.

ADDENDUM
1984 EDITION

Dearest Judy,

When I dropped by Brentano's and saw that another Abigail Knightley book had been released, I snatched it up, as I always do. Of course, I had no idea you'd be telling our story, which is why, after all these years, I'm writing to you. I know it's what you want me to do.

At first, I was furious with you for harvesting my diary entries without my permission. I'd assumed they were lost, destroyed, or, at least, buried in a deep hole. I can't believe you kept them all these years, which I suppose I should be flattered by. Your "journal entries" were a lark. You never kept a diary, at least I don't remember it.

To be honest, I resisted the story at first. I'd toss it across my study and curse you. It seemed like you'd thrown together a perverse Man Ray collage of our lives. Gradually, I began to get it. I remembered how you would poke and prod me, even rebuff me, to get my attention. It was at once irritating and exciting—but clearly a sign of affection. Warmed by that thought, I'd rise from my chair, walk across the room, and pick up the book again.

In your final chapter, you invited me to offer my account—or offer corrections. Your book isn't accurate in every detail—well, many details. I'm not interested in nitpicking. It's beside the point. However, I want to comment on several significant changes you made and posit a theory:

First, Bogdan never saw himself as Orpheus. He wrote Анка or Anka, a diminutive form of Anna, not Эвридика, on the bodies of all those girls. The police didn't make a mistake. It was his sister's name. You added a flair to his killings that wasn't there. While I appreciate the literary flourish, it comes close to romanticizing him. He was cruel and thoroughly despicable, but I'm telling you what you already know.

Second, after Halo fell from Hill Estates, you wrote that you went to check on him to make sure he was dead, but you omitted what happened. You see, I followed you, which you didn't know. I never wrote it down. I understand why you didn't include it. It would've greatly colored the reader's opinion of you—of the "character" of Judy. They would've had the image of you discovering Halo Closs mortally wounded but still alive. Instead of seeking help, you picked up the wooden plank that had served as our bridge—our gangway to safety—and cracked him over the head with it.

This leads me to my theory, which began to form as I read your book. I hope you'll indulge me. So, what if you knew that Elaine Closs was your mother much earlier than you let on. What if—and I have no way of proving this—when you rifled through Bart's desk the day we broke in using a bobby pin and our true crime know-how, you found more than you let on. In addition to an adoption document with Charlene Peters's name on it, what if you found your birth certificate with Elaine's and Halo's names on it? Certainly, Elaine wouldn't have mentioned Ellis Baker's name. Whatever it was, something could've pointed you to Elaine.

What if you visited her on your own, and when you did, Elaine, who must've had some inkling that Cleve had Charlene's diary, gave you her journal—which oddly, or perhaps suspiciously, you've never let me read in its entirety. After all, once Charlene knew that Cleve had it, wouldn't she have approached her sister about it?

And this diary, what did it contain?

Here's what I think: Charlene *did* use you to blackmail Moira, and she came back to DC to sink her claws into Halo and, perhaps, blackmail the family again. That's what Cleve knew and why he was furious at her and at you. That's what you found out, which of course, would've been devastating.

Growing up, you were used by other people time and again, especially parental figures: Bart, Edith, Halo, Elaine, Moira, and yes, maybe even our beloved Miss Martins. If she turned out to be a villain—as I think she did—it would've pushed you over the edge and changed you. With Elaine whispering to you and offering you the proof of Charlene's deception, I see why you'd want to punish her and the Closes. I can also understand why it's a secret you could never tell me.

It makes sense: If Charlene knew her sister killed Cleve, which surely Halo told her about, I can't imagine her letting her into her apartment and serving her Ovaltine. But I do see her letting you in for a morning confab. Elaine knew what you were going to do—perhaps it was even her idea, and she gave you his shamrock tie to frame him—but you did the deed. Meanwhile, she directed the FBI toward Halo, who were happy to do whatever it took to shift focus from Bogdan to someone else. They didn't care who killed Cleve or Charlene.

You probably learned that trick for moving the body in the same first aid class that I did. You knew how to stage the scene. We'd already verified that AHKA was written on Cleve. It was the perfect double revenge. You framed Halo as revenge for deserting you, and freeing Bogdan was a kind of revenge against the Peabodys for inflicting Jackie on you. Knowing the truth about Bogdan, I'm sure you regret that now. As in life, during that whole episode of the book, you were in real pain. But it wasn't the grief of losing the person who called herself Miss Martins; it was the grief of losing the idea of Miss M.

Your revenge against Elaine was more complicated. If what I'm writing is true, you knew she had love for you, as muddled as it was. What did you propose to her? Or she, you? A suicide pact—and I was supposed to be the witness? The great recorder of the melodramatic gesture? Was that why she was so accommodating when we arrived at her door? Oh, I just thought of it: Did *you* send *Love's Last Move* to me with the Ovid inscription after filching it from Charlene? What a brilliant way of nudging me in the right direction!

As soon as you produced the moon pin—the one you nabbed from Charlene's apartment after killing her, not, as you wrote in the book, the one you grabbed from Elaine's jewelry box—she knew you hadn't come for a suicide pact, but a confession and an execution. From the beginning, you seemed in control of that confrontation, even manipulating it. Sure, Elaine had a few things to confess, but perhaps she also redeemed herself by confessing to killing her sister, absolving you. Maybe it was an act of true motherly love. It's unfortunate that she's been locked up at St. Elizabeth's Hospital for over a decade, or we could ask her. In your "journal," she inquires, "Are you going to tell Philippa everything?" What if that *everything* wasn't just that you're mixed race, but that you helped murder your aunt, our esteemed Miss Martins? We'll never know, will we?

Finally, about the episode with the plank: Both of our feet were on it when Halo went over! You claimed that it was *only* my foot on the beam, that I'd acted on impulse, that I'd prized my secret so highly I'd killed a man. But your foot was on that board, too. Our eyes met. To this day, I still see their depth and clarity. I don't understand why you altered it—after all, it was a defensive gesture. Unless you killed him because he knew about your involvement in Charlene's death. Come to think of it, if he did know, he might've meant to harm us that day.

I understand why you edited out finishing him off with the board, and any evidence that you were involved in Miss Martins's death, but why this? Was it so I would feel compelled to write this letter correcting the omission and, in writing it, proclaim that you eliminated the instant that linked us together forever, which of course, has the ironic effect of reaffirming our bond? Or was it because you did it, *you* jostled the board, not me? Was it that, back then, you were lonely in your guilt and needed me to be a murderer, too?

So, there you have it! Is it the truth? Only God knows, Judy. The years have changed us. Are you the swallow? Or the nightingale? Remember, the myth is told both ways. But no matter how it's told, only the gods deliver justice in the end, not us mere mortals.

What do you say, shall we meet up again? There's so much to talk about, more stories yet to tell. Let's say September 20th in front of Lincoln. Perhaps you can finally settle it for me: Is he freeing the slave or making him beg for his freedom?

Love, Philippa
September 1964

ACKNOWLEDGMENTS

The Savage Kind pays homage to and re-imagines the femme fatale character from classic American crime fiction and the great films noir of the 1940s and 1950s. I've always had a strong affinity—and sympathy—for these kinds of characters. As a gay man, I've experienced a degree of the oppressiveness of our patriarchal culture, which often belittles and vilifies feminine characteristics and sensibilities. When I read these novels or watched these films, I saw the femmes fatales doing illegal and immoral things but sensed that, just under the surface, they were struggling to find agency. After all, these women were strong, intelligent, and witty. Why shouldn't they have more power? Why did the men around them inhibit them? Why were they consistently punished by the narrative in which they found themselves? I always rooted for them, even if that wasn't the intention of the story.

Powerful, complex, and passionate women have played a significant role in my life. Without my mother-figures, my teachers, and my peers, gay and straight, I would be utterly lost. I wouldn't have had the inspiration to write this novel or, frankly, any others. I'll always be in their debt.

Although writing is often portrayed as a solitary activity, in truth, writers would be nowhere without family, friends, agents, and editors offering criticism to help them mold their vision into its best form. I appreciate my generous friends who read early—and *very* rough—sections or drafts of this book and gave me detailed comments: Matthew Ferrence, Tara Laskowski, Bernadette Murphy McConville, Frances McMillan, Dalynn Knigge, Maya Shanbhag Lang, and Jessica Hendry Nelson. Especially, I'm grateful to my sensitivity reader, the fabulous crime writer Penny Mickelbury, for her essential and instructive feedback.

A resounding thank-you to my miraculous agent, Annie Bomke, who knows all too well the evolutionary journey of this manuscript. I sincerely appreciate her enthusiasm for these characters and her patience with me while I navigated this story's many complex layers. I couldn't ask for a better guide through my publishing journey.

Thank you to the fantastic Pegasus team for believing in this novel, notably my talented editor, Nick Cohen, who offered his clear-minded support and direction, Derek Thornton for the gorgeous cover, Maria Fernandez for the elegant interior design, and my publicists, Jenny Rossberg and Megan Swartz Gellert, for their hard work in spreading the word about the book, the importance of which should never be underestimated.

I'm also grateful to the LGBTQ+ writing community and the crime writing community, from bloggers to podcasters to instagrammers to organizations like Lambda Literary, Queer Crime Writers, Sisters in Crime, and Mystery Writers of America. I'm particularly thankful to Al Warren, true crime writer and radio host extraordinaire, who allows me to co-host on the House of Mystery Radio Show, even though I'm far from a typical radio personality!

It should never go without saying: thank you to all the librarians, teachers, bookstore owners, and avid readers who've read my work and the work of other LGBTQ+ authors. Without your support, well, where would we be? Keep reading widely, keep reading diversely!

To my family—my immediate and extended family, my blood-related and chosen family—thank you for your love, kindness, and support. Finally, to my husband, Jeff, whose own story echoes through the pages of this book, thank you for insisting that I stay the course with my writing—and for all the love, endless patience, and yes, food-preparation skills! Without you, I would starve . . . in more than one way.